SURVIVAL

SURVIVAL

PHYLLIS BOTTOME

Little, Brown and Company · Boston
1943

To
those Pilgrims of Eternity
whose home is Austria

SURVIVAL

10th April 1939

A GREAT interest has always been taken in what living people think or feel about ghosts, but the other side of the picture has remained unpainted. We do not know what ghosts think or feel about living people.

Now I — Rudolph or, as people in Vienna used to call me, "Rudi" von Ritterhaus — *am* a ghost; and therefore what I think of these people who inhabit that small island off the coast of Europe called England — where I am doing my haunting at present — may be useful to my sometimes unwilling, and yet always kindly, hosts.

I am an admiring, an affectionate — even, in a way, a grateful — ghost and all that I shall say in this record of my daily life here is written with the aim of being of use to these particular Islanders. For although I have ceased to survive as what people call a "real" man, I still survive as an observing animal and my observations still have the value of a trained psychiatrist's. That is the curious part of it. The normal house-to-house ghost is a spirit of what was once a man, without a body. I — on the contrary — am the body of what was once a man, without a spirit. I am not out of my mind at all. I was never saner. But I am — I suppose I always shall be — out of my spirit.

What happened in Vienna on 11th March in 1938 when my spirit was driven out of me, I shall touch on as lightly as possible since it is not part of my purpose in writing this record of the English people; but what I once was has to be mentioned since at least half of what is observed is in the eyes of the observer. You do not look at a thing without an eye, and whether this is a bird's eye, or a brute's eye, or a human eye, has its significance.

The occupation of Abel by Cain which took place when the German Army flung itself upon undefended Austria, the people of Great Britain and France at that time preferred to call an act of unity.

If the meal of a cannibal upon a murdered brother *is* unity — they defined the German occupation rightly. The plebiscite took place, but it was Hitler's plebiscite — not Schuschnigg's — and it took place under the engaging care of the German Army.

I was at the time a useful and even privileged person. Nor was I ill-born. My father had been a General in the War of 1914. My mother was a beautiful actress who had been legally married to him. She was so lovely and had had such a successful stage career that no one in Vienna had ever noticed that she was a Jewess. Her religion was that of all artists — obedience to the laws of her creative art. She died when I was ten years old and my father remarried. My stepmother was what would be known now as a full Aryan, and she was so good to me that I confused my two mothers in my mind, and for the sake of these two tender-hearted women, I looked upon all women henceforward as my friends; indeed, I have never altogether lost this sometimes dubious habit.

I was a diligent schoolboy; pleased with my work and my comrades. My father was not at all stern in spite of his military training. He was as staunch a friend to me as my stepmother. Fortunately they both died early in the 1930's.

I had already become a biologist attached to the University of Vienna, but I added psychology to my other field of research, and it became more and more engrossing to me. So without giving up my special science, I took the practice of psychiatry as a profession.

I had all the patients I could manage and access to what was then — however poor materially — probably the best ground for psychology in the world.

I worked with, and for, Alfred Adler for three years before he finally went to America in 1934. He wanted me to go with him, for he foresaw what was to become of Wien; but I refused. Klara had already promised to become my bride and her whole family was bitterly against such a separation. They told me what a complete and united strength such a family as theirs could be to their future son-in-law, and to his children. If I remained in Vienna I could count on an early appointment of phenomenal importance to so young a man. "Provided that you can keep it," Adler said to me with his curious hooded look that seemed to pierce deeper than the bones of the present, into the heart of the future.

I felt deeply injured. Adler sometimes said cruel things which turned out afterwards to have been the truth, and which, if one had not thought them at the time *only* cruel, might have saved one from subsequent disaster.

Klara and I therefore remained in Wien. We were married in 1935, and within a year Andreas was born to us. The next three years substantiated all my hopes. It was wonderful to watch my dreams change to reality and yet not lose their bright transparency. I received my appointment. I had a large circle of congenial friends and colleagues. My love was like the food I lived on.

Neither Klara nor I paid the least attention to politics. We amused ourselves with the old Viennese quip "In Germany the situation is serious but not desperate; in Austria the situation is desperate but not serious."

We thought Schuschnigg a clever dog, though we disapproved of his earlier agreement with Dollfuss, which threw the working people of Vienna to that Wolf, Mussolini. The attack on the Goethe Haus, and those other memorable workmen's dwellings, sickened all thinking people in Vienna. It was as senseless as cutting off one's right hand in order to make oneself into a complete entity. A few months later Dollfuss paid for his timid treachery with his own blood; that indeed struck some of us as a more fatal event, though it was in reality far less fatal, than the slaughter of our own work people.

Anyhow, we told ourselves that Schuschnigg would last our time and was a good deal cleverer than Dollfuss. His acrobatic antics to keep Austria from the lethal threats of the two gangsters on either side of us thrilled us all, as a gladiator show must have thrilled the Roman Populace. We did not realize that we were to be thrown to the lions ourselves as a grand finale. But being Viennese, we did at least realize that Hitler and Mussolini *were* wild beasts, which was more than the Great Powers did, who persisted in trying to believe them rather a bluff new form of Sunday-school teacher. And yet, what was the use of our knowledge — for the whole monstrous swindle caught us by surprise in the end, after five years of wolf crying!

It was as if one moment a man were driving along in his own little car to a known destination on the right side of the road, with the sun shining down upon him, and in command of all his faculties and possessions — and the next moment the car was changed into a man-eating tiger, and the driver, with all his possessions and his faculties, crunched up together inside the tiger.

People think of Refugees as unfortunate people who have lost their homes, suffered various painful experiences, and been driven out of their country in a moneyless and embarrassing condition — embarrassing of course both for themselves and for their hosts — but we are something quite different. We are human beings changed in essence. Many people have left homes before and started penniless new lives in foreign countries after bitter personal experiences, and yet remained much the same people that they were before these events took place. But those whom Hitler and Mussolini drove out passed through a unique experience. The web of their lives was torn before their eyes into useless fragments. There was no security of soul, mind or body that was left to them.

For never — until the Nazis had prepared and trained themselves into one united weapon turned against the heart of man — had any ruler commanded the full resources of a civilized state. Germany gave Hitler this power; and this was how Hitler used it. He could not create man, as God once did; but he could uncreate him. I know this as a fact because he uncreated me. I did *not* survive what happened to me. I do not know one single Refugee who has wholly survived it.

To uncreate man is what Hitler set out to do, has done, and will continue to do, as long as he can control the resources of the German Reich. Mussolini was more modest, or had the sense to know that no Latin country can be forced to give up its individuality completely. However, he must not be underestimated. He did the worst he could with less malleable material.

Hitler has always disliked mankind; not intermittently with one of his faculties as most human beings dislike their enemies, but continuously with all the faculties he possesses.

The sun does not divert Hitler from his hatred by shining, nor does he forget his preoccupation with murder in order to take a dog out for a walk or play a hand at cards. Hitler lives in a state of continuous movement towards a self-directed goal. He hates from morning till night; and he acts with the whole of himself upon what he hates. Suppose a Christian were to follow his creed like Hitler, with love as his aim instead of hate — we should see another Christ! But this time we should know better than to let him live for thirty-three years; and have his story published after his death. He would be put straight into a concentration camp from the moment he began to improve upon the teachings of the authorities; and anyone who dared to make his story known would risk being put away himself, as well as having his book burned.

But in Europe in 1938 no one thought of behaving like Christ. Schuschnigg went to Berchtesgaden and Vienna trembled like an ox when he reaches the slaughter-house; and those who saw Schuschnigg after the famous interview knew that the axe had already fallen.

I shall not write of those loud days and nights that followed. Our ears were less stunned by Hitler's bombers than our hearts were by German cruelty. It would have been better for most of us had our hearts remained stunned.

I had my father's name and my University appointment to protect me; I only lost, like all the rest of us, the sense of all moral and physical security. I knew that all I had hitherto believed was a lie. Man was *not* a benevolent animal. Friendship had no foundation in fact. No one could be relied upon, because courage was a drawback, involving danger to others.

Mercy was out of the running with cruelty; nor did justice come into the picture at all. When we met a friend in the street, we did not dare to look at him. We were too ashamed.

For quite a long time I was uninvolved in any personal disaster. I went on from day to day doing my work, loving my wife and child with a desperate intensity, and being loved by them. I saw very little of my friends; nor was I quite sure who they were.

We knew that we had the Family behind us. Klara's people bore a great name; and we supposed that it still had some significance even to the Nazis. Perhaps it had.

One day I left Klara and little Andreas as usual, telling them that I would be back early for it was his third birthday, and we were to have had a picnic in the Wienerwald.

When I hurried into the house at four o'clock I found they were not there. We lived in the Hohe Warte, close to the Vineyards of Grinzing. Schubert's and Beethoven's footsteps were all round us. We could almost smell their music when the apple orchards bloomed and the vines turned green. Our little house was not quite empty. A new servant, a country girl, was in the kitchen. She stood by the sink crying. Country people change very slowly; she still had a heart; and it was for me that she was crying. I asked her what the matter was. She said, "The Family have called. They have taken the Gnädigste away with them; and the Herr Baby — and even his birthday cake."

They never came back.

After walking about for an hour or two in the Vineyards — thinking things over it used to be called, when one was allowed to think — I went round to the Family's great apartment opposite the Staats Park in the centre of Wien. They had forgotten that they had once given me a latch key; so I was able to get inside.

I found Klara in the bathroom, and Andreas in a green-tiled bath with steps leading down to it, like a pool. Andreas was enjoying it very much. He had the boat I had given him that morning as a birthday present in the pool with him.

I said, "Klara!" but when she turned and looked at me, I saw that there was no such person.

It was quite unnecessary for her to explain to me what she felt, after that look. Nothing really need ever be explained by people who have once been in love with each other. Because if there is still love — nothing else matters; and if there is not still love — then also nothing else matters.

Klara had been dispossessed, and so, in a flash, was I. Only the child wasn't. He held out his arms in an ecstasy and cried, "Daddy! Daddy! Sail my boat with me!"

Klara had not been able to show him how it moved, so I kneeled down on the splashed floor, and showed Andreas. Afterwards I got out of the house somehow, but what had really happened beyond the mechanical movement of getting away (I wasn't even arrested) was that I knew, then, I wasn't any longer "myself." I was a disintegrated atom that had once belonged to a part of a civilized world.

26th April 1939

IT was such a little blur when I first saw it on the horizon that I thought it only a thicker part of the mist. All I could see was a smudge of cloud above, a smudge of cloud beneath; and something a trifle thicker in between. I could not guess it was the Island itself till a man next to me — rather a low-class type of Viennese Jew — burst out sobbing and cried: "That's England!"

"It's too small! It's too small!" I thought to myself in an agony of fear and rage. "It's too soft!" I felt as if my heart, beating up into my ears, would burst through my flesh, to warn it.

England was the only hope I had. I knew that if it didn't hold against Hitler, nothing else would. And how could one be sure of any country ruled by Chamberlain and his gentlemanly officials, who had so confused and cotton-wooled the minds of their people that they believed the Nazis would let them choose which they wanted — Peace or War? I had no belief in France. My French colleagues had told me. It was already too late. The poisoned fangs of Abetz and Laval had gone too deep. The Communists — never accustomed to think — only to act without thinking — were actually supporting the Bankers. These swollen magnates, as usual, kept their hearts in their pockets and were prepared to part with anything in the world except their money.

The Bankers of France — her two hundred Ruling Families — openly said: "Rather Hitler than Communism!" The Communists said: "First Hitler, then Us!" France said nothing.

There were a great many sea-gulls floating about in the white mist; and then as we approached the harbour a little breeze sprang up, and blew the clouds apart, and I saw that blunt square tower on a green mound that is Dover Castle.

Somehow or other, just the sight of its age-old unaggressive strength steadied my nerves.

I remembered Adler had once said to me of these Islanders: "They are a benevolent and powerful people; and will not yield lightly to Dictatorship."

The docks looked unprepared for our landing. There seemed no one whose business it was to look after our approaching ship. Suddenly — as if from nowhere — two men sauntered towards the dock's edge; our sailors threw a cable toward them — they caught it; and without a word or a gesture, the ship was moored.

The docking of this large steamer hardly seemed to require an act. The ship — the land — they came together in a flash — as if they had happened to meet.

"Are they *accidentally* right, these Islanders," I asked myself, not without anxiety, "or is their skill so deep that it has become unconscious?"

This is a question I have often asked myself since; for as a people, the English have no method, only a kind of working confidence.

"In what have they this confidence?" I still ask myself. "In themselves — in each other — or in life?"

James and Eunice waved to me from the dock. There was no one else on it, except the two men who had helped to dock the ship.

Mr. and Mrs. James Wendover had been very great friends of mine. They had also procured my English visa for me; but, of course, friendship, for me, was now purely problematical. I neither expected it, nor even hoped for it. Perhaps I rather dreaded it. I believed that it was a mirage — a will o' the wisp — something that the moment the Nazis came, would automatically disappear; and I was not anxious to watch it disappear a second time.

James and Eunice had once, four years ago, come to me in a moment of dire human emergency. I had never come across a similar case in my own countrymen so that I had been specially interested. Fortunately I had been able to clear up their trouble; and our curious three-faceted friendship followed.

I deeply liked and respected them both, but I should have had no reason whatever to suppose that they liked me in return — except that they had a way of turning up on their holidays, as they explained to me, "by accident."

I had received a telegram from them the day after my wife left me, saying that they had got my permit to enter England, although I had not asked them to obtain it for me. I might suppose it was another of these "accidents."

There they stood and waved cheerfully at me from the dockside, as if I were about to pay them a normal friendly visit — such as I had often planned, and never before accomplished. I could not reach them until I had passed the Passport barrier; but it made it easier to know that they were there.

To my surprise, everything went very smoothly though it was almost terrifying to meet the eyes of officials as if they were human beings. When I had passed the barrier I was trembling so that I could hardly stand.

James said: "Had a decent crossing?" and Eunice, who was always, if anything, the more inarticulate of the two, said nothing at all. The short strong grasp of their hands, however, reassured me. I found out afterwards that Oxford, where they lived, was a long way from Dover, and that very few people would meet a visitor by coming all the way to the landing stage.

A porter took my suitcases. They had a car waiting outside the station — a big comfortable car that ran like cream over the smooth wet roads. They did not seem to think it necessary to explain anything to me, but I had to say, "I am going to London — perhaps I could find lodgings there — " Then Eunice spoke for the first time. She said in a shocked voice, "Oh, no! You are coming to us! Of course, if you want to, later on, you can go to London. But if you don't mind Oxford, we have heaps of room — "

Were they quite mad, I wondered, as well as kind? What better place could there be in the world than Oxford? My eyes filled with tears, and I knew that if I spoke I should not be able to control my voice, so I tried to smile instead. After a long moment I found that my eyes were shut, but I do not think I had fainted. I quite well remember getting into the back of the car with Eunice, and a porter lifting in my suitcases.

The soft wet wind blew against my face; and out of the mist that still hung over the land, I could distinguish gentle, huddled trees above green earth. Although the summer was far advanced, the colouring of the woods and fields might have been June — it was so fresh and full of life.

I do not know for how long James drove us through the open fields and the small villages that grew into little towns, and fell back again into that soft misty greenness, before Eunice said, "We'll stop at Sevenoaks for tea — it's my mother's home — but she's away on a visit so there won't be anyone there!" From the first, Eunice understood that I was like a raw egg — quite unable to stand the pain of new approaches.

Sevenoaks was a town turned into a garden, and the house we stopped at stood in a garden of its own full of late-summer flowers. There was no harshness in their gaudy reds and yellows because of the soft light that rested on them. This island light seems always to come between you and the sharpness of things.

"England," I said looking round me at the garden and the rolling hills, "is a country without edges!"

James, shutting off his engine, laughed and said, "Well, we do rather like slipping in and out of things without cutting ourselves."

Eunice opened the front door, which was not even locked. Servants, of course, I did not mind, especially not the English kind of servants, who did not look as if they noticed you any more than — if as much as — the plate of thin bread and butter they put upon the table. We had brown and white bread and butter, potted meat and honey, jam and three kinds of cake. I thought, "I must write and tell Klara what a feast they had prepared for one insignificant stranger!" And then I remembered that it was Klara who was now the stranger. A dog turned up from somewhere and helped us a great deal.

"The first time you came to see me," I reminded them, "we spent the whole time talking about my sheep dog, Luchs."

"Yes, he was a grand fellow," James agreed, "pity that we have that heavy quarantine law so that you couldn't bring him with you!"

I didn't tell them that I'd found Luchs hanging under my window with a paper round his neck on which was written *Jews* are *dogs — they have no need to keep them!*

I had already begun to edit my memories, and to say to myself, "This you *must*" or "This you need *not* tell them."

The one question I dreaded had to come sooner or later, and I almost welcomed it when it did come — in order that it might be over. It was Eunice who asked me in a way that gave me a chance to say nothing but "Yes," which was all I could say: "Your wife and Andreas are all right with her family, aren't they?"

I said, "Yes," but I am afraid I held on to the arms of my chair while I was saying it. They never asked me any more questions about Klara or Andreas. But they wanted to know whether three hours more in the car would tire me.

"I don't feel as if anything in the world would tire me again — " I told them — "not at any rate in this country."

They both looked away from me, and from each other, in that curious embarrassed way they have whenever I say anything to them that I mean — with emphasis. That is another thing I notice that the English seem to be without, emphasis. No edges, no emphasis. It will be better if I make a list of all these differences.

"He speaks English rather well for a foreigner — " James said to Eunice after a pause — "makes everything a damned sight simpler, old boy, all round!" And he smiled his funny little twisted smile, as if he wouldn't let himself be amused, for fear of giving himself away, even to his own thoughts.

"But it couldn't be simpler, Rudi," Eunice said turning to me with her gentle urgency, "than to have you with us for as long as ever you care to stay. It's what we've always wanted!"

"Just till I get some work," I muttered guiltily, because you feel guilty when you have no work, "it would be heavenly to be with you."

I don't say that a weight was lifted off my mind although I only had twelve marks with me, and as far as I could see, beyond selling my gold watch and cuff links, no particular way of getting any more; but the lack of money was only part of the trouble.

My real relief was that I didn't have to make any fresh arrangements about anything so totally uninteresting as my life.

His life is not a thing about which a ghost can be expected to take much interest. Just to stumble back into the blessed silence of their car, and be carried along through moist floating space without so much as lifting a finger, was a sort of dull felicity.

It was growing dusk when we reached Oxford.

We have cities in Austria that are as beautiful as Oxford perhaps — Salzburg and Innsbruck — Vienna itself — are still as beautiful; but this was not like a city. There were elms and rooks among the towers and ancient buildings; the old walls melted into gardens. The narrow congested streets led straight to meadows, or to the side of a silvery winding stream that they told me was the river Isis. I never saw so many young men on bicycles before either, except in Holland; but there it was not *only* young men who rode bicycles, so that you did not have the feeling of picked intelligent youth tumbling over each other in a stream flowing towards the future, or is it towards the past that this stream is flowing?

Looking at their young faces, as they slipped by us in the waning light, I found myself urgently hoping that it was towards the future.

"These faces," I said to Eunice, "are each so different from the other. I find that very exciting!"

She looked surprised for a moment and then she said quickly, "Oh, I see what you mean: they haven't that drilled-into-sameness look of American gunmen like the Nazis. I once saw a Nazi film . . . " She stopped as if she were afraid of hurting me.

"But we *must* talk about the Nazis," I told her earnestly. "I shan't mind, in fact I'd mind far more if we didn't! It's one of the things I came to England for — to talk about the Nazis! You see you *can* only talk about them while they are not there!"

James spoke in his half-soothing, half-sardonic drawl. "But of course we'll talk about 'em!" he promised me. "We'll talk about everything under the sun; that's what we've always done with you, isn't it? Why I remember dragging my soul out by the roots as if it were a turnip, and handing it to you to look at, and you put it in again very neatly with a nice little trowel, as if you didn't think it very different from any other turnip! Have you still got your little trowel, Rudi?"

I heard a sound as if someone were laughing. I suppose it must have been my laughter, since the sound hurt me. It is curious when you begin to think things funny again; and know that they are not.

We began to climb a hill that had substantial houses on each side of it, standing each in their own grounds, like all English houses, as far as possible hidden from their neighbours. We stopped outside a blue door in a wall. A gleaming white stone house stood at the end of a crazy pavement stretching between high box hedges.

I had to remind myself, "There will be a child in that house!"

I think they had not meant me to see Rosemary till the next day; but she showed herself. She stood at the top of a flight of stairs leading into the hall, with the light on her fluffy yellow head like the down on a young chicken. She gave a high squeal of rapture at their homecoming.

I was glad she was a little girl, and except for the colour of her hair, not like Andreas.

"I'm coming down on myself!" she warned us — and very nearly did; but I caught her before she fell. She did not seem to mind the arms of a stranger. I was just, as I hoped to be in that house, a convenient way in which to reach her mother and father.

8th May 1939

I FIND the Next World very difficult to believe in — even though I am there!

Its superficial resemblances to my former life are so misleading: work and food, sleep and speech, go on as usual, and yet nothing in me grips them or is gripped by them. All the processes of life slip on me or off me, like the water that slides off a duck's back.

Yet the differences are certainly a relief.

Instead of harsh rigidity, a mild vagueness; instead of shattering sounds, silence; instead of a wall of hate, the spacious formlessness of an almost universal goodwill.

There is no stress at all under this particular roof. James and Eunice go about their business as if it is not merely nobody else's, but hardly their own. When they leave the house it makes no perceptible difference except that I am alone with the Child. Rosemary is fortunate in both her parents. James, who shows a great respect both for his own will and for the wills of others, does nothing to violate or drive the will of his only child.

Eunice has perhaps suppressed her own individuality a little too vigorously, so that Rosemary has less to learn from her mother's reactions to her behaviour than is normal for a child.

But to possess a mother who is as impersonal as a draught of air and as unspectacular as a drop of water gives a child a wonderful field for its own creative and controlling powers. Nevertheless Rosemary has her own difficulties like the rest of us. She resents that her mother, having taken complete charge of her till she was two years old, has now restarted her work as a teacher, handing the child over to the care of a nurse.

Rosemary has developed a trick of constant attacks of acidosis in order to meet this problem.

Instinctively, a child realizes the anxiety of its mother that it should be nourished.

Food is a symbol of life; it was not for nothing that that great teacher, Jesus Christ, on the eve of His departure from this world took bread, and breaking it, gave it to His disciples, saying, "This is my body," in order to show them that He was now leaving His very life to be shared by them.

Deep in every woman's heart — deeper perhaps than anything else — is her desire to provide food for the being she loves. When a woman has ceased to make a man happy, she will still try to make him comfortable; and she will be even more sharp in her passion to satisfy the needs of her child.

The child, therefore, when dissatisfied, or anxious (perhaps the man also — for what are men but children of a larger growth?), reacts by refusing to take this food from the woman. Either he will not eat at all, or if he eats, he cannot digest, or else he will not take what is provided for him but asks for different food.

Rosemary has reached the stage now, whenever a new nurse appears (and as they are all failures, many new ones appear), of automatically replying by an attack of acidosis. By this illness she achieves two objects. She receives instantly the full attention of her mother, who promptly gives up her work to nurse her; and she makes things quite extraordinarily difficult for the interloper.

I have set myself the task of relieving Eunice of this anxiety.

A ghost is a good attendant for a young child. Rosemary finds me there like a shadow, without the pressure of a personal substance. I only remove, if it is necessary, some of the perils that beset the path of her experiments. Usually I try to show her how to overcome these dangers for herself. She prefers this — since she is a courageous child. She is already attaching herself to me though I have only been here about two weeks. I do not think she has any great affection for me, nor is such an affection necessary when you are young. You love more that which you can control, and Rosemary knows that she cannot control me; but she seems to have a certain confidence in me because now when she comes into any new situation she looks round her immediately and demands, "Where's man?" and if I am absent, she turns away from almost any pleasure, however promising, until she has retrieved me; then she takes no further interest in me, which is as it should be. I look after her therefore, and I work in the garden, also I am learning how to typewrite.

I know that James and Eunice are trying to re-establish me in my profession although they do not speak to me of their efforts, for fear that they may fail.

The occupation of foreign doctors with their different habits and their faulty English is a difficult problem, and one that any Refugee ought to be able to understand. The behaviour of the German Refugee doctors during the first persecution of 1933 accounts for some of the General Medical Council's intractable rigidity. They admitted quite generously nearly two thousand of their German colleagues who in return – many of them – behaved with their usual German egocentricity. They undercut the prices of their British colleagues; forced themselves upon the practices of other men by tricks and subterfuges; and often when positions were obtained for them, threw these over at a moment's notice to go to better-paid jobs in America.

The General Medical Council – in fact most of their fellow Islanders – seem hardly to be aware that Austrians are no more like Germans than they themselves are like Americans; even less like – for Americans are sometimes an improvement upon their Anglo-Saxon heritage, when it *is* Anglo-Saxon, whereas I must say – though it sounds like conceit – that Germans are seldom an improvement upon Austrians. Einstein or Thomas Mann can be cited against me – but Einstein is a Jew and Thomas Mann a genius. Such people have very few, if any, national traits.

When our Austrian persecution started in 1938 after the Occupation, the General Medical Council refused to open its doors again, except under such conditions as rendered the re-entrance of all their most famous Viennese colleagues into their profession almost impossible.

Of Freud, who was dying, they made their one generous exception. But he had only time and breath enough – old hero that he was – to make a last joke before he died: "Now at last I will consent to say, '*Heil Hitler*,'" he remarked when he saw the home and garden prepared for him by his English hosts.

Julius Bauer, the greatest gland specialist, and one of the best teachers in Europe, could not even continue his research work in Great Britain without passing, at fifty years old, a students' examination in midwifery in a foreign tongue which would have taken up at least a year of his life. England lost him to America though he asked for nothing better than to devote his whole time, and every gift he had, to the country he loved.

Löwenstein, the discoverer of Anatoxin, lived from hand to mouth in London while his old friends fought for his right to work. They did not obtain it. He, too, was lost to England and went to California.

Heinrich Neumann, our throat-and-ear specialist, a big burly Czech peasant, universally famous, was first imprisoned by the Nazis and when ultimately released (though his surgical instruments were confiscated), died; thinking it, I imagine, hardly worth while to go on living in such an unworkmanlike world.

It did not occur to one of the generous rich men of this country to start Research Fellowships in connection with the Universities, or to endow any Institution for the homeless scientists of Vienna. What a marvellous future such a research hospital might have had — started by these picked Viennese scientists co-operating with the heads of the British Medical Profession!

To their honour, James told me, the Regius Professors of both Oxford and Cambridge as well as many individual Heads of the Medical and Dental Professions, with a still larger proportion of the rank and file, offered us strong support.

But they fought the General Medical Council in vain.

When people are not individually responsible for their actions, they cease to practise any disinterested morality.

So we of Vienna, who led Europe in our profession, are now rendered useless to our English friends. We can give no contribution to the country we long to serve. We who were the children of Science and had thought her to be the universal source of Truth, have found her, upon these shores, a constipated British Nationalist.

Many of us became embittered by these restrictions and inhibitions; and by what ultimately followed from them — the suspicion bred in the mind of the ignorant, against all Refugees.

But I shall try not to sink into a morass of envy and self-pity in this diary, since I have a feeling that the heart of the British has not yet been reached. These people live far down beneath a surface of privilege and security. One day Hitler's bombs will reach their core. The crust will break up then and we shall find authentic fires burning — not of Hitler's making! Fires which will in the end destroy both Hitler and the selfishness which was the true cause of his wholesale power.

James and Eunice are like most of the thinking people in Great Britain, greatly disturbed by the blindness of their Politicians, but not even James and Eunice are disturbed enough. I find everyone we speak to expecting War; but since no one wants it, the Politicians, filled with the selfish arrogance that has already wrecked Europe, believe that they can avoid it.

Their War preparations are on a par with their wish-dreams. They have perfected their Air Raid Warnings, James tells me, but refused to prepare any shelters in which those they warn may achieve safety.

Fear, rather than the courage which earns its own security, is the Leader of British Policy, and since their War strategy follows this aim, it, too, is weak and fearful. Perhaps the little neutrals are not so silly after all when they refuse the form of collective insecurity *now* offered them, rather than what they asked for *before* Hitler was equipped to strike them down!

James tells me that the Rulers of England have been gradually smoothing out and deadening the truth for years, gagging the Press and deafening the people by telling them that there need be no War, or alternatively that if War is thrust upon them, it need only be an economic one in which flesh and blood will be spared — though why Hitler should provide himself with thousands of tanks and aeroplanes and a whole galaxy of lethal weapons in order *not* to destroy flesh and blood, has not been explained to them by these golf-ball thinkers! I watch, with rage and horror, these belovèd and threatened Islanders, who are our only hope still — and their own! I forgot that I am dead; how foolish I am to speak of hope!

If the War were over and the last German had retreated to his own borders, should I return to Vienna?

Never, now — not for my own sake or because of Klara's, or the child's, but because every stone is slippery with shame and broken faith — because I could never look at St. Stephan's tall spire without tears.

There are some things too terrible to have happened until memory itself has grown into thin air. In the Campagna about Rome even now the ghosts of long-forgotten crimes jostle the wayfarer. They talk of "Roman fever," and this fever has baffled physicians for many centuries. Those who once take it are always liable to catch it again. Well, now there will be for certain men a "Viennese fever"! And it will not be safe for travellers who are sensitive to germs from the past to linger in her streets or visit her Palaces. I would not wish them burned or destroyed, for many people are immune from such attacks; besides, I am not a pessimist. I can believe that men may, in the far distant future, reconsecrate Vienna by love of their kind, and by the acts of love. But for me they cannot do this. For me the desecration will last as long as I live.

I had a strange experience to-day. James and Eunice took me to a party.

There has been a mission from Poland sent to London to find out what their new strong ally is prepared to do for them.

The Poles want a loan of eight million pounds as well as aeroplanes, tanks and guns. It seems to me they are a little late. They should have thought of these requirements before Beck jockeyed France off the inside lines; and fouled that good horse, Czechoslovakia!

The Poles are a brave and romantic people who have never known what co-operation means, nor what other people are up to.

Now they have a new rich friend and expect her to hand them over the moon, without knowing that the substance of this moon has precisely the nature of green cheese.

I do not like parties any more but I consented to go to this party given to the Polish Mission by James's rich friends in Berkeley Square.

When you go inside such a house you see why England allows

herself to be ruled by obscurantist humbugs. It was museum-rich.
The food was the best in England, the wines exquisite; and there
were speeches made about how nice the Poles were and how
brave and valiant England expected them to be. I enjoyed listening to the speeches because they were really humorous — but not
so funny for the Poles. The name Sienkiewicz was of course mentioned. The young Poles ate what they could get hold of; and
looked glum. When they found I was an Austrian, they got me
into a corner where we could not be overheard — or understood
— if we were listened to — since we talked German — and demanded to know if the British were completely mad or wholly
insincere.

"Do they not know," one of them asked with passion, "that
we are *doomed* if they do not act immediately, and give us all the
help we need? We can fight *with them* but we cannot fight *for*
them, and the Nazis are at the door! What have the British got,
for us, or for themselves? Yet when we ask them, they refer us
to the City and when we ask those in the City, they talk to us of
Security! It is to Hitler they should talk about Security — God
knows no Pole has it!"

Another told me, "Last night we were taken to a meeting of
young men like ourselves. They were debating whether, if War
should be declared, they would fight or not! They were *men*,
young ones, like us! What do they think will happen to them if
they don't fight for England, that they will escape fighting? Not
at all: they will be made to fight for Hitler, or else be murdered!
Once Hitler gets in, they will have no souls to call their own,
and no tongues they can use to talk about them. These English
fellows are not drilled — or armed. God! Have they never seen
or heard or smelled a Nazi over here?"

"Not for what he *is*," I told them; "only for what he *isn't*.
Ribbentrop has been here."

"Have the British gone Nazi in their sleep?" another demanded. "Will they sell us out?"

"I think not," I said. "Some of them might — a Dean here — a
city magnate there — but not the country. The country, whether
you believe in them or not, has men who, once awake, will fight

till they have only bones left to fight in. I can very well understand your feelings, but I do not share them. I believe that England will fight, and fight to a finish; but, alas, about one thing I
agree: she has not yet started! Go home. Prepare to shed your
blood, perhaps in vain, but remember that England will soon stop
her lying and hiding, because this that you have seen, these kind
ladies and gentlemen who entertain you with pity and champagne,
represent, in the end, nothing but themselves. You have not seen
the real England: she is, as usual, hiding behind her little hedges
in the damp fields, or at work in her great factories, or digging
under the earth for coal, or facing the seas and all that is under
the seas, upon her merchant ships. This is a great England, and
she still exists; but you will not find her in City Offices, or in
these drawing-rooms. Perhaps she has not yet found herself, but
Hitler will find her!"

"For us — too late!" they said in a chorus round me.

I did not say to them, "You also are too late, for your brothers,
the Austrians and the Czechs!"

To-night they go back, these Polish boys, with nothing but a
stunned sense of having to choose between suicide or slavery.
It is to the honour of Poland that they will choose suicide. But
perhaps hardly to the honour of this British Government that
she is offering them an alternative that she knows does not exist.

3rd September 1939

THANK GOD, it has come at last! All this year-long feverish tossing from side to side of a sick-bed is resolved into the healthiness of cool decision.

Hamlet speaks for these Islanders at their every crisis, through the voice of Shakespeare. From the moment I landed, I seemed to hear him say: —

"But thou wouldst not think how ill all's here about my heart."

Now instead I hear — as clearly as one can hear in our mountains of Tirol the voice of a waterfall at midnight when the frost releases it — the bell of action.

"We defy augury: there's a special providence in the fall of a sparrow. If it be now, 'tis not to come; if it be not to come, it will be now . . . the readiness is all."

War in England has the silent quality of growth. It has broken like a slow dawn. As the darkness thins, I see the blurred faces grow clearer and find that all are turned in the right direction.

There will be no retreat now. No politician can for long deceive these attentive people; or dare betray them. This is what I came for; this is what I believed in; this is what made me die every death, except the easy one of oblivion. I am content at last. I am among them. I will give them all I have.

Yet there is still reason to fear because none of them know, yet, how tremendous, how equipped, how single-minded is their enemy! But a reasonable fear is an ally to a fighter. Such fear knits the heart rather than unravels it; and I believe that no enemy, however tremendous, can now tear this aware and living tissue from its rock.

The seas roll between England and her enemies; and astride the seas are her sons.

Hitler has made two mistakes — mistakes that come from the natural indecency of his corrupted heart. They are both psychological mistakes and therefore will be fatal. Hitler believes that enduring courage can arise from hate. It cannot! Enduring courage arises only from love. Hitler has taught his docile people how to hate; these indomitable people here will teach themselves how to love. Also Hitler has forgotten, if he ever knew, that the British are, by religion, sportsmen.

A strong animal easily devours a weaker animal; but it takes a very strong and a very astute animal to destroy a hunter.

I have not very much admired, nor do I now, those sportheaded men of Britain, who merely hunt, shoot birds, and fish as if their lives depended on it, when they do *not*. But a country where the love of sport is the deepest instinct *is* an active and courageous country.

Every one of those forty-two million Islanders thrills to a risk, and they thrill in common. Down go their class barriers, their blind arrogance of privilege; even the smug selfishness of the rich! The people of Great Britain thrill together, aim together, face in skilled unison together, the Beast of Prey that threatens their homes and the inner freedom of the hearts that built them. I even think to myself, "I am glad their homes are so uncomfortable; that they are always going out into the garden; and do not know how to cook — Because of these things, they can endure hardness!"

It is strange, too, how in a few hours their faces have become alive; and their conscious chilliness has melted away from them. Now they look at each other with bared, friendly eyes. They have indeed much to shake off, and much to awake from, these merry Islanders; but they will be clean when they are stripped. They will be dangerous.

"We may as well stick round the radio," James said to me rather apologetically this morning, Sunday the third of September.

The French windows were open. James employs a boy to help me work in the garden. He spends most of his time watching birds and playing with Rosemary; but he is a nice boy, and even comes in Sunday mornings to help me water the flowers. This, he was doing now, as the slow sunny minutes ticked blindly on.

Our suspense was like a colic. We had spasms of it, and in between looked at each other in premature relief.

Eunice was, as usual, the quietest; only once I saw her hands open and shut, when there was nothing in them.

We were afraid that there might after all be *no* Declaration. We were afraid of a wrong Declaration. The Poles were already three days gone in their mortal agony. The heart of France within Daladier's closed fist beat intermittently, and faintly, like a dying man's.

Eunice slipped away at the last moment into the kitchen. She and the cook came back hand in hand together. James beckoned Edward in from the garden while Big Ben was still striking. Rosemary went on playing by herself on the sunny lawn with a toy set of gardening tools I had given her. I watched her yellow head bobbing up and down like a transmuted speck of dust in a sunbeam. I reminded myself that to keep that bright dust moving in the light was what we were fighting for.

Mr. Chamberlain spoke. His meticulous, stinted voice hammered the stillness to pieces. At this hour he spoke well — or else the hour spoke for him.

But I believe the veil that has for so long obscured his eyes has at last fallen.

I have often said to myself, "If they really see — these British Politicians — they will try to stop what Hitler is doing!" but after watching them for a long time, I had to add — "If they know how to look!" We are, after all, responsible for what we look at, since there is something behind the eyes that look, which alters the shape of any object to our vision, although the object itself is unalterable.

When the Declaration and the speeches were over, the people all over this little Island sang, "O God! our help in ages past." But I fancy that as they sang, they changed their minds about God; and realized that His help would come only from the hands He had made for that purpose.

They also sang their King's song. It is very fine to mix music and the heart itself; since one is the true speech of the other.

The child went on playing in the sunshine with her back to us — building up her wise dream world. I was glad they kept her out of the World that was responsible for War.

The two women looked frozen together where they stood. James spoke first. Edward had a bewildered expression, and kept glancing at James as if for reassurance. James was smiling with his eyes and one corner of his mouth.

"*Our* time, Edward," he said to the boy, "but not Peace in it! Well, it wasn't the *Lord's* Peace that we were having anyhow, was it? I expect we've got to patch that Peace up for ourselves later on — you and I!" James was twenty-nine and the boy seventeen.

James did not look at his wife, but I did. I am in the habit of looking at Eunice first, when a thing happens, because I have never seen her think first of herself. She didn't now. She said to the cook, "You know, Jane, your young man is such a good signaller that I feel sure they'll keep him in England!"

The cook, who had become angry — as most uneducated people become when suddenly moved or surprised — said, "Well, Ma'am, I must say I thought Mr. Chamberlain would keep us out of this!"

Then everyone went about his usual business.

We spent the evening, after the nine-o'clock news, discussing Rosemary's acidosis, and how to deal with it.

There seemed no use talking about what the Nazis were doing to the Poles.

15th September 1939

YESTERDAY was Rosemary's third birthday.

Perhaps she had even from the first too much excitement. I had made her a doll's house with electric lighting. Eunice had bought the furniture and a family of little dolls. Her father had provided the contents of a farmyard neatly painted in wood. Beyond the fact that a cow and a cock were of much the same size, nature had not been falsified in their reproduction.

It was a perfect summer morning, and Rosemary took the day like a bird. After we had each had our little success with our indoor offerings, she ran out into the garden, to be met by the boy Edward, who presented her with a tall white tulip in a pot. This tulip bulb had been kept dormant in a greenhouse by an expert gardener friend of Edward's specially for this occasion; and now it bloomed as in May. This was the peak of her rapture. Something that grew — that was beautiful — that was hers — how can we tell what reaches swiftest the core of a child's heart? But we know when it *is* reached! I watched a little anxiously the opening and shutting of her hands: her whole being vibrated and trembled with ecstasy. Edward planted the tulip in a bed of its own, which he told Rosemary was to be her garden. She was to have complete charge of it and I left him explaining to her what care it would need.

Rosemary often plays alone in the walled garden, while Eunice is at her work; and one of the maids in the house is supposed to keep an eye upon her from the windows.

It may have been an hour later that I looked out and saw the tragedy happen.

Edward had gone home to lunch, and it had occurred to Rosemary, left alone with her treasure, that she was responsible for its well-being, although Edward had already supplied it with everything a plant required.

Time is nothing to a child one way or the other — they live in
eternity. "Now," Rosemary must have thought, "I have to do
what Edward told me — I must water this flower immediately, or
it will die!"

Unfortunately Edward had left a full-sized watering can upon
the path, nearly as large as Rosemary herself. It was a miracle
of effort that she succeeded in carrying it across the little terrace
to a tap in the wall. What it had cost her to reach the tap, and
turn it on — for it was stiff — I dare not think, but she had succeeded, although she had not been able to turn the tap off again,
and had wet herself to the skin. Somehow or other, she then
carried the can full of water across the sun-baked terrace, to the
bed of the white tulip; and then while I looked on in dismay too
far off to stop her, the whole contents of the can lurched forward over the doomed flower.

The proud, beautiful head shook — sagged and toppled over
into a muddy pond at its root. But I had no thought to spare
for the fallen tulip; the real tragedy was in Rosemary's eyes.

The whole of joy, the whole of security, that inner confidence upon which Life itself is built, fell with that tulip; and
Rosemary had caused the fall.

She knew herself responsible for the death of what she loved.

I never moved quicker in my life than down the stairs, to
reach the child. She stood stiff and silent in her horror — with the
water still pouring over her — and her eyes transfixed with grief,
bent upon the broken flower. But when I reached her and caught
her up in my arms, she buried her face upon my shoulder; not to
see it any more, although she wanted me to see it.

"Look!" she cried between her sobs. "Look!" and perhaps
that I was there to see it with her, comforted her a little.

"You see it was too much!" I tried to explain. "Edward was
right: water is good for tulips — but not too much!"

But this did nothing to lessen her agony — if indeed it reached
her understanding. A less sensitive, a less loved child, might not
have thought it so terrible to kill a flower; but this child did.
Nor perhaps was it only that the flower was dead, and by her
act, that most troubled Rosemary. Edward was wrong. How

could she ever trust anyone's word again? She did not doubt
that Edward, like herself, had acted in good faith. In no sense
had this accident altered her love for Edward. She moaned in her
grief, "Poor Edward! Poor tulip!"

Edward as a garden divinity, had, as far as Rosemary was
concerned, ceased to exist. A god that cannot control his own
laws is himself in danger — so is his worshipper.

Cats could eat birds; birds could eat worms; anything could
happen now to anybody, in the sunshine, under a blue sky.

I felt that I held Austria in my arms, when the Germans occupied her, and the Democracies would not even try to keep
their promises to save her.

Rosemary stopped crying very quickly; but the joy had gone
out of her day; and nothing could replace it.

That night the illness started; for a week acidosis played
havoc with her. Rosemary was as ill as a child can be, and
recover.

It was that first fortnight of the "phoney war" when only
Poland was in agony.

Eunice and James and I said very little about the fall of
Poland — it was like the fall of the white tulip — irreparable. We
merely nursed the child, night and day, till she recovered, and
decided to digest her new, insecure universe.

"There are two things we can do to fight any return of this
illness," I told her parents, on the first evening when we were
sure of her recovery. "One is to give her more courage; and the
other is to make her less precious; and one to some extent depends upon the other."

"You must explain," James said, lighting his pipe, and smiling
at me, over it, so that I saw he already half understood what it
was I meant. But Eunice would not understand. She set her
brave lips rather more firmly than she need have done, and
blinked at me through her glasses as if she did not like looking
at me, which I could well understand. Eunice always keeps
her reluctances out of her speech, but they are none the less
visible.

"Rosemary has recovered physically," I said after a pause,

"but she is shaken, because such an incident can knock the bottom out of a child's universe. You think she showed great courage and initiative in dragging that great watering can to and fro to water her white tulip. Certainly she took her responsibility in earnest and her conscience was good. But to make such frantic efforts — to feel so responsible — was in itself a sign of mistrust. She did not think Life could even look after a tulip for half an hour, till Edward came back. She had to take everything upon her own shoulders; and she had to do it at once.

"It is true she did exactly what Edward had told her to do. She watered the tulip in order that it might live; and she watered it to death. So we all do, when we try to manipulate Life, rather than find out what Life itself demands of us. All that courage, that obedience, those great efforts, resulted in the exact opposite of Rosemary's intention. So the German nation to-day desires to spread light over all the world, and spreads darkness, because it does not realize, and has not had the confidence in Life itself, to find out what the world asks of it. To find out what Life demands of us, and to train ourselves to fulfil these demands, that is a long and humble business!

"To force upon Life what we ourselves happen to possess is, so we sometimes think, an intelligent short cut; and it is not only Germany that will have to find out that it is not intelligent! But of one thing I am very certain — that the Germans as well as Rosemary will live to see their white tulip — the *Kultur* — that the best of them seek to spread — mysteriously, viciously, cruelly die — by their own hands.

"That too will be a solemn tragedy — though you will not find any Austrians or Poles that will greatly regret it — perhaps not enough!

"You may think this incident for Rosemary is a little thing, but I assure you it can lay her moral universe in ruins. Rosemary is now in the same position as Germany was after her defeat in 1919, when Hitler first began to take advantage of her great weakness; and subsequently of ours. Whatever you tell Rosemary to do, will seem to her dangerous; and if she does not do it, she knows also that it may be even more dangerous. This is a time in a child's life for wrong decisions; decisions in her inner life that you will not even know *are* happening.

"She may say to herself as I think she did to this illness: 'Why not then be so ill that no further efforts are possible? Even if necessary? Why not be ill whenever things become too difficult for me?' She is too young for such thoughts? But *is* she? What do we know of the thoughts of a child? Must they have a vocabulary? For that I grant you she is too young, but those thoughts can govern her nevertheless, without words — they stir in her blood, unspoken impulses of fear, reducing her powers of resistance to any poison that seeks to invade her. And Eunice is a perfect nurse. How wonderful to be nursed by Eunice, who will otherwise teach strange children and leave Rosemary face to face with the horrible experiment of a *new* nurse, who, not being a mother, is far from perfect!"

James's smile broadened. Men are always jealous of the attention a wife gives to a first child — they like to see it attacked by an outsider; and sometimes they are right — although jealousy is seldom a wise guide. Eunice's lips took an even straighter line. "Do you mean," she demanded, "that I should not nurse my own child when she is ill?"

"That would be difficult," I admitted, "and I would not ask it, for no nurse is better than a skilled mother such as you are; but when the worst of the illness is over, as it now is, I think we should make her convalescence a little quicker by making it less inviting! I should advise that we leave her alone now, and cease to amuse her. Also I think she should have the care, but no more the special privileges, of her illness. Then she will not stay delicate quite so long, and she is less likely, when a fresh conflict comes, to revert to illness, as the best way out of it. We have now to start an education towards courage. Adler used to say 'The only good education for a child is an education towards courage.'"

Eunice frowned. "You speak as if the child was not brave enough," she protested, "but I think she is only too brave — she has no fear of anything! I have tried to keep her so, because I know that you always thought I did not trust Life enough, but I have sometimes thought it a mistake!"

I laughed a little both at myself and at her, for I knew that Eunice takes too much pains over everything; and I perhaps too little, but over some things, such as this plight of Rosemary's, I am prepared to take great pains.

"She must not be too precious," I told Eunice, "but do not think I wish her to be less loved! Only you must not be selfish about this business of loving — give Rosemary herself more of it to do, that is what will increase her courage! It must not be easy loving either, like that she gives you and James and even myself. We do not challenge her enough. She should have someone of her own age, who will quarrel with her as to who is to have a yellow cow and who the red. Even I, a stranger, am quite useless because I am indifferent about the colour of my wooden cow. Another child is not indifferent! If she mixes with other children she will cease to be a queen. The one child of a household has always a court; and is always being protected by someone. Rosemary must fight for her own status, on her own feet, with her own equals — then she will feel both less threatened and less precious!"

Eunice ceased to look so severe, but she was still searching about in her mind for fresh objections that might still keep her in control of her loved object. James took his pipe out of his mouth and said: —

"Well, what do you propose to do, to lessen this Queen Complex? We cannot invent a family in a week or two, even if I earned money enough to support one. Tom has all the money in our family. Eunice and I are supposed to have the brains; you should have lived long enough in this country to know that brains are a drug on the market. Nobody wants them, except those who have already got them, and can seldom afford their upkeep."

"What I would suggest would not cost you money," I told them. "All that is necessary is to start a nursery school for children under five, here in this house; and if you have no other teacher in view, I will teach it. After all, I know very well that you cannot reinstate me in my own profession at the moment — but the study and understanding of children is at least as vital

as any other part of humanity — and I will gladly undertake it.
Half a dozen children from two to five will be enough for us.
Probably their parents could afford to pay us ten shillings a week
each for the full morning hours. I would — if they live in a near
neighbourhood — collect and return them to their homes. I could
then pay for my board and feel independent. I too must not be
spoiled. What do you think of this plan?"

We discussed it all the evening and they thought well of it.

In the end Eunice went even further than James, and pur-
sued with unflagging zeal a search among her friends for the
children.

Now this little school is established and running with success.

At first Rosemary was flurried and hostile. I had to make her
understand that she was not dispossessed; her home was her
own, and only shared in the morning with the other children.
Then she became too important as a hostess and wanted to
arrange all that they did — where each one was to sit, etc.,
but this the children themselves reacted against sufficiently
strongly so that I did nothing in the end but watch Rosemary
adjust herself gradually to *not* being the centre, "the middle
point" as we used to call it in Vienna, of every occasion. It was
difficult for her of course, but companionship soon makes up for
this loss of central significance; and Rosemary becomes every
day more hardened to the world — that would I knew have been
tougher still for her, if she had come to it isolated and exceptional,
expecting all to be roses, mother love, and appeasement.

She has her rights; and I see that she gets them, but she must
fight for them like the other children, and if now and then
she gets outfought, she must learn how to fight better next
time.

"Fearless courage": is that of real use in this world of to-day?
Not without equipment; not without training. "Gallant little
Poland," they say in this country, or did till she was beaten!
Well, Poland *was* and *is* gallant, but she believed in horses; she
persecuted Jews; she kept her press in a straitjacket; and refused
her duties to her allies.

To be fearless is not enough, or is it perhaps too much? The courage of Poland became her grave; and how many other people's graves this uninstructed courage can dig, we shall find out sooner or later while this War lasts.

How brave that tall white tulip looked before the floods drowned it!

15th October 1939

I DO not write often in this diary because things happen very slowly here. There is no War yet — except upon the unquiet seas. Often I feel myself to be in a "slow-motion" picture. We take a jump — the British Empire and myself — but remain in the air until all notion of where we shall land is forgotten.

Corruption is stealing through the divided mind of France, while Hitler eats into its shaken heart. Soldiers who do not fight paralyze the people they are there to defend; and I believe that France is becoming paralyzed behind the Maginot Line.

"An economic war is enough!" the myopic rulers of these two great Democracies still shout across the Channel to each other. They have not even confidence enough in themselves, or in each other, to tunnel the Channel.

Does a defenceless householder win an economic war against an armed burglar?

It is laughable, if what must happen should these two fail to defend themselves were not so horrible.

These soft autumnal days are as gentle as the smile of the old, when they are happy.

Is not Oxford the soul of England? A little commercialized with its red-brick edges; within, its splendid monuments — somnolent, ripe, secure?

Every time I walk through its narrow streets or melt into the college gardens, I feel afresh how benevolent, how wise, through what twists and turns of unconscious beauty, these ancient people have preserved the best gifts of their private lives. Each stone has its single history. Men, always brave and often wise — but somehow different from other men upon the mainland of Europe — have ruled here, and been trained to rule, by the profound unrigid wisdom of unspoken laws.

There are no names upon these colleges. A stranger cannot

find his way about in the streets or between their walls. But here strangers do not matter, except to themselves. After all, they can ask; they can be told; the others know.

In the end I find myself thinking, "How different *ought* men to be from their brothers?" Is this what we are fighting this War to find out? It is surely part of it; since there are two wars going on in the Democracies: the War against Fascism, which is a Lie; and the War against isolationism, which should no longer be a Truth; and some of us get confused between these two issues; or some of us take one side and some the other. We have not the same Faith. But the Nazis have only one issue — their war against isolationism is already over. They fight to maintain and spread their Lie, which is also their Faith, that the German people should have the command of the whole world; and since theirs is one issue only, and an issue of Faith — it makes them dangerously strong.

Rabelais said: "Science is wisdom; conscience is a greater wisdom; if there should come a time when these two should be divorced from each other then Hell would be let loose on earth."

Well as I see it — this War is the Hell in which men have ceased to believe; and it *is* let loose upon the earth — because science *has* been divorced from conscience.

When I wake in the misty mornings and look out at these mauve-grey colleges, their mullioned windows and vivid walls, their lawns smoothed out by centuries of easy living, I ask myself if I am not already living in a dream — which will be to-morrow, or the day after to-morrow, merely a memory perpetuated perhaps by Hollywood.

Have not I, and all the other poor rats with me, left our sinking ship only to postpone our doom? For is it not humanity *itself* that is sinking?

And then I go downstairs to breakfast — the English breakfast. Still bacon and eggs upon their tables, and toast and marmalade; bad coffee if you can drink it, or if you can drink it, good tea.

Eunice's little attentive tilted face, smiling up at me behind its twin mirrors — James giving me a curt nod, entrenched in *The Times*. Then Rosemary dances in, all curls and laughter; and eats the tops off our eggs, singing her way through a new world, which does not exist for us, and may not for long exist even for Rosemary. James has been asked to leave Oxford to take on the Turkish and Arabic broadcasts for the B.B.C. so we discuss living in London, and omit to point out to each other that there may not be a London in which to live.

But Oxford — I doubt if I could explain even to James that there might be no Oxford! I go on eating my breakfast after Eunice has taken Rosemary upstairs; and James reads on, having handed me Eunice's paper, the *New Chronicle*, considerately across the table. But I do not read papers at breakfast, having no train to catch. I go on thinking instead how different this university city — and Cambridge its twin brother — are from Paris, say, or Heidelberg — or Vienna. You cannot imagine Frenchmen studying here for long: Oxford is too quiet, too remote, for a French brain. It has no fierce brawls, no national current running through it. It is not beaten against by the street wits of Paris. Here the towers of Oxford's churches influence still what goes on under its college roofs.

Yet Oxford is not blinkered as German universities are blinkered by student corps or the spirit of militarism. Nor is it always open to the movement of men's minds in their café lives, as we Viennese always had our student days, so that we did our best thinking to the smell of coffee.

The training of men's minds, and the personalities that rule these minds, produced the psychological school of Vienna. Freud and Adler sprang fully armed from the cafés; and all the thinking men of Vienna, writers, journalists, young politicians, joined their wits with those of these two great dynamic beings. Perhaps Freud caused Fascism itself by disrupting the entire intellectual life of Europe with his vicious question: "Why should I love my neighbour?" There was dynamic poison in that sentence; but a Europe that was not rotten would not have been disrupted by it. The iron of defeat and hate was still hot when Freud struck that bitter question out upon its anvil.

Europe was in the habit of forcing its libido towards hate and death; it was not yet ready for Adler's counterblast. "There is a *Law* that man should love his neighbour as himself!"

The tragedy was that Freud himself — though a Dictator type — was big enough, as a man, finally to adjust to the lessons of Life; and honest enough to admit that in the first élan of his great psychological discoveries he had been wrong — or only partially right. Adler he never forgave, or admitted to have been right, but Freud nevertheless came to believe, before the end of his tortured existence, that man must be trained towards Social Interest; or die in his own blood.

But the Oxford scholars took no part in this great struggle. I doubt if they knew that it was going on. They continued to pigeon-hole their knowledge as if it bore no relationship to their personalities, or to life itself. They resolutely turned their backs on the future; ate their great dinners; told their ripe jokes; polished the jewels of their scholarship. Except for a few brilliant heretics, such as James and his friends, these twin universities remained precisely where they were when Edward VII was their unwilling student, until another Edward, two generations later, became another still more unwilling student, finishing his education more happily in the trenches.

James laid down the *Times* and said: "Now I must catch my train. There's no news." He looked at me speculatively with his raised intelligent eyebrows as much as with his keen unrestless eyes.

"When it comes it will be bad," I told him bitterly.

"It *must* be bad," James agreed in that voice which is as soothing as if he were saying his prayers.

After he had gone I went out to bring my babies to their nursery school; and on my way I met Nathalie Winterstein.

It is curious when you first meet a fellow exile. It is no comfort to either of you.

I had last seen her at a masquerade ball in Wien, where she and Klara were the chief beauties.

"I think — it is Rudi!" she said and burst into tears. I took her by the arm and led her out of the busy High Street, into a little stone alley where people seldom passed.

There we sat down hand in hand, on a low wall, though it was a little damp. Still we could not afford a restaurant, and there was nowhere else to go. It was very private and still, sitting there together in the autumn mist.

There she told me all that had happened to her since we last met. She is alone here with Willy, who is now nearly five years old. Our good old Fritz, Nathalie's husband, was beaten to death in their flat opposite the Votiv Kirche; because of Nathalie's escape with the child. He had been very clever, for he had put a little money into the Bank of England for them, and got them out safely into Switzerland, before the Occupation; but not quite clever enough. It seemed he had stayed a day too long to wind up his affairs; and the Nazis caught him.

When she had finished telling me everything — how her old mother is safely in Switzerland now — how her father it seemed died of shock — and how she has had to give the money to the old mother to live on, and is on very short commons herself, I ventured to ask her if she had seen Klara since we parted. They were bosom friends; and though Fritz was a full Jew, Nathalie had only one grandmother tainted.

She said, "Yes, I saw Klara once." She hesitated a little painfully, then she said: "Perhaps she did not see me."

"Did she look unhappy?" I asked her.

"Not exactly," Nathalie told me. "She looked hard."

"When one lives in the company of stones, one should be hard," I told her. I did not ask her about Andreas.

I took her address before I left her, and that night I told Eunice and James all about her.

To us, I mean to those who are called Refugees, any other exile is an object of immediate solicitude. We are safe. Some of us like myself are even — comparatively speaking — in Heaven. Must we not then share our Paradise? But also must we not remember that our safety has been paid for by our English hosts, and that those whom we solicit must pay still more for the safety of another person?

The government of this country, archly through its Minister Hoare, referred to a "crack in the door" through which a few chosen Refugees might be pulled, by the great exertions of a few private good Samaritans. Neither the Church nor the State was at all prepared for any form of less limited Christianity; so the Refugees did not have as a rule too easy a time of it. Some of them were interned; some were sent without wives or overcoats to Canada; and some were drowned in the *Arandora Castle*. They were also herded together with Nazis, which they had reason to dislike even more than the Atlantic Ocean, or a Canadian winter without an overcoat. Some of them committed suicide like Stekel. I was therefore a little nervous before I appealed to James and Eunice about Nathalie and little Willy; partly that I did not want them to say "No," nor did I think it likely that they would — and partly because I did not wish to urge them to say "Yes" — as I feared they might — since that created fresh expense for them; and was, for me, a fresh obligation.

But I need not have hesitated. They said, "Of course. What shall we do?" with the desire to do everything possible. It was therefore easy for me to say, though still a little painful, that Nathalie, who was also one of Adler's students, could do for the children in our nursery just what I was doing. I did not want to give up the children, since, apart from the money, they were a great creative interest to me. I thought of them and indeed treated them as a New Europe; and I taught them, on that Law of Adler's, through their acts, their games, their every occupation, to love their neighbour as themselves: not better, but as well. Nor is this so difficult as you might think, with children under five years old.

Now I must find something else to do; and the activities of Refugees are highly suspect to the British Government. You are even forbidden to land, if you express the desire to work for them.

For a fortnight I tried to translate Heine — which is always impossible because it looks so easy; and read out loud to the blind. This is an activity that I enjoy because the blind are practically the only people who know how to listen.

A few weeks later James came back from the city looking more cheerful than usual. "Rudi," he said to me after we had finished supper, and Rosemary had been put to bed, "my brother

Tom is, as perhaps you remember, Treasurer to the X Hospital in London. I have for some time — even before you took up the children — tried to get consent for you to work in their Research Department. At last the permission *has* come through. I can't get you a salary even now, but there is a visitor's grant that will cover your travelling expenses and even provide you with a few shillings pocket money. Whether we go to London ourselves or not, we shall have heaps of room for you, so from our point of view nothing could work better." I did not say anything. I buried my face in my hands. Dante was wrong: the stairs of an exile are not too steep, they are too easy; and the bread not too bitter, it is too sweet. James left the room but Eunice sat by me. By and by she asked me, "Rudi, has James ever told you about his brother, Tom?"

"I know that Tom Wendover is an eldest son," I replied, "and that he has a big place in the West Country; and a rich wife whom neither of you like, so that you seldom visit him. And of course, when I was working with James, I realized what this elder brother — with all the family possessions — and full of manly excellences — had meant in his life. James secretly adored his elder brother; and was still more secretly much depressed by him."

"Yes," Eunice agreed. "James *was* discouraged, of course, but, as you used to say, '*innerlich*' James is much stronger than Tom. Tom is just one of those striding persons whom everyone is afraid of, but he is most of all afraid of himself!"

I took my head out of my hands in order to explain better. "Probably he never goes near himself," I said. "That is why he is afraid. It is always the Unknown that frightens us. Most of all what is unknown to us about ourselves. I once knew a young girl who nearly drove herself mad because she was so afraid that if she met a danger she might not be brave. 'Until you can meet the danger of not knowing whether you'll be brave or not,' Adler told her, 'you will certainly fail, if you have to face any other danger.'"

Eunice smiled. "And if we know ourselves," she asked, "do we then become brave?"

"Well," I said, "if one takes all that trouble — one has learned something! To be *less* interested in oneself for instance, and to be less vain, makes one much less frightened. What a price to pay for a little self-knowledge — to be less interesting! Is it any wonder that so few of us are willing to pay it?"

"Tom is vain," Eunice admitted reflectively, "and he's not a bit interested in other people — that's quite true. Least of all — at the moment — in Frances — that's his wife. I don't really dislike her though, Rudi — I only don't see how to get on with her — she runs over me like a lawn-mower runs over a daisy!"

"You should not be so easy to run over," I said a little severely, for it is true that Eunice is, especially when she dislikes any-one, deceptively insignificant.

"James does *really* dislike her," Eunice went on, keeping my reproof to herself, "because he thinks she does Tom so much harm — and of course she does." Eunice paused, and then added what really touched her most, as if it were an afterthought, "And there are the children."

"*Little* children?" I asked, for I had forgotten how much older Tom was than James.

"No, that is the worst of it," Eunice explained. "They aren't little any more — they're noticing everything — and of course taking sides. Gillian is nineteen and Adrian eighteen. They haven't the ghost of a chance really to find their way about in life. They've been falsified by their parents' tempers and buried under special privileges ever since they were born. Adrian — being the only boy — is the most spoiled. He has great sapphire eyes like his mother's and he's vain and hard — much harder than Gillian. But perhaps I don't understand boys as well as I understand girls. You might think that Gillian was harder; but anyhow she's not vain."

"You love this girl — Gillian?" I asked her.

"James and I both love her," Eunice agreed, "but I admit she's difficult to know. You see what emotion she has had has always hurt her; so naturally she takes precautions against having any fresh emotions or even showing those she already has. She is not, I think, at all at home in the world. Perhaps she is not

unlike what I used to be, Rudi, before you taught me that Life
was a friend — and not an enemy."

"Did I teach you that?" I asked incredulously. "Well — I
think it is true — though I have not experienced it."

We were both silent. I was trying to remember what I used
to think and why I used to think it. It must have been something
like Wordsworth's, my old idea of life.

> Serene will be your days and bright
> And happy will your nature be,
> When love is an unerring Light
> And Joy its own security.

Joy is not its own security now. But perhaps this truth was
limited even when Wordsworth lived. Life is not careful of
her single specimens — only of her Laws. Of these she is careful, and they are universal. If we do not accept them universally, we cannot expect safety. The *whole* world must learn
its law of love "unerringly" before one man or woman can
be, for even a fragment of a lifetime, free from torture or disaster.

"You were not hard," I told Eunice, smiling at her, for I saw
that she was looking at me anxiously, "and you always had
courage — that amazing Ariadne thread of courage that some
women — women like you, Eunice — always carry about with
them — a thread too strong for anything to break, and which
brings them safely out of all their difficulties in the end. Let us
hope this girl Gillian also possesses the Ariadne thread. But why
do you tell me so much about these people?"

"They have got into a specially bad sort of tangle," Eunice
explained, "and James and I have been thinking you might be
able to help them out of it!"

"Eunice," I said, "pupils often go a great deal further than
their teacher. It was not I who taught you that when a man
is bowed down with gratitude, you should free his heart, by
giving him a chance to serve you!"

Eunice flushed and turned her head away from me, as she
still does when she is talking about anything she feels deeply.

"No, no," she murmured. "Only naturally Tom means a

lot to James and me, and so do his children. If you are working for Tom's hospital you see, sooner or later you'll get in touch with him, and then he's sure to ask you to stay at Silver Fountains! I can't tell you any more just now because that's James coming back, and he hates talking about his family, but of course he wants you to *know*, though perhaps not just yet!"

I too heard James's footsteps. Men may deceive themselves and others by their words, but seldom by their physical characteristics. When a man walks down a passage, shakes hands with a friend, or laughs at a joke, he gives himself away. A man who shuffles, who tramples, who creeps, who tosses his footsteps away from him, is showing you just what he is. A man with a false laugh is not wholly true; a man who cannot shake hands with hearty goodwill is certainly more or less hostile to other human beings.

James's footsteps are always lifted a little higher than need be, as if he wants to make quite sure where his foot is going to land, before he puts it down. On uneven ground this might be a wise precaution; but the passages of this house are flat.

I did not think he would be ready to talk yet, with me, about his brother; and his brother's difficulties.

20th May 1940

I HAVE waited for six months for James to speak to me about his brother.

There is a stir of evil things in the air. The planned tragedies of Norway and Finland have drawn to a slow finish. The Democracies did nothing much to help about them. They could not; and — while they struggled in vain — I left the private record of my emotions unwritten. To tell the truth I acted like Hagar when Ishmael was dying in the desert, I found myself repeating constantly: "Let me not see the death of the child." And I shied away from any sort of self-expression. A cowardly prayer as I have always thought, and quite useless, for the eyes of the mind not only see all there is to see of evil but, not being on the spot, often fail to see what there is of good to counteract it.

Churchill arose out of the effete blundering of Norway; and out of Finland sprang the splendour of a small nation's unbeatable courage. A little light to lighten the darkness of the whole world. Finland was equipped, ready, alone. She was *not* taken unaware by her great Enemy; and she made a miracle out of her defence. She fought unaided, and won her own hard-bought security. She has been in a sense beaten, but she is herself still licking wounds that are just not mortal.

Russia has crept back behind her new frontiers, having won Stalin's game; but spent rather more than he meant to pay over the candle.

The blundering Democracies just failed to make a fatal blunder — by walking into the trap Hitler had no doubt helped to prepare for them. They left Russia alone, exasperated, but not incurably attacked by her natural allies, to think over her next move against the Nazis. It is true the Democracies had to sacrifice Scandinavia and the Low Countries, who have no faith left now even in themselves; but I do not see that Great Britain and

France could have done otherwise; under the leadership of Munich they had grown too used to the sacrifice of others.

Now at last this country that I love is free to act from its own nature and to sacrifice — if need be — itself — upon the altar of Freedom.

Never in my life have I seen a stranger or a grander thing than Churchill ruling over the hearts, as well as over the persons, of his countrymen.

How did he get there, in one bound? He — so long ignored except by his enemies! Was he always dumbly loved — powerlessly longed for? Who has put him where he is? What hidden wave suddenly weakened the shelving sand of his appeasement foes? Not the act of War, for then he would have taken the place he had earned by his prescience on 3rd September 1939. Not the long-drawn-out decrepitude of this past year's phoney fighting — for that was the mere pussy-footing of the city gangs in Paris and London, forced against their own wills to meet Hitler as an enemy rather than to greet him as a friend.

Was it that last vainglorious ineptitude of Chamberlain's "Hitler has missed the bus!" slapped back at him by Destiny? Who can tell the cause? No outsider can know the heat at the centre of a Briton's heart — perhaps not even the Briton himself knows it.

Suddenly one day there is an explosion where no one knew there was a fire.

A voice caught up an old and living word of Cromwell's and threw it across the floor of the House like a javelin: "For God's sake go!" and that poor, self-complacent little nut-cracker, doubling up under the blow, found itself hollow, and sank into its own ruins. "J'aime Berlin," as the French used to call him, never, so to speak, moved again. Yet I believe he loved what he thought was England. He even believed that he himself was a symbol of the land he loved; and indeed he had some reason for his faith, for it had seemed that Britain *was* behind him while he sold us out for safety, and the Czechs, upon our doorstep.

But Britain had moved away on tiptoe from him after all — under the cover of darkness — without either her friends or her

enemies being aware of it; and after Norway, Chamberlain
found himself a man without a country. There was Churchill
instead with Britain massed behind his broader back. She had
chosen this great personality and fearless representative, when
she herself was at last prepared to say "No" with her blood. But
how England got behind Churchill, or why she was not there
before, a poor devil of an Austrian will certainly never find
out! James and Eunice say when I ask them: "Well — that
umbrella — the things Chamberlain didn't say — it reassured most
of us — we thought, 'Thank God *he* couldn't be a Dictator';
and then he promised us the smooth things we knew we all
wanted — for we *did* all want them — peace — prosperity — to be
left alone — only we forgot that we should have to pay for them.
Some of us thought that Chamberlain, being a business man,
though nothing else, might be able to fix a reasonable price with
Hitler and Mussolini, and so no doubt he might have been able
to fix one if he had had another business man to deal with.
Unfortunately he was no crime expert, and it was criminals
with whom he had to deal"; and then I say, "But what made
Britain think after such a criminal record as Mussolini and
Hitler had already shown that she was dealing with anything
but criminals? Is a man only a criminal if he attacks *us*, after
having destroyed, spectacularly one by one, with monstrous
efficiency and publicity, friend after friend, while we sit staring
at each other and gasping: 'Am I my brother's keeper?'"

One can say these things to James and Eunice, because they
know they are true; but even *they* cannot explain to me how
they have ceased to be true. For the people themselves *have*
changed. Churchill *is* England! All men *are* brothers! Even I
— in my new Laboratory life — find myself a brother!

It is six months since I started my work in the X Hospital.
That first day I was so nervous that I could not work. I was
like a man when life has been too suddenly restored to him.
In fact that is what I am, for my life has always been my
work.

I cleaned test tubes; I checked retorts; I sterilized instruments
and laid out plates — I said to myself "I know nothing! I have

forgotten everything! I am no longer a scientist!" But the smells, the reactions of mixed chemicals, the faint odour of the Bunsen burners, soothed me like the voices of old friends.

I arrived, that first day, so early that there was only a servant in the Laboratory; and he was of course a little suspicious of me with my foreign accent. But by and by a colleague entered. He was polite to me, he showed me where I might work and what instruments I could use, and left me to my own devices. I felt like a new boy in a school. All day long, I watched what the others did; trying to take in their ways and their customs without showing any of my own. Under my fright I was happy, and knew that I should soon feel braver. Nobody noticed me; but now I am used to being left alone in this country and no longer resent it; because I realize how much they themselves like this feeling. It is a compliment to a stranger when an Englishman takes no notice of him. It is as if he said: "You are one of us! You need no help!" Yet how ready he is to come to your assistance if you ask it! He only does not want to insult you by supposing that what he knows by heart, is unknown to you. For him it would be a lasting disgrace that he should not know where to hang his hat; or how to address a superior or an underling. He does not wish such shame to rest upon you — stranger though you are — so he shows you only what you have asked; and swiftly removes even the witness, to your ignorance. But after he has removed himself from you, and because he has told you what you needed to know, a bond has been established. Next time he meets you he will speak.

It is not difficult to know these Islanders. It is only difficult to *get* to know them.

One might perhaps have supposed that since it was by his influence that I was working in the X Laboratory I should soon have met James's brother — Tom Wendover. But though I have worked here now for six months, and I believe that he is often in London, I have never yet set eyes upon him.

"Does your brother avoid me?" I asked James last night on my return home. "I hear to-day again that he has been at the Hospital, but he has never so much as put his nose into the

Laboratory where he knows I am working. And yet I do not think that they are dissatisfied with me there!"

Eunice was putting Rosemary to bed, and James and I sat over a wood fire in his study. These early spring days are light and cold; and curiously long. I find myself shivering even over the fire, but perhaps I am not really cold, perhaps it is only Rotterdam.

"Well, he wouldn't," James said eventually, referring to Tom. "I mean he is no expert; why should he bother you? He's only there to sit on some governing board or other. But it's funny your bringing this up to-night. He *does* want to meet you. I had lunch with him to-day, and he told me something I've got to put before you, but you needn't do it, you know, if you don't want to. Eunice hates the idea, and I don't like it much. Still, they're all I must say in a devil of a mess down there at Silver Fountains. I can't help them out, but perhaps you can. It's like this — " After he'd said it was like this, James proceeded to do almost everything rather than tell me what it *was* like. He poked the fire; put on fresh wood; lit his pipe; marched up and down the room with his hands in his pockets; took them out; fiddled with the black-out; and at last having got rid of all possible postponements sat down in his favourite chair — and with exquisite gentleness dislodged the cat; took out his pipe, sighed deeply and murmured: "Love — how any sane, middle-aged, *occupied* person can fall in love — under the present circumstances — beats me to imagine! One would think Hitler was enough!" As I knew that James and Eunice are fathoms deep in love with each other, and — since there is no possible point where their aims differ — likely to remain so, I felt at peace. James was distressed but he was aggravated rather than agonized. His deep-set, colourless eyes rested on me with a gleam of humour. "Can you see any excuse for it?" he demanded. "Middle-aged people," I remarked cautiously, "are much the same as other people. They have more obligations than the young, but the same emotions. Besides perhaps Tom, if it *is* Tom, wants an antidote to Hitler! I should suppose falling in love might be a good antidote to being wrapped in hate."

"Well, it *is* Tom, or I shouldn't bother," James explained, taking up his pipe again. "I mean it's normal for Gillian or Adrian to lose their heads or their hearts — or both together — and none of our business what they're up to at their age — but to break down family life — and for a girl it's impossible he can marry, and unthinkable he shouldn't — if he's making — as I fear he is — serious love to her — well, it's serious for everybody, isn't it — and we've got to do something about it! Of course I needn't tell you it's entirely Tom's wife's fault. He's had nothing of a marriage from the start; and I suppose when you get over forty you feel time's a bit short, for picking anything up; but where on earth do you suppose he's started looking for it? He's had the idiocy to fall in love with a young girl, who's the clergyman's wife of his own parish! If you knew what that meant in an English country place! She's got two kids under six too; and says she's in love with Tom. I can't believe it. I don't think Frances knows, mind you. But it's a queer thing, in however bad a married life, how little you can hide anything being wrong with you, from your partner! Frances doesn't know who it is, but she feels it's something. She has gone all over ill, with God knows what; and sent off the family doctor with a flea in his ear. Nobody knows if Frances is dying, or merely trying to put the whole family on the spot. She might be doing both simultaneously. I wouldn't put it past her; anyhow, Tom suggests that you join Barrow at the Plymouth Lab and carry on your research there. He's heard all about what the X men think of you in London — and he's keen as mustard on keeping you at your own job, so you won't lose by it. He'll put you up at Silver Fountains and give you a first-class screw, for any help you can give to Frances. Of course I've just thrown in this love business for what it's worth. It might have nothing to do with it; but Eunice thinks it has."

"I remember once telling Adler a malicious patient of his was in love, and he said, 'Against whom?'" I told James, "Perhaps your brother *is* in love now *against* his wife — if she has cheated him. Has she been, or is she now, unfaithful to him?"

"How can one tell what unfaithfulness is, in anyone but oneself or one's own wife?" James intelligently asked me. "I know when I'm being unfaithful to Eunice. I'm unfaithful when I like looking at a girl without eyeglasses; and I should know at once if Eunice were unfaithful to me. I remembered getting terribly agitated when she took a fancy to the Apollo Belvedere at the Vatican. We went to Rome for our honeymoon and I said, 'I can't see why the devil you want to look at that statue for *so* long — I have a good torso too!' There are these moments, no doubt, in every real relationship. But in a good marriage one gets over them quickly. I knew Tom was in trouble, but I gave him six months to sweat it off. Now it's over six months, and Esdaile — the parson-husband — is on his hind legs. I rather like the parson; and he wouldn't get on his hind legs easily. Most of the time he's thinking about God, but it's a pity the girl he's married is at least fourteen years younger than he is!"

Eunice came in then, and we discussed Rosemary, and the babies. I have not ceased to be as interested in them as when they were my chief work; and as for Rosemary, I think I must confess that she is my greatest friend. This is no disrespect to her parents, but they have each other, whereas Rosemary thinks I was made entirely for her.

At last I said, "Well — I will sleep on this new project. You are offering me money to do a thing which I am very unlikely to be able to do, and I am now doing something which I *am* able to do, without money, and I must admit I infinitely prefer doing it!"

They looked at each other, and then smiled.

"Well," they said, "only *you* can do this other thing," and I saw, because after they'd said this James stopped smiling, that they wanted me to do it.

4th June 1940

THE incredible is happening. Somehow or other Dunkirk is being evacuated! The stunning explosion of the Maginot myth has *not* broken the B.E.F. It is coming across (as the British say in that dangerous but splendid phrase they so often use) — "somehow." The men are pouring over, not in tens, or even hundreds, but in tens of thousands. Almost the whole of the British fighting power *is* being saved, by her sea units.

So great is the miracle that this astounding island has already ceased to observe that miracle or no miracle, Dunkirk is a defeat. The men are saved; but their fighting tools are not.

Truly this is not a military-minded people!

James and Eunice see further alas! They have the bitter powerlessness of the intelligent minority. They know very well what each loss and failure mean, and in what direction they are leading. We do not speak of it much to each other; all assemble at the hour of the chief radio messages: eight o'clock, one o'clock, nine o'clock. They go about tight-lipped and Spartan all day giving me, and each other, when we meet, their grim humorous smiles, as if they said each time they passed a comrade: "Well, we have something within us stronger than hate!"

To such people the death of the body is but a cruel incident. No one can kill the spirit; they cannot even demoralize it. Not when the spirit is undivided, and confronts the final issue. Torture I have taken care to see that none of us shall meet. If the Nazis win, we can all four die — the child without consciousness, even of death. I have also provided Nathalie with what is necessary for herself and Willy.

It is wonderful what a calm this brings to the nerves. Now we can attend with concentrated faculties upon *not* letting the Nazis arrive!

We live precisely as we did before danger had risen above

our horizon. Every evening when I return from London I go
to see Rosemary before she sleeps. Sometimes she says her prayers
leaning against my knees. She gives us this privilege in turn, as
the fancy takes her, but I notice though she adores James, who
is her favourite playfellow, she chooses him for this particular
favour less often than myself.

Perhaps she senses that James despises the idea of a Deity,
whereas Eunice and I would — had we any authentic information upon the subject — welcome it. Both of us, even as it is,
accept the Christian ideal, whereas James has a sort of cold
disdain towards all Religions, including the one he invariably
practises.

Rosemary enjoys her prayers, and firmly believes in this
pleasant invisible guide, to whom she talks night and morning
with her usual freedom and enthusiasm.

As this is my last night at home, Eunice suggested my putting
Rosemary to bed, as I often do if the others are busy, alone.
Her prayers took their usual course. She mentioned the death of
a goldfish that had happened during the day, an act I think she
took as showing carelessness on the part of the Deity; and she
reminded Him that there were two others in the pool in the
garden, still open to His ministrations.

I am relieved that Rosemary has slightly altered the sequence
of her prayers. She used to insist first, "I want man back — "
referring to my leaving the babies to Nathalie. Now she is
reconciled to Nathalie and prefers Willy, a silent and likable
boy, to any of the others; and has put off her request for my
reinstatement till the last.

We took two celluloid ducks and an alligator into the bathroom with us. Perhaps I shall remember as long as I remember
anything this June evening, when the last of the B.E.F. must be
streaming back to their homes from that inferno, with eyes
amazed at the sight of their untouched serenity.

Rosemary has a perfect little body; each limb is in due proportion, and blooms with care and health.

There may be children this evening as beautiful upon those
fatal motor roads of France; but I hope not. I know ugly children

can suffer just as much, but there is a point beyond which I refuse to let my imagination go if I can help it.

No alabaster vase holds light with the same bright flush as that with which the rounded body of a child holds the blood that gives it life.

Rosemary has no ounce of superfluous flesh over her shapely limbs, but everything about her curves, as a rosebud curves cleanly into itself. She has a straight back; on her neck the little shavelings of her golden curls lie flat against the whiteness of her skin. Her legs are finely formed to hold the body's slender weight; her feet are as beautiful as her small clutching hands.

I persuade her to do everything possible for herself; and to-night I watched with pride the careful skill with which she handles the small cake of soap I bought for her, putting it back in its own dish, when she has finished with it. Naturally she soaped both the ducks and the alligator, after she had soaped herself.

We filled the bath towards the end, and I gave her a lesson in floating. The sight of her own body rising upon the water, and lying securely upon it, with only the touch of my hand under her neck, filled her with awed delight.

The drying I had to take a hand in; but while I dried her she dried the ducks.

She is a most active, energetic child; and completely fearless.

I remember that Andreas would not let himself float. I think he did not believe only my finger could hold him up. Little girls are more courageous than little boys, because they take for granted what little boys first try to prove to themselves — that life is favourably inclined to them.

I had made up my mind to take this last evening as if it were *not* the last, so that no hint of adverse emotion could reach the child. We laughed at all our usual jokes with as much appetite as usual; and even invented fresh ones; but after she was in bed with her Teddy-bear on one side of her and her rabbit on the other, Rosemary suddenly asked me, "Man, is there going to be anything sad in this room?"

I pretended to look under the bed for this strange animal

"Sorrow." It was not there! Nor in the cupboard, nor anywhere I looked, while she prompted me. I looked till I proved to her that it was not in the room at all — but still she looked at me dissatisfied; and when I bent over her to kiss her good night, she clung to me, and whispered: "It's in *you!*" So she knew my secret, and would not rest until I had pretended to take it out of my pocket, and laid it under her pillow. "Now it will go to sleep," I told her, "this bad dog Sorrow — and in the morning when you wake it will be gone."

I found Eunice downstairs sitting alone, by the open window, for it is one of James's late nights in town.

The little garden was quite light, and we could see the tall blue delphiniums, standing like towers, against the pink flush of the sky. The birds were calling their last short messages.

We took out the map of France, and traced, in the lessening light, where the French Army were retreating.

We tried to believe France might not fall; but I think we knew she had already fallen.

We Austrians have always a special feeling for France. I do not say that I prefer her to the rest of Europe, but when I see, among all the flat mediocrities of Potsdam, the bust of Voltaire on Frederick the Great's table — I know where I belong.

I used to spend my holidays in France; it was there in the Vosges, and once in Provence, that James, Eunice and I took our tours together.

I had worked also for two years at Salpétrière; so that I had known always what was happening to France. She had been conquered long before the German Army crossed her frontier.

Laval had conquered her in Abyssinia; and Chamberlain on the frontiers of the Rhine.

One can say that she has been beaten by herself with the help of her friends — so that the mere shadow of an enemy was enough to turn this secret defeat into an open rout.

On one of my visits to Paris, I came face to face, in the Louvre gardens, with the terrible statue the French nation abased itself by putting up after 1918. They called it "La Victoire." So shockingly vulgar and trivial is this little block of stone and so alien to the lost spirit of France that I felt myself blushing as I looked at it.

It was as if an artist had taken to represent his country not as a mother — but as a prostitute. But perhaps he had to take it, for artists must produce truth: perhaps France herself had chosen a prostitute to represent her? It was for no such Victory that those French boys, with their white gloves on, died at Verdun.

"Is it true," I asked Eunice, "what people over here keep telling me, that you prefer Germany to France? I cannot believe that you do not love best the most tragically intelligent country in the world!"

"James and I love France," Eunice said slowly, putting down the map, "though we loved Germany too, what we *thought* was Germany. I know you never did: you used to say that a goose-step was the most dangerous form of acrobatics in the world. I suppose we didn't take it seriously, that goose-step. But we always took France seriously. She is not easily understood — one has to love her, as it were, without understanding her. I think I can see why our unread, untravelled people *should* prefer a country that they know is cleaner, tidier, perhaps more honest, and a good deal less intelligent! Besides uneducated people always suppose the French are immoral. They do not realize that French immorality is merely what the French people provide for us, because we wish to have it on their side of the channel."

Eunice is very rarely cynical, but I have always noticed that when a woman is cynical she often speaks the truth. James on the other hand is cynical when he wishes to avoid speaking the truth. "Besides, there are the politicians," Eunice went on after a pause. "They have betrayed us into a sort of appeasement tenderness for Germany. This has been going on for a long time. We are a simple people and really know very little about foreigners, so that Hitler could play on us, as he chose, egged on by our own leaders. Besides you must admit the French themselves, as represented by Laval, Flandin or even Daladier, have not given us objects *to* love! I had always hoped Reynaud — "

I too had hoped Reynaud —

"Well," I said, "I suppose it was a case of a right man too

late, or perhaps only a man who would have been right with sufficient support. The support is not there, and I believe that he has a mistress who wishes France to be beaten. Reynaud is a man who has few men friends — none of equal capacity to himself — such men are generally at the mercy of a foolish or wicked woman. France as a country has the same character — she too stands alone and has few friends. Such people — or such countries — accept bad advice very readily."

"But Churchill, can he not still save her?" Eunice whispered.

"We have to save ourselves," I reminded her. "No one else damns or saves us, though many may hinder or help us on our way to damning or saving ourselves!"

"I know," Eunice murmured, "you told me that long ago when I was desperate! I loved James so much too much, but I didn't know how!"

"He loved you too," I reminded her, "and didn't know how; but you both took a good deal of trouble to find out! France and Britain avoided such trouble. They did not love each other enough to find out. Neither would give the other what he most needed. Neither fully trusted the other. The British naval treaty with Germany shook the confidence of France. Laval's swindle over Abyssinia broke the confidence of Britain. They patched up things on the surface, but you cannot patch thin ice; any unexpected footstep may always go through."

"Then you think," Eunice asked in a voice I heard shake for the first time, "you really think France *must* fall?"

James had come in without our noticing him. As I looked up I saw him swaying like a drunken man; but I knew he was not drunk. "To all intents and purposes, France *has* fallen," James said; he still held his hat in his hand, as if he could not give up something he could crush.

I have seldom seen a man suffer an impersonal pain as if it were a personal one. The fall of France ravaged James. He was not thinking of the safety of this Island, nor even, for a moment, of Eunice and Rosemary. He was thinking solely of France.

"Tom says," he added, sitting down with the careful stiffness

of an old man, "that he has seen Vansittart — well Vansittart
knows everything. Behind the tinkle of tea-cups at the Foreign
Office they've been crushing him to death to keep him silent,
all these bitter years. Well, now it's England that will be crushed
to death, by these same little men!" He looked at Eunice accusingly, as men always look at the wives they love in sudden
adversity. Is it not she who gave him all the joy in the world
once, and is she not forever after responsible for all his pain?

Eunice got up, and came back with drinks and glasses. It is
not the custom to drink alcohol in this house, but to-night we all
drank it, and were thankful to feel physical warmth at least
come into our cold hearts.

It was a curious, long evening, because we said so little. James
sat quite still and stiff, with the veins standing out on his thin
temples, as if his arteries were seventy years old, and not only
twenty-nine. Eunice shivered from time to time, although it
was a warm and chill-less evening.

As for me, I did not feel anything very much — for me the fall
of France was an anticlimax.

I had seen Austria sold out and raped before my eyes.

France only came through the same gap made in my heart.

If Austria had tried to save herself even as much as France,
I could have borne it better. As it was, everything had fallen
for me on 11th March 1938 — even France.

But I have hope now. I know the country I am in will fight
on. Drugged, stupefied by lies, and unequipped — she is still a
fighter. The strength is there, the blind strength of Samson,
the swift agility of David. I put my trust in these people. A
country dies when, like France, it has retreated till its back is
against a wall. But Britain has no walls. Her first and right im-
pulse is to take, and keep, the seas. The issue of this War is
whether she *can* keep them.

We spent the hours of the last evening in saying things to each
other like "What is to happen to the French Fleet?" We measured
Weygand. We took out the map again. Neither Weygand nor
the map were very encouraging.

Finally, we went up to our own rooms. All three of us had

forgotten that it was my last evening. But I remembered when I found myself alone. No man ever had better friends than these two are to me. It is strange that I should have forgotten even for a minute that I am to leave them.

The moon shines on, with its serene exactitude, over this small sweet-scented spot. Below my window are the towers and walls of a dream city.

Curious that Oxford has not meant more to me than it has actually meant — I shall miss the sinks in the Laboratory more than I shall miss these ancient monuments. I have dined in halls; I have heard the famous choir sing. I have talked with wise old scholars in evening dress over their rich port; and all the time I have been saying to myself: "The Nazis are at the door!" and when I tried to say it out loud, they stared at me as if I had said something that was indecent — and not even true. No, I do not mind leaving anything here but my friends. Nor have I found anything else here. In London in the Laboratory I worked again. But even that has never been vital to me. What is vital is how I can reach these men and women, and make them understand! I do not mean only understand the Nazis, but *themselves!* It is *they* who are really their own danger; the Nazis are the mere opportunity, presented to them a little suddenly, in order to prove if they can meet the real danger or not.

1st July 1940

I AM writing in the train on my way to my new task. I did not say good-bye to Rosemary because we thought it was better to avoid a parting scene, but I left her Andreas' cuckoo clock. I bought one for him last Christmas in Switzerland. The cuckoo had a really good musical note; and Andreas used to watch the hours for its appearance.

When I found Klara had not let him take it to his new home, I wanted to smash it to pieces under my feet; but then I had another feeling that it was perhaps for my sake that she had left it. The child had loved it and she had left me nothing else of his; so I packed it carefully in my collar box; and when I came on it, when I was repacking last night, I thought it might soften the parting for Rosemary.

She is interested in birds and Edward is teaching her all their different notes, so that it will act as a kind of messenger between us; and I shall remain in her mind, not as a friend lost, but as part of this new interest.

Ghosts do not like to change the place and people they have been haunting. Naturally in spite of my hopes for this brave Island I fear the Nazis may at any moment act in some bestial and incredible way with all their stirred-up strength; and that this unprepared and peaceful people may be taken by surprise.

There is not much limit to the Nazi power now they have the pillaged resources of Europe at their disposal, and the terrible prestige of their victory over the Maginot Line.

What can stop them now? Only England herself — this small Island!

But the British are a curious people. They took Dunkirk as a victory though it robbed them of at least forty thousand men, their whole military equipment, and their great ally, France. Dunkirk *was* a miracle; but it was not a victory!

"Now we know where we are!" they say to each other to-day smilingly; and where are they? In the Jaws of Hell — and alone against the Devil Hitler and all his company!

I am glad that I persuaded James to take a cottage on Hampstead Heath instead of a city flat, before I left them, because if they bomb London, Eunice and Rosemary will have a better chance with the open country round them; and he is determined to take this new work, which necessitates a move to London.

Personally I am very fortunate to be going to the West of England, which I have never seen, for I hear it has hills as well as the sea. A man who has been used to mountains all his life feels strange when he lifts up his eyes and finds the sky empty. I suppose too that the Nazis may be taken a little by surprise over their own success; and delay their next onslaught.

This train is passing through many small cities without distinction, but soon we travel into fresh fields; and now there are the Downs, soft, green hills, round and low, but quite empty — except for here and there a little village dropped like a child's toy.

Even while I write, all the earth has turned a bright and vivid red and we come to the coast again. It is the red of the Dolomites after rain, and the formation of the rocks is a little like our smallest mushrooms and chimneys among the foot-hills.

The sea is the colour of churned turquoise — and there is not a single sail on it. How these Nazis have dehumanized the world!

Midnight: Silver Fountains, Fittleham

There is no news to-night. France has the Nazis' hands about her throat. She will not speak again.

I cannot sleep for the thought of all I have seen and the people I have met. They tingle together in my head! It was late afternoon when I arrived here.

First I saw this great pile of buildings, gleaming between the trees, set high on a little hill, and then it vanished. It was as if the house faded suddenly into the side of the hill. I suppose it was only that the road twisted. But to see it so plainly like a great pearl hanging there against its green setting, and then nothing — it gave a shock to the heart. You cannot take your eyes from all the things that grow in this West country, and there is always a sweetness in the air, so that not even the scented lilies of Corsica can be sweeter.

I do not like the house. It is too large for private persons, like some great luxurious prison or hospital, but unused. There are people in it of course, but they get lost.

I cannot imagine James ever liking it, nor has he spoken of it to me except, once, to say that he was thankful it belonged to Tom.

I cannot believe that I shall be worth what they have offered to pay me, even in the short while that may be left to me to serve them.

No member of the family received me, but a manservant took my suitcases immediately to my room and wanted to unpack them for me, although I would not let him. I wanted to be alone in this lovely room. It has flowers in it, and a window looking out over the Park. Small and dappled deer slip between the golden trees. The sunset light is beautiful. It is much softer and less sure than our mountain light. I could not believe it was real.

You have to study the beauty of this clear-rose–tinted room with its four square windows, each holding a fresh picture, to believe in it. It is well arranged for comfort, either to sleep or to work, and fresher and cleaner than anything but the flowers they were so kind as to arrange for my welcome.

I was astonished at such luxury and thought how Klara would have made me enjoy it — with her jokes and her exclamations. But I must not remember what it feels like to see with a double vision nor how dull and empty all single vision seems for ever afterwards.

Very soon there sounded a little knock at my door, and when I said, "Come in," a lady entered who said she was Lady Wendover's secretary. Eunice had told me about this Miss Fitchett — a truly devoted and good worker, the right hand of my patient — perhaps a little too devoted.

Miss Fitchett is very small and quiet, about forty years old with soft-brown hair and eyes, and a little girl's kind anxious face. She told me that Lady Wendover would see me now, but that she was very ill — far more ill than Lord Wendover realized.

I saw at once that there was a difference between the husband and wife and that Miss Fitchett was used, possibly by both parties, to make this difference wider.

I followed her over deep carpets; the balls of my feet rose to their springiness, as if heather were under them. We passed through a room full of pictures with a most lovely bloom on them; and then into an even larger softer room, but I did not notice very much what was in this second room because I was looking at my patient.

There is always between a doctor (who is a real doctor) and his patient a direct relationship. The doctor is immediately aware of his patient's need for him and this makes him at once into a friend. I could not dislike a patient any more than a trained sheepdog dislikes the sheep he would risk his life to save.

I knew instantly as I looked into the glazed and tortured eyes of this poor woman, Frances Wendover, that I should be her friend.

In Germany there are many clothes made of glass, for until the victory over France the British blockade pressed on the country heavily. It was as if my patient had dressed not her body only, but her whole being, in a glass dress, behind which she lived, very unhappily.

She whispered as I stood at her bedside looking down at her, "I am *really* very ill!"

Miss Fitchett left us. I said, "Yes, I can see that you are — and we will now find out together the reason for your illness; and then how to cure it!"

I could not know, until I had made a physical examination, if her illness were organic, or if she were ill because she was in such a state of mental turmoil and conflict that none of her organs could function properly.

To all patients, it is their symptoms that are most distressing to them, and every doctor should realize this fact and pay suffi-

cient attention to the patient's account of them, even though in
reality such details may be unimportant, and are nearly always exaggerated. Still, the doctor has to study first the patient behind
the illness; and almost anything that the patient does, looks or
says, is a key to his personality. So I sat down by Lady Wendover's bedside and listened to her recounting all her sufferings;
and they took her a long time to describe because she was ar-
ranging them in a very intricate and involved pattern, in order
that I might recognize her as a heroine.

When she had finished, I asked her leave to make a physical
examination; and it bore out my expectation. There was no sign
of any organic weakness or progressive disease; but none of her
organs were functioning normally. She had fever, her pulse was
a hundred and twenty; there was distension and weariness all
over her. She was only thirty-eight and had a beautifully made
body, too thin and under-nourished but that of a young woman
still — a young woman accustomed to every care; and supported
by every luxury. Yet in another sense I do not think she had
understood her body at all, or cared for it properly. This woman
had never accepted her body as the blessing such a beautiful
gift of nature should be considered. I doubt too if she had ever
shared its beauty or enriched its life by an easy and happy life
with a mate.

She had, I think — poor woman — in every way stinted and
violated the morality of nature. I could tell by the way in which
she took the examination I made that she resented and even
despised this beautiful physical instrument, and had never learned
how to use or to control it. A man who loves the working of a
good machine feels injured and exasperated when he watches
a bad driver dislocating or neglecting a good car by careless
driving. So a doctor like myself feels when he examines a neglected or ill-run body.

When I had finished my examination I sat down once more by
her side and told her that I would try my very hardest to bring
her relief.

I looked at her very earnestly and with the affection I already
felt for her, so that she might trust me as her friend. Her pulse

actually quieted after I had said this. She looked into my eyes and saw that I respected her, and her illness.

Then I bowed, and left her.

I found Miss Fitchett standing in the corridor outside the door, her hands pressed close together as if she were in great anxiety or danger.

"You believe she is really very ill, don't you?" she pleaded.

It was almost as if both she and my patient thought that to be very ill was an achievement.

I said, "Yes, I do find her in a very serious condition and I will do my best to alleviate it; and you, I am sure, will co-operate with me?"

This she instantly promised.

I told her that she might care for our patient by day, but that I would, for a week at least, procure a night nurse. I did not want Lady Wendover left alone at present, nor did I wish her visited by any member of her family, or friends. I wanted her to be spared all telephone calls, and letters — in fact, any fresh call upon her enfeebled strength.

All of these things I could see Miss Fitchett was very pleased that Lady Wendover should *not* do; but she told me at once that Lady Wendover did not like trained nurses. That I could well understand — they had a weapon that she herself had not. Lady Wendover had never been trained.

"Nurses are not all alike," I said to Miss Fitchett, "and if she is only on night duty, when I hope Lady Wendover will be sleeping, the nurse cannot be much trouble. Besides, we will give orders that everything shall be as much as possible what our patient likes, and about this you can be of the greatest help to me."

So it was arranged, and I went downstairs to find Lord Wendover.

3rd July 1940

HE was standing with his back to an empty fireplace.

I shall always connect Lord Wendover with the smell of leather — old, well-polished leather. Skins of animals lay on the hardwood floor; and their antlers decorated the walls. Three live dogs stood stiffly at attention near him. I found them to be well-mannered, carefully brushed and most affectionate animals — two red setters, and a black cocker spaniel; and I have every reason to believe that he is fond of them.

It was not a large room, and Lord Wendover and the dogs seemed to fill it.

He looked straight at me, but he neither returned my bow nor held out his hand to me, until I reached him.

Then he offered me a drink. This I took, though I dislike alcohol, but I saw that my taking it was a relief to him.

Never have I seen a man more unlike his brother. Both are silent men unless roused by a direct interest in some statement made by others; but whereas James's silence comes from a strange spiritual reticence, as well as from the fact that he is highly intelligent and anxious not to presume upon it, Lord Wendover is, I think, silent because he wants the other person to give himself away. He also is intelligent, but it is the intelligence of the hunter — a sophisticated cynical hunter — with the hunting instinct running raw, under his carefully courteous manner.

"I have seen Lady Wendover," I observed, when I came to the conclusion that he was not going to broach the subject, "and I am in a difficult position as regards her. Legally, as you no doubt realize, I have no right to advise or prescribe for any patient, or to act as a doctor in this country; though, as James will have told you, I am a qualified physician from the University of Vienna. I can only act here as a lay psychiatrist, and at present your wife has severe physical symptoms which must receive attention before any psychiatry can be attempted."

"What do you propose doing then?" Lord Wendover demanded with a sort of cold amusement in his clear pale-grey eyes.

"Two courses are open to me," I replied cautiously, for I saw that any decision made in his presence had better emanate from him. "I may hand her over to another doctor and await her extremely doubtful recovery, for unless he is, as well as a physician, also a trained psychiatrist, her recovery *is* doubtful; or I may ask you to connive with me in compounding a felony; and treat her myself against the letter of the Law."

"Let's hear a little more about the felony first, and what it implies," Lord Wendover said, setting down his glass and producing a pipe. "I come from a race of smugglers and pirates, and though as a general rule I uphold the Law, I have in exceptional circumstances no fundamental unwillingness to evade it."

"If you know an English doctor," I explained to him, "who would be willing, after due consultation with me, to write any prescriptions I consider suitable, I think between us we could soon allay the physical symptoms from which your wife is at present suffering."

Lord Wendover did not speak, but he raised his eyebrows in a significant manner, and the faint smile in his eyes deepened. It was plain to me that he was only too ready to discount Lady Wendover's physical sufferings.

"You must not doubt, Lord Wendover," I told him, "that her present condition is highly serious. She even requires a night nurse as well as Miss Fitchett's complete attention during the day. Indeed I should recommend rest and careful nursing for several weeks."

Lord Wendover's eyebrows sank to their natural level, but he continued to look amused while carrying out those slow pleasant processes that are an intrinsic part of pipe smoking. He settled down in a large leather-covered arm-chair opposite my own with his very strong glass of whisky-and-soda within reach of his hand.

"There's James's friend," he said between the slowly igniting puffs of his pipe, "Barrow — the head of our private research laboratory in Plymouth. I could get hold of him for this evening. Perhaps he'd help us."

He might just as well have said, "He's got to do what I tell him!" as "Perhaps." It was what he meant. He stretched out his hand to a telephone on his desk.

It interests me to watch him move. He has complete muscular control and that economy of movement only common to a trained athlete. At first I had thought him a young man, but as I watched his face I came to the conclusion that Wendover was in advanced, rather than young, middle age. He may even be fifty, but he moves like a man of thirty.

"Look here, Barrow," he said into the receiver, "if I send a car at once will you come to dinner? I want you to meet James's Viennese friend — Yes! Well, that's all right. Come just as you are; it's wartime!"

He laid down the receiver. "Nice fella, Barrow," he observed. "We'll talk it all over with him." Then he took up the receiver again, and switched onto a house telephone, and gave orders about sending the car. His voice changes a little when he speaks to servants. He is still polite but he is curter.

"I am interested in what you say about my wife's condition," he then observed after a pause, which may have been for his pipe to draw properly. "You say she is physically very ill, though I gather you think she is a fit subject for the practice of psychiatry. What then is the matter with her?"

"Probably you know that better than I," I told him. "We cannot pigeon-hole the symptoms of a human being. Her mind is just as real as her body, and not disconnected from it. When a person cannot digest her food, or sleep, has fever and a weak and rapid pulse, she is certainly very ill; but I do not find any organic cause for these symptoms. There must therefore be some deep stress or threat to her security in her present circumstances."

"Other than the Nazis?" Lord Wendover said with his former lift of the eyebrows.

The English have a way of referring to the Nazis as if they

were a distant and rather ludicrous subject which I find very disconcerting, for I have known the Nazis when they were neither distant nor funny.

"Other than the Nazis," I repeated gravely.

"There must be professional secrecy, of course," Lord Wendover said indulgently, as if he were referring to a child's game. "I have no intention of asking you to break it, though I am naturally interested in finding out what you think the exact cause of my wife's illness to be, since she sent off, with a flea in his ear, rather an honest doctor who has been attending to our whole family for years with unqualified success. He had suggested that her illness *had* no cause."

"In that I find she was right," I replied, "since all illnesses have a cause."

"Could they not be invented?" Lord Wendover suggested.

"There would have to be some cause for their invention," I answered, "but do not think your wife is malingering! Her physical symptoms are involuntary; but for all that they may very well be produced from other than a physical cause. Shock or conflict can set up and maintain almost any set of severe physical symptoms. If you can throw any light on what special shock or conflict exists for your wife at the present moment, I can then tell you how we may treat this illness — and what to expect as to its course."

"I should prefer to let you find out from my wife herself," Lord Wendover said after a long silence, "but I will mention, for your guidance, since you ask me for help, that my wife believes herself to be a victim of almost wholesale persecution by her entire family. Miss Fitchett is probably the only person at the moment in whom she has complete confidence — arising no doubt from the photographic accuracy with which Miss Fitchett presents (for my wife's inspection) the most flattering image of herself! I do not know what effect Joan of Arc had upon her family, but I believe the origin of witch persecution in the Middle Ages to have been that certain women were uncommonly difficult to live with. According to my wife, I ill-treat her, poison my children's minds against her, incite her servants to

rebellion, and generally play the devil with our mutual responsibilities. She accuses me of ruining my daughter and corrupting
my son. Perhaps some of these ideas may be upsetting to her.
You never know with a woman of her carefully trained susceptibilities. I leave it to you to find out what basis her theories have
in the region of fact. Our family doctor was so misguided as to
inform her that her family resentments were inventions."

Beneath the careful indifference of his manner, I could see that
he was at breaking point, or else he would not — in spite of the
fact that James is my best friend — have given me this sudden
overflow of confidence.

When a household has had to bear for any long period the
attacks of a patient in an advanced state of neurosis, each member of it becomes slightly infected and is liable to some form
of explosion.

As a rule it is the patient's mate who has to bear the full
weight of a neurotic's disintegrating powers, although the worst
destructive effects are generally to be found when a neurotic
acts upon the raw susceptibilities of a child.

"If she takes any of these ideas for facts, she might well be
ill," I admitted to Lord Wendover, "and yet it is generally the
patient's opinion of herself that is the core of all such illnesses.
Your wife is a discouraged person who needs to be very well
thought of by those she loves. If someone who has hitherto believed in and cared for her suddenly believes in and cares for
her no more, a person like your wife is shaken to the foundation
of her being. She has built herself up upon the respect of others
rather than upon her own, and she finds herself as it were like a
captive balloon — let loose upon the air.

"There need be none of the outside factors that you have retailed to me. She could become very seriously ill simply because
she was no longer accepted by a loved object, at her own valuation. Unfortunately when a dramatic, highly dynamic person
such as your wife becomes demoralized by a nervous shock of
this nature, she can easily become the centre for demoralization
in others."

"Oh, yes, my wife has great powers," her husband said sardonically, "but I am amused that you should call her 'discouraged.' She is, I assure you, well aware that she possesses these exterritorial gifts; and she is accustomed to make use of them without scruple."

I did not dispute this assertion; although I believe that a person's emphasis upon their own powers is seldom a sign of their belief in them. I saw that, about his wife, Lord Wendover had an habitual resentment which was misdirecting his otherwise sound judgment. It is useless to argue with a permanent condition of the mind, and does nothing but strengthen any fallacy by which its owner seeks to support his error.

I merely repeated, "It would help me greatly to know what has actually taken place, as regards any of her main relationships lately."

"She tells me her main relationship is with God," Lord Wendover informed me, "but whatever has taken place between her and the Deity, she is unlikely to divulge it to me, since I am unable to take very seriously the particulars of such an imaginary relationship. She might however talk more freely about it with our Padre. She is very devoted to him and as I thought it might be useful to you to meet him, I invited him to dinner to-night with his wife, who is a friend of my daughter's. You will find they run in and out of the house a good deal — both of them."

I was interested in the last part of Lord Wendover's observation because I have often noticed that when anyone informs you of a fact which you are bound to observe for yourself, it is because they are laying a particular stress upon it, and would be glad for you to do the same; or else perhaps they wish to excuse some motive of their own which lies behind the fact that they have, superfluously, presented to your notice.

At this point in our discussion the dogs, who had recovered from the intrusion of a stranger, and were now sprawling across Lord Wendover's feet, suddenly darted to the door in an ecstasy of welcome. It opened, and a girl in a very short white-silk tennis skirt, no stockings and a pale-yellow shirt open at the neck, stood in the doorway. She was not at all like her mother but I guessed she was Lord Wendover's daughter.

"This," he observed, "is my child, Gillian, known by her intimates as Jill. Well, Infant, this is your Uncle James's friend, Dr. von Ritterhaus of Vienna. I've just asked Barrow to dine to meet him, but you needn't dress."

The girl withdrew.

She had glanced at me, with eyes of a deeper grey than her father's, but quite as cold; and she just smiled. She neither spoke, however, nor offered to shake hands. She disappeared as I bowed, followed by all three dogs, although one — the black cocker spaniel — returned shortly and re-settled himself across his master's feet.

"That's my ruined daughter," Lord Wendover observed. "She relaxes occasionally into tennis, while acting as a V.A.D. at the Bodmin Hospital between 9 A.M. and 6 P.M."

I was glad to hear that there was one member of the family who took the War seriously. There was a curious look of shamed pride in Wendover's eyes as the door closed after his daughter. Pride I could understand — but I wonder why he is ashamed when he looks at her. She is a pleasant sight. There is a fresh and intrinsic dignity in a young girl who is at the same time a healthy creature with all the materials for earthly happiness under her command. I felt my heart full of respect and good wishes for this young girl's future. She does not need to have beauty, nor do I think her beautiful.

Her father got up very soon after she had left us.

"Well," he said, "we dine at eight. I hope they've shown you your room?"

We were crossing the hall, a great open room full of trophies of the chase interrupted by old family portraits, when I saw the boy.

About *his* looks there was no question. He was the most beautiful young human being I have ever set eyes upon. He has crisp black wavy hair; and eyes like his mother's. They shone with the glancing fire of a sapphire. He has his father's height, but with the slenderness and grace of a trained adolescence. He had obviously just been bathing; a wet towel was twisted up in a neat roll under his arm. Something else had happened to him besides his bathe; he was rapt in a sunny dream. The light of it rested on his sparkling eyes, and curved his parted lips. There was about his whole figure a visionary beauty, neither of the air nor of the earth, but as if the spirit within him had suddenly been set free to enjoy both — as they are rarely enjoyed except by the most pure and the most sensitive of human beings. Experience had not yet sullied the clear pool of his attention, and all the forces of hope were intact in him.

He stood there, not seeing us, but looking back over his shoulder into the last cold light. His head was poised upon his slender throat in a proud and shapely manner. It seemed as if he could not quite tear himself away from what the day had held. The door was open behind him, and in front of him was a great bowl full of tall, late-summer flowers. I did not want to see his dream disturbed. There was so much bloom and so much rapture in the boy's backward glance; and then I suddenly realized that his father wanted to break his dream.

Wendover broke it roughly — and as if he were at the same time afraid of the boy's beauty; but whether for the sake of the boy, or for his own sake, I cannot be sure.

"What the devil are you staring at?" Lord Wendover demanded in a hard exasperated voice.

The boy started, and flushed to his forehead. He muttered something, and would have sprung up the stairs and away from us, if his father had not forced him back by saying, "Where are your manners? This is James's friend, the doctor from Vienna!"

The boy swung back then and gave me his hand. It was ice-cold; but I do not think it had been cold until his father spoke to him.

The boy said, "Is she — is my mother any better?"

I liked his voice; I liked his self-control, for beyond that first angry start, he had shown no displeasure with his father, and had instantly obeyed the dictates of a host.

"For a few days she must be kept very quiet," I told him reassuringly, for I formed the impression that he, alone, really cared how his mother was. His father did not believe in her illness and the daughter had not made any enquiries about her mother. "She will soon be better, I hope; indeed, I am sure that she will!"

The boy nodded in a relieved manner, glanced at his father for permission, and then ran swiftly upstairs.

"That's the corrupted youth!" his father said dryly. "Now you've seen the lot of us!"

"It is curious," I found myself saying, "that you should — any of you — feel that you have anything of which to complain. One would say, superficially, looking at this house and its surroundings, and after meeting its inmates, that you possess the best this world can give; and the power to dispose of it to the finest advantage!"

"Does the possession of such objects, and the power to use them, imply any particular sense of security, or even of satisfaction?" Wendover asked me, but more as if he were speaking to himself than to me. "I have not found that the power to dispose of such possessions is acquired by possessing them; quite the contrary, I assure you!"

His eyes followed the slim young figure disappearing up the shining staircase.

I had thought that he loved his daughter better than anyone else, when I had seen him look at her; but now I do not think so: I believe that he loves his son as I loved Andreas, when he was my son.

19th September 1940

I was late for my first dinner at Silver Fountains. My patient, two hours after I had left her, had a sudden palpitation of the heart.

I gave her *sal volatile* mixed — as we generally mix it in Vienna — with bicarbonate of soda. It acted "like a miracle" as Miss Fitchett expressed it, although nothing could really be less like a "miracle" than that by dispersing gases pressing upon the heart, you should cease interference with its normal action.

This "miracle" gave Miss Fitchett sufficient confidence in me to submit to a mild and camouflaged form of "third degree."

I saw her alone in that lovely room with the shining Reynoldses and Gainsboroughs, and went over with her, word for word, what had taken place in the way of conversation between her and my patient, after I had left her in so peaceful a condition.

The first time I think Miss Fitchett was wholly "unconscious," as we call it, that she *had* left out a salient fact. She did not hesitate, and assured me with great co-operative eagerness "*Now* I've told you every single word either of us said! I knew you didn't want her to *talk* — but every now and then of course, you have just to *speak* a word to a patient."

"You are perfectly right," I told her. "Indeed, to be unnaturally quiet has a perturbing quality."

Then I took her through the whole conversation again.

The second time, her eyes wandered a little and she played with a paper knife. Still, her account was substantially the same.

I apologized for taking her over the same ground a third time, explaining that such questions were like a net thrown out to catch a shoal of minnows — even a second or a third throw of the net is necessary, since some of the quick little fish of memory each time dart through the meshes and escape.

Over this third account, I saw her pause at a point where she had not paused previously.

"Lady Wendover asked me if her daughter had come in, and I said yes, I thought she had."

I stopped her altogether here.

"What made you think her daughter *had* come in?" I asked her.

Miss Fitchett hesitated and flushed a little.

"Well," she said, "didn't I tell you I had to run into the passage a moment — and I met Jill. She told me Dr. Barrow was coming to dinner. I thought I had better not mention this fact to Lady Wendover for fear she'd think it was a consultation with you, and that you thought her even *more* ill than we had feared. So I didn't tell her, and I suppose that was why I forgot to say I'd been out of the room at all! It was only for a minute anyway!"

"You were most wise," I told her, "not to mention the matter of Dr. Barrow's visit to our patient. And was that all that passed between you and Miss Gillian in the passage before you returned?"

"Well, practically," Miss Fitchett said. "I did just say, 'You haven't much time to dress, dear, have you?' and she said, 'Father said I needn't — there's only Virginia and the Padre coming, as well as this doctor man.' She didn't mean *you*, of course!"

Very naturally, Miss Jill had forgotten even the shadowy presence of the Viennese ghost. It would not have been worth while to dress for him.

"But you *did* mention to Lady Wendover that these two other guests were to dine here?" I asked her.

Miss Fitchett wanted to say "No." She very nearly *did* say "No," but fortunately she belongs to a type whose loyalty is greater than its cowardice. To serve Lady Wendover she would, I think, face a trouble greater than embarrassment. Nor has she much vanity; indeed to look a fool is almost painfully natural to her.

"Well — I *did* just say that the Padre and Virginia were coming to dinner," she admitted. "However ill Lady Wendover is, she likes to hear little things like that about the house."

"But she had not herself invited them?" I suggested.

Miss Fitchett coloured again.

"She hadn't exactly *asked* the Padre to dinner," she admitted, "but you see she'd never *mind* his coming! They're the greatest friends! He has a standing invitation to any meal, though it wouldn't be usual for him to come if she wasn't downstairs. Still, he might have to, in order to see her. He's terribly busy just now, and a meal hour might be his only free time!"

"But with his wife it makes it more formal I suppose?" I persisted.

I got then what I wanted.

"Oh, Lady Wendover wouldn't be likely to ask *her*," Miss Fitchett said — and then hastily amended her speech. "She thinks Virginia isn't good for Jill — or Adrian — but of course if they invited Virginia — any of them — she wouldn't dream of objecting. She's so wonderful that way; you've no idea what she puts up with!"

"And as a result of putting up with these things," I thought to myself, "she has these severe palpitations of the heart!"

I knew all that I needed to know now, so having reassured Miss Fitchett by telling her that she had behaved faultlessly, that nobody was to blame for Lady Wendover's attack, and that we must expect little ups and downs, I hurried to the big dining-room that leads out of the hall.

Everyone was already at the dinner table; and I had missed the first two courses. Lord Wendover wisely told me to take my place without further formalities, and introduced me to his guests while the meal continued.

On one side of him sat the beautiful girl who was the Padre's wife. Dr. Barrow, one of those lean dry men with glasses who seem specially attached to Science in this country, sat on the other side of her. Jill sat on her father's left and beyond her was a man whom I at once guessed must be Mr. Esdaile, the Padre. My seat was between him and the boy Adrian's. I was glad to sit between them for I do not think they like each other. The boy, at any rate, was stiff with a kind of inner fury; and I knew that it was not for me that he felt it. There was already a bond of sympathy between us. I think he felt that I was taking his

mother's condition seriously; and he wanted it to be taken seriously. It is a curious fact in this household that both the members of the family who like my patient seem to want her to be
very ill; whereas the people who, for some reason or other, are
in opposition to her, rejoice to think there is nothing the matter
with her.

The Padre's wife wasn't only lovely: she was American. Instantly I felt in her a sort of central freedom completely missing
in my English hosts. It was like having another Viennese at
the table. She behaved — as we all used to do on social occasions
— as if she enjoyed herself; and was there for that sole purpose.
She *was*, in fact, a social occasion!

Out of the five men at table, four were spellbound by her.
The fifth, her husband, was not. Jill seemed to share his freedom from enchantment. They spoke to each other in low tones
with their eyes turned away from her, about Girl Guides and
bomb-proof shelters.

It is difficult to describe a charming girl — one who knows
exactly what weapons she possesses — and how to use them.

Virginia's clothes, her features, the way her hair was dressed,
the vague scent and shine that hung about her, were all directed
to one aim. The song a bird sings is not for mere selfish rapture.
He, too, is using it to attract. The bloom upon a fruit is not
empty of the same purpose. Why must a young wife cease to
attract because she has a husband? Virginia is enchanting partly
because she knows how, and partly because she has a good heart.
I think this gay and brilliant girl thinks it her duty to give
pleasure to all who are about her.

I do not quarrel with a girl who acts upon this theory; nor
could I see why her husband should quarrel with her. But he
was quarrelling. Perhaps he was jealous *of* her — as well as *for*
her — since she held the attention of the entire table and he did
not. He had the face of a man in great pain, who is using infinite
self-control in order to hide it. This pain of his was chiefly envy,
but he would have been ashamed to call it by its real name. He
had a beautiful smile, grace and good looks. I do not yet know,
but I should take it from his scholarly, distinguished face that he

has a far better-used brain than his young wife; but I can see that he does not forgive her her dreadful power to charm.

Perhaps he suspects that she may do harm to others by it; but at the moment she was only harming him, and perhaps the girl Gillian; and this was their fault rather than hers.

In general, the English seem to think that a great deal of damage is done by falling in love. The damage that is done by *not* falling in love, is what principally strikes me about them. All these over-devoted little dogs on leads are not a happy symptom.

I watched Lord Wendover laughing at a story of Virginia's till the hard lines of cynicism and self-importance vanished from his face, and it became as innocent as an eager schoolboy's. She was making Barrow, too, feel young and attractive, neither of which things, I should suppose, he had ever yet felt; and as for young Adrian, well, I am afraid I now know the source of his dream!

As for me, she made me feel at home. Just such girls, only perhaps a little quieter, for Virginia's voice was rather penetrating, were a part of our old background in Vienna. Just such a girl — radiant, equipped, enriching — was once my wife.

I could have gone on my knees and thanked Virginia for making those big eyes, for her infectious laughter, her generous flirting, and the way she swung us all into that lost world of the Strauss Waltzes and Lehar. It had once, after all then, existed — that world set to music where the blood raced, the eyes shone — and there was no shame or fear. There might even still be something besides the blank rigidity, the crude antagonisms, the sickening sadistic cruelty that is turning the earth into a shambles. I felt as if she had lit a fire before which we could warm our frozen hearts.

"What vitality Americans have," I said in a low voice to Adrian.

"Oh, but not all," he murmured back. "She's something rather special, isn't she, even for an American?"

"Yes," I admitted, "to be *yourself* is special; I fancy that is what she is doing for us. She knows that none of the rest of us *are* ourselves, so she is giving us the chance to take a holiday!"

He looked at me as if he were grateful for my appreciation.

"I'm glad you think that," he said. "Some people, you know, think she puts it on!"

"Not at all," I said laughing, "she puts it *off:* chains, fetters, formalities, they all fall away from her. Look how she moves: she is not extravagant. She is just natural! It *is* after all natural for us to move, since we are not vegetables!"

It was quite true that all the rest of us looked terribly *still!* The kind, cold Saint upon my other side suddenly asked me when I had left Vienna. He did not of course mean to be cruel, nor to make my blood, which had felt warm for the first time for many months, run cold again. I became a Refugee. I answered all his questions.

I am sure of this — if people who do not know you *have* a misfortune talk of it, you do not feel greatly hurt. If they *know* you have a misfortune and purposely avoid talking of it, you feel it more; but if you have a misfortune and anyone deliberately keeps the wound of it open from mere curiosity, then you feel it most. I am however sure that the greater part of this man's cruelty is unconscious; and arises from his having been intensely cruel to himself. Still, there is an antagonism between us of which I, rather than he, am aware.

When dinner was over, he asked me if he might visit Lady Wendover. He thought she was expecting him. Now, on many accounts I did not wish this visit to take place. My patient really needed complete quiet. He was in himself a point of conflict, since his presence suggested that of his wife. Further still, I knew that Lady Wendover's religion was an alibi — a flight from the responsibility of her too dominating temper, and its natural results. This Padre manipulated her religion and increased in her an intense sense of superiority.

Religion in itself should be the best ally science has. The root of true religion and the root of true science is exactly the same — a truthful obedience to ascertained Law.

But many people make religion act *against* science and in support of their own aims. God is the ace they keep up their sleeve to cheat with. I am under the impression that my patient props up her nerves by her religion; and that in order to get rid of the one, I shall have to attack the other; and I think that this priest, with his beautiful *forced* face, is largely responsible for both her illnesses.

Lord Wendover overheard Mr. Esdaile ask to see his wife, and gave me an opportunity to refuse without discourtesy.

"I fancy," he said, "that Dr. Ritterhaus is rather against my wife's seeing visitors at all, at the moment. I know the household is forbidden!"

I saw the priest's face set against me, like a raised weapon; and I changed my mind. I will not refuse him anything that is not vital to my patient's security. I want to keep in his good graces; and it is important, too, that he should not try setting her, at this early stage, against me — as he could do very easily. I could not isolate her permanently from her spiritual adviser. I therefore said quickly, "It is quite true what Lord Wendover says, Mr. Esdaile, but you are an exception, since my patient would feel her mind set at rest I think by your ministrations. I should be glad for you to spend a few minutes with her this evening, and I am sure you would not allow any question to arise which might disturb or unsettle her night's rest."

He gave me a quick friendly smile, and left us. Lord Wendover's eyebrows rose again, but he made no comment upon my surrender.

"You two medical Johnnies," he said, "had better get together in your own lingo. The news is at nine o'clock in the hall if you want to hear it."

Incredible for him to speak on this night, with London threatened, as if there could be any choice! Hour by hour their life as individuals as well as the life of their nation is at stake — and yet these English people eat and behave as if nothing at all unusual is taking place. They could even ask if one wanted to hear the news!

It was a curious comfort to be alone with Barrow. We could talk as men talk who have the same aim and use the same tools to carry out their purposes.

I know that I shall find him a true friend, as I have found

James. He has no rigidities, no personal vanities, no greed.

For a few brief minutes we forgot the Nazis, but at two minutes to nine I laid my hand on his arm and said, "None of this will be of the least use to mankind unless we can destroy Hitler!"

He nodded, and we went out of the doorway in silence together and into the hall. Last night was the heaviest, up to that moment, of the attacks on London. One by one the bastions of that great city are being struck and fires rage like great streams; the little lovely churches fall — the lives of harmless citizens are trapped, and buried beneath their homes! I was glad I had forbidden my patient listening to the radio. The news is enough to make a strong heart break.

I watched the reactions of this group with interest, as well as a sympathy I already knew that I must not show.

Barrow, who was beside me, simply looked bored. He had his hands in his pockets and hunched his shoulders slightly together. The Saint stood there with his head bowed and his eyes closed in prayer. He had shut himself up with God — and away from the rest of us. And yet, if there is a God, such an attack upon mankind should draw his children together, and start up in us such a passion for our brothers that nothing should ever tear our hands, our eyes, or our hearts, from them, ever again! Lord Wendover leaned against the side of the radio which he was supervising, motionless and stiff, I think, with fury. The boy pretended not to care. He leaned back in a low chair, waggled his foot, lit a cigarette and smiled reassuringly across at Virginia. Her great blue eyes were wide with pity and horror, the sweet curves of her generous mouth, more generous. She was a young girl, but she was also a mother. Her whole heart was in that hopeless battlefield among people's shattered homes. She was frightened too, but she did not look for reassurance to her husband with his shut eyes.

Lord Wendover is not her husband. She looked at him.

The girl Jill sat there tight-lipped, and as still as her father. Her eyes were on the floor. I do not know what she saw there. I saw only that this thing was happening to England because she had trusted her brothers in Germany, trusted them when they were acting infamously to the rest of our human family. People say, and I for one do not wonder at them, can we ever forgive these Germans, who broke the trust of all mankind? But we should not forget that we also are responsible for their power. It is our selfishness — our fear — our idleness — and our greed that fed Hitler's hungry vanity!

Before we dare trust anyone else, we must ourselves have become so trustworthy that no one has a weapon strong enough to bring against the weakest brother in the world.

21st September 1940

ALL through this last week these terrible bombing attacks continued — upon England's air fields, and upon her heart — London. I could neither write nor sleep while this last citadel of freedom shook to its foundations. I attended to my patient, and I visited the Plymouth Laboratory daily. Lord Wendover gave me a bicycle on which I ride the ten miles in and out of Plymouth. He saw also all the local authorities for me; and I am freed from many of the severer alien restrictions and allowed to continue my research work, covered by the Wendover name.

He himself went up to town to see the damage of the bombing at first hand, and though this I think never occurred to him as his real motive, to share London's danger. I do not think Lord Wendover would ever take into consideration, while carrying out any of his plans, a little thing like danger, either his own, or perhaps anyone else's. He is a forceful, shortsighted man, typical of this people. I do not think that England herself yet knows that she is being shaken to her foundations. The radio and the newspapers give only soporific hints. The people go stumbling on with cricket bats and tennis racquets in their hands, gas masks on their backs; and their strange hearts full of an incredible optimism. This, of course, I cannot share, since I know the Nazis, and that they are wholly equipped and prepared for the final logic of their brutal adventure. There is nothing that they will not make use of in order to win this War, including undue British optimism. Hitler's secret weapon is that he truly understands all the weaknesses of his opponent; and has learned how to profit by them.

My patient is suffering greatly, although her physical symptoms are clearing up. As one by one they disappear, her mind becomes more aware of its hard core of pain. From the moment her husband left the house, she began to talk freely to me. It was as if a gag had been taken out of her mouth. Watching Lady Wendover writhing against the sense of her inner defeat, I can well believe what my brother Oskar told me when I saw him at Dachau three days before he died from the effects of physical torture.

"Acute physical pain is less terrible than the pangs of shame one feels at having tortured the being one loves!" He referred, of course, to his wife, Lisa — a possessive nagging woman (though they were devoted to each other) to whom he had been unfaithful. She had committed suicide — which at that time, and for that cause, I did not think at all necessary. She killed herself, I feel sure, merely out of a desire for revenge.

I know now what Oskar meant. He *was* partially responsible for her suicide, although to my mind Lisa was equally responsible for his having been unfaithful to her.

The torture I see in Lady Wendover's face is that she too *is* responsible for her own sufferings. She has, by her intemperate vanity, shocked and estranged her husband; and what most hurts her at present is that he no longer accepts her at her own valuation. He once adored her almost as much as she wanted to be adored; and now she has to face the fact that he no longer even admires her. Nor is it any more within her power to give him any happiness, or even unhappiness.

No doubt she was once more beautiful than she still tries to be, and he gave in to her and spoiled her for the sake of her beauty and in order to gain from her the very stinted pleasures she was prepared to yield to him, in return for his devotion. I do not think he had the best of that particular bargain, but on the whole it has demoralized him much less to lose *her*, than it has demoralized *her* to lose him. She is being driven frantic by her uncontrolled wishes which she disguises to herself as virtues; whereas he still has his work in the world, a position he has earned; and I imagine many sincere and active friends. Besides — he has the love of both his children.

This she, poor woman, has alienated by her attempts at domination. The boy still has that uneasy half-deluded love a man never wholly loses for his mother; but I should suppose that the girl

Gillian has emptied from her hard little heart the last traces of her childhood's affection for her mother. Both children were no doubt used as active recipients for their parents' conflict. They were filled, poor little empty cups, by their parents, with the poison of their differences; and then passed from one to the other.

Lord Wendover may have struggled to retain his loyalty to his wife and to allow her the almost unlimited rights of a mother over her children. But he had had to step in and take control when he saw that his children were being ruined by her; and he could control them only by showing them his love, and so winning theirs.

It appeared to my patient that he was deliberately using every unfair and evil wile in order to tear her children from her living heart. In reality, of course, she had never loved anyone except herself; and her children were merely the most highly valued — if they were even that — of all her possessions. She *had* suffered physically in order to produce them, a fact that still seems to occasion her an indignant surprise, but subsequently all further care and inconvenience were taken from her by paid assistants. She might, in fact, never have had any children, for all the influence they have had over her undisciplined and dominating instincts.

It is curious, but apparently this whole independent class of non-working Englishwomen have never been trained except to exert their powers of attraction. To claim and hold the attention of others is their chief spiritual activity. On the part of prostitutes, such an aim is considered unworthy, but on the part of British wives and mothers it is apparently accepted as virtuous — at least if it is confined to the members of their own family circle. It is of course more injurious here than it would be anywhere else. Our Austrian women at least add to their power over their domestic circle very expert knowledge of how to expend money for the best interests of their whole household, as well as how to cook, and maintain in great beauty and order every article in their homes; added to which they very often play a musical instrument nearly as well as a professional. Sport they accept from their earliest years, in the sense that Englishwomen also accept it. They swim, ski, walk and play tennis with sufficient skill. They do not take so large a part in politics as Englishwomen — perhaps they are not as charitable — but on the other hand, they companionate men more by giving them far greater pleasure. Austrian women know their *métier femme* almost as Latin women know it; and far more thoroughly than German women (who are greatly discouraged by their men, and so cannot practise what charms they possess) know it.

I do not say that Austrian women are the most attractive in the world. I only say that since to attract is not their *only* aim, it is astonishing how much better it works with them than with Englishwomen of the upper classes, who have never had to do anything else.

My patient, for instance, cannot make a bed, cook a meal, or create a costume; she plays no musical instrument; and as far as attracting men is concerned, she only wishes to attract them by what the English would call "innocent" flirtations.

She told me with pride this morning that she had never been physically unfaithful to her husband. She has, of course, never been physically faithful to him either.

To a scientific mind, these empty incitements to sexual impulses are inherently vicious. By them, there is no doubt, my patient helped slowly to poison her husband's heart, and gave the gentleman she distinguished by her preference no satisfaction whatever.

The desire to dominate is not a sexual instinct, though it can be, of course, and often is, used sexually. Beauty was in Lady Wendover's case an accidental, and by no means favourite, weapon.

What she wanted was to be a combination of Helen of Troy and the Madonna — with Joan of Arc thrown in. But it has not occurred to her that there are any steps, physical, mental or moral, which have to be taken in order to reach these special goals — or indeed any other goals.

She has an immense fortune, organized and looked after by her husband. This has enabled her to carry out most, if not all, of her lesser wishes. She has, she tells me, established a sort of *salon*, and wishes to lead and attract a band of young and devoted men — perhaps also girls — upon intellectual lines. The mistake she makes is that her husband also has an intellect and a highly trained one, so that the young men are often so ill-advised as to listen to him, as well as to her.

Nor has her career as a speaker been an unqualified success, except upon charitable occasions where the funds at her disposal allow of her speaking at almost any length, upon almost any subject.

The intellect is a ticklish business for an untrained mind to attempt to corner. My patient has, from the long stories of feuds and shocks she has retailed to me, failed to obtain the food her insatiable vanity has sought. She has therefore decided to give up intellectual adventures, or at least to lower them in her scale of values, and to take up the Deity instead.

Religion, she tells me, is now her "all-in-all." No one but God knows what she suffers. She prays to Him almost without ceasing; and He always listens. He is more reliable even than Miss Fitchett, who has to have her meals sometimes.

Mr. Esdaile has, of course, been the greatest possible help to Lady Wendover: he has understood where and how everything in her has broken down; and his power of reconstruction is only limited by the frail material of her dwindling physical strength.

I learned to my consternation that she has now reached the exact position always craved by a neurotic. She has applause without earning it, since whenever it comes to producing the acts of virtue demanded by Mr. Esdaile from her (as necessary portions of a Christian's career), she can be too ill to carry them out. I was afraid — when we had reached this point — that except as a fellow High Priest, I would be unable to be of any use to her; and I am not constructed upon sacerdotal lines. However, we had not yet reached the bottom of my patient's basket. Mr. Esdaile himself, she has now confided in me, has become, at least vicariously through his wife, a problem.

Unfortunately Mr. Esdaile, though a Saint, a great preacher, and an unflagging social worker, made one flagrant error. A few years ago he married a girl fourteen years younger than himself and wholly devoid of any moral standard.

He looks upon divorce as a mortal sin; so does Lady Wendover. Nor, I gather, are they in love with each other in any sense in which a Viennese would understand the word. The affinity between them is purely spiritual. Each realizes the other's tragedy; each leans upon the other's soul. There is nothing earthly or possessive in the deep affection which binds them to each other. They merely back each other up. Neither Lord Wendover nor Virginia have the slightest grounds for objecting to this form of sublimated friendship. Still, I gather both of them do object to it; and with great strength.

Lady Wendover, rather to my surprise, is not at all jealous of Lord Wendover's physical affections straying. In giving up her own youth, my patient has apparently also given up Lord Wendover's. She accuses him of every other form of marital wrongdoing; but she does *not* accuse him of any undue interest in other women.

It simply hasn't occurred to her that Virginia Esdaile, whom she looks upon as a vicious and irritating child, could be attractive to her husband, in spite of the fact that Virginia's own husband is only a few years younger than Lord Wendover — still less, that Lord Wendover could lose his heart to a girl the age of his own daughter.

Lady Wendover's quarrel with Virginia is over her children, over both of them apparently. Gillian, Lady Wendover tells me, is a difficult, headstrong, hard-hearted modern girl without deep affections, completely insensitive to beauty or tenderness of any kind. She has formed herself upon her father and is an exact replica of him. A dissatisfied young married woman is a bad companion for her; and Virginia and Gillian are, in so far as either possesses anything so soft as a bosom, bosom friends. I ventured at this point to ask Lady Wendover why she considered Virginia to be dissatisfied. She promptly became vague and somewhat chilly, telling me that she had to keep Michael Esdaile's confidence. However, it appears that Michael Esdaile and his wife have not lived together for some time. A young and innocent girl, Lady Wendover told me, should not discuss these questions with a no less young, but wholly initiated, married woman. That they *do* discuss the subject she was very sure from the extremely realistic remarks dropped by both girls in unguarded moments. But Lady Wendover has an even stronger objection to Virginia. Adrian, a mere child, is breaking his heart over her. Virginia's influence over Lady Wendover's peculiarly beloved and sensitive boy is appalling. Michael Esdaile is doing what he can to separate them; but it has not yet amounted to much. Lord Wendover merely shrugs his shoulders and turns the other way, as if he were not even interested in the subject. Perhaps — I thought to myself — because he is too much interested in it?

Lady Wendover told me with sincere, if jealous, anguish that she was certain something terrible would happen soon. Her mother's heart warned her. Also the situation is highly injurious to Michael Esdaile; and the whole parish is talking about it. Love affairs in London are one thing, Lady Wendover admitted with a streak of common sense which I privately applauded, but love affairs in the country are quite another, and a far more serious, thing.

I know that she is not without grounds for this latter anxiety although I think she misjudges and exaggerates its importance.

Miss Gillian, I feel sure, is getting no harm from Virginia. I have a very strong impression that she is at present getting nothing at all from her.

Whatever may have been their former relationship, I do not believe there is any love lost between these two young girls at the present moment; certainly not upon Gillian's side. They only speak to each other in public, and remarkably little even then; both are passable actresses, but they are not sufficiently skilled to hide from an intelligent onlooker that each finds serious cause for annoyance in the other.

Adrian is, of course, head over heels in love with Virginia. He is a healthy young boy of eighteen and it would be shocking had he no love affair, preferably of an inconclusive nature, to carry on at such an age. A married woman who is six or seven years older than he is, and whom he cannot turn into a permanent shackle, while she is no drain upon him financially, is, I should suppose, exactly what he needs. I only hope, for both their sakes, that this love affair exists, and is mutual. As a matter of fact, I am afraid that only Adrian is in love. I fancy that Virginia has quite other fish to fry, and is intent upon frying them. However, I rather doubt if she is heart and soul in love with anyone. If she were, would she attempt to draw even a poor dead fish, like the writer of this diary, into her delicate net? I cannot well mistake the beautiful pleading eyes, the fleeting gesture of her hands — as if her heart too were fluttering, when I approached her. Poor lovely, silly child, what does she want of me, in addition to all her other victims?

Last night when she had finished playing tennis with some young people who had come to tea, she sat down on the grass at my feet.

"I've got to ask you something," she began with a little troubled frown across her silken forehead. "Ought I to keep my babies in England? Or ought I to go back, *home* — to America with them? Which do you think is safest? You know the Nazis! What ought I to do? It is hopeless to talk to English people about danger because they don't believe in it — though you'd think they would have found out by now how *appallingly* strong the Nazis are! Or if they do believe in danger, they still won't *act* on it. My husband tells me to trust in God, who will protect us whatever happens. But He didn't protect Poland, Holland, Belgium or France, did He? And yet I suppose some people trusted Him, in all those countries, not to mention Austria and Czechoslovakia! If I ask Lord Wendover, he isn't really sensible because he's English, I mean about England he isn't sensible; about everything else he is. He just says, 'We must trust in the Navy. After all, the Channel is a good tank trap.' All English people think their Navy is almighty, but is it?"

"It is the best weapon the English possess," I answered cautiously. "I admit it is at the moment under-equipped either with sufficient anti-aircraft guns or with planes to protect and guide it, let alone enough ships to carry out its activities. Nor do I know what are the possibilities of naval construction in this Island. But I do not see how Britain can stand a chance unless your country acts, on sea, at any rate, to help them out. After all, it is equally to help themselves, since they possess only one fleet and have two oceans which they must in some manner defend. The Nazis have, for the last six years, concentrated upon the moral selfishness of all the Democracies; and when they were fully equipped themselves, have always struck at their lack of unity. Nevertheless your country and Great Britain have preserved what human decency there is in the world to-day, still allied to sufficient power — if they act in unison — to carry it on into essential victory. I do not speak of Russia because the deluded ruling classes upon both sides of the Atlantic minimize her powers and overlook her purposes; but though Stalin may fear and dislike the Democracies for their insensate attitude against his country, he does not hate them in the dispassionate and realistic way in which he hates Hitler and the Nazis. Of this I am very sure; but the Democracies it appears are not!

"As you see for yourself I have nevertheless sufficient faith in the triumph of human decency — safeguarded as it is, at present, only by this one small Island — so that I propose to stick to it — and add to it what powers I possess. But you are in a different position than I. You have your children to think of first. You are a mother, and it is only natural a mother *should*, I think, always put first the helpless children committed to her responsibility. In my mind, the dangers are so even that you may safely study your preferences. The sea is a danger to cross. This small Island, undefended from the air, is a danger to live upon. Choose which you like, and remember not to be unduly alarmed by danger, since life is not worth the fear of losing it!"

Her beautiful eyes, upturned to mine, swam in tears. They were quite genuine tears though they were only meant to move me; and they did. She said softly, "Have you been so unhappy — that you really think life is not worth living? You are so young to have been so unhappy."

"I have not said that," I answered as coldly as I could. "I said life was not worth being *frightened* about losing! I *am* living, and that I think proves that I think it worth while, under almost any circumstances, to go on living; but not under *all*. I should not attempt to live under Nazi rule for instance. It would seem to me degrading to live in a world where such ideals were the forcible bread of any human being."

"I see," she murmured, hanging her lovely head, and playing with the blades of grass under her delicate fingers. "I see!"

But I knew that she had *not* seen!

All that she saw was that she had wanted me to confide in her and that I had refused.

Perhaps fortunately for me, Miss Fitchett arrived at this moment to say that my patient was anxious to see me.

As soon as I return from the Laboratory, and before I go, I am always at Lady Wendover's disposal. Often she rings me up in the middle of the night to ask me some frivolous question as to whether she should drink her milk hot or cold. This does not at all disturb me for I think she should know that there is one person other than Miss Fitchett and more accessible than the Deity upon whom she can rely. I believe that Lady Wendover already feels she is my friend; and I know that I am hers.

2nd October 1940

THE first news we had of Lord Wendover was a long-distance call from London. It was to me he made it. I was astonished at the clearness of his voice because the telephone is often out of action at present between London and the West Country, yet I heard his resonant, not unpleasant voice as if he were in the same room.

He made no personal enquiries and volunteered no information about himself. Immediately he knew that it was I at the telephone he said, "I want you to consult with Barrow and my daughter Gillian how best and quickest to turn Silver Fountains into a hospital. We must get our own London hospital removed, after an incident — personnel and patients — as soon as possible. I am making legal and medical arrangements this end and shall have to stay here for the present. The hospital is sending you a list of all they need to have provided on the spot; and of what they can themselves bring or send. Barrow will tell you what firms to deal with in Plymouth and it will be well to get estimates both for storing our furniture and for getting the necessary reconstruction well in hand. Expense is no consideration. If my wife objects, remove her, by ambulance if necessary, to the Dower House. She'll be quite comfortable there. Got what I said? All right," and his voice abruptly ceased.

One has to remember he is a man of business and of high political importance. He has, too, a big fortune of his own, founded upon large oil concessions in America; as well as his wife's. Yet even for what he is, Tom Wendover is curt. James too economizes in speech but he is always unhurried and courteous, rather as if he were playing a game with his own parsimony. James would never dictate to any person — he would not even dictate to a word.

I did not hurry, for I had to think things out. My patient was doing very well and the relationship between us was firm and happy in so far as a relationship with a neurotic can ever be either firm or happy. Yesterday she sat up without ill effect, for several hours.

I am now allowing her to read her letters and make her own telephone calls. She is accustomed to talks on the telephone to her friends all over the country and at great length; and the War restrictions trouble her greatly; but I do not like to stop any of her activities now that she is stronger; none of them are useful — except to her — but they *are* activities.

I wanted to get her goodwill about this affair of the hospital, but how, under the circumstances, I asked myself, to do it?

I went out into the Park among the changing trees. If one empties the mind and watches trees and birds and the slow movement of clouds, while at the same time oxygen flows through the lungs, I find the brain soon becomes clearer.

The motions of life, with all their endless variety, ease the troubled heart. In nature nothing remains static for long; there is a blessed periodicity; and in the human spirit too, neither grief nor anxiety, nor even fear, are permanent visitors. I like to realize that we are not in the passing moment; it is the passing moment that — for a brief interval — is in us.

Nevertheless, I was greatly troubled. To any man, interference with the progress of his task is an irritating factor. I wanted my patient to improve; and she *is* improving; and now it seemed to me that this improvement might be thrown completely out of gear.

Lady Wendover is *not* a person to whom things can safely happen, unless she feels herself to be in control of them; otherwise, she throws herself against these things in a hostile manner and breaks herself to pieces in the process. If only I could make this sacrifice demanded of her appear to be taken at her own volition! I have no theory against lies, except that if there is the slightest possibility of their being found out, they are useless; but I cannot think of any lie about this plan which would be foolproof enough to be useful.

For a while I let myself forget my problem while I watched

the early autumn light softening the first frost upon the yellowing leaves. I had not to think about breakfast, for I have a standing arrangement with the cook, who is a kind woman when approached properly, to allow me to make my own coffee on an electric plate whenever I choose. I see my patient every morning just before I start on my bicycle for Plymouth. I take the side roads where there is little traffic and I can enjoy the landscape.

This West Country is like a garden; but a garden belonging always to someone else. There is so much privacy that very little of its beauty can be shared with the passer-by. Here and there is a gap in a hedge or a gateway over which you can look at the wide mild land, gently peopled, with vague colours washed over it by invisible sea breezes. There is never anything brutal or mean in this country, except the brutal and mean rows of little houses that form part of every city, great or small. They, alone, are insults to human intelligence, and even more, to human kindliness; and why should we separate the two — since they are not meant to be separated.

This morning nothing stirred in the Park. The leaves breathed themselves open to let a robin or a chaffinch through, and closed again without a sound. I strolled down a wide grass path which the children call a "ride"; and before I knew it, I found myself by the little grey-stone church dropped just within the Park gates.

Here I met Mr. Esdaile, who was just coming out of it.

In these country places the church definitely belongs to the Vicar rather than to God or to His People. The church is, technically speaking, "in the gift" of Lord Wendover — and the person to whom he gave it was Mr. Esdaile.

The moment I saw him, I knew what to do. I said, "There is something about which I should greatly value your help and advice!"

Instantly his face, which had worn a stern and slightly disagreeable expression, became beautiful. This man *likes* to help his fellow human beings; not only because it feeds his sense of superiority, so that he is reassured by feeling that he can look down from above to below; but also because he possesses a passion of deeply frozen tenderness which such an appeal readily releases.

He cannot give his heart to *one* other — but to *all* others he can give pieces of it.

"There is nothing that would give me greater pleasure," he told me, "than to help you. I am wholly at your disposal since my daily Celebration is now over."

I knew that he took this "early Celebration," as it is called here, fasting; but that he did not mind prolonging his fast, I also knew. So we paced the wide grassy path together beneath the yellowing chestnut trees, while I told him of Lord Wendover's sudden plan. He listened in silence with bent head, his harsh face beautiful with sympathy.

"Yes — yes — " he said at last, when I had finished. "It is unfortunate that Lord Wendover *should* issue commands rather than make appeals. He is so strong that it does not occur to him that it is a weakness not to seek the co-operation of others. It is also a great pity that he should force an invalid to change her surroundings in so sudden a manner. I can feel for your distress as a doctor; but Lady Wendover is a person accustomed to make great personal sacrifices. She has a wonderful nature. Her strong will is harnessed to spiritual laws. I do not anticipate that she will suffer physically from this change if it appears to her — as I must confess it does to me — as a direct call from God — a call to act with even greater generosity and courage!"

"That," I said quickly, "is my own hope. You can do what it is frankly impossible for me, as a mere medical man, to achieve: you can inspire her to make this problem into an opportunity! The field of sacrifice — of generosity — and even of courage *is* spiritual. It would be impertinent for me to suggest to my patient a moral reason for her making this effort; although I myself believe that the safety of one must never be set against the safety, or rather, the desperate insecurity, of many. Lord Wendover did not, of course, say anything upon the telephone as to what he found in London. It would not have been possible, but he must have seen fearful things!"

Mr. Esdaile nodded gravely, but hardly as if he resented the danger to which Lord Wendover is personally exposed. He said reflectively, "He thinks a great deal of this place. I suppose what he suggests will completely spoil the house from a private point of view, at least for a very long time?"

"It will," I agreed. "You cannot turn such a house into a hospital without changing it from roof to cellar. It can be done though! I had been thinking the matter over, even before I received Lord Wendover's message. This great house with its two wings, its big central rooms, the servants' offices, and out-houses, would make a very good hospital. In the stables also, kept as beautifully as the house itself, doctors and nurses could have excellent quarters arranged for them. But what we must do in order to get everything ready in time, with the telephone working so badly and Lord Wendover necessarily in London, rather alarms me!"

"About practical matters you will find that Gillian will be a great help," Mr. Esdaile told me reassuringly. "She is her father's right hand and will have full authority to act as you both think best. My wife, too, I feel sure, will be highly useful. Both these young women are extremely competent and intelligent without any — as we say here — nonsense about them. Perhaps they have not got quite nonsense enough!" he added with a charming whimsical smile. "We, who are older, go about our business with less despatch, and a little more consideration for the feelings of others."

As I did not wholly agree with this remark, I said nothing, but I hope I looked impressed. I am not at all sure that competence and despatch are not better signs of a co-operative spirit than what is sometimes miscalled "consideration," which may only be a pandering to fruitless emotions upon either side; although I do not consider tact to be useless when it is coupled with sincerity.

Mr. Esdaile impressed me still more by saying, "I will go straight to Lady Wendover while you tell Gillian. She passes close by here — through the drive, by the South Gate — to Bodmin at nine-fifteen. That is the sound of her car! If you stand here, you can stop her while I go on to the house. I will meet you in the hall in half an hour's time!"

He was off in a second, bounding like a boy, through the thick bracken. He has such eagerness, such enthusiasm, when he is on an errand of mercy, and all his errands *are* of mercy; only within himself is this narrow rigid space of inhibition that leads to cruelty; only for Virginia, his wife, he has no mercy.

I stood in the middle of the road while Gillian stopped her car for me, unsmilingly, with a little frown of impatience.

"Do you want a lift?" she asked ungraciously. "I'm a little late already!"

"I have a message from your father," I told her. "I will be as quick as I can." And I gave it to her.

Immediately she stopped her engine and sat quite still in the car, looking straight in front of her.

"And he said," she repeated slowly after I'd finished speaking, "that Mother could live in the Dower House — did he?"

"He said it might be necessary," I agreed, "and indeed, I think it will be, for a large London hospital means three to four hundred beds and you will need all the room there is in Silver Fountains. Even perhaps tents will have to be put up on the lawn. No one yet knows what intensive bombing upon open towns may produce in the way of casualties. In any case, a lot of reconstruction will be necessary and should be begun at once."

"I think," Gillian said after a pause, "you'd better get in. I'll telephone to my hospital and get a day off, and then I'll take you to Plymouth. We shall need all the time there is! What about Mother?"

"I think Mr. Esdaile will talk to your mother," I explained. "He believes that she will agree to the plan from a religious point of view. I met him just now, and he offered to put it to her in this sense — and he will let us know the result as soon as possible."

"I see," Gillian said dryly. "Well, get in! We'll have to go back to the house anyway for me to telephone."

I got in and barely had time to close the door, before she had swept the car round across the turf, and was streaking up the drive at a pace that deprived me of breath. Yet Gillian is not a mad or careless driver. She knows exactly what she can do —

and what she can't. It is only that her capacity for speed is startling. One does not expect so quiet and controlled a girl to act at such a formidable pace.

But I have already discovered that she has a fury in her. She became impatient after receiving permission to take the day off from her hospital.

"God always seems to take such a long time," she observed to me, "besides, I think it's silly! The thing's got to be done, hasn't it? Why don't you wait to find out what Mother thinks about it till we get back? We can leave a message for Michael!"

"No, I shall wait," I told her. "It is more respectful to your mother. One does not go faster or more smoothly when one drives across the feelings of others."

Gillian said, "Pooh! All these feelings — when things have to be *done!*"

"Some things can be done," I suggested, "while we are waiting. If I might have some paper, I would begin to make lists of what we shall need to find out. You also could help me by making a rough sketch of the inside of the house: its rooms, stairs, and passages."

Gillian gave me a sudden smile that lit up her face as if a cloud-shadow moved away suddenly, from a bed of flowers.

"That's an idea!" she said and ran to fetch us both paper. Soon we were working away like old friends — she upon her drawings, and I upon my lists, though until that moment I had thought of Gillian as the only hostile acquaintance I had at Silver Fountains. Perhaps she was never really hostile; only the unsmiling face of a girl is so unlike those I was once used to; besides, to amuse or please Gillian is always a little difficult. Eunice had told me, "She is a very good girl, only some of her is frozen; and some of her is not yet awake."

Mr. Esdaile took exactly the half-hour he had foreseen; and I saw by his face as he came downstairs that he had succeeded. He leaned over the table we were working at, and said half to Gillian and half to me, "Your mother is marvellous! She is willing to move almost immediately, and even suggested going into the gardener's cottage."

"And where would Elwin go, poor dear," Gillian demanded

ungraciously, " and all the little Elwins? Of course she knows the
Dower House is both comfortable and empty!"

"Well — I reminded her of it," Esdaile said good-humouredly,
"and all she asks is that you, Doctor, would just take a look at it
on your way to or from Plymouth, so as to let her know how
suitable you think it, and which room you would suggest for her.
She is prepared to further our purpose in every way; and even
hopes in a few weeks' time to take over some administrative post
in the hospital."

"That's the last thing they'll want her to do!" Gillian said in
an exasperated voice. "There'll be rows all over the place if she
does that! After all what does she *know* about hospitals anyway?
There'll be matrons and all sorts of swagger experts buzzing
about; and they'll do all the proper things in the proper way. If
Mother starts telling them off, there'll be merry hell! You ought
to know that yourself, Michael!"

Michael Esdaile looked at her with a twinkle in his eye which
greatly surprised me.

"You run along, little tartar," he told her genially, "and leave
your mother to us!"

Gillian accepted this admonition with a sudden friendly smile,
as if she were not at all offended but rather relieved to be treated
like a child; and indeed one has to remind oneself, so wise and
practical is she about all material and mechanical matters, that
she is very little more.

"All right!" she said. "Tartar yourself, Padre!" and then to
me over her shoulder, "Come on!" and again we whirled off in
her little car, licking up the miles to Plymouth at a rate that prevented conversation although it did not seem to prevent a certain
increasing sense of companionship.

Barrow, too, gave up his day's work, and the three of us went
through this commercial and prosperous-looking town with a
fine-toothed comb.

Gillian and Barrow quarrelled briskly over my head since each
felt he knew better than the other where to go and what to do.
But we lost very little time over these bickerings for both of them
knew a great deal. When they reached an impasse I was elected
to choose between them; and I chose as impartially as I could.

I think between us we succeeded in making every preliminary investigation and arrangement possible.

The Plymouth people say they must have ten days to do all the removing and reconstruction necessary; but Gillian beat them down to a week. She insisted on seeing only the heads of firms; and by turns she wheedled and stormed them into acquiescence. Fortunately there is as yet no great curtailment of either man-power or building materials in this rich country; or else they do not yet realize what a great deal there will be for both.

I must say for so young a girl, Gillian shows a great deal of character and none of that mildness in action that I should have supposed natural to her.

We shall need extra lavatories, showers and sluicing facilities, kitchenettes and a complete theatre installation.

Gillian put in a long-distance call at noon, and in two hours' time she was connected with Lord Wendover, and had a further consultation with him. It was singularly short, and I thought on her part, cold. She did not ask him if he were safe, or would be in any way secure for the next few nights. Of course one might say that no one can tell what security or what danger are likely to exist — but I thought at least a suggestion of anxiety upon her part would have seemed natural. But Barrow told me, when she left us for a few moments, that for an English person to show anxiety about a loved one is *not* natural.

On the way back I had to insist with some urgency that she should stop at the Dower House. For some reason she seemed to wish to avoid this inspection greatly.

"It is always in order," she told me impatiently. "We could all move in to-morrow if we wanted to! Mother knows exactly what the rooms are like — and will sooner or later take the best of them. Why worry?"

"We promised Esdaile," I reminded her. "Besides, I think your mother has a right to ask this little attention from us!"

"All right," she said reluctantly, "if we must, we must! Nobody would mind doing what she wanted, if she ever wanted anything sensible!"

This was the first time I had seen the Dower House. It seemed to glow in the late-afternoon light as if a living strawberry had been crushed into its neat red bricks. It is a comfortable house with big square windows, standing in a secluded, deeply walled spot close to the West Gates of the Park, nearly a mile away from Silver Fountains. It was locked, but Gillian had the key with her. I thought it a charming interior; square, high-ceilinged rooms that looked as if they had never had secrets in them. I liked the old-fashioned furniture, and the wood it was made with, not dark, but rather bright, and as it were polished with age. The whole house is very well cared for, and even has about it an air as if it were already lived in.

Gillian rushed me through the rooms in a breathless hurry.

I was specially pleased with the main south bedroom which I saw was most suitable for my patient. It was there we came across the yellow scarf.

It was a lovely daffodil shade of yellow. It lay across a dark shadow on the carpet; and looked made out of light. Both of us knew it by heart. It was Virginia's scarf.

Gillian gave a funny little gasp; and looked down at it as if it were a rattlesnake. Her eyes were horrified. She had more colour than I had ever seen in her face; but she said nothing. She simply backed away from that bright scarf to the door; and closed it quickly after us.

"Don't tell Mother we saw that!" she said when we were once more in the car; and then added: "Nor anybody else!"

"I will tell nobody," I assured her. "But what about Virginia herself?" I added as an afterthought.

"Oh, I'll deal with *her!*" Gillian said with a vicious twist of her soft lips that made her for a moment remind me of her father. I must say I have never in any other country come upon a young girl with such gentle and refined behaviour, so low a voice, so unassuming a manner, who yet holds such capacities both for action and for fury! Only to-day, after a fortnight in the same house with her, has she let me see either of these qualities. She is, of course, far less docile than I thought her, but from henceforward I shall rely on her more.

22nd October 1940

LORD WENDOVER, with his usual lavish directness, sent the hospital lists from London by special messenger. I was therefore able, by working through the night, to get the final Plymouth orders ready for to-day.

Just after midnight a knock came at my door; and Adrian strolled in. I thought he had just come in from the garden, for there was a strong west wind blowing, and his hair was ruffled.

"Sorry," he said, a word used by the English oftener than any other, except perhaps the word "Thanks." "Sorry if I interrupt, but if you have the time I thought we might have a little chat. I'm off to-morrow."

I have not mentioned that Adrian and I are on very friendly terms because I hardly knew till last night whether we were or not. My instincts told me that the boy, in some curious way, both liked and leaned on me; but he did not express any such feelings or even seek my company particularly, so that I had concluded he was simply a less hostile human being than his sister, Gillian.

He possesses what is called "the Eton manner," and this also is apt to be misleading. "The Eton manner" seems to combine great polish of behaviour on certain occasions with equal casualness upon others — and at any moment can turn from the suave to the insolent. One might say that this manner provides the maximum of defence for the Etonian and the minimum of security for the outsider. It can, however, be very agreeable; and accompanied, as it is in Adrian's case, with great personal beauty, it is often most disarming.

I put aside the lists I had been working on and told him that I had reached a good moment for a break, and would be glad of a cigarette with him.

He took out his slim silver case and offered me one, taking

trouble to light it for me; then he flung himself into a massive
leather arm-chair, with one leg over its arm, and lit his own.
Extreme hardness on furniture is another mark of the British
young. No European parents would ever permit such rough
action towards household treasures.

"I suppose you don't happen to know when my father is
coming back," Adrian demanded nonchalantly.

"No," I admitted, "your father has called up three times to-day
but he has not mentioned any personal plans."

"He wouldn't," agreed his son gloomily. "He doesn't have
plans — he just goes ahead and kicks anything in his way out
of it! Is it really necessary to swamp this place into a hospital
and deposit the family, lock, stock and barrel, in the Dower
House? I ask you! It seems rather hard on Mother too; but I
understand you've squared her by appealing to the Almighty."

I did not know whom he had understood this from, since he
did not seem to be on speaking terms with his sister, and had
certainly not yet seen his mother, though he was to pay her a
farewell visit before going back to Eton. However, I thought it
best not to ask this question but to stick closely to facts; so I told
him with a glance at to-morrow's programme, typed for me by
his sister, "The furniture vans arrive at 8 A.M. to-morrow. The
men are to clear all the unused rooms first. The day after, they
will empty the reception rooms, offices, etc. on the ground floor.
The third day I fear the family move must take place. Reconstruction begins the day after to-morrow, but it will be confined
to the downstairs rooms. I have satisfied myself that your mother
can be moved to the Dower House without danger."

Adrian jumped up and walked restlessly about the room, his
hands in his pockets, examining everything as if he were looking
at it for the first time. On Lord Wendover's instructions, I am
working in his library, which is entirely cut off from the rest of
the house. It has its own offices, a separate door into the garden,
and a small bedroom, bathroom and kitchenette attached to it.
Even the telephone upon his vast desk has a line of its own and
is not connected with the house telephone. I find that riches in
England are seldom used for display, but always for increased

privacy; and it would be hard to imagine anything more private than this special apartment of Lord Wendover's.

"You think my mother really on the mend?" the prowling youth asked with his back to me. He was examining a Chinese elephant, a small bronze of the fourth century — an object of extreme value — and he came back with it in his hands and settled once more into his deep arm-chair. He had chosen one that was in the shadow, so that I could not see his face, but the light from my reading lamp shone on his long slender fingers playing with the elephant.

The veins should not stand out on a boy's hands as strongly as they stand out upon Adrian's.

"Yes," I said consideringly. "Your mother is better. But there are disturbing factors in her case. When I say she is better, I do not mean that we have yet removed these factors; and as long as they are there, we cannot prevent the recurrence of severe physical symptoms at any time."

"What are these mysterious factors?" Adrian asked a little superciliously. He seemed to think that he had a right to ask, and that I should be obliged to answer any question he might choose to put to me. This also is part of the Eton manner. It always assumes privilege on the part of the person using it.

Nevertheless, I decided that I would answer him fully. I have a great respect for the young. I think they should, whenever possible, be told the exact truth; also there was an air of greater maturity about the boy to-night than I had ever seen in him before.

"The factors against your mother," I said to him, "are three. She has had a false bringing-up; her nearest relationships have suffered lately from some form or other of breakdown; also she believes that she can — and indeed *ought* — to have what she wants. The world is not built on these principles for any human being. I cannot obtain for her what she wants, nor would any other medical adviser. What I *can* do for her is to show her how to adjust to *not* getting what she wants; but I cannot, of course, promise that she will do this adjusting, even after I have shown her the necessity. All I can tell you is that if she chooses to make these adjustments, she will be able to avoid the recurrence of her present symptoms, since they are the result and not the *cause* of her illness."

"Is that all psychology can do?" Adrian asked with an irony that just touched insolence.

"Psychology," I told him, "is a science, not a sort of Savonarola. It cannot reform people against their wills. It can only provide a better method of mixing the human ingredients presented to it. As it is a social science it must depend as much upon the patient's willingness to be cured, as upon the physician's skill in curing. There is neither force nor magic in psychiatry."

"And if the patient is too ill to make an effort, or doesn't particularly *want* to get well, then I suppose she just doesn't?" Adrian persisted.

"Probably not," I admitted, "but of course other fresh factors or new incentives towards recovery might crop up. There is no truer saying than 'While there is life, there is hope.' "

The boy whistled rather disconsolately.

"I am in rather an awkward fix," he stopped whistling to explain. "I know why my mother's upset. *I've* upset her. She mayn't have mentioned it to you, although she probably *has*, but I happen to be in love with Virginia — and she doesn't, of course, like it. The Padre is her particular spiritual pet, as no doubt you have discovered, and as he rather naturally doesn't like it either, it's a sort of double soup to be in!"

I merely nodded. When a reserved person once begins to talk, nothing can stop him; and he does not want to have to listen, until he has quite finished his unfamiliar exertion.

"It's quite true, I *am* in love with her," Adrian admitted, putting down the Chinese elephant with exaggerated care upon the edge of the desk nearest him. "I'm damnably in love with her. I dare say it seems rather odd my spilling the beans like this to you, but you seem to be fairly deep in the family councils already, and I can see you like Virginia. That makes it easier — for everybody else in this house now seems to have a down on her! Gillian has behaved like a beast about the whole thing — I can't think why, for she usually has some sort of 'stand-intogetherness' with me about our bad half-hours! I don't expect Mother to like it, of course, but our generation usually keeps clear of moral taboos. However, this seems to be altogether too much for Jill — and I admit it's more serious than if it were just me. I might keep a stiff upper lip and get over it. 'Men have died and worms have eaten them — but not for love.' I know all that! But you see Virginia cares too, that is to say she has been so good as to tell me that if she wasn't six years older than I am, and the mother of two children, she'd divorce old Esdaile and marry me to-morrow!"

I was not altogether surprised to hear this statement. I had an idea that Virginia might have made it before, to many other men. Nor should I have been surprised if she added me to this collection of flattered confidants. But I should be really startled if she meant to marry a boy of eighteen, and give up her house, her family, and her financial security.

"The trouble is," Adrian went on after a pause to relight his cigarette which had gone out, "that old iceberg, Esdaile, won't divorce! Have you ever come across Saints before? I'd prefer a brute any day. You could knock a brute down and jump on him, but you can't very well knock down a man who starts praying for you while you're knocking, and who won't lift a finger to defend himself. Mind you, Esdaile's no coward. He'd fight like hell to defend anyone else! But that doesn't prevent his being awfully cruel too. He gets under one's skin! What Virginia has to suffer and *how!* Until you came, she simply hadn't a friend in this house. What I want to ask is, will you stand by her, *for* me, since I've got to go back to Eton? She told me to come to you herself!"

Well, of course, women will do these things — I couldn't help smiling.

"Set a thief to catch a thief!" is a good English saying, but to ask a thief to *support* a thief: is that quite so good?

Adrian and I are both thieves, for Virginia belongs to Esdaile.

Actually speaking, we all belong only to ourselves; but Virginia has, alas, not learned to belong to herself; nor does she want to. She prefers to let this painful responsibility rest upon the nearest adoring male; only I don't think the nearest adoring male of the moment is either myself or Adrian.

"What about your father?" I permitted myself to ask. "Won't he stand by you?"

Adrian's eyebrows shot up into his hair, exactly like his father's, and this is the only time I have ever seen the faintest resemblance between them.

"No, he won't," Adrian said curtly, stabbing his cigarette end viciously against the bronze elephant he had handled so carefully a few minutes earlier. "Nor should I dream of asking for his support!"

He got up once more and began moving about the room. He seemed to prefer shooting this part of the conversation at me over his shoulder.

"My father," he added, "is a bit of a problem to me at the moment. Up to now, he's been a pretty decent parent; coughs up when necessary; and doesn't ask questions. In fact, Gillian and I wouldn't have quite known where we were without him. I'm fond of my mother — Gillian isn't — but you know what I mean. My father's all there, and can be counted on to take things in, whereas my mother is generally somewhere else, and only takes in what she wants to think is there, and nine times out of ten, it just isn't!"

He glanced back at me over his shoulder with eyes that shone brightly and wildly like an animal's. I nodded reassuringly, for I knew that he had described his parents with remarkable shrewdness.

"Another thing I'd like to know," he jerked out, after a somewhat prolonged pause. "Does a man of forty-five have to lose his head about girls? Is it physically necessary like old David in the Bible, and all that? Why doesn't a man like my father take to women if not of his own age, at least reasonably nearer it, between thirty and forty, say? Virginia's only twenty-four! Not quite that — and I'm eighteen which is grown up really if people would only see it! After all, I'm considered old enough for the 'Drink' in a few months' time, aren't I?"

I had to find out at this point what he was talking about. It seems Adrian is joining the Air Force when he leaves Eton, and he meant by the "Drink" that he expects to be drowned. It is quite probable that he will be either drowned or burned within the next twelve months. The psychology of intelligent boys in Great Britain to-day cannot be normal when we consider this premature doom hanging over their heads.

"Men of your father's age," I told him, "don't unfortunately feel old, any more than boys of eighteen feel young. You, who are going to learn how to ride the air, at the rate of three hundred miles an hour or more, must already know that age and time mean nothing. We have got rid of them both; and at least half the world has jettisoned its conscience with them. We presumably belong to the other half. We have kept our consciences. That's our problem. If we too throw our consciences overboard we shall be left the victims, not the masters, of our great discoveries!"

The boy shook his head impatiently. He did not seem to think that conscience was the kind of thing to be applied to a personal problem.

"Well, my father doesn't seem much troubled by *his* conscience!" he remarked rather acidly. "I needn't say more than that he definitely bothers Virginia. That's why I want your help. There must be someone to stand by and take care of her — since her husband won't. Let *her* talk to you about her difficulties, and if you don't mind, sometimes talk to you about *me!* We need to feel we have some sort of a link between us, in this damned intricate and yet hostile household: someone who isn't trying to get us both down!"

"I shan't try to get either of you down," I said, after a considerable pause, "but I can't promise to be of much use to Virginia. Have you tackled your father directly about her — so that he knows your feelings?"

Adrian turned to face me. He stood quite still. His brilliant eyes met mine in a long look that was, I think, the saddest look I have ever had to meet from so young a human being, and that is saying a good deal.

The eyes of the dying are grave, but they are not so sad. The

eyes of the disinherited are desperate, but they are not dis-
illusioned, for they have not seen their inheritance turn to ashes:
they have only been deprived of it; but this boy had seen his
father's love crumble beneath him like a burned-out stick.

He shook his head and murmured, "I told him all right, and
he laughed at me!"

Power makes men very cruel. That is why no one should have
it over the destinies of others. I found it hard to forgive Tom
Wendover for laughing at his adolescent son.

"I can tell you what I know," I told him. "That is all the help
I can be to you. I believe — whatever wild intemperate fancy
your father may have for other women — he is still tied to your
mother. I don't know why, or how; but I am quite sure that no
man tries to hurt his wife and no woman tries to hurt her husband
unless they are still, as we say, 'in love' with each other. There
is no real indifference between your father and mother: it is
War to the Knife."

"And you think *love* is War to the Knife?" he asked me
incredulously, his dark thin eyebrows rising, without insolence
this time, in a sort of pained wonder . . . for Virginia knows
how to make men happy.

"Love *can* be used as a weapon," I answered him, "but I do
not think war is the purpose of love. On the contrary, I think
the purpose of love is to produce life. It is only death for which
we need weapons. I suppose that Freedom means we not only
can control such a force as love — but that we *must* control it, or
else, like electricity or any other natural force, it becomes dangerous!"

He turned this comment of mine over in silence for a long
time; then he said, "I think I see what you mean, but it's not
much good to me, unless you can get my father to see it too!
If he's trying to flirt with Virginia, and he *is* trying to, you
don't deny that, and I can see it for myself, why then he'll
never do anything to help me! And you see I need a certain
amount of help. Virginia has no money. We can't get married till
I'm on my feet — even if she'd take me. Well, it's up to either my
mother or my father to provide for me. Both have promised me a

decent income when I come of age — but I'm at their mercy about
it; and I doubt if it comes to Virginia and I setting up together, if
either of them is going to show any mercy! Of course as soon as
I have my wings, I'll earn something, and it isn't as if either of us
cared a damn about money, but naturally as I may get done in
before very long, I don't want Virginia to starve!"

I very nearly smiled again, at the thought of Virginia starving
under these, or any other, circumstances.

The boy, however, was deadly serious, so I simply told him as
reassuringly as I could, "In my experience, parents always give
in to the *fait accompli*, in the long run, that is!"

"Yes, but you see," the boy replied with ruthless logic, "my
run isn't likely to be a very long one, is it? Divorce takes a hell
of a long time to put through, especially as Old Man Esdaile is
going to dispute it. I've got to have some sort of support to bring
anything off, what you might call, even at my age, reasonably
soon!"

I tried another tack altogether.

"Must it really *be* marriage?" I asked him. "Whichever way
you look at it, Virginia has two perfectly good children which
she took the responsibility of bringing into the world. What do
you propose she should do with them now: desert them?"

The boy winced.

"They'll be well taken care of," he said stiffly, after a pause.
"Esdaile is, after all, a just beast; they're his children."

Of this I was not perfectly sure. The younger of the two
children bore a marked resemblance to Lord Wendover.

"Nature," I said, "provides children with mothers. You must
forgive me, but I am a scientist, and I believe in nature, so that
mothers are the only provision for children that I am inclined to
think *is* satisfactory."

"Then you'd tie her up to that stick Esdaile, for life?" he asked
with an indignant flush.

"Not particularly tightly, I wouldn't," I reminded him. "But
I would expect that anyone who took his place should accept the
children as his wife's, and therefore care for them as *his* — if
re-marriage, that is to say, were contemplated."

"Well, I'd do that," the boy agreed with reluctance, "if I had the money. But don't you think some women aren't meant for mothers? Virginia married at nineteen. That's awfully young to know what you're in for, isn't it? Esdaile insisted on their having a child at once. He has some fool notion that you can't lie with a woman without. Of course, everything he thinks *is* bunkum, but he sticks to his bunkum like a leech! He hasn't lived with her at all since the last child was born. You can't very well call it breaking up a marriage, for her to take a fresh start with me, can you?"

"No," I admitted, thinking of my own wife, Klara. "I should even expect it, but not this dropping down, into the nearest gutter, of the child or children for whom you are responsible! After all, the love of a husband whom you have wholly repudiated must be looked upon as a moral gutter. Esdaile is quite likely to punish the children for their mother's leaving him, while thinking that he is doing his duty by them. There is another point to consider. You realized what I meant about your father and mother — well, have you thought it might also be true as regards Esdaile and Virginia? Have you thought that man may be a monogamist, by instinct? Not that he *need* have only one woman in his life: that depends upon *when* he has her, and what he thinks of her; but there really seems to me to be a natural difficulty in replacing a woman who has been the centre of a man's life, the mother of his child, the core, as it were, of his main responsibility on earth, by any other woman, while she lives I mean, and is accessible."

He lit another cigarette and thought this over in silence.

"Couldn't one make even a *first* mistake?" he then demanded. "Certainly, what you say might be true if one could be sure of making the right choice early enough, but one doesn't grow wise as quickly as all that! How can one be sure, until one tries it out?"

"One *is* sure," I said, with a physical pang that quite literally shook me, "if one has lost a wife and child; and when they *have* been the core of one's life. I suppose that your father and Esdaile *are* sure. I think your mother, too, half realizes it. I think Virginia may know it; or that if she left Esdaile and the children, she might find it out. Have you read *Anna Karenina?* It is the best treatise on the subject that I know. I don't think Tolstoi loaded his dice against his illicit lovers. He found that such a situation just didn't work; and he shows us why. Yet one always respects the lovers, who were serious people, and took all their risks with courage. Of course you realize that there is an alternative to Virginia's leaving her home. Any generous woman who is in love with you, will be your mistress. Esdaile has only himself to thank if he is replaced as a lover, since he will not act like one."

The boy turned his back to me, and said, "There is a perfectly good moon, and it's damned hot in here. Would you mind turning the lamp off, so that I can put the curtains back?"

I thought to myself that he was a reliable fellow to have remembered the black-out at a moment like this. I turned the lamp out and he threw open the French window, onto the moonlit terrace. Then he came back to his chair. I could not see him any more but I could tell by his faint movements after this that he had sat down. I think he put his head between his hands and cried; but he made no sound.

For a long while we sat together in the tempered darkness.

At last, he said, "Well — that's that!" — an English expression that I have never fully understood.

He got up and drew the curtains back again. I took this as a tacit permission to switch on the reading lamp, upon his father's desk.

"Well," he said, strolling back to his former chair but not sitting down in it, "we've had the deuce of a pow-wow, haven't we? I think I must be getting along to bed now. I hope I haven't bored you! Anyhow, you'll stand by Virginia for me, won't you?"

"Yes," I said, "I will stand by Virginia."

I, too, got up. I expected him to shake hands, or to make some other sign of partnership, or at least farewell, but he simply wandered slowly across the great room towards the door — and without turning for so much as a final glance at me, closed it softly behind him. We had cleared up none of his difficulties;

nor had he informed me what he intended to do, or even what he wished me to do for him.

In what, for instance, did "standing by Virginia" consist?

This young man has saddled me with a responsibility for a difficulty he himself created; but the boy is young and cruelly ridden by a passion that cannot take its natural course. Full responsibility is the grown man's perpetual task. If Andreas had asked such an obligation from me, how gladly would I not have undertaken it! Well, I *will* stand by Virginia, for Adrian's sake, as the English say — "somehow."

23rd October 1940

I WAS not wholly surprised to find my patient less well to-day. The limelight is now off her. No longer can she shine as the heroine in the act of giving up her hearth and home to the injured. Shining must stop, and steps have now to be taken to carry out her sacrifice. Everyone else is too busy taking these steps even to notice whether she is being picturesque or not.

I had hardly reached Lady Wendover's bedside before she began to find fault with the arrangements she had been willing for us to make the day before, in order to remove the furniture.

"Please bring me the Inventory!" she demanded. "I wish to see *exactly* what things you propose are to leave the house; and what are supposed to remain."

I brought her my typed copy. It runs into many pages, so rich is this great house with all its treasures! The picture dealers are to take the famous pictures away to their own picture vaults for the duration; and half a great warehouse has been reserved for the furniture.

The removal vans had already come. Gillian and I were directing and supervising the packers, when I was summoned again to Lady Wendover.

This time she was much more displeased.

"The work must be stopped at once!" she said. "I cannot possibly have these things taken away so indiscriminately. I should have been consulted first, and I must have several days at least in which to make my choice. Certainly I shall not part with the Sir Joshuas! It is ridiculous to think of removing my boudoir furniture in this manner — in fact every room in the house has pictures in it which I might specially need, or miss. Tom always takes this high-handed way of doing things over my head when I am ill, but at least I should have supposed my own daughter, or my own physician, would have shown a little more consideration for my needs and feelings. You have taken a great deal too much upon you in carrying out this move wholesale, without consulting me! No doubt I did say that Silver Fountains should be used as a hospital, but not that its contents should be emptied out, onto the nearest dung heap. Am I not the mistress of my own home? Surely I have the right to say which of my things I wish to give up, and which I wish to have remain within *my* *reach?* How do you know that I should not prefer to have the Dower House furniture warehoused and some of this — with which I am accustomed to live — moved into its place?"

I thought it better not to remind her that she had said yesterday that she would give up everything she possessed; and begged us to undertake the removal without further argument or discussion with her, since she was too ill to pick and choose. She would be content, she had told us, with a cottage and a crust, in order to save the London hospital.

"Surely, you have every right," I agreed readily, "and I will see that the work is stopped at once. Shall I send away the vans and the removal men? They will not be able to come again for several weeks, and the hospital staff is arriving in a few days' time. Would it not be wiser to telephone to London to give up the whole scheme? The nightly bombing is, as you know, continuous, so that the staff should make other arrangements immediately."

Lady Wendover tossed her head back on the pillow and bit her lips. Her eyes looked as if they were held open with pins, and had a distracted furious expression. She was in a highly destructive state of mind; but she could not afford to show that it was destructive; and this of course annoyed her even more seriously.

"Fidget!" she cried sharply to the adoring shadow at the foot of the bed. "I wish you would keep still, and stop opening and shutting your mouth like a fish — you're driving me mad!"

"Fidget" as a pet name for Miss Fitchett is one of Lady Wendover's jokes; and although she was in no joking mood this morning she still used it.

"All this is a terrible shock to me!" she said bitterly, directing her unhappy face towards me. "I feel my generosity has been taken gross advantage of! I could not sleep all night and now my heart is leaping against my side — I think I am going to faint!"

I motioned to Miss Fitchett, who fluttered towards her, to leave the room; and rather to my surprise, she obeyed me.

I then took up the lists that had fallen off the bed onto the floor; and turned away as if I also were going to withdraw.

Lady Wendover whispered, "Doctor! My heart!"

"You would perhaps like a glass of water?" I asked her, and fetched her some from her bed table. I did not offer her anything stronger because as soon as she stopped trying to be breathless, I knew that she would feel less faint. Her palpitation was produced by anger; but it is not any use reminding people not to be angry.

After drinking a little water, she said in quite a strong voice, "You are not going to leave me in this condition surely — where is Fidget?"

"I suggested that she should leave the room," I explained. "I could see that she was annoying you; and since you are in the right position for your heart, and with plenty of fresh air blowing in upon you, you will soon feel better. I will therefore leave you to lie quite quiet, while I carry out your instructions!"

She said, "No! Don't! I haven't given any instructions yet. Give me the list again."

I did so, and she sat up as if there were nothing the matter with her, which was indeed the fact.

"At least you might give me an hour or two," she said petulantly, "to go over these wretched lists, so that I can put a mark against what I want at the Dower House, what is to be kept elsewhere, and what the men can take. You seem to forget that I have just had to part with my only boy — I saw him last night — who knows if not for the last time? And under the most distressing circumstances! No one takes the least care or notice of my feelings, but I am used to that! I had however supposed that as a doctor, you would show some consideration for my state of health, and not bring the house about my ears while I am still prostrate!"

I handed her a gold pencil; the lists; and arranged a bed desk upon which it would be easy for her to write.

"Do not fatigue yourself unnecessarily," I told her. "I will go now and give the order to the men to stop working immediately. Your health *is* my first consideration, and I am more than anxious that you should not overtax your powers while carrying out the magnificent sacrifice you are making for the bombed-out citizens of London. It is necessary that we trust each other, however. I will see that you do what you have undertaken to do without too great a risk — if you will try to believe that I am a capable judge of what you *can* do! Believe me, I am watching you very carefully, and if you follow my directions, you will achieve your purpose."

"What do you mean by my purpose?" she asked in her sharp, bullying manner; and it was the point, for I knew quite well that she *would* achieve her purpose, which was to upset the whole household one way or another, unless I was able to give her an even more important rôle than that of being a public nuisance.

Still I felt moderately certain that she would now alter the lists without undue delay. She has great executive capacity, which she is capable of using to good effect, if her authority is not threatened.

While I watched her, her eyes became calmer; and more accessible.

"A little chicken broth," I suggested, "and then — the effort! We shall all feel the happier for your being able to help us about what to retain of these great treasures. I must admit I had not thought it possible for you to make these decisions so soon after the parting with your son — but courage achieves miracles!"

She smiled, and said graciously, "Well, I will try not to be any longer than I can help, and if Fidget brings the chicken broth I will take some of it!"

The workmen, after due consultation, agreed to work on after their usual hours in order to make up for the present stoppage. I was empowered to spend what I thought right; and I made it worth their while. Gillian, however, proved a real problem, nor could she be paid into complaisance.

She went with me into a small visitors' room off the hall where we could speak in private, while I told her what had taken place. The absorbing hot anger of the young swept over her.

"The men can't be stopped like this," she told me furiously, her small hands clenched, her grey eyes blazing. "Yesterday Mother told us to do whatever we liked — with everything! She *can't* take back what she said, now — and begin picking and choosing! Every hour is precious — you know what there is to do! Doesn't she understand that to hold up the work is to lose lives? You don't know what she's like — she may spend days deciding what she will, or won't, have taken. You have my father's orders, and ought to *see* that they're carried out. Let her keep her own two rooms full of her favourite stuff if she must — but the house is a Wendover house, and the things in it belong to Wendovers. If you're afraid of her, let me go up and tell her what I think! You're *some* kind of a doctor, aren't you? Surely you can tell her she's not well enough to alter lists!"

There was the same agony of thwarted power in the daughter that I had noticed in the mother — but the daughter was the more adjustable. The mother only wanted to have her own way; the daughter wanted to have her own way too, but she also wanted to save the hospital. I hoped that she wanted to save the hospital even more than she wanted her own way.

"You must ask yourself," I said firmly, "which it is you wish to relieve: your own temper, or the situation. Your mother is even now making her alterations in the Inventory. If we leave her to do this, unopposed, I believe they will be moderate. The men have agreed to work overtime. We have therefore nothing to lose — except our tempers! But one foolish word to your mother, one hint of opposition, and once more the fire will be over the fat!"

I knew that this was incorrect English for this homely saying; but it made Gillian smile. She ceased to launch herself into a good imitation of a ramping Hitler.

"Wait a little," I urged gently, "and meanwhile help me in

another matter. I think it wiser to have your mother moved to-day. There will be fresh trouble to-morrow if she is on the spot. I had hoped to let her have a few days more in her own room here, but she can be moved very quickly and easily to the Dower House, and there she will find a sphere which she can turn upside down at will. If she stays here, she will either endanger our plans, or have a serious relapse into illness."

For a moment I thought Gillian would say, "No!" I even saw her lips form the stubborn word. A furrow crossed the lovely line of her brow. She wrinkled her small, pugnacious nose.

"But," she said, "the Dower House is not in order — it should be aired all day first! I know she *could* move in, but I had meant to do a lot to make it more comfortable — and now — "

"And now — " I said — "could you not mean something different?" Sometimes when I looked at Gillian I thought of Rosemary watering her white tulip to death. Both had the same energetic instinct, and both the same distrust of Life.

"But you don't know Mother," Gillian expostulated. "She will find fault with everything and make so much trouble! She will need everyone to wait on her all at once; and besides, if she really *is* ill, oughtn't she to find everything properly prepared for her, and go straight to bed surrounded by everything she is accustomed to, in the way of comforts?"

"Not at all," I said, "it will do her a great deal of good to find fault, and to have to re-arrange matters. The house is warm and dry. It is still summer weather. The cook and two maids can go on a few hours ahead of her. Miss Fitchett will accompany her after tea, to run her errands, while you can drive them in perfect security to their destination, only at a slower pace than usual. Then you will return as quickly as you like before the complaints begin! You have perhaps already seen that the scarf is removed?"

The colour swept up to her forehead, over her pale, clear skin.

"It *is* removed," she said, and shut her lips as if nothing on earth would ever make them open again.

It spoils the smooth curve of her lips, when she shuts them so tightly. The upper lip is very short and well-shaped. It is a pity that she is wholly without the warmth and seductiveness of Virginia.

Gillian *did* open her lips again after a long, cold silence to say, "If those are your orders, I suppose I must carry them out. I should have thought if Mother *could* become seriously ill at a moment's notice, it would be a risk to get her up after weeks in bed, and hustle her into a house not fully prepared for her. I suppose you know she staged another row with Adrian last night. She hasn't seen *me* yet — so I expect you thought *that* would be even worse for her!"

How jealous children are of their parents' love, even when they do not love their parents! Gillian made me think of Andreas when I kissed his mother. Yet he loved me nearly as much as he did his mother; and I loved him as a man loves his only child.

I did not answer her at once, not until she turned her offended wintry eyes directly upon me. Then I smiled at her, perhaps too tenderly, for I was still thinking of Andreas.

"It might be worse for *you*, rather than for her," I ventured. "But at least you would not become seriously ill from falling into a temper. That would only happen if you were her age and had worn yourself out by having had your own way all your life!"

It is beautiful to see the stillness of human eyes flash suddenly into movement; but I was sorry that anger, rather than pleasure, made Gillian's eyes change so swiftly as they met mine.

"You have no right to speak to me like that!" she said, which I suppose means that I am a servant and paid for my services rather than for my opinions.

I made no answer, for it is always better to let others have the last word if you are angry; and I knew that I was very angry.

I went about my business, and all day long I felt sad and heavy and did my work less well for my foolish anger. The displeasure of a young and attractive girl can be very galling, I find — even to a ghost. I wished that I could have told Eunice about it. She has that strange gift in a woman that she non-conducts all undue emotion. James, who is the least exaggerated person I know, although one of the most sensitive, has greatly profited by Eunice's complete absence of reaction. She feels *with* him, but retains her power to make all such feeling light. I used to be a little like this myself; but pain has made me very vulnerable to pain; and what is anger, in oneself or in another person, but an uncontrolled and intemperate pain?

After all, I had succeeded in easing our situation enough so that we could carry out our job, and that is my only business here — or elsewhere. My patient soon decided upon what pictures and furniture she wished to retain; and I altered the lists accordingly, so that the workmen only lost two hours of their daylight time; and this they made up during the black-out.

Gillian moved her mother at teatime quite successfully, but in tight-lipped silence, to the Dower House. Miss Fitchett telephoned me at 9 P.M. to say that my patient had eaten her dinner; and was wonderfully well, considering. She had found everything in a dreadful state; and had to change all the existing arrangements before she could think of resting.

"She will rest all the better," I said to Miss Fitchett, "for having had to make these changes; and now you will give her the sedative I ordered, and perhaps get a little rest yourself. I can imagine that you need it! To-morrow you may find that she is still more active."

Miss Fitchett did not laugh; in fact I have rarely seen her smile, and never heard her laugh; but she made a little sound that I heard across the wires, as if she agreed with me and was even a little amused, with the completeness of her agreement.

I find that Miss Fitchett and I understand each other very well, for both of us are devoted to my patient although we do not think that the end of the world comes when she thinks it does.

24th October 1940

LEFT alone last night with the rather complicated lists of my patient's wishes, it seemed to me simplest to collect each piece separately from all over the house, and assemble them together in one of the already empty rooms. I could not be sure that anyone — except Miss Fitchett and myself — was really anxious to carry out my patient's wishes; and I have always noticed that when people do not want to do a thing, quite important details may get confused or overlooked.

I am physically a strong man, and heavy weights laid along the base of the neck and the spine rarely strain a healthy human being, so I put on my bedroom slippers and carried the furniture piece by piece.

I thought of what was happening in London, perhaps last night, where men struggled to lift the beams of fallen houses off human beings — under a hail of bombs. My work seemed trifling in comparison, and I was sorry that I was not helping or saving anybody, only property. Still I have never despised property. Men have a right to collect what they like and need for living purposes. All well-made things have a sound human value. Nor are they only *things:* they are the work of man's creative mind. One should believe, I think, in the validity of the object, and give it the care and protection it needs. But whether any one man should possess quite so many objects or quite such precious ones, or indeed any which require the care and protection of others apart from himself, is another question.

My patient has never taken any trouble for her possessions. She has always paid for others to care for and protect them. Yet they are hers alone, to enjoy — or to control.

I do not think I ever thought so much about property before, as I did last night, carrying those chairs and tables, cabinets and pictures. I did not envy the Wendovers their possessions; indeed

I rather liked knowing that I was independent of the things I carried. Perhaps we never know the intrinsic value of a beautiful thing unless it does *not* belong to us. But I could not help wondering if owning valuable objects might not make a person feel that he was himself valuable when he was not. There is a certain arrogance in rich people that I am sure is quite unconscious, and I think it may come from their confusing what they happen to own with what they happen to *be!* There is another thing I have noticed living here in this rich household: the property of the Wendovers seems to act as a screen. It hides from them the needs and wishes of others. Perhaps it hides from them even their own. If this War is won in any real sense I think they will not reach this goal without parting with their present sense of Possession. Production rather than profit should be the aim of a living Democracy.

While I was carrying a flawlessly inlaid Buhl cabinet on my back, and edging down the main staircase with it, Gillian came out of her bedroom onto the landing. It must have been about three o'clock in the morning.

She wore an extremely well-cut black camel-hair pyjama suit with flame-coloured collar and cuffs; and it brought out the colour of her hair and eyes very pleasantly.

She did not speak; she just looked at me, and followed me downstairs into the billiard room where I was making the collection for her mother. She closed the door very softly behind us, and stood with her back against it.

"What on earth are you doing?" she demanded accusingly, as if it must inevitably be something wrong.

I explained, but I could not tell from her expression what she thought. She keeps her inner life as closed as if she locked the family jewels behind the screen of her young features.

I got rid of the cabinet, which had a marble top and was heavy, and seating myself on the edge of a solid Davenport lit a cigarette.

"Why on earth," she repeated, "are you carrying these things about — instead of waiting for the workmen, or the servants, to remove them to-morrow? It is fantastic of you to work by

night as well as by day. And, anyhow, moving furniture is not
your business."

"If I think it will result in benefit to my patient, I find that it
is my business," I replied firmly. "I happen to think that human
affairs do not do well in pigeon-holes. What I have done to-night
saves time; that is to the good of our common purpose. And it
might also save muddles; that will be to the good of my patient.
She might resent it if her wishes were not carefully carried out."

"You mean I should not be careful about my mother's wishes?"
she asked angrily.

"Care might not be taken — " I amended. "To-morrow there
will be a great many workers doing a great many things. To-
night there has only been one worker doing one thing, and that
is nearly finished. There remain, to bring down, only two Sir
Joshuas, the Gainsborough, and the little Fragonard over the
drawing-room mantelpiece."

"Did Mother *know* you were going to spend the night carrying about all this furniture?" Gillian then asked me.

She stood very stiffly against the closed door, rather, I thought,
like a young Saint in a niche over the doorway of Chartres;
although naturally enough the young Saint wears a robe of ribbed
stone, rather than soft pyjamas.

"I felt free to carry out your mother's wishes as I thought
best," I told her smilingly, for I can never help smiling at a
young woman whose wish is to be fierce and whose appearance
is so pleasant. Besides, why should a girl be annoyed when she is
young and good to look at, and sees that the man she is speaking
to is enjoying her society?

"Ever since you've been in this house, you've interfered with
something!" Gillian burst out.

She was evidently in a much more serious rage than I had
thought.

"I am always finding you helping the cook, talking to the gar-
deners, or fetching and carrying for Fidget! It is so unnecessary
— and rather impertinent — besides, do you *never* sleep?"

"I relax in various ways," I told her. "Last night, for instance,
Adrian came and talked to me, and to-night *you* are paying me a

visit. I shall sleep later on. It is only three o'clock. In Wien we begin our café life at about ten, and often talk till morning. If one works all day, it is a waste of time not to spend part of the night for pleasure. Besides, I have no habits; such things as habits belong to old men with beards whose muscles are stiff!"

I wanted her to smile, but she wouldn't. She said just as angrily, though the thing she suggested doing was kind, "Well, at least since I *am* up, I shall get you some soup, or coffee. Please come with me into the kitchen!"

She would have spoken in a far more friendly way to a dog.

The kitchen is a charming room, and very well kept by my friend Caroline, the cook. It is quite true that I have taught her how to make an *Apfelstrudel*, as well as pancakes soaked in wine, which the peasants in Tirol call "Drunken Brides"! She is an intelligent and friendly girl whom I respect greatly.

It was obvious that Gillian knew nothing about the kitchen; and I preferred to make the coffee myself.

"Soup," I told her, "is not a dawn dish. If you wish to eat, I will scramble some eggs. The bread is in the larger of the two blue tins on that table."

Gillian bit her lips and frowned; but she brought me what I asked for, and soon we had a good meal, made with perfect ease upon an electric cooker.

I was hungry and I rarely enjoyed a meal more. I found some hothouse peaches and grapes in the Frigidaire, and these went very well after scrambled eggs and coffee.

There is as yet no food shortage in England; but it is bound to come, later. The rate at which the ships are being sunk is terrible. This everyone knows, but what it must imply they seem not to understand. I hope they will never lose their spirit of optimism, these English; but optimism without foresight, or the energy to take the steps that alone can justify optimism — this might spell their doom!

Gillian began to look less frozen after we had worked and eaten together. I made her put on Caroline's apron, while we washed up our plates and cups. When we had finished she said, "Now I will help you carry the pictures."

We found a step-ladder and took it to the drawing-room. Last of all, I lifted down the lovely little Fragonard.

"How the French understand the combination of pleasure and dignity," I told her. "The little figures in this landscape are as responsible and natural as the trees and flowers. They are in order, and yet they dance. I sometimes think, Miss Gillian, that in this country you hardly rate pleasure high enough — your idea of it is strenuous and yet irresponsible. It seems to depend always upon other things: a ball, a gun, horses or greyhounds. Yet we ourselves can make pleasure! You English are not always very human, if I may say so!"

Gillian sat on the floor, close to the step-ladder, while I sat on the top of it, with the Fragonard upon my knees.

"I'm human enough," Gillian said without looking round at me, "and I could be gay too — if I were happy!"

"You are troubled about Adrian," I said. "Perhaps you think as I do, that he drove away very early this morning, in his fast sports car, to some station at which Virginia joined him, and that they spent a wonderful day together before he returned to Eton!"

"How did you possibly guess?" she said, the lovely, furious pink creeping up to her forehead.

"I guessed," I explained, "because had I been Adrian, I should have done exactly the same, if you were Virginia, of course!"

"That's nonsense," she said sharply, and would perhaps have stamped her foot, a thing I have read about in English novels but not yet seen done, had she not been sitting on the floor. "You don't even mean it, you would have *preferred* it to be Virginia! Oh, if only Uncle James were here!"

"Why do you not send for him then?" I asked. "The Dower House has seven bedrooms."

"I did send for him, in a way," she explained. "I wrote a postcard. I said couldn't they come down sometime for a week-end! But they didn't!"

"Upon this famous postcard, you did not perhaps say *why* they were to come?" I ventured.

"Oh, well," Gillian answered, "they might have guessed.

Adrian is such a *fool!* He can't see Virginia doesn't mean anything! He won't let me tell him the truth! We always used to share things, and say everything straight bang out to each other. You see there *are* only the two of us. Now he's gone all frozen and polite and says nothing. As for Virginia — well, obviously she *knows* what I think of her. She was my friend first! It was so wonderful, her being American, and such *fun!* I always stood up for her, whatever she did. Now it's all horrible, and I'm just ashamed!"

Perhaps she wanted to cry, but she did not cry, only I watched her eyes fill, and then empty again. She gave a little hopeless, exasperated sigh, sadder than tears. She is far younger than a Viennese girl of nineteen could ever be. I am quite certain that Gillian has never had a lover. Admirers of course, by the dozen perhaps, but so far off! Her heart is as untarnished and immaculate as a mountain peak after a first snowfall.

I thought it was best to speak to her with absolute directness. "You feel ashamed?" I asked her. "But I cannot see quite why. To be a little hurt, because people in love are very selfish and have shut you out, that I can easily understand! To be apprehensive, because behind this young affair of Adrian's there is something more serious between Virginia and your father, that too, I can understand; but of what are *you* ashamed? Cowardice and treachery are shameful things. I do not know what else is, except the most shameful of all, perhaps, cruelty to each other! You have not shown these qualities, except perhaps unconsciously the last!"

"It is a sort of treachery," she said in a voice so low that I could hardly catch her words, "what is happening — and I have to feel in it too, because I *am* my father's daughter! What he does, really happens to me as well. Besides, I may laugh at my mother, I may be angry with her, for so much of what she says is rubbish and she *will* order me about, but after all, she *is* my mother! I've always taken Father's side when they have had rows, because I've known he was right. He orders me about too, but he's sensible. But this — this business about Virginia — it's changed my whole life!"

"Ah, one's life!" I said unsympathetically because I felt she needed me to make matters lighter for her. "It is always necessary to change it! But it should never, except very superficially, depend upon the lives of others. Are you not making altogether too much of this business of love-making? In one sense you can't make too much of it. Love is our daily bread. Without it life is worthless — it is not even life. But you make it too romantic! Look at the facts carefully, and you will feel better. Since Adrian was ten years old, and he is now eighteen, your mother, a highly attractive and physically competent woman, refused to live with your father. She has been perfectly faithful to him, if to be stagnant is to be faithful! No other man has so much as touched her. This friendship she has with the clergyman, Michael, is a subliminal liaison of an atrocious innocence. Please forgive the strength of my language, but I am both a man of science and a Viennese — therefore a healthy instinct translated into a spiritual flirtation is far more immoral to me than any physical relationship.

"Your father suffered as only a forcible and healthy human being can suffer. You have only to look at his face to read the lines of his torment. What then could be more natural than that he should seek release, from a young and healthy girl — also deserted — who is the actual wife of the man to whom he owes his defeat? After all, husbands or wives are defeated when their mates find any other companionship preferable to their own. It does not matter if this companionship is with someone of the same sex: even a dog can be made to hurt a lover, or a book, or a musical instrument; or the record of a gramophone. It is what takes the place of an old joy that is so cruel a wound. The intention is all that matters. Your mother and father unfortunately now wish to give each other pain instead of wishing to give each other pleasure. They have turned their love inside out. It is a pity, and it certainly makes a complication for their children, but you have to free yourself, and to help Adrian free himself, of this complication!"

Gillian turned her head round so that she could look straight at me. She had never done this before, except in some sideways insignificant manner, as if she were observing the room I took up in the space surrounding us, so that she might not find me in her way.

It is shocking to me to realize that at nineteen any human being can be as regardless of sex as this child is. The facts she has doubtless known for many years, but their spiritual significance has wholly escaped her.

"But how can we free ourselves?" she asked me. "Father is married to Mother — we both belong to them! This *is* our home! We're very fond of Michael, all of us, even Father! He prepared Adrian and me for confirmation. He's been in some ways our best friend. He's not only religious: he's great fun. I don't think you understand about Michael: he can be quite awfully respected! Virginia thought he was a Saint, and wanted to marry him, as you would a film star. It was a sort of stunt, she told me, to see if a Saint *would* marry her! Well, he did, and she didn't like it because there was always God, and Michael was so particular. She ought to have known he would be, oughtn't she? She told me once he stopped being her lover when she only flirted! I *do* see a little what you mean about Virginia — only *not* Father!

"Naturally I don't know very much about my parents, but they've always seemed fond of each other! I mean they've had rows and Mother's always interfered too much, and she doesn't understand, as Father does, what people need. Father's been everything to us! But Virginia's *our* friend, she's not his; she's *young!*"

"Yes," I agreed, "of course that makes such a relationship aggravating and highly inconvenient to you. It might even make life tragic if you took such a relationship too seriously. If your mother were to realize, or worse still, perhaps, if Adrian did, there might be great troubles; but I don't think, as yet, either of them do. Your mother is concentrated on the annoyance it makes for her to see Adrian in love with Virginia, and Adrian himself is too much in love to realize anything, except Virginia.

"I'm not quite sure that although Virginia *is* your father's mistress (and no doubt has been so for some long time) that she has yet become Adrian's!"

"Oh, no," said Gillian with a little gasp of horror. "No! No! Of *course* Adrian doesn't know about Father — *no one* else does — only *you* know — because I couldn't help it — you saw the yellow scarf!"

"There is no reason why you *should* help it," I told her. "I am here to make the relationship between your mother and father better — not worse. I may not succeed, but I shall do the best I can and in any case, I shall hold my tongue. That is what doctors are for!"

She nodded.

"I know you'll do that," she agreed, "but it's no use pretending it isn't awful. They used to meet in the Dower House — that's how I found out — only two months ago. I had shot a rabbit, and heard it squeal, so I ran to look for it and found it close against the library window, in a patch of fern. I broke its neck, and then I looked into the room, and saw Father with Virginia in his arms. It was dusk. They didn't see me. But afterwards, I told Virginia I knew! Of course she must have told Father; we haven't spoken to each other since, except in public: how can we, ever? That's finished too! Everything I *have*, is finished!"

"It has not yet begun!" I told her impatiently. "You both exaggerate and confuse what has taken place between your father and Virginia. That was a yellow scarf you found on the floor and *not* a rattlesnake!

"Virginia is not an evil witch dropped into your household out of an old ballad — she is a lovely and beautiful girl, without a real home — in a foreign country. Your father is a man of great strength and courage, occupied vitally in helping to save England from the Nazis; and you are to him what you have always been, his only daughter. It is Adrian, not you, whom I find in a bad position. He does not know the truth and he is not likely to find it out in the best way. Probably you should have told him!"

"Oh!" Gillian exclaimed indignantly. "How could I? Besides, he wouldn't have believed me! He thinks I'm disgusting to Virginia because I'm just jealous! Perhaps I *am* jealous, too, but not the way he thinks!"

"Well," I said, "it is now nearly five o'clock, and our work is finished. We should get some sleep. To-morrow I will write to James and Eunice myself, and tell them that things are very complicated here, and that if it is possible, we need their help. Is your father fond of James?"

"Yes," Gillian said, "in his way he is, awfully! I mean, in a sense, he thinks James rather a poop, but he does admire him *intellectually*, if you know what I mean!"

People in England always speak of the intellect as if it were some queer excrescence to the rest of a person, rather like an ingrowing toe-nail. They think people who have it should be ashamed of it and hide it as much as possible.

"Father *talks* to him — " Gillian went on after a pause — "he doesn't to most people — he just *tells* them things. But he lets Uncle James tell *him* things back."

"That is an advantage," I agreed rather dryly. "As for us, we cannot settle other people's affairs for them; but we can perhaps bring unknown facts to their notice. The decision — what to do about the new facts — must however remain with them. Miss Gillian, I know very little about life. All that I once thought I knew I now realize was built on an insecure foundation; but this has not yet been proved a lie to me, that man must live this life on his own responsibility, and upon nobody else's! For you to talk of happiness having finished, or your affections being already lost, is a nonsense, for you have had as yet no life. Your affections are as unfurnished as an empty room; but they are not broken; they will need to be re-arranged a little, that is all! If the Nazis do not come, they *can* be re-arranged. Our immediate object however is to see that the Nazis do *not* come, and this hospital that you are to work in with me will be our part in the defence of this Island. Let us be friends and work well in it together!"

Her eyes left mine, but she did not lower her head.

"Thanks," she said finally, "I feel better somehow. But actually we *are* friends, aren't we — or I shouldn't have talked to you like this?"

She got up. I liked the quick way she rose. All her muscles co-ordinate and move smoothly. They are very healthy, these

English girls, although they are so physically incomplete. This one will work hard for her country; but as yet she has no realization of what she is working against.

These lucky Islanders are so wholly accustomed to freedom that they no more think of losing it than a fish thinks of losing the water it breathes in — or a bird the air. Yet they have come within an ace of losing what they breathe. Sex must go on, and no doubt will go on, Nazis or no Nazis, but the element of freedom hangs by a hair!

28th October 1940

EVERYTHING from the medical point of view is now ready for the opening of the hospital. Gillian is supervising the final cleaning of Silver Fountains from cellar to garret.

To-night the ladies upon whom the work we are to do largely depends arrive from London: the Deputy Matron, Sister Tutor and Home Sister. These titles are of course unfamiliar to me, but Barrow has explained the very responsible and important duties that these three ladies will fulfil.

The housekeeping and administration of the whole hospital rests in the hands of the Deputy Matron. Sister Tutor watches over, and lectures to, the nursing staff. The Home Sister has varied and intersecting tasks suitable to the name given her.

In the last resort, I am the final authority for the well-being of the patients; but Barrow assures me that the routine work of these skilled and trained women will lighten my responsibility in a manner unknown in my own country.

I set out, therefore, to see my patient at ten o'clock this morning with my mind emptied of anxiety. If a man understands his work and is assured that there will be no extraneous obstacles to his carrying it out, I think his heart is always at peace.

There was a heavy dew on the ground; and twisted here and there across the golden bracken, the red leaves of brambles sparkled with crystal drops. There was no distance, and the great oaks and chestnuts seemed painted in against the background of lilac mist. Robins sang their abrupt sweet songs, and the light came slanting through the trees a little thickly, like run honey.

I had a sort of upspringing of hope in my heart. Is not England still miraculously preserved? Beyond her vigorous guarded seas, she is still free to breathe deeply, and to grow ever stronger against future attacks. As yet there has been no attempt at invasion; and in a few weeks' time it will be too late to attempt one against the shortening stormy, winter days. The American destroyers, too, spell decisive hope; surely this great people will soon join us? Yet America is, perhaps even more than this country, a peace-loving land — incredulous and disconcerted at the thought of War. She is, alas, too intelligent to believe in it! It is our tragedy in Europe that the stupid should also be the strong. How helpless Austria was in 1938 — although I could almost say that every Austrian must once at least in his lifetime have outwitted a German, probably as many times as he has met one! But all the wits in the world did not save our intelligent Schuschnigg when he came to Berchtesgaden and found himself surrounded by wild beasts.

I was trying not to think of these things, in the still sunshine, when I heard a strange sound coming from an invisible glade.

It was the hoarse barking of two stags fighting. This is the time of year when these very picturesque animals, with their ferned horns, fight for their mates, head to head and heart to heart. Gillian has told me these Park animals are fallow deer. They are less big and wild than the red deer that live their more natural lives on moor and mountain. But Tom has among them some of the wilder species, though they are few and difficult to catch sight of, on account of their more independent lives. These stags now fighting were red deer.

I turned aside down a grass ride, deep into the bracken, till I came to the beginning of the beech avenue. The trees stand there like the pillars of a great church, with a space under them. There the two stags fought. One must not go too near such a battle for these queer, archaic gentlemen are dangerous.

I kept to windward of them, meaning to sit down on the trunk of a fallen tree and watch them for a few minutes, when I discovered that someone else had forestalled me. A girl lay twisted, face downwards in the bracken, her head in her arms, sobbing. Only a few yards from her, the stags fought, hoof to hoof, eye to eye — antler against antler; yet she seemed as unconscious of their presence as they were of hers.

It was a curious sight, and I might have stolen away and left her to her tears, if I had not suddenly realized that the girl was Virginia.

I moved forward then very quietly and, bending over her, said her name. She started up, stared at me, and threw herself forward into my arms.

Poor child, she was very unhappy; and with it, as always, very impetuous! It seemed natural to hold her in my arms, while she clung with her face against my shoulder, still shaking with sobs.

"Be quiet," I whispered, "for the stags are fighting too close to us for safety."

She moved her head and looked at them with startled eyes. I think it seemed strange to her that anything mattered except her grief, or that even a beast could be so oblivious as to think of its own concerns, when her heart was broken. Yet the stags had their own love affairs to think about, and they were absorbed in their combat. One was younger — and at first sight stronger than the other. He had no moss on his horns. The other must already have had several seasons' fights, for his great fronded antlers were chipped and twisted from former battles.

Somehow, these two stags reminded me of Adrian and his father; and I watched them, wondering whether the younger one, for all his fresh pride and strength, was a match for his astute and toughened elder.

"Which do you wish to win?" I asked Virginia; and she cried, "Oh, must one of them lose, Rudi?" and I saw that she too had recognized the likeness; and knew that her own heart was at stake.

"Yes, one of them must lose," I told her rather sternly, for she had provoked the battle.

The younger stag pressed forward with terrific fury and directness. He was all ardour and anger, and it was from him those hoarse, fierce cries sounded. The older one was silent but he pressed firmly forward, the muscles standing out on his great arched neck, so that you could see them move under the hide.

He seemed to let himself be pushed back a little towards the trees, away from us, as if he were reserving his full powers until he had found the best position for exerting them. I could see that — in a flash — when the moment came, he would push past the antlered guard of the younger one, and do him some great injury.

Virginia saw this also, and cried aloud, "Oh, Rudi, stop them fighting! You must stop them!"

The stags heard her cry and broke apart, pawing with their hooves into the soft ground, and lowering their antlers threateningly towards us. I seized a stick and flung it at them, fortunately hitting the younger one. He bounded off through the trees, the elder following him. In a moment they had vanished so that we could not tell which would be the victor.

Virginia gave a deep sigh of relief. "Perhaps they won't fight again!" she said pleadingly. "I am so glad you came, Rudi! Adrian said I might speak to you — but I haven't had a chance! Lady Wendover sent for me at breakfast time this morning. I went at once, and found her dreadfully angry. She said awful things about me and Adrian, things I couldn't bear, but I had to because of Adrian, and because of course she doesn't know, not really, what there is to be angry about! She told me I must let Adrian go — Michael would never divorce me — and he's going to give up this living, and go up North right away from everything into some horrible Newcastle slum! It will be awful for the children, and besides, they don't know, she and Michael, but Adrian won't be here long. He's going to enlist in the Air Force — he's only a year under the age — and he thinks Tom will let him — and that I'll come to him in a few months' time. But of course I can't!"

Virginia began to cry again, wildly and out loud like a child; but like a child, she listened through her sobs when I said to her, "What will stop your going to Adrian, Virginia?"

"Oh, you know," she sobbed. "You know Tom won't let me go! I don't know if he can stop Adrian joining the Air Force, but he can stop *me!*"

"I do not think he can," I said slowly, "not if you wish to

go to Adrian, I mean, not if you wish it above everything else that can happen to you, or to anybody else."

"But that's just it," Virginia said, brushing her tears away impatiently, "I *can't* do what I wish! Tom will tell Adrian that I'm his mistress, and I am! And then Adrian will never forgive me!"

I think I never saw such hunted eyes as hers. Poor Virginia! Those who cut across obligation in order to do what they desire always find themselves trapped sooner or later in the inescapable torture of their own wishes. She has the most beautiful eyes — dark-blue, not bright and hard like a forget-me-not — but like the deep sky above a mountain pine.

But the spirit behind their beauty was desperate and in flight. Virginia does not know what she wants most, or what will hurt her least. She thinks that she loves two men, but perhaps she really loves neither. What she is longing for is some escape into a happier and easier way of living.

I can easily understand this — for her husband, Michael, is a hard man who would demand of her an equal hardness. I wondered if the doe awaiting the outcome of the stags' battle felt herself a driven victim like Virginia. She too could not intervene, but, happy animal, she would, I hoped, be content with whichever stag proved himself the stronger!

But Virginia would not be content.

At the moment she preferred the younger and the weaker of the two males who were fighting for her; but I thought it would be the stronger who would keep her, in spite of her preference.

"You need not continue to be Tom's mistress," I told her gently, "unless you wish to. Such relationships can always end at the will of either party. After all, you were the wife of Michael, and you are *not*, to all intents and purposes, any more his wife. This with Tom is a lesser tie!"

She moved uneasily; her eyelids fluttered like the zigzag wings of a chased butterfly.

"If Michael refuses to divorce me, how can I marry anybody!" she said nervously. "I think it's wicked of him, but he's like that! He has a grudge against me because I can be happy

without him, but he thinks it's because of the Church. It makes
him behave like a stone, and be proud of it. Besides, there are
my babies; you can't think I *want* to leave them!"

"Yet they are also *his* babies," I reminded her, "and you cannot take them away from him."

She blinked and would not meet my eyes, and I had again the
idea that perhaps the younger child was Tom's.

"I suppose," she said after a long silence, "that I shall just put
Adrian off! I can't marry him, and because of the children I
can't even live with him — so I must just go on waiting for something fresh to happen. Perhaps Adrian will get killed or Tom
be tired of my always being upset! Only *must* we go to Newcastle? Can't you stop Lady Wendover's sending us away?"

"Not if your husband wants to go, I can't," I told her. "Besides, do you not yourself think that it might be best? I take it
Adrian does not know about his father, or his father, beyond
thinking you've flirted with him, about Adrian?"

Virginia nodded. "It — it just happened!" she murmured. "I
didn't mean it to happen, Rudi! You see, Adrian always played
with Gillian and me, when he was a boy, and suddenly, one
day, he wasn't a boy any more. He had grown up, and Tom
was away all last winter and spring because of the War; and I
was frightened, and so awfully lonely and dull, and then Gillian
stopped being friendly and there was only Adrian. You do see
how it *could* happen, don't you? I know it was awful, but when
you're in love and know what a man wants, and there isn't any
other way of making him happy except by giving it to him, and
being happy yourself *with* him, is it so dreadful to do what you
both want? Gillian thinks it is, even though she isn't religious.
But then she hasn't been a wife, and then for so long, *not* a wife,
not anything! That was how Tom happened, and I got used to
him, and it seemed all right. I couldn't feel very wicked, because,
after all, Michael didn't care! Besides, if you're going to be as
good as all that, and try to force somebody else to be good as
well, you have to pay for it, don't you? But I was mad to let
Adrian love me! I had thought of him as just a child — and loved
him like that for years, ever since I came here; and then, just

last Christmas, I found he was older than I was, and I *had* to
do what he wanted!"

"It's not so dreadful," I said gently, "but what might be really
dreadful is Adrian's finding out suddenly about his father —
it might be such a terrible shock to him!"

"It would be a shock to Tom as well, to find out about
Adrian," Virginia said defensively, as if something within her
were trying to protect the rights of this old lover whose claims
she had so casually violated. "More, in a way, because I've belonged to him for two years. I was terribly fond of him, and
he's given me everything he could — always. He'd marry me to-
morrow if either of us could get free. In a way it was so funny
talking to Lady Wendover this morning, and knowing that I
had the whip hand of her all the time whatever she said, only I
couldn't use it!"

Her eyes, not yet dry from tears, brimmed suddenly with
laughter.

"Oh, Rudi," she said, "do you think I'm very wicked? You
don't look at me as if you were despising me, and yet I suppose
you do? Or is it only the English who despise people? You see
the awful part of it is that both Tom and Adrian would despise
me if they knew!"

"Oh, no, I don't despise you," I told her. "In my country
we do not like venal women — but you are not venal. You like
to give as well as to take, but I must admit that I think you have
put yourself into an unfortunate position, because you can get
into a much worse difficulty from *not* having spoken the truth.
You see the truth is always much more embarrassing when it has
not been spoken than when there is nothing to hide! And also
it concerns others — they are not free when you have fooled them
by a lie; and it is always very dangerous not to leave a lover
free. If I were in your place, whether I told Tom or not, I
should tell Adrian!"

"But why Adrian, and not Tom?" Virginia demanded.

"Because," I said, "if Tom finds out, or if you tell him, he
can take care of himself. Tom is an important person, to his
country as well as to you! In a sense, also, he deserves no better

than that you should leave him. He is twice your age, and I take
it you were true to your husband until he made love to you,
therefore he broke your marriage. The breakers-up of marriage
cannot expect their own love-loyalties to remain intact."

Virginia looked grave. "But — " she said, and stopped, as if to
speak hurt her, and then added, "Yes, I *was* true to Michael. I
flirted, but I was true to him. Tom knew I was true to Michael,
but Michael didn't! Tom believed in me, more than Michael!
He does now: that's why I mind as much, or more, Rudi, than
I mind for Adrian, or for Michael. Tom is more like me; he isn't
as particular as Michael and Adrian, he knows flirting *is* only
flirting. But you see I've really let him down now!"

But though she spoke of Tom, I had the feeling that of the
three of them, the one whom it hurt her most to think about was
her husband. Tom had spoiled her, but Michael had not spoiled
her; and it was for this she could not forgive him. But I said nothing to her of these things then since they were not my business.

"Adrian," I said firmly, "ought to be told by you at once about
his father, because you must help him over the knowledge. You
— and only you — can show him how to bear the thought that he
has been deceived by you. If he finds out from anyone else, he
may not be able to bear it!"

Virginia leaned once more against my shoulder, as if I were
the bough of a tree, and not a man.

"Oh, Rudi," she said, "I can't ever tell him! *You* must tell
him for me. If you think he's really *got* to know, I mean! But
why should he be told? They may send him overseas soon; that
would make such a difference. And I can pretend to Tom, I can
go on pretending! After all, it isn't as if I didn't like him, is it?
Just because I'm not interested in him any more isn't the same as
if I didn't like him!"

"He might notice the difference," I said a little dryly — thinking of Klara.

There had never been a time when she was not interested in
me, nor when I would not have noticed if she had ceased to be
interested; until in a flash, an hour, a summer afternoon, I had
become a Jew.

"It's such a pity," Virginia said after a long silence, "that *you* aren't my lover, Rudi. You know you could be — quite easily — if you wanted!"

"Easier than you think!" I thought to myself, but not aloud to her.

"That also might lead to embarrassments," I said aloud, "for then you would have three lovers to explain to yourself, instead of two. Besides, I should always know if you were interested or not. I am not a good man to lie to!"

Virginia moved her head from my shoulder and looked at me with eyes that were pleasant to drown in.

"But I should rather like to have *one* man," she said with a little smile, "to whom I *must* always speak the truth, and who wouldn't believe me if I didn't!"

"You can have him to tell the truth to without making him your lover!" I answered.

Virginia was again silent.

This looking for lovers to help her evade difficulties was presumably her life-plan, and with her looks, it could not have been difficult to find them. On the whole I thought her rather a good girl only to have had the two Wendovers as lovers, with that stick, Michael, thrown in as a husband.

"You're so much more the right age," Virginia said at last. "Tom and Michael are too old for me, and Adrian is too young; but you really know what I mean!"

"Do you yourself know what you mean," I ventured to ask her, "or even what you want? Think for a moment! You do not wish to leave your children — yet you would leave them if Michael released you. You wish to give up Tom, and yet you have not made up your mind altogether to renounce him. You wish to go to Adrian, and yet you are sitting here, under these great beeches that are rather like a church and must sometimes remind you of your husband, except of course that you are sitting under them with another man!"

Virginia laughed out loud, and I laughed with her. She is all that she ought not to be perhaps, but it is easy to laugh with her.

"Well, I *do* know what I want really," Virginia told me, when she had finished laughing, "I want you to tell Adrian about Tom; and I want you to prevent my having to go to Newcastle; and I want you to come to lunch with me to-day — before you have the whole hospital pulled over your ears!"

I was glad that she had reminded me of the hospital. It was a great help to me.

The fact that I have no human relationships that are my own I find makes me very vulnerable to emotional contacts. I could, I know, easily be true to a wife whom I possessed, but hardly to a wife whom I no longer possess. I would make any reasonable sacrifice for my son, but without Andreas sacrifice has a sterile look.

I wished more than ever that Eunice and James were within call. Still, I reminded myself I had a certain definite loyalty to Adrian, and I mean to keep it whatever Virginia may mean; so I agreed to go to lunch with her to-day, that being the easiest of her wishes to grant, and I hoped the least harmful.

1st November 1940

I AM not certain why Virginia wanted me to lunch at the Rectory. Did she feel naked after her confidence to me, and want to re-clothe herself, and perhaps impress me by presenting herself against the background of well-bred domesticity — as the mother of two healthy, handsome children, the mistress of a charming house, the wife of a man I had only to look at in order to respect? Or was it that she wanted her husband, Michael, to see yet another man brought to heel by the attractions he would not so much as acknowledge?

The house *was* charming; so were the children whom we saw for brief well-timed moments before, and after, lunch. So was the lunch itself, and above all, so was my gracious scholarly host. But all that these pleasant accessories accomplished for Virginia was to show me how completely she failed to be part of them. She might have been a wandering air blown in at one window and out at the other.

The servants looked to their master for suggestion and approval. The children were governed by their firm and placid nurse. The little girl leaned against her father all the while she was in the room, not troubling to hide the suspicious and hostile feeling she had for her mother.

The little boy ran towards Virginia with some show of affection, but he soon moved away from her as if he found her presence did not add either to his security or to his entertainment.

Her husband treated her with the scrupulous courtesy due to the mistress of the house; but without overlooking any of her prerogatives, he managed to convey that she was wholly incapable of carrying them out.

I have never seen a more relentless exposure of inefficiency taking place under the mask of protective kindness.

Virginia was not naturally inefficient, even domestically; of this I was assured by her work in the hospital. She was an impetuous, untrained girl, and like all discouraged persons, liable at times to become careless and unreliable. Sister Curtis, who was a good judge of character, had already told me that Virginia would make an admirable nurse — with careful training. She has courage, generosity and kindness. These are three fine qualities. But a woman whose main desire is to give people pleasure, and to save herself pain while doing it, is likely to fail overwhelmingly where she is not appreciated.

I had not been half an hour in Virginia's house when I realized that her servants despised and disapproved of her; her children were estranged from her; and her husband was relentlessly destroying and undermining all her capacities for usefulness.

He never looked at her, but I think nothing she did or said escaped him.

While she was pouring out sherry for us before lunch, for instance, her hand trembled among the glasses. Instantly her husband moved the tray to a steadier position on the table; and finally removed it from her altogether. He was on the *qui vive* to supplement or replace anything she overlooked, or to rectify any little slip she made. In the same way he edited her speech, so that whatever Virginia said — and she is a copious, picturesque, often inaccurate talker — had to pass through the fine-meshed sieve of his mind in order to be cleansed from its impurities.

Once the little girl said, "Oh, Mummy, how silly you are!"

Her father instantly rebuked her. Virginia flushed, as if both her husband and her child had struck her.

Against the subtle tactics of her husband's superior and controlled intellect, Virginia was as helpless and inexpert as a bird that has flown into a room and cannot find the window through which it came in order to fly out again.

I can imagine no greater spiritual torture to a spirit unsure of itself and relying upon the appreciation of others than to live among a group of people none of whom admire or even respect her. No doubt had Virginia earned her own self-respect, she would have been less harrowed and flustered by the chronic disapproval of her household. Perhaps even if Michael's antagonism had taken a more aggressive form, it would have roused her courage to fight back. But even the babies — and they were little more than babies — under their father's watchful eyes, though they paid her a sort of lip-service of obedience and affection, obviously regarded her as an ill-behaved animal to whom their father had taught them to be kind.

Nor could one deny that superficially they were in the right. Virginia *had* broken their laws. No doubt, too, she often upset the regularity and routine of the nursery by haphazard entrances and exits. No doubt she sometimes forgot the necessary duties of a mother and the mistress of a house; and without doubt she is a faithless wife.

In order to carry on her intrigues, she must often have told lies; and these lies must sometimes have been found out. Perhaps no one under the Rectory roof knows for certain that she is any-one's mistress, but they are all more or less conscious that she is not truly her husband's wife. Nor can any of them forgive her this desertion since her husband is apparently the best of men, the kindest of fathers, the most considerate of masters.

So Virginia, who wants to be more right than she need be, is where she loves most considered more wrong than perhaps she actually *is!* For few human beings — certainly not this exiled child Virginia — are wholly in the wrong, however badly they may elect to behave.

A man whose every exertion is bent upon showing up the flaws in his wife's character must be at least partially responsible for some of them.

Nevertheless, I must admit, against my will, Michael *is* what he claims to be, a good man. The love and respect he has built up for himself in his home, and throughout his whole parish, is justified. Personally he shows me great kindness, although I am a foreigner and a stranger, and he might well have considered me an active rival upon his own preserves; but he has treated me from the first as a friend. He has added to his own daily work hours every evening, helping us over the preparation for our hospital. Gillian, who has known him intimately (and while Virginia was her best friend), would not have said, "Michael is to be respected," if she had not had a good foundation for such a statement.

After lunch was over — and every mouthful of the very excellent food nearly choked me — Michael walked back to Silver Fountains with me through the Park. The last light of the day shone through the trees. The mild moist air was motionless. In the distance, the stags were still barking, and I wondered if the question had yet been cleared up between our two fighters as to which was the stronger.

Michael talked to me freely of Lady Wendover and the problem of what position to find for her in the hospital. He showed great penetration and wisdom as to her character. Now that I no longer had to watch the vivisection of Virginia take place under my eyes, I enjoyed his conversation; I even felt from time to time as if I were talking to a fellow psychologist. But one cannot talk for very long to most clergymen without stubbing one's intellectual toe upon the sacerdotal obstacle. The moment always comes, sooner or later, when the Priest ceases to trust to knowledge and replaces it by what he would term "principle." A "right" and "wrong" has crept into the region of abstract fact. Instantly the atmosphere changes, and one knows that one is talking to an unconscious liar.

Virginia, poor child, lied because she felt too weak to get on without the support of a lie; and her husband lies because the tenets he supports are not strong enough to be accepted without one. Both secretly deny to themselves the validity of the object — which is the God of things as they are.

In Austria the sacerdotal claim is so fully understood that no sensible man would attempt to discuss any abstract question with a Priest, unless he accepted the Priest's framework of authority and revelation.

"Naturally," any Catholic would observe, "if you do not believe in a Priest's God, you should not discuss either the Creator or human nature with him!"

What is the use of discussing sex, for instance, with a man who has violated the laws of sex? You should therefore put God and Nature to one side, and converse with your Priest about anything

else that turns up. But most English clergymen, although at heart
they have the same desire to shirk the main laws of life, its uncertainty and its dependence upon a physical law, do not set
them wholly aside. They marry, and think they can arrive at
purity by underestimating the love of women. They arrogate to
themselves a sacrosanct atmosphere founded upon their arbitrary
faith in a benevolent Deity to whom they attach mainly human
attributes, sometimes their own. By the help of this imaginary
Person, they think to escape the dangers and tasks of common
humanity and add to their own authority by using an omnipotent
Being to reinforce the weakness of their arguments. Religion —
and I look upon some sort of religion as vital to every man —
is surely the relation between the individual soul and his standard
of good and evil. It is this standard which is all he can know
of God; and anything higher and more workable as a standard
than the teachings of Jesus Christ is unknown to me. I could
therefore be in complete accord with almost any clergyman who
based his opinions upon these great utterances and gave up the
sacerdotal and revelationary claims; but the longer I talked with
Michael, the less I felt we were even vaguely in accord, about
religion or anything else. No one could behave, even to an out-
cast, as he behaved to his wife and have the right to call himself
a Christian. The picture we make of others can be even more
false than the self-portrait we believe to be ourselves; but surely
we owe to every human being a basic respect *as* a human being,
which it is terrible and disintegrating to refuse to the worst of
criminals? It is in fact precisely what the Nazis are trying to do
to humanity at large. I therefore felt that of all the human beings
I had so far come across at Silver Fountains, I was least in fundamental sympathy with Michael Esdaile. I could very well understand that Virginia, made to feel like a Magdalene when she was
only a naturally attractive young woman a little too free with
her gifts, in self-defence might have had to take a lover such as
Tom Wendover, who would certainly not think the less of her
because she knew how to attract him; but I must admit I saw less
reason for her swerve from Tom in the direction of Adrian.
Adrian has all the hard rigidity of youth and the cruel idealism

of first love. He will not let Virginia off cheap. To my mind, she would be wiser to break with Adrian rather than with Tom. Nevertheless, since she has supplanted Tom by another Schoolmaster, it may be that she still needs Schoolmasters? Perhaps she does not really care deeply for either of her new lovers, except as punishment for Michael, or as an escape for herself?

I looked with fresh interest at the features of this hard-worked Saint by my side — chiselled and thinned down by self-torture. One had only to observe the set of his thin lips to see how cruelly and chronically he controlled himself. Nevertheless, I was aware of a strange power in the man's face. There was a light in his eyes and a curious freedom, in spite of his physical frustration, about his whole attitude, as if, deeper even than his sufferings, he had access to a hidden fount of serenity.

Was it just that his spirit, by his severe exactions and self-martyrdom, felt itself bought off from individual responsibility?

Michael told me, when we had reached the steps to the terrace, that he was going on to the Dower House, so I decided to walk part of the way with him.

"Lady Wendover," I said, to test his iron self-control, "I found rather perturbed this morning over her son, Adrian. She thinks he has let himself fall in love with your wife. Such romances take place very easily at his age, when there is constant propinquity. In fact in my country we think a young man often trains himself to be a very good husband by first caring for a woman already married."

Michael's face set like stone. I know now what it is about his face that has so haunted me. He is the image of the sculptured Knight upon an old tomb in the village church.

"I hope that Lady Wendover is mistaken," he said quietly. "I knew she had this anxiety but I could not fail to consider any such emotion not only wrong for Adrian himself, but culpable on the part of my wife had she aroused it! A married woman, above all a mother, should be far too careful of her dignity — and far too certain of her duty — to let such a fancy arise at all."

"She is not veiled," I remarked a little dryly, "nor kept behind a purdah, therefore Mrs. Esdaile can hardly be held accountable if a young man, with whom she is brought into almost daily contact, should fall in love with her."

Michael flushed and I watched the fine blue veins upon his forehead thicken and stand out like cords. He was a highly sensitive man, and so jealous that no woman could fail to understand how best to wound him.

Still, Virginia was probably unaware how mortally she *had* wounded him.

"It is difficult to discuss such a matter with an outsider, even a doctor like yourself," he said with courteous severity. "I have not mentioned it to my wife; indeed I think that to mention it would be to insult her. I believe Lady Wendover *has* mentioned it, quite against my wishes and advice, to Adrian! If she is right in her conjecture, the only course I could consider would be to give up this living and go elsewhere. I am considering it."

"I speak of it," I explained, "because it affects my patient. Lady Wendover is your friend. For many years you have been her faithful counsellor and adviser, and she would naturally feel it deeply if you were to leave the vicinity. A doctor — above all a doctor who is a stranger — can only advise what is best for his patient's physical health; but physical health is, as you know, a highly dependent portion of a human being; and what it is oftenest dependent on, is the secret aim of the whole personality. This secret aim is sometimes not quite so hidden from one's intimates as from ourselves — and certainly not hidden from a spiritual adviser such as yourself."

"Lady Wendover's aim," Michael said stiffly after a long pause, "is, I am sure, to be a good woman. Even her faults, and I admit that she has great faults, are, as it were, upon the right side."

I made no answer to this statement because I did not suppose we had a common definition for a "good woman" or a "right side."

"It is true, I have tried to help her," he added, turning back with me, as if he still did not think that we had said enough to each other. "She has many difficulties and problems, but after all, my first duty is to my young wife. I cannot allow her to be put into an invidious position either by her own fault, or — if you choose to consider it so and indeed it may *be* so — by her misfortune!"

I remained silent, for on my part I had nothing further to add.

I should believe Virginia to be at fault if her husband were her lover, and knew how to be an acceptable lover; otherwise, and I believed it to *be* otherwise, I should consider the chief fault between them to be his. But I did not think I could express this point of view acceptably to Michael Esdaile.

However, he continued to walk towards Silver Fountains with me; and began to talk about the hospital. He showed such sympathy and understanding for the ordeal that awaited me that I felt again how hard it was not to be able to like him.

Indeed, it is as if this good and interesting man understands everything except himself.

6th November 1940

FOR three days Silver Fountains has been a hospital. The Wend-overs and their problems have slipped from the foreground to the background of my mind. I am a doctor again.

It is not organizing the hospital that has made me one; nor even the valued co-operation of those three splendid, but very curious, women, Matron, Sister Tutor and Sister Lawrence. I suppose that all pain makes one the more vulnerable to pain. As I examined my patients and found each of them alone in his separate hell, I knew that I must break down its walls and join them.

Adler used to say, "Cruelty is a bridge to death," and for a long time — until I saw a man tortured by the Nazis — I did not know what he meant. The man who was being tortured looked so ashamed: not of anything he had done, for he was wholly inno-cent, but because another man was willing to hurt him for nothing, out of cruelty. Dogs and children have the same look of sick remorse when others are punished in their presence, perhaps for the same reason. They are suffering for the Torturer, who is incapable of suffering for them.

I think now that Adler's saying meant that every cruel action a man performs, perhaps even every cruel word he says, is taking him away from the mainland of human fellowship, and connecting him with the solitary island of hate. A man is de-humanized as a man little by little each time that he crosses the bridge of cruelty, until only the animal remains alive.

When I examined my first English patient, I knew that it was into my real life that I had passed again. I had to be with him in his pain, and since he was alive and must be kept alive by my skill, I could not be a ghost any more.

More than half of our patients are Raid casualties. We have one Ward of very severe bone injuries; one of septic cuts and burns; and one for shock patients. Then there are the usual Wards of growths, tumours, intestinal and stomach diseases, as well as a T.B. Ward, mostly abscesses; and one specially for children.

In each Ward there are from forty to fifty patients. We use the three great rooms, ballroom, billiard room and first-floor drawing-room, for the Raid patients. The others we have grouped in the smaller rooms, each Ward on its own floor.

For each Ward there is a Sister-in-Charge, a staff nurse; one probationer, and one or more V.A.D.s.

The Chief Surgeon from Plymouth gives me his invaluable support, and London sent me a good third-year student on the surgical side. Otherwise, I have an excellent resident woman doctor besides myself, and two consulting men physicians who visit us from the immediate neighbourhood, from time to time.

The patients came by special ambulance trains with their separate Ward staffs, spaced over the last three days. Like all British organization, this plan ran extraordinarily well. The plan itself might easily have been bettered, and was not really very thoroughly worked out; but whenever there was a hitch, someone used his emergency wits, and removed it.

It occurs to me that probably the British lack of foresight and preparation arises out of their strength in action. Perhaps they rely too much on last-minute illumination and suffer unnecessarily heavy losses in consequence. Yet I find myself admiring the spirit that springs up to meet the onrush of catastrophe in such unshaken creative energy!

I put the children's Ward in the billiard room, next to Tom Wendover's special quarters, which I am occupying at the moment. I could get the children out from this room more easily than from any other; and when I hear a child crying in the night, I can easily slip in and soothe him.

They are mostly Cockney children from Bermondsey and Bethnal Green, very under-nourished and sickly-looking little ones, but of an extraordinary toughness. It is perhaps the life of the streets that gives them their sparkling courage.

Some of them are terribly injured, and it is only upon the

interest they have in life that we can count for pulling them through.

Adler once said to me, "When you go to see a new patient, ask yourself first, 'How much health has he in him?' — and then find out what is his disease; for it is of secondary importance what is the matter with him but it is of the first importance that he has the will to live. Courage is the health of the body."

Fortunately these suffering and injured little citizens of London have still a great deal of courage!

I have to be severe with myself not to give these children too much of my time, for I find each little boy is Andreas — and each girl, Rosemary. I have not mentioned Rosemary often in this diary, for I have not wished to stress how much I miss her. I must admit that not a day has passed since I left her, when I have not thought of her — as a man misses a lost limb.

Eunice and James I also miss deeply, but we write constantly to each other, whereas the bond between a child and an adult depends wholly on physical presence. If the child is not with you, there can be no communication, so that none of the first-hand observation which is the increasing life of such an intimacy can take place.

When I come into the children's Ward, I stand for a moment looking at the children; and considering to myself what each one needs. All their heads turn to greet me, if they can move at all. Some cannot move, and with those I stay longest.

There are many doctors who think it necessary to lessen children's pain by drugs; and of course in many cases it is absolutely necessary to give sedatives; but often a word will help more than a drug, or even a glance, from man to man — so that the child knows his suffering is shared and understood; and his courage appreciated.

It is easier to wake the courage of a child than of a grown-up person; and even more vital for its recovery. Once a child realizes the power he can rouse in himself to meet his suffering, using it becomes a kind of splendid game.

Sister Curtis, who is the Sister-in-Charge of the children's Ward, asked me if I could manage to come in every day while the dressings were being given; so if I am not operating, I choose this hour; and the most painful dressings I do myself; but it is the *children* who teach *me* how to bear pain — not I, them. I am only their willing pupil.

I suggested that Virginia should work by day in the children's Ward as a V.A.D. She is a little impatient as a learner, and I have had to point out to her why such exactitude is necessary in a nurse's training. It is not only vital for the patient, who must depend absolutely upon the nurse's skill and common sense; but the untrained nurse herself suffers from two great disadvantages. She makes unnecessary efforts because she has not learned how to economize her own strength by knowing what she must do, and what may very well be left undone. This produces undue fatigue and constant tension of spirit. She suffers also from uncertainty as to her own part in any emergency. In most cases it is less than she thinks, when once she has learned how to meet her problem with precision; but she wastes life as well as time if she has to make rash experiments.

In life, as in literature, there is only one *mot juste*, not dozens.

When I first met the three superlatively trained women who run this hospital — for I do not run it, as I should if I were in Vienna: I am run *by* it — they surprised me greatly.

I do not know why, but I had expected dominating women — probably plain — certainly middle-aged; all three authoritative. I supposed that I should have to cope with them much as I try to cope with my patient, Lady Wendover. But they are not at all of the same type.

The Matron, Mrs. Price, is quite a young woman. She has a charming pleasant manner, great quickness of mind, and though I imagine she could act with spirit and decision if any need for it arose, the prevailing impression she makes on one is of great tact and good humour.

Sister Tutor, a Miss Bartlett, is perhaps thirty; a great personal friend of Matron's, with a dry cold manner lightened by irony. She is obviously highly intellectual, and she could have been very attractive, if it had ever occurred to her.

"Gosh!" Virginia observed after her first sight of Sister Tutor, "what a fish!" and it is of some cold, powerful incisive fish that she reminds me. I should like to ask James if it would be possible, even for an Englishman, to make love to such a woman. I should gravely doubt it.

Nurse Lawrence, our Home Sister, is wholly different from the other two. Gillian tells me that she belongs to a lower social status, but I should never have supposed that she was anyone's inferior. She is perhaps forty, with the face of a reliable and healthy child — though rather too stout a body. But it is her heart that is so admirable. She has the maternal instinct at its best: controlled by wisdom. There is not a patient in the hospital who is not the better and lighter-hearted for her presence. She is not sentimental, but she has a smile that drives out unkindness. I have never seen her linger over a pleasant task or hurry over a disagreeable one. To each person alike she gives her full skill and attention with the selfless impartiality of a mother. Yet nothing escapes her that should *not* escape her.

With such women as fellow workers, my job is light indeed. The Sister in charge of each Ward comes with me on all my rounds, and it is to her I give my orders for the patients. She alone is responsible to me for how they are executed.

I have not yet discovered one of my wishes that has not been carried out promptly, with the requisite care and skill.

The theatre Sister, Sister Peters, studies the methods and tastes of all the operating Surgeons with great attention, and meets them as best she can. Of course, our theatre is not like the great theatres in most London hospitals, filled with every up-to-date appliance known to the mind of man; but it works well, and requires only a little extra forethought and skill to make up for mechanical defects.

Each Ward is fitted with its own sluice, kitchenette and bathroom. I did not think we could get these constructed in time, but Gillian saw that the work was done and stood over the men while they did it.

Tom Wendover arrives next week, and I hope that he will be satisfied.

Gillian surprised me very much by volunteering to act as my

secretary and accountant. I find this life-saving for there are many difficulties of language and custom which I have not yet mastered — for all these, she acts as a wise and accurate interpreter.

"Rudi," she said to me the day before the Matron arrived, "I make rather a bad V.A.D., and anyway they don't really need me at the Bodmin Hospital, but I believe I should make you quite a good secretary! You see, I can tell you more or less how we do things in this country, and what people mean by what they say, or don't say!"

"Particularly, I hope, by what they don't say," I answered her, "for that is what I find it most hard to understand! What you yourself, for instance, don't say puzzles me greatly!"

Gillian hardly ever looks at me. It is one of the chief differences between her and Virginia. Virginia looks at me all the time; and knows how to do it. I have not discovered whether Gillian avoids meeting my eyes from shyness or austerity, but she certainly avoids meeting them.

On this occasion she looked out of the nearest window and said, "There must be more that one *doesn't* say, of course! You might try to remember that I do not know very much except about country life, fishing, hunting and shooting, and apparently *you* know nothing about *them* and a great deal about lots of other things! If you will tell me what you want done, I will try to do it — that's all that really matters, isn't it?"

I am afraid that I sighed with some regret, for after all a good deal more matters to a man like myself who is sensitive to friendliness. I shall certainly be glad of her services, and I know that she will carry out my orders efficiently. But I give very few orders. I have always found that people work better if they are, as far as possible, left to discover what to do and how to deal with it, by their own individual methods. If they will not accept this amount of responsibility, they are unlikely to make good workers at all — even if told exactly what to do.

I know that Gillian is a superlatively good worker, for without her terrific energy and thorough local knowledge, we could never have fitted Silver Fountains into a hospital, literally a nine days' wonder, in the time demanded by Tom Wendover. But I am far from thinking that such admirable driving power is enough.

"What matters most," I said, "or perhaps I should say seems to me to matter most, is that fellow workers should be friends."

Gillian has a very pretty nose above an extremely short upper lip. It is not too sharp a nose at the end, and not too straight: if anything, it turns a shade upwards. I have invariably noticed that these tip-tilted noses are a sign of courage in a human being, sometimes accompanied by a not very even temper.

Gillian made a little sniff with this nose, and said shortly, "Well — I don't see that we need to make a song and dance about what we call it anyhow! Do you want me to be your secretary or not?"

"I do!" I said hastily; and then to my surprise, she blushed.

It is very difficult indeed to know what is in the mind of a young English girl.

I find Lady Wendover a great deal easier to understand than her daughter. She has improved out of all knowledge physically during the last ten days; and now demands to take some prominent part in running the hospital.

After the stags' fight in the glade, I had gone straight to my patient. We discussed at some length Michael and his wife, and the plan of removing them from the neighbourhood. I must admit that I was surprised that even to get rid of Virginia, Lady Wendover could envisage parting with her favourite Priest. But while I listened to her, I found myself wondering if now that she had a new adviser in myself — one much less strict and far more, to all appearance, malleable to her wishes — she did not feel herself sufficiently supported to manage without her friend — the Saint. After all, Michael *is* a Saint, a man curiously inflexible to himself, but also to others. I have observed already on several occasions that the fact of his disliking any course of action did not for a moment deflect him from following it.

Lady Wendover expressed herself with great force against Virginia; and it was instructive to listen to her. She did not only speak with the jealousy of a mother of her only son, but also spoke with the suppressed resentment of a beautiful woman who had never used her beauty with the reckless successfulness of the culprit. Suddenly to realize that it might have paid you to be reckless

— when you have *not* been reckless — must be a secret annoyance to any virtuous woman.

"As long as Virginia stays here," I eventually suggested, "you can see more or less how this affair with Adrian goes; and to a certain extent you and Michael Esdaile, between you, can limit it. Once you have Virginia completely beyond your reach, you cannot possibly tell what Adrian will do, or how completely they may not, between them, hoodwink her husband."

Lady Wendover seemed to be struck with this idea and I did not add to it. Instead, I took up the subject of her desire to run the hospital, for this of course was what her demand for work implied.

I begged her to remember that she had barely recovered from a severe illness, and should not rush into a new task without conserving more energy.

"Energy!" she exclaimed impatiently. "I am full of energy. What I need is outlet! You had better send that Matron — Mrs. Price — over to see me. I will discuss the situation with her!"

I did not mention that at the moment Matron was working sixteen hours a day, and I hoped sleeping the other eight.

"Wait for three days more," I pleaded, "before seeing anyone beyond your family. After all, you cannot embark on any new job until you are able to take a little physical exercise. I should not agree to your doing any regular work unless you could walk at least a mile a day without undue fatigue."

Lady Wendover looked stubborn, and I could not help thinking how plain even good-looking women manage to appear while they are making up their minds to do what they want against all opposition. I smiled at her, however, as if I found her — as I usually do — very attractive to look at; and at last she smiled too; and I saw with relief that this first round of a difficult matter was won. She would wait at least three days before upsetting any apple cart in Matron's vicinity.

"Can I take a walk to-day?" she demanded pleasantly.

"Certainly," I told her, "if you will take Miss Fitchett with you," for I knew that Miss Fitchett had not been able to take a walk for a good many days. "You will need an arm to lean on."

15th November 1940

NIGHT by night these German devils still bomb London. Their attacks spread too, from city to city all over the Island — tearing out their hearts. How long can this small country stand these furious and devastating raids? Very little is said about them. Those who know most what dire destruction is being caused — to their shipping, to their vital industries, to their food situation — say least.

I think I have at last discovered the real reason for the inexpressiveness of the British. They understand each other so well that all explanations between them are superfluous.

Outside this Island, they have not wanted to be understood. This has cost them the friendship of France, often the sympathy of the United States; even their own Empire sometimes reels under their self-oblivious arrogance. But within this little Island the English need hardly lift an eyebrow, or change the tone of their voice, in order to make their basic wishes known.

They have been brought up in an intensive social system regulated long ago to suit the habits of a small but all-powerful class. An Englishman has but to show that he belongs to this class, or is within visiting radius of it, for everything essential about him to be understood; and since understood — catered for.

It is not surprising that those who belong to this class should have an unstressed, complacent, implacable courage, for they have never had to take the harsh realities of life unpadded, and need fear no wounds except those that they inflict upon each other.

But I should not have expected to find the same courage — a sort of dauntless ferocity — among the slum dwellers of great cities. Yet this hospital is full of such courage although when their small homes were reduced to ashes, it was all my patients had — or are ever likely to possess in the future. Yet those who have lost all have not given in. They still say, "Let's see which'll get tired first — us or 'Itler!"

Perhaps this strange untutored courage comes because the world of sport, pleasure and social privilege in this Island, though only occupied by the few, is open to the many. Every citizen has what they call here "a sporting chance" to reach the top of the ladder, although perhaps only one in twenty thousand ever reaches it.

The rest are still immersed in the strange romance of their exclusive wish-dream.

There is however a danger that these perpendicular advantages may one day topple over. The ideals of the British people may change faster than the static minds of their ruling class.

This is indeed, whether the British yet realize it or not, everybody's War; and it must lead to everybody's peace. But if it is to be a democratic peace, not Totalitarian State Slavery, we must first arrive at something better and more generally advantageous than the fake democracy now practised for the good of the few at the expense of the many.

I always remember that last night I spent in Vienna. I was stumbling about its little friendly streets behind the old University in the moonlight. They were quite empty, until I came upon a blind beggar. He had turned a dustbin into a musical instrument and was trying to make music out of it.

That blind beggar, I have sometimes said to myself, is at the bottom of the World War. We are all blind and have tried to make music out of a dustbin.

It had been arranged that Lady Wendover was not to visit the Hospital until I considered her strong enough. This promise — for she had given me her promise — she broke without even letting me know that she was going to break it.

I had just finished my morning round, and was taking off my white coat, when Gillian burst into the room.

"Mother's come!" she exclaimed. "What are you going to do about it?"

She appeared to be prepared to support me in any extremity — even that of physical violence. Her clear grey eyes danced with the light of battle; her cheeks were faintly flushed. Excitement was extraordinarily becoming to Gillian; but I had to damp it down.

"Perhaps," I said, hanging up my coat, "you will be so kind as to ring up Matron for me, while I receive your Mother. Please tell her that Lady Wendover is here and that I am about to show her over the hospital. . . . I shall be greatly obliged if Matron would join us, in my room, in about an hour's time and take a glass of sherry with us."

Gillian frowned. "Why don't you tell Mother," she said, "that she must *ask* Matron for an interview — like anybody else! Matron's got a room of her own, hasn't she? Why should she be sent for as if she were the housemaid? It would do Mother good to be sent for herself!"

I did not stay to discuss what particular "good" would be served by this act of self-humiliation on the part of Lady Wendover; but hurried out into the hall to receive her.

I found her standing in the middle of the hall trying to intimidate one of the nurses, with Miss Fitchett in the background.

"My good child," I heard Lady Wendover say, "run along at once, please, and take my message to Dr. Ritterhaus and Matron. I know they're busy at this hour of the morning, without your twittering about it; but they won't be too busy to see me!"

"There!" whispered Gillian just behind me. "What did I tell you? She means to be nasty!"

"Go — and telephone to Matron!" I whispered back. Gillian, if reluctantly, obeyed me; but she was, I knew, gravely disappointed. She had expected me to withstand her mother in some heroic manner. I can imagine moments when to be a hero is an unavoidable necessity; but I did not consider this to be one of them.

I came forward smiling, with my hand outstretched. "My dear Lady Wendover!" I exclaimed. "You have indeed given us all a pleasant surprise! And you have come at a very fortunate moment for me, since I have just finished my rounds and can now give myself the satisfaction of showing you over your own marvellous gift — the hospital — for the first time!"

Miss Fitchett's face changed from that of a rabbit's frozen with terror into that of an exceptionally nice woman forced to behave improperly and not daring to apologize for it.

"Oh, there you are!" Lady Wendover said rather shortly, ignoring my outstretched hand. "This young woman seemed to think no one dare approach either you or the Matron, or even set foot inside this house without getting leave from one of you, in spite of the fact that the house happens to be my home! Where is the Matron?"

"Let us see over the hospital first," I entreated her. "Matron is looking forward to meeting you and hearing your impressions after you have seen it. I hope you will grant me the privilege of showing it to you myself, and what, owing to your generosity, we have been able to make of Silver Fountains *as* a hospital!"

A faint wintry sunlight may have been said to flicker over Lady Wendover's expressive features, although I cannot say that she carried this as far as an actual thaw. Her manner still remained bitterly frosty.

She was beautifully dressed, and looked, I thought, handsomer than ever in her outdoor clothes; but suddenly I found myself feeling profoundly sorry for her. For a beautiful woman to grow old and lose her beauty has always been accepted as a major tragedy in her life; but Lady Wendover was not yet old, and she had retained much of her youthful beauty. Is it not a greater tragedy for a woman when the heart she once held so easily in thrall no longer desires her beauty or considers her wishes?

I forgot Gillian — I forgot Miss Fitchett — and the difficulties that lay ahead of us when Matron should make her appearance upon a field which she considered her own. I only remembered that Lady Wendover *had* given up her home; and the great uses for which she had sacrificed it. As we went through the Wards together, little by little I had a feeling that she too began to see how great these uses were. The changes in the house itself were too wholesale for the comparison to be a pain to her. The great rooms retained only the beauty of their spacious lines, and lofty height; otherwise, they had become simply conveniences for mercy.

I took her first to see the Raid victims in the men's and women's Wards. The dining-room is the men's Ward. It opens on to a terrace overlooking a distant sheet of water. The Park, the deer, the distant hills were all free to their astonished eyes. These slum dwellers saw at last the full beauty of England under its low soft skies. Some of the men had never seen it before, and some only as children. All their lives had been spent trapped in great cities between the walls of narrow streets.

The women had the drawing-room on the first floor. The walls and ceiling were a faint dawn-pink, and the polished parquet floor sparkled with cleanness. The patients looked out upon a rose garden, where late autumn roses still bloomed, and the last flowers of the year thronged the broad herbaceous borders. I dare say they would greatly have preferred their own shop-filled streets in more normal days — but just at the moment they valued the silence and the sense of space. Beauty had a favourable chance to besiege and lull their shocked and tortured senses.

I do not think I ever saw women look more at peace than these Raid victims at Silver Fountains. Some of them were terribly injured, but they lay there looking out at the November flowers in the pale sunshine with every nerve at rest.

I whispered to Lady Wendover, "You see, you have given them peace!"

Her eyes filled with tears, for she was a kind woman and had recently been very ill herself. She moved forward beautifully into the middle of her great drawing-room, and of her own accord told the Ward who she was. She seemed to find with ease the right words to say to these women.

"I want to welcome you," she said, "into my home. If I hadn't been ill myself, I would have helped to get it ready for you and greeted you when you first arrived. Now I want to tell you that it makes me very happy to see you here, and I want you to stay until you are all quite well!"

They loved — these poor women who had never shared great

clean rooms or fine clothes, or easy words — to think they were in this great lady's home, and that she was glad to have them there. They could see, as plainly as I could, that she really *was* glad. Even Miss Fitchett had forgotten how difficult it had been to make her glad, and she was beaming with reflected glory. She looked like a good nurse when the child she cares for, and often finds it difficult to care for, suddenly shows to great advantage before strangers.

Lady Wendover went from bed to bed, finding kind and appropriate words for each of the patients.

I had been afraid that she might hurry her visit, and then be impatient and angry if the Matron, who could hardly free herself before noon, had to keep her waiting; but instead, it was difficult to show her all that she wanted to see in one short hour. Still, I think it was perhaps enough.

We finished off with the children's Ward, and this moved her so deeply that I feared she might become exhausted physically by so great a strain upon her sympathies. But the emotions that we feel for others seldom have this effect. Lady Wendover had made a great effort and seen that it was a great success; and I could see that she was now in a mood when even the importance of another woman would glide harmlessly off her.

Almost as soon as we had reached the library, the Matron knocked. She came in looking every inch a Matron — her white uniform dazzling; but her charming face under her cap and veil had a graver expression than usual. She could not afford to be too humble, for the rights of the hospital were in her charge.

Lady Wendover looked across her glass of sherry at the Matron with frosty appraising eyes. She smiled, however, quite pleasantly, without getting up.

Matron came forward to the middle of the room, but no farther; I made the introduction; Lady Wendover waved her hand towards the nearest chair; Matron hesitated a moment and then sat down in another chair, a little farther off.

I think that before she sat down they may have shaken hands, but as I had turned away from them at that moment to pour Matron's sherry, I could not be sure.

Lady Wendover said at once, in rather a dry, offhand voice, "Well, Matron, I hope you like Silver Fountains!" It was as if she had said, "Only an idiot *wouldn't*, but how am I to know that you are *not* an idiot?"

Matron has a low gentle voice and she answered a little slowly, but as if she were wholly at her ease, "You have made it into a wonderful hospital for us, Lady Wendover. I am indeed glad to have this opportunity to tell you how greatly we appreciate all that you have done for us — and given to us! It is the greatest relief to the Staff, and to myself, to think that all our poor harrowed, menaced patients now have the chance of getting well in safety!"

Lady Wendover was not perhaps quite sure whether she wanted the Matron to be what English people call "a real lady" or not; but I think she knew that Mrs. Price is one.

"My husband and I wanted to give England what we had," she answered quite simply; and I think she really meant it. I do not say that patriotism was what she had given up Silver Fountains for — in the first instance; but since she had seen the Raid victims — especially the children, whom I had kept to the last — Lady Wendover had grown larger-hearted.

"There's something I want very much," she went on rather hurriedly. "I know this is *your* hospital, even though it *was* my home, and naturally I do not want to intrude upon you in any way; but I do want somehow or other to find a niche in it again. Cannot you and Dr. von Ritterhaus give me something to do for the patients that will give me a right to feel that I can still serve them as, in a sense, their hostess?"

This was the crux of our difficulty. The Matron is the hostess of a hospital, nor can she resign from being its hostess without ceasing to be a Matron. Everything depended upon the goodwill between the two women. A man is helpless in such matters. If he intervenes where two women are at variance, he is sure to annoy one or the other of them — probably both. I therefore said nothing and left the matter to the Matron. They were not, I knew, suited to run in double harness: one of these two women knew how to work, and the other did not; one acted as an impersonal authority, set in a framework of carefully constructed and practised rules — the other was a despotic, untrained personal Power, entirely motivated and controlled by her own wishes. How could they work together?

Matron hesitated, looked at me, and then back again, very kindly and earnestly, at Frances Wendover.

"I can understand perfectly how you feel," she said, "and I believe you could be of real help to us! And indirectly, perhaps, to our patients. They have to be cared for on professional lines, and their routine, and ours, is already fixed by the London Committee's regulations for this hospital which we all try to carry out to the best of our ability. But Silver Fountains is rather a lonely place for our nurses, and I wonder if it would be at all possible for you to organize a few amusements for them. This would make a great deal of difference to us all, and, I think, react very happily upon the patients. I know you are not strong yet, after your recent illness, but if you could be the leading influence in any such plan, you would be doing the hospital a great service — would she not, Dr. von Ritterhaus?"

I hastened to agree with Matron enthusiastically.

I don't quite know what part in the life of the hospital Frances Wendover had envisaged for herself; perhaps it was in the children's Ward that she had seen herself ministering and — if ministering — more or less ruling. But I think in the long moment that followed she was reluctantly relinquishing a pleasing rôle; and I admired her greatly for this renunciation — as much as I admired Matron for making it easy for her to renounce it.

"Yes," Lady Wendover agreed at length, "I *will* organize some social life for you all, and I am grateful to you for the suggestion. There is, however, one more way in which I believe we could be of service to you. You have, I am sure, already met Mr. Esdaile, our Rector, who has agreed to act as your Chaplain, and you must have been struck with his wonderful powers! He is a real shepherd of souls, and I believe you would find him of special use in the 're-training' — as Dr. von Ritterhaus, I know, calls it — of your shell-shock cases. He has promised me that he

will undertake this task, for which he is so specially suited, for
you! Could not you and Dr. von Ritterhaus use him — unofficially
as it were — as a lay psychiatrist?"

This was a great shock to me. I had expected her to ask for
another power-loophole — probably quite unsuitable — for herself.
This might have been difficult to parry but considerably less
difficult, since the Matron had so skilfully fallen back on the
London Committee regulations as a means of escape; but Michael
Esdaile — already accepted as a Chaplain — would be hard to
keep out of the shell-shock Ward, regulations or no regulations;
and I did not want him working in it.

There might, I considered, be certain cases in which his help
would be valuable, but there would be far more patients in whom
the mere approach of a religious teacher would set up an endless
train of guilt complexes, unpardonable sins, or dangerous alibis,
none of which Michael Esdaile, or any other untrained person,
could be expected to understand.

How were we then to look this particular gift horse in the
mouth, and refuse it with sufficient grace?

Miss Fitchett choked over her sherry.

I don't know quite what she feels about Michael Esdaile; she
may have some secret cult of masochistic worship for him, but I
am pretty sure that she knows that I have not.

Matron fixed her eyes expectantly upon my own. She had taken
her fence; this, her eyes seemed to say, was *mine*.

"I am sure," I said at last, "that Matron agrees with both of
us that we *are* exceptionally fortunate in having Mr. Esdaile
as our Chaplain! I doubt if we could possibly have had a wiser
or more discriminating Priest to officiate for us. I shall particularly value his service in the children's Ward as a great educational force. As to the shell-shock cases, they are at present being
very expertly handled by my woman colleague, Dr. Reed, who
also allows me some little say in the matter, for I have had some
experience myself as a psychiatrist in the Viennese schools. We
might, I feel sure, be glad to discuss some of our problems with
Mr. Esdaile, but I think the actual treatment of the patients is
better left in the hands of medical experts themselves. However,

we are about to open a school of occupational therapy for our patients, when we have found a suitable room for it, and perhaps Mr. Esdaile might be of great assistance to us there. We shall be in need of any skilled teacher in arts and crafts, and it is possible he may be a master of one of these crafts, and be prepared to teach it?"

I did not dare to glance at Matron for approval, but I felt that she had relaxed in her chair as if she thought the worst was now over, and our difficulties — if not solved — fairly well evaded.

Lady Wendover rose, and Matron followed suit. I saw that my patient was not pleased with me. She glanced in my direction, but she did not look directly at me.

"We must, of course," she said coldly, "be guided by Dr. von Ritterhaus' opinion." She did not say by my authority. I suppose she thought it difficult to imagine that an Austrian Refugee doctor had any authority even in his own hospital.

Matron said nothing.

Miss Fitchett knocked over her glass of sherry and broke the glass.

"How extraordinarily clumsy of you, Fidget!" Lady Wendover exclaimed sharply. But I think the incident was a relief to us all, and I am not at all sure that Miss Fitchett did not contrive it with that purpose. She may look like a fool; but she is very far from being one.

The Matron and I escorted Lady Wendover to the front door. I took her down the steps and put her into her car.

"Thank you for coming," I said to her. "You can make a wonderful Christmas here for the children."

Her face became suddenly human again. "Oh, yes!" she said. "I *will!* Thank you for showing me the hospital!"

After they had driven away, I was afraid to go back to my room to work because Gillian would be there to scold me. She would, I knew, have wished me to keep her mother altogether out of the hospital; and I had not done so. I had not even *wanted* to keep her out of it. I *had* wanted to keep Michael Esdaile out of it — and this also I had failed to accomplish. In fact, I had done nothing for which there was any hope I could escape a scolding.

I ventured instead to knock at the door of the Matron's Office, and she called out, "Come in."

I found Sister Tutor with her, and they were both in fits of laughter. They were, however, too discreet to reveal to me the cause of their mirth.

"Poor thing," the Matron said, "you look as if you needed some of the Wendover sherry you forgot to give yourself in your own room. Take some of mine instead."

I drank it gratefully.

They are very nice women, both of them, whether they are ladies or not.

28th November 1940

THE last load of personal anxiety has been lifted from my heart. James is going to bring Eunice and Rosemary to Silver Fountains and will leave them here till the War ends.

Almost every night, when sleep at last overcomes me, I wake sweating from a dream in which I have been trying in vain to push away bricks falling upon Eunice and Rosemary. James and I work together side by side, but the harder we work lifting them, the more bricks fall.

I hurried from the Wards to share my joy at their coming with Gillian; but she had not forgiven what she looked upon as my ignominious surrender to her mother the day before; and I found myself an enemy upon the battlefield of her displeasure.

She said unsmilingly yes, she had heard that her uncle and aunt were coming and would make due arrangements to receive them; then she passed me the many forms I am supposed to fill in daily in order to assist those regulating the administration of the hospital. Almost anybody but a doctor could do this mechanical work exacted from the House Physician better and more quickly than he could do it for himself. I spend approximately ten per cent of my working life over clerical work; and this extra ten per cent of an expert's time is wholly wasted.

If I had been British, I should have let Gillian go on steeping herself in her displeasure while I filled in my forms, but though I am a ghost, I am still the ghost of a Viennese, so instead of filling in the forms in a dignified silence, I sat down opposite her, pushed the forms aside, and lit a cigarette.

"You are still angry, then," I observed, "that I showed your mother over the hospital with all the honours of the occasion? But your mother, after all, has her rights. We cannot keep from her all share in this handsome family contribution. Think, too, what a help she can really be to us by entertaining the nurses.

Nurses need entertaining more than most people — I need it myself sometimes — and I have been told that your mother's entertainments have always been considered among the best in London."

Gillian frowned severely. "Naturally she gives good entertainments," she said dryly, "she has a first-class cook and oceans of money — why shouldn't she? All her dice are loaded. But you ought never to have let her into a place where real work was going on. She will demoralize half the nurses in the hospital once she gets hold of them. Besides, Father wanted the hospital to have no dealings with her at all. I thought he had made this perfectly clear to you!"

I felt extraordinarily annoyed at being spoken to as if I were a servant, and a defaulting one at that, although in a sense I am the hospital's servant, but I do not believe that I am a defaulting one.

"Real work," I answered, taking hold of the only piece of her criticism that I could try to cool myself by thinking impersonal, "can protect itself. It is only when work is unreal that it stands in any danger from anyone else. Your mother might make some of the nurses misunderstand their duties, but I assure you Matron and Sister Tutor would soon put their misconceptions right again."

"So *you* think," Gillian said bitterly. "All I can say is — you don't know Mother — even if you are a psychiatrist! She'll be all over the place interfering with everything, and no one will have a moment's peace and quietness, and all because you hadn't the common sense or the moral courage to stand up to her!"

"But I couldn't stop her!" I replied, now thoroughly irritated, "and even if I could have stopped her, I wouldn't! Neither situations nor people can be altered by the interference of an outsider. If they are to be altered, that alteration must come from within. The most I can do is to show your mother what her situation really is. She, and she alone, can bring about any change in her own attitude towards it. My task is difficult enough without your seeking to throw upon me problems that are beyond either my power or my responsibility."

I was far beyond common sense myself by now. The whole
Medical Profession had taken upon itself the halo of martyrdom.
I saw myself as a Siegfried dedicated to the death of Dragons;
and the young girl before me, with her flushed face and her grey
eyes sparkling with anger, was sufficiently disguised as a Dragon.
I had entirely lost that placid unconcern which should rule the
scientific breast; or perhaps the breasts of scientists are less
scientific than I had thought.

"I should have supposed that as a doctor it *was* your responsibility to prevent your patients from doing damage either to
themselves or to others," Gillian said nonchalantly; then she
added with an inconsequential ferocity that completely deprived
me of breath, "I never *have* believed in the Medical Profession —
and now I never shall!"

I was wounded to the quick because I was of course by now
"the Medical Profession"; and it was in me that Gillian had ceased
to believe.

"Doctors," I told her savagely, "work to improve the condition of their patients; and to defend them against the dangerous
interference of their relations!"

It was War to the Knife between us, and yet there need have
been no war if I had explained the simple truth that every
neurotic in a household is a potential volcano; and that as Gillian's mother happens to be a volcano in a chronic state of eruption, the best thing for all of us is to organize some outside interest
that will cause her to erupt a little less in the tormented bosom
of her family; and a little more, if necessary, in the larger and
tougher bosom of the outside world. But no angry man ever
wants to say what he should. He says what he thinks can wound;
and as for an angry woman — she is, or should be, satisfied if she
has made a man angry; for an angry man is always at the mercy
of the woman he admires.

Gillian now became perfectly cool, and looked out of the window in an interested way at an utterly uninteresting robin.

"Is there anything more you want me to do this morning?"
she asked meekly, after a prolonged pause. "I was thinking of
working on the files."

"You can work on what you damn well please!" I suspect that I shouted; and Gillian shuddered as if the word "damn," one that she would have used herself in a friendly moment, had an unnerving effect upon her. I got up and left the room; probably I rushed out of it and banged the door after me. I cannot now remember exactly how I left it; but I found myself in the hospital, standing at the entrance of the T. B. Ward which I had already visited. The cool enquiring eyes of Sister Tutor brought me to my senses. I made a hurried exit in the direction of the theatre; and was relieved to find that I could be of some slight assistance to my colleague, who was about to operate on a stubborn case of adhesive tonsils.

Slowly, my mind cleared under its accustomed opiate. I remembered that Eunice and James would be with us soon, with all their power to soothe. They are a singularly non-conducting couple and I cannot imagine better people to have about in an emotionally disturbed atmosphere.

I now began to remind myself that it was only natural that Gillian should be bitterly annoyed by this eruption of her mother into our hospital life. At this moment the hospital is as much an escape for Gillian as it is for me. If my work is an opiate — so is hers. And, poor child, she has had pain enough to need an opiate!

A neurosis in a family always reminds me of the statue of the Laocoön in the Vatican. The father and his two young sons are caught together in the grip of the huge serpent. The father, one feels in order to save the sons, stands in the thickest of the coils; and is wholly doomed. Yet he is struggling with terrific and hopeless valour in order to free his sons. One child is beyond help; one still perhaps could be saved if some outsider — risking personal involvement — should come near enough to strike off the outer coils.

A neurosis threatens in the same manner all within its reach; and all within its reach may be drawn (by any weakness in themselves) into the battle. Yet a neurosis is but a phantom animal, and there need be no battle.

The poet Shelley, himself a neurotic, but with the courage to understand his own disease, writes truly: —

'Tis we, who, lost in stormy visions, keep
With phantoms an unprofitable strife,
And in mad trance strike with our spirits' knife
Invulnerable nothings.

Psychology teaches us that there is no knife; there is no enemy
to strike at; there is only a certain lack of social interest in the
Visionary.

This War, too, bears a similar resemblance to the Laocoön.
It is the neurosis by which the world at large has been caught;
and against the coils of which we are all to-day so uneasily
struggling. War also — once understood — is but an evil phantom
in the mind of man; and can be, in the same manner, cured. The
neurotic's cure lies in realizing that his vision *is* imaginary, and
in having the courage to come to a better understanding of the
world about him; when he becomes friendly, he becomes cured.

It is the same with the world: it is no use talking of Peace until
you have made a more friendly world.

I wanted to go back to Gillian and to apologize for my bad
temper, but I did not do this because I thought to myself, "I
do not yet know what *she* wants!" Her methods are other than
mine, and no doubt better for her than my methods.

I went to the Dower House instead and had an hour with my
patient, listening to all her plans for the nurses' entertainment.
I am not of course quite sure what entertainment they will afford
the nurses; but that they have already afforded Lady Wendover
entertainment, and of a most beneficial kind, is obvious.

I found that she had given Miss Fitchett a morning off.

"You have heard," Lady Wendover said as I was about to
leave her, "that James is going to bring my sister-in-law and their
little girl to stay with us till the end of the War? We shall have
to put up with it of course for the sake of the child. I never can
think why James should have married that little nonentity with
eyeglasses."

28th December 1940

DUSK had fallen when I left the Dower House to-night; a great windy darkness shook the Park, sounding through the trees in a thousand voices.

The wind was not cold, but every now and then the rain splashed against me in a wild whirl of icy drops, blowing inland from the Atlantic.

Always in this West Country you are reminded of the sea; the smell and feel of it is in every breath you draw. I find I have grown to love and watch for this sudden control of the neat land by its wild playfellow. To-night not a star was visible, but half a battered moon lurched through cloud wrack intermittently.

I saw a tiny gleam of light approaching me through the trees and heard, between the shouts of the wind, Virginia's voice calling. I stood still showing my flash lamp till she came up to me and touched my arm.

"I've just left the Ward," she told me, "and I thought you might be coming back this way. Do you mind if I go with you?" Her voice sounded as anxious as a chidden child's.

I drew her hand through my arm for answer and we struggled on against the rain and the wind together. She did not say why she wanted to be with me, but I think I know how lonely she feels because I too sometimes have the feeling that I am lost in an alien planet. The life in this Island is remote and private. The people are, I think, the kindest in the world, but they live their lives behind walls of special custom, and ancient habits. They seldom see over these high walls — into the customs and habits of their more open-living fellow mortals.

Austrians who inhabit the centre of Europe, Americans who live in a continent without frontiers, are always more at home with foreigners and strangers than the English. They too were strange and foreign not so long ago, and may be soon again, but these Islanders, if they leave their country at all, move like hermit-crabs with their nationality like a roof upon their backs.

While Virginia and I struggled in friendly laughter through the wet windy darkness, she spoke of her home. She did not say much, for we could barely hear each other speak, but from the fragments of her scattered words I built up a picture of the little Southern town, upon the Mississippi River, where she had been brought up.

I seemed to see, with her eyes, the warm gardens without walls or hedges running into each other, the high magnolia trees and stout camellia bushes with their red flowers and flat burnished leaves. Virginia had been the leader and the beauty of this small provincial town. All the other girls had identified themselves with Virginia; her triumphs were theirs. They rejoiced in her old family, her school successes in the big Southern city of Baltimore; her social victories in Washington when she came out in her early youth, and to her little town's delight, married at nineteen a saintly English Preacher whose brother was in the peerage. Their warm Southern loyalty to the old country which had been once their homeland, and had still a memory of home about it, had set a halo round Michael Esdaile's classical head. This was the kind of marriage that they had wished Virginia to make.

Virginia did not actually tell me these things, but her nearness, and the talking voices of the air, brought the sense of them to me. I understood how she had always had a proud and friendly audience. Life had been for her a succession of dramatic stages — each stage a little larger and more important than the last — and never lonely, because each part she played had had the admiring chorus of her friends and home ties to support it.

In the ordinary sense of the word, Virginia is not an actress; she is an extremely sincere and honest girl, but she has been shaped by applause, and at the height of it, suddenly transported to a country where the one thing missing, the one thing the English really resent and dislike, *is* applause. Few people in this country wish either to applaud or to be applauded. Applause involves publicity, the expression of a personality, the acceptance of a public rather than a deeply private value, all qualities that the English dislike in themselves, and for their implications. English people, even when forced to applaud, suspect the object of it. When anyone is too interesting, too attractive, they say to each other in hushed voices, "Brilliant — but unsound"; and it is, to them, one word. They cannot conceive of a *sound* brilliance; while dullness on this Island is inclined to become an actual symbol of virtue.

I do not know how much of the causes of her social failure Virginia had grasped. Between the gusts of the gale, she talked of surprise parties, clam-bakes, barbecues and other strange ceremonies of her childhood and early youth. She said once, as we stood for a moment under the sheltering silence of the beech trees, "You see, where I lived we were all friends — even when we didn't particularly care for each other, still all of us were parts of each other's lives. I thought it would be the same here, but it isn't. At home I was never frightened *once* — not socially frightened I mean! I was Virginia Rose Western; and now I am Michael's wife and I've got to behave properly; but I didn't have to behave properly when I was Virginia Rose!"

It is very easy to understand how, after her first disappointments and surprises, rubbed in no doubt by Lady Wendover who had no wish for a triumphant social success on her doorstep, Virginia had lost courage. Once she had lost it, the only way she found to restore the heady exultation of her old career — the stream of the life that *still* ran through her, and demanded freedom — was by the underhand victories of her flirtations. She had no work to raise her self-respect by an absolute standard. After all to men — even to Englishmen — her beauty was still a potent attraction. That Idiot, Michael Esdaile, behaved as if it didn't exist; he fought it away from his heart. Well, it became, Virginia's beauty, which should have been his pride and his joy, his deadly enemy. It is not surprising that he has lost her; nor do I particularly object to his loss. What I object to, is that Virginia has lost herself. For to use your beauty to get the better of other people, rather than to serve and enjoy life by it, is a pitiable limitation. This girl has no sloven's body — nor, if she chose to use it on anything besides her body — a sloven's mind.

Even in the darkness, I felt that the figure I could not see was firm and resilient.

Virginia walked close by my shoulder with the light free swing of well-used limbs. Physically she had neglected none of her possessions. A doctor realizes the care needed for complete physical success. Virginia's unpinched feet, her sound teeth, bright hair, and smooth polished nails, the good clear colour in her cheeks, are all the result of intelligent and careful attention.

I remembered, as we stood together in that sudden stillness beneath the great antlered trees, that line of Byron's poetry: "She walks in beauty, like the night."

Virginia asked me, as we neared the solid blackness of the house, "May I come in with you, Rudi?" I had to say, "Yes," though I did not want to say it. I was tired and I had many things to plan and think out before I took my last round of the hospital.

Tom had given me the key to his special private door. A path through a covered hedge led straight to the library. In a minute we had stepped out of the loud singing world of wind and darkness into the dense bright stillness of that thick house. Perhaps Virginia knew this room I worked in better than I did. She stood before the blazing wood fire looking about her with a funny little smile before she threw off her turquoise-coloured rain cloak, and the hood that hid her shining hair.

She knew where Tom kept his cigarettes and took one, before she sank onto a low wooden seat built round the great fireplace.

I was not wet through but I was glad of the fire's warmth, for it was a hostile night, and the flames were friendly. Once more I thought, "We are both fugitives! All this warmth, this light, this deep private kindness, does not belong to us. We have no real place here."

"What do you think I wanted you to see the day I asked you to lunch?" Virginia suddenly asked me. I had not yet made up my mind what she had wanted me to see, so I shook my head.

She smoked for a little in silence, and then flung away her cigarette. "Did you say to yourself," she began, " 'What a lovely home she has! What beautiful healthy children! What a devoted husband! Surely she has no excuse for not being as happy as a queen.' Did you say these sensible things to yourself, Rudi?"

She pretended to laugh; but I would not pretend to laugh with her. I said as gravely as I felt, "I saw that you were terribly unhappy in your beautiful home; and I saw that your husband was intentionally hurting you. What else was there for me to see?"

"Then you *did* see — what I wanted you to see —" Virginia said eagerly in a low voice — "just that I hadn't a home at all! I am a complete failure, and that's why I'm so unhappy! Jill thinks I'm just a tart, and of course Michael does, and Adrian *would*, if he knew. But I wanted you to see for yourself so that you could understand why there was first Tom, then Adrian, or anything or anyone, just to fill up the time, and to take the taste of that damned failure out of my mouth!"

Virginia didn't look at me, only at the fire. The clean blaze swept straight up the chimney in a single flame like a sacrificial fire. The glow shone back upon her face. The only other light in the room was the reading lamp on the big desk, just as it was when Adrian talked to me, only that night had been almost a summer night, very still, while now the gale flustered and shouted through the chimney; and the rain hurled itself, as if someone had thrown the entire contents of a bucket, against the windows.

I did not answer her at once. I was wondering how sincere she was, and what kind of a fool she wanted to make of me. What power she has — and in spite of her sincerity, was she not using her power simply to make me the servant of her beauty as she had those two other men? I did not blame her for this, though for both our sakes I intended to resist it. A violinist loves his instrument because he knows how to play on it. Virginia's body was her instrument; and she knew how to play on it like a virtuoso.

The firelight deepened the red of her lips, and brought out the golden shades of her brown hair. All her limbs were long and slender, and had been unhampered. I thought of the long hot summers she had told me about, swimming and surf riding in the rough Atlantic breakers; and how beautiful she must have looked, white as the spray she rode through. She wanted me to pity her, but there were so many people under this roof so much more pitiable. Besides, I did not want to feel much to-night, beyond what was reasonable.

At last, she turned her misty-blue eyes to mine; they had not the clear whites of Gillian's eyes, nor the cool grey round the dark pupils. Virginia's eyes were a luminous blue, like the horizon on a summer's day where it meets the sea, and you cannot be sure which is sky and which is ocean.

"Tom may be coming soon," she said, "and I'm so afraid! Adrian *has* been allowed to join the R.A.F. in spite of his age! He'll be home for his last leave before he's posted. And it's all going to begin all over again!"

"Why don't you go away?" I asked her.

Every free place in the world, and there are many free places still open, is free to her, and yet she wants to remain glued to this one spot where she is in trouble; and can make more trouble! I could not help remembering all those who were not free to move, under Nazi tyranny — the pillaged, the threatened, the tortured — Ah, if those who needed it most could but possess her freedom! I did not remind her of them, for what good would it do? Looking at her, I realized that we are none of us more free than we allow ourselves to be. Virginia cannot help making trouble. She is a lightning-conductor; and wherever she went, she would attract the lightning.

"Tom telephoned me last night," she went on after a pause, turning her eyes back to the fire again. "He's suddenly decided we ought to divorce, and to marry each other! It's a thing he's never even suggested before! He hates to see me, he says, at a loose end. Of course he's jealous, and now that Jill knows about us, he's lost his last home support. He can't *bear* Jill's knowing. I understand that, for I can't either, although it couldn't be safer. She won't open her mouth ever. But everything is gone for Tom now, except me; and I can't make him see that I'm gone too, really, and oh, Rudi, I am! I'm gone! Gone! Gone!"

She didn't cry this time or try to cling to my shoulder. I should have felt it less important if she had. She spoke in a dry whisper, her hands twisting round her knees. It was like watching an inexperienced diver diving from too high a springboard. He tenses his muscles unskilfully before he plunges. He is acting against his instinct — and that adds to his danger. I had the feeling that this love affair with Adrian was against Virginia's instinct. She did not know how to take the depth of the water that lay beneath her.

"You mean you are so much in love with him?" I asked her.

"So much!" she whispered. "Too much!"

How could I say that it is not love to harm another human being, as she must harm Adrian if she turns him into an escape? It was from Michael's stinging scorn that Adrian's adoration was to save her; but from her own scorn it would not save her. Tom was safer, but a too familiar refuge. He had none of Adrian's blind faith in Virginia; and it was from the pure and perfect devotion of a boy, who had no knowledge of fellow weaknesses in a woman, that Virginia longed to draw the spiritual sustenance she lived upon. Adrian would have to pay a heavy price for Virginia's self-respect. Poor lonely silly child — she could not bear to fall from grace; she wanted to fall *with* grace, and she did not realize that the act of falling is never graceful.

"It would annoy Michael equally," I said after a pause, "whoever you go off with, but I think perhaps the insult would be greater to him if you deserted him for a mere boy — without money, position, or even the prospects of keeping you in moderate comfort! Perhaps you have come to the same conclusion?"

Virginia dropped her hands from her knees, and sat bolt upright; the appeal of suffering that had made her eyes so tragic and beautiful was now replaced by a sharp anger.

"What on earth do you mean?" she demanded.

I chucked my cigarette into the fire, and leaned forward towards her.

"Look here," I said, "you're young enough to be told the truth, aren't you? When I was at your house I saw what you meant me to see! I think your husband *was* trying to hurt you in every conceivable way — but has it never occurred to you to ask why?

You seem to me to have counted a great deal too much on his Sainthood!"

She stared at me, bewilderment driving back the anger in her eyes.

"Hadn't you first outraged the sacred Image of you he set up in his heart?" I demanded. "I'll admit that it's never very fair *to* set up a Holy of Holies, and expect a human being to officiate as an Image; still, you chose the type of man who worships, you wanted a Saint, and presumably that's what you wanted him *for*, so that he should worship you! Well, now you've discredited your own Image, in his eyes, and so you have at your heels not only a cheated husband, but a far harder judge, a cheated worshipper!"

"But, Rudi," Virginia expostulated, not angry at all now, but deeply interested in justifying herself against my unexpected attack, "Michael gave me up — for nothing at all! I *wasn't* unfaithful to him till he *had* given me up! For two years I'd been, or tried to be, every damned thing he'd wanted; and believe me, he wanted a whale of a lot! I never knew which was Michael and which was God, and I had to obey both! Then a boy turned up, who was a good dancer, and I danced with him — and I may have flirted with him a little too, by way of relief — awfully little really if you realize what I'm used to in the way of flirting! Michael wouldn't remember I'd been used to beaux all my life, and knew how to handle them. He just froze straight away from me. Nothing I said would make him believe I wasn't plumb unfaithful. But Tom believed in me! After I'd had an awful scene with Michael, I just couldn't bear it, and I went to Tom, and he understood everything! That was how it all began. There's something about being trusted that *makes* you care for a person, isn't there? Especially when the *one* person who ought to have trusted you won't!"

"Yes," I said, "and since neither of these two men had the slightest reason to trust you, you must like being trusted by one of them better still, I suppose!"

She leaned forward and struck me with the flat of her hand across my cheek. I hoped it would relieve her, and it made me

feel distinctly better myself. I caught her hand, and pulled her
back into her seat, for she had started up, to leave me.

"No," I said, "don't go yet! It isn't over. You had better hear
the whole truth — however angry it makes you. You can't hit
truth away, and it's only fair to Adrian to listen to it. I suppose
you *do* mean to be fair to him, don't you?"

She said in a choked voice, "*Of course* I mean to be fair to
Adrian," though I knew she didn't.

"Well, then," I said, "why don't you tell him the truth? If
he wants to wreck his life for his father's mistress, let him: it's
his own lookout! But don't ask him to wreck his life for an
imaginary woman, the faultless victim of a cruel sadist! Michael
is as cruel as he's hurt; and you hurt him because he locked you
up like a sacred Relic instead of letting you run about like a
human being. But he wouldn't have treated you like a Relic if
you hadn't wanted to look so sacred, and you needn't smash
Adrian's life, unless you've got to be sacred still. These pretty lies
that we tell each other, they cost too much. Is it worth while to
lie at all, quite apart from the mess it makes of Adrian? You see,
he'll hurt *you* by and by, every bit as much as Michael has hurt
you, worse perhaps, for he's younger, and isn't a Saint. Why not
get out of this false situation and stand on your own feet: then
you needn't despise yourself any more. That's the only thing
that really matters. Those men don't matter, it's only *you* that
matters —"

She stood up, and I stayed crouched down on the little seat,
feeling cold in spite of the fire. For a minute I think she wasn't
sure what she was going to do with what I had given her. Probably she thought that I meant that the men didn't matter to me;
and that *she* did; and this may have helped to steady her, but
what I believe — and the only thing that prevented me from
making love to her — is that it only matters when we despise
ourselves. Other people we can get rid of, but ourselves we cannot lose. I should despise myself if I made love to Virginia. I can
see that behind all her fear, her home-sickness and her vanity,
she is a good girl with courage. She has never used this courage
except to conquer men's hearts, an easy prey when a girl so

beautiful concentrates her whole being for that one purpose,
but useless too because conquered hearts don't keep conquered.
Virginia could do great things if she worked hard enough. I
don't know what it is that stops her unless it is her inability to
work without applause.

For a moment, I think she saw herself as free from both men,
to choose her own life and live it from the centre of her being,
by her own wits and strength; and then she remembered her
loneliness and the price we must all pay for freedom.

She covered her face with her hands. "He won't let me! He
won't let me!" she whispered.

I knew that she meant Tom Wendover, not Adrian or Michael.

"Don't ask him to *let* you!" I said, getting up and standing
beside her. "Act at once, on your own initiative. Tell Adrian
the truth first! If he sticks to you, break with his father. If
Adrian can't face what you tell him — well then, you've freed
both him and yourself. You won't feel ashamed any more; and
when you don't feel ashamed, you *can* stand up to Tom Wendover. After all, he'd no right to persuade you to break your
marriage, and therefore hasn't any right to force you to make a
new one!"

She dropped her hands. "I'm hideously afraid, Rudi!" she
whispered. "Afraid of them both! And I shall go on being afraid!
These Englishmen, I don't understand them. You can't make
them laugh at you or hit you, or break down and love you; they
won't even be really friends. And I don't suppose there's any
hope for me about anything now, because I'm so ashamed!"

I looked at her for a long time. All the feeling I had for her,
a deep respect because I know that she has courage and generosity, was in my eyes, as well as that homage a man feels for any
woman who has shown him what is most desirable in life, and
been willing to share it with him. There was, too, the pity I felt
that she had put herself under the harrow of her miserable marriage. For whatever Michael Esdaile himself had suffered, he had
driven her by his cruelty out of her home.

I knew that she read this homage and this pity in my eyes, for
she put out her hand to me. I took it; kissed it; and dropped it.

"You have everything," I told her, "and you will still have everything, even when you have cut your life free from its human entanglements. You have tremendous powers!"

"But have you thought," Virginia asked me anxiously, "what I'm to do with an angry cheated Tom, who *never* worshipped me but *does* love me? And perhaps even if he finds out about Adrian — will *still* love me?"

"That's your business: what you do with Tom Wendover!" I told her. "But you can at least remember that he's a strong man and knows that his country needs him. It is his job to save England. It is *your* job to save yourself!"

"Won't you even help me to save myself?" she pleaded.

"Let's stick to helping Adrian first!" I said.

She winced as if I had struck her. I had meant to strike her, because it was my only way of getting rid of her.

She went quickly to the door, and I opened it and helped her on with her rain cloak. I gave her the torch; but I did not offer to go home with her, through the storm and the darkness; this must have struck her as being very unchivalrous; but I thought it, at the moment, more chivalrous to remain where I was.

19th January 1941

IT is more than a month since I have written this private record. During these weeks I have been unable to observe or to relate my daily happenings; but I have been able to carry on my work in the hospital just the same. I have even been particularly successful with my shell-shock cases.

Over this period the Nazis have continued, night after night, their terrific hammer blows upon this country. There is a great weight of pain now upon this land; and people no longer speak readily of other things.

In the air they are not yet strong enough to return the Nazi blows. They have no prepared and equipped army to match the trained forces of the Reich. Their life as a nation — and even as individuals, did they but know it — depends wholly upon their ships; and week by week, these ships are being sunk.

As we live near a great port, I come into contact occasionally with these men of the sea, Naval or Fishermen. They are quite unlike any other men whom I have ever met. I find it difficult to describe them. They have a gentle ferocity; a sort of gay readiness to take or to receive mortal blows that has nothing to do with either fear or anger. They are combative without being aggressive. On the surface, apart from their work, I find them merry, simple men with easy manners; but a discipline so great controls their activities, and their whole outlook, that I hesitate to set any limit to their powers. I find them capable of more than human endurance; and of great creative adjustability. Their discipline is the exact opposite of Nazi discipline. They seem to have no fear of what is in themselves. Obedience is, of course, a part of their discipline, but obedience is never an aim — whereas with the Nazis obedience is always the chief aim of their discipline.

British seamen act, at it were, for the sake of the thing in itself;

and in each one, however deeply hidden, lies a guardian quality. A good mother, or a good sheep-dog, has this same selfless power; but never before have I found it in a number of men working upon a common task. Perhaps British seamen retain their power of individual initiative because the sea, rather than any officer, is their real master. It is from an unpredictable element that they learn to meet and overcome danger.

The Nazis are shaped by the Known; and as far as this takes them, they are iron men, terrible in their controlled obedience. Nothing can stop them, except perhaps the Unknown. This is the one poor chance our small beleaguered Island possesses; for the Unknown will not stop British seamen or their brothers in the air — the Unpredictable is their element.

When I am not working, I try to keep my mind upon these men, because I am alone now upon an uncharted sea. I have lost James and Eunice.

I was out early as usual, for a mouthful of fresh air before work began, when a boy on a bicycle stopped me, with his little brown envelope. I supposed it was from James to mention their time of arrival, and opened it eagerly; but it was from Tom Wendover.

PLEASE BREAK NEWS TO GILLIAN AND HER MOTHER. JAMES, EUNICE AND ROSEMARY KILLED IN LAST NIGHT'S RAID. TELEPHONE COMMUNICATION OBSTRUCTED. INSTRUCTIONS FOLLOW.

I read the telegram twice through without the feeling of shock; then I put it in my pocket and watched the boy jump on his bicycle and ride off.

They were all three dead — and they were noble people. Each had a special value, the child a promise, the parents the fulfilment of promise. They had gone out of this harsh world harshly.

At first, all I could think of were the details of the Air Raids I had read about. The slow accumulation of horrors that the last months had built up ran like an incessant tape before my eyes. There had been four months of them, and all the worst horrors of these four months I saw fall upon the heads I loved. I could not see anything else for a long time. Later on I had another sorrow, but this I did not remember at first for I was crushed under the weight of the house that fell upon them. I had lost not only the best friends a man ever had, but the only people who knew what I once was — the service I gave my country — the Rudi who lived in the Hohe Warte and sang Schubert's songs — who possessed and was possessed by Klara and Andreas . . . he was alive to them! This Rudi died again in their deaths. He died finally, I hope, for though man has but a brief span, he seems to have in him the faculty of a cat. He can lose many lives.

This is a selfish and incurable part of my grief; nor have I hitherto succeeded in getting the better of it. Quite soon I remembered the poor angry child Gillian, who must be told of her loss by a delinquent messenger.

I do not believe there is any way of breaking bad news; it breaks itself. What preparation there can be is only that one should give the attacked heart room for its own courage.

I found her already awaiting me, seated in front of her typewriter, very still, very composed, very what she always is, ready. But alas, for what I had to give her, how could she be ready?

She said, "Good morning," without raising her eyes when I came in. I stood before her until she looked up at me, a little annoyed at my silence; for I had not answered her greeting.

When she met my eyes, she said quickly, "What is wrong?"

"There is a telegram from your father," I told her; and I gave it into her hands, so that she could have control of at least that little piece of paper, and make the words her own, without the interference of an alien voice.

It is very terrible to watch the young when for the first time they become aware of the fundamental insecurity of life. Their world reels away from under them, and their hands clutch at emptiness. Gillian sat rigidly still, reading and re-reading those bare words of her father's; then she did a very surprising and beautiful thing. She sprang suddenly to her feet and put her hands on my wrists.

"They were your best friends!" she said; and in that standing away from her own grief to reach me, grief became suddenly natural to us both; so I took her in my arms for a short moment —

and she came into them willingly, as a child that hurts itself seeks the nearest human refuge.

"Not Uncle James!" she sobbed against my shoulder. "Not just *now* — Rudi!"

I let her go quickly, for I knew that she is a person who would not care to be held for long.

"Fortunately there is a good deal to do," I said. Instantly Gillian tossed back her tears. "You'll tell Mother?" she demanded anxiously. "Yes," I said, "at once, and while I tell her, you'll let Matron know, and any of your father's people whom he would wish to know directly from you. The rest you can leave to me."

"I'll tell Michael," Gillian said quickly, "and I *would* ring up Adrian if I knew where he was. He ought to go to Father now. Father cares awfully for Uncle James. There were only the two of them."

"Probably your father will telephone Adrian himself," I suggested. I had the feeling that Gillian knew as well as I did that her father at this moment could safely rely upon his only son. They would be nearer to each other during this family crisis than Virginia was to either of them — though only for a moment.

As for me, my heart had ceased to feel like a stone that I was carrying about slowly because it was too heavy for me. I think Gillian had saved me from some kind of breakdown by letting me share her grief. It was all she had to give me, but it was a great gift; and only a very brave and generous girl would so instantly have given it. I had felt out of everything in the whole world until she drew me, by that touch of hers, back into life. Now I knew there was something I could still share; so I felt human again; and hurried off to the Dower House to see my patient.

Lady Wendover's reactions were quite predictable; but not very sympathetic. She was deeply injured. Here was something spectacular, if fatal, that had happened to somebody else. Here was a grief she could not even claim as a personal tragedy, since the loss of James and his family was more her husband's than hers.

I saw her turning over in her mind whether she could not beat

up some special tie between herself and Eunice — but she remembered in time that she had described Eunice as "a little nonentity
with eyeglasses." I am afraid that I might have reminded her
of it, if she had failed to remember it herself. Still I felt pity for
her. Imagine what a great film star would feel if any very remarkable disaster befell her understudy! She would of course
be sorry for the understudy, and might even be seriously ham-
pered by her loss, but would not her prevailing feeling be —
"All that publicity — wasted — when it might have been *Me!*"

It was harder to excuse her next reaction. She fell back upon
displeasure, as many people do who wish to belittle the tragedies
of others.

"So stupid of them," Lady Wendover told me, "to have stayed
that extra night! Why ever didn't they come here sooner! I must
say I think Tom might have done something more energetic
about it. Poor dear Eunice was always so supine! You yourself,
Doctor, might have written *more* urgently, mightn't you, because I really believe you had *quite* an influence upon my poor
brother-in-law. It was James who urged me to have you; doesn't
it seem *queer!* We should never have met each other, if it hadn't
been for James!"

I bowed. What really *did* seem to me queer was that we should
be alive instead of James. But it was not the sort of queerness
that I could take any steps to alter; or to explain to Lady
Wendover.

"I don't want to blame them," Lady Wendover went on, for
it seemed necessary to disguise the fact that she *did* want to blame
them, "but I myself, of course, would *never* have risked Rosemary — think of that poor child — " I suppose I may have winced,
for she added hurriedly, "I daren't *let* myself think of her! We
must have a Requiem Mass. Ring up the Rectory for me, will
you, and say I must speak to Michael. It's no use my asking
Fidget to do it, for she'd start crying into the telephone. I can't
think why she was always so fond of James and Eunice; they
were infrequent visitors, and she must have seen very little of
them! I do so dislike one's servants taking fancies to one's relations, don't you? I'm trying not to cry myself, because it won't

do any good, will it? I realize how bad such a shock is for me; it couldn't have come at a worse time, could it? Just as I had made every arrangement too for their comfort! I think the extra food ought to be countermanded at a time like this, don't you? Please ring the bell for Fidget! Of course *she'll* have to be told sooner or later!"

I rang the bell for Miss Fitchett.

I was sorry not to be able to tell her, alone and quietly, of the loss of her friends. I could only, as she came into the room, greet her with more than usual emphasis. I succeeded in holding her eyes for a long moment so that she could be warned of some evil thing by the pain in mine; and I think that she was perhaps a little prepared for the next moment's cruelty.

Lady Wendover said, "I've got horrible news for you, Fidget — and if you feel it, you can just imagine what it means to *me* . . poor Tom too, and the children, they've always been so devoted to James! He's been killed, and Eunice and the child too, quite awfully, and we know no particulars, but they were probably buried alive under their burning house! Will you get my *sal volatile* and put some bicarbonate in it? I'm sure Dr. von Ritterhaus would wish me to take it, I feel so absolutely done in!"

Miss Fitchett went straight to the medicine chest, and got out the right bottle. Her hands shook a little, so I took it from her and mixed my patient the required dose.

As soon as I could, I got Michael Esdaile on the telephone and he promised to come round immediately. It was all that I could do for Miss Fitchett as I had to return to the hospital for my morning rounds.

Later on that day Tom Wendover got through on a long-distance call. His voice sounded dead and flat; but as usual, authoritative. Whatever happened to him, or to anyone else, I felt sure that Tom Wendover would go on giving orders; and that they would be the right ones. He asked how Gillian was, and said that Adrian had joined him; and would attend the funeral with him. They would be with us in three days' time. He gave me all his further directions; and finally reached a point where I think that he found speech unbearable. As long as one can think of something in a death that is not the person, it is possible to go on talking and planning with composure, but when only the Image of the Dead is left — close against the heart — then there is no agility left in order to avoid the full impact of grief.

Tom Wendover at length reached the point where there was nothing left between us but his brother James — he then disconnected the telephone. Perhaps he did something else after that, but I did nothing else; I was left alone with James.

23rd January 1941

WE had a little trouble about the Requiem Mass.

Lady Wendover wanted it to be a family function. She had the idea that it should be a sort of emotional miracle driving all the family back into their right holes and corners. She wished Lord Wendover and Adrian to attend it; and she put a good deal of energy into this idea, though the rest of the family disliked it very much.

Tom Wendover refused to come home until the Mass was over; and Adrian remained with his father. They had a Requiem Mass of their own in London; and it was not my business to remind them that as James and Eunice had no Church interests whatever (merely putting the religion they possessed directly into their lives) a Requiem Mass was not appropriate to them. Nor was it appropriate to Rosemary, who — alive or dead — was too young to take advantage of Church privileges.

I have never limited myself in any way by the precepts of the Catholic Church, though I have always admired its functions. Such a service was a last public honour to my two friends; and I gladly made a point of being present.

It was the first time I had been inside an English church, or seen Michael Esdaile conduct a service. The church itself was an interesting symbol of these very private and domestic Islanders. With us, the village church is an open affair — a sort of spiritual Inn. People come and go as if it belonged to them, and make what use of it occurs to them, within reasonable limits. But in this country the "Inn" element is absent. The church is very little used except on Sunday. It belongs to a small select circle, organized by the Priest, and carrying out his idea of what the Anglican religion considers respectable. The element of universality is wholly absent.

Nothing could have been more dignified, more profoundly

skilled and easy, than the way Michael Esdaile carried out the ceremony. We had Bach's music, the most suitable in the world for Death, since every law is simple to this great Lawgiver; and the process of death as natural to him as the rest in a bar of active notes. The choir was excellently trained; and Eunice and James would have liked, I knew, the clear sexless quality of the boys' voices.

I had to feel angry with the words of some of the hymns they sang, for I did not think the deaths of my friends were really well chosen; and I was wholly unreconciled to them. I thought they were a horrible accident.

The congregation did not fill the church, although out of compliment to the Wendovers, many of their friends came who must have been strangers to James and Eunice. Some of the hospital Staff were present; and many of the Wendover dependents.

Lady Wendover, Gillian and Miss Fitchett sat in the front pew to the right; Virginia in the front pew to the left, and a young V.A.D. friend with her.

Sometimes I watched their faces; and sometimes I attended to the service itself. I was anxious to divert my mind, and not to be too greatly moved by the beautiful old English words. I could not take comfort in them. Constantly there was the refrain "And may perpetual Light shine upon them!" but my friends had been thrust into perpetual darkness.

A beam of wintry sunlight stalked like a searchlight across the shadows of the South Aisle. I watched the dust weave its strange pattern in and out of it, and remembered how, as War was declared, I had seen Rosemary's yellow curls dance by the open window. She had seemed to me, then, outside the realm of those horrors — but she had been drawn into them. Darkness, and not light, had caught her after all.

In a sense, I was accustoming myself to the deaths of James and Eunice. They had achieved a very fine pattern of human life. To a friend like myself, it was an irreplaceable and unforgettable pattern, but they had achieved it. At thirty, and both were nearing thirty, you have fulfilled yourself, although your work may still be stretching usefully ahead of you for more than twice as long. The unbearable loss, to me, is Rosemary. She is a promise unfulfilled, a promise broken.

For James and Eunice, it is still in my power to do something. I know what their wishes were: they wanted me to assist in solving some of the Wendover problems, to carry on my science, to fight for all that the Nazis are fighting to destroy.

But for Rosemary — what can I do? I do not know what Rosemary would have wanted. And what an insult to love it is, not to be able to carry out the wishes of a Friend, dead or alive!

I could not help wondering what the rest of this decorous congregation was making of the unutterable blunder that had brought us there. I do not think most of them were thinking either about the Dead, or even about death at all; the business of living was too important to them for the death of unknown people seriously to impinge upon it; a painful thought or two flashed through them, but no more.

Sister Tutor and Sister Lawrence had made a great effort to be there, as well as to free several of our Staff. Sister Lawrence's round good face looked a little heated still with the struggle it must have been to get the duties of her morning safely accomplished in an hour short of their usual time. She looked grave, as if she were in church for that purpose; but her chief concern was still with life, and I think she felt a little disappointed that she was interrupted from carrying it on. I liked to watch her efficient way of taking the responses. She made them so promptly, with a sort of spectacular neatness, nothing slovenly or left out — almost as if she were tidying one of the patient's beds.

Sister Tutor also followed the service carefully but she did not sing, or recite the Creed. She looked neither happy nor unhappy; a muscle sometimes twitched at the corner of her mouth a little mockingly. I do not think she has a reverent mind. Once I caught her eye. She wears a glass monocle in one eye that I usually find a little intimidating; but I had the feeling that in some ways we thought alike about this Requiem Mass.

Gillian had no colour in her face at all; and was bent upon driving all the emotion she felt into some secret hiding place. She was, I could see, desperately anxious not to break down and cry;

because her mother expected her to, and would indeed have been
highly pleased with her if she had. A good deal of Gillian's mind
was taken up with grief for her uncle's loss; but much of it was
occupied with her chronic desire to disappoint at all costs the
sentimental claims of her mother.

Virginia cried quietly into a succession of small lace pocket
handkerchiefs; and must have felt relieved that while keeping in
tune with the occasion, she could display her actual emotions
without concealment. The death of Rosemary had, I knew,
struck raw on her nerves. I think there were no tears shed for
Rosemary more bitter than Virginia's, whose children were alive.
She was a mother and afraid to love her children because of the
responsibility this love entailed. Yet in rejecting the responsibility, she could not wholly reject the love. It tore at her now
under the disguise of pity for the dead child.

Miss Fitchett, to use a good English phrase, was "dissolved in
tears." It was a luxury she really needed, and probably seldom
took, for her whole life must have been a series of minor disappointments and outrages. Among these domestic atrocities,
Eunice and James had moved reassuringly, and with perfect tact.
They had not made their sympathy dangerously apparent; but
they had not failed to understand that Miss Fitchett was a sort
of Saint Sebastian bound to a tree, and pelted with arrows. Even
I, though it is true I see Miss Fitchett always as a human pin-
cushion, do not give her the sympathy I know she got from
Eunice. I am always very sorry for people who cannot leave their
troubles, but I am less sorry for those who carry their troubles
with them as if they were important personal luggage which must
not at any cost be mislaid, or left behind. Lady Wendover, I
admit, is responsible for the arrow shooting, but why should Miss
Fitchett let herself be bound to the Silver Fountains tree? I doubt
if Saint Sebastian chose his tree; but I am certain that Miss
Fitchett has chosen hers. Nothing will induce her to leave Lady
Wendover, and Miss Fitchett ought to know by this time that
nothing will induce Lady Wendover not to shoot arrows at her.

Lady Wendover, I think, enjoyed every moment of the Requiem Mass. I doubt if the thought of James or Eunice, in any

real sense, crossed her mind. I do not think her religion means everything to her, but I am sure that it means a great deal. I could see that she was filled with emotion, much of it pleasurable.

She was the Chief Mourner. Gillian, it is true, was the blood relation, but Gillian is only a child; and has not known her uncle anything like as long as Lady Wendover has known her brother-in-law.

For the moment, Lady Wendover must have forgotten that she disliked James, and barely tolerated Eunice. She saw them as they never were, but as they might have been — the brother and sister whom she had never had, and never could have had, since if such relations had existed in the flesh, she would have bullied the life out of them. But for these enthralling strangers and their tragic end, Frances Wendover wept bitterly from time to time. She was carried off her feet by the spell of the beautiful and luminous words, with their comforting suggestion of what the hereafter was at least as likely to be as anything else. Behind all this surface flow of emotion, I knew her to be a deeply unhappy human being who could see no way out of the human difficulties she had made for herself. I feel for her a deep and profound sympathy, for are we not all as Meredith, the English poet, has said, "Thus blindly with our blessedness at strife," and can any one of us, looking at the blindness of his own heart, not realize that we too "are betrayed by what is false within"? This woman was brought up in a wrong way, to think that she could achieve success by accepting her wishes as a standard, and her beauty and money as weapons to fight with, in order to carry out this selfish standard. She has fought hard and well but her wishes were of no value — even if she could have achieved them — either for herself, or others. She was the exact opposite of my two dead friends, for Frances Wendover fights rigidly for her own good, and they fought with elasticity, for the good of others; they even knew what this good was because they took, objectively, the trouble to find out.

As I believe the world, in this mortal struggle, is writhing rather more in their direction than in hers, I am not altogether sure that the Requiem Mass was not for Frances Wendover after all, while Eunice and James can still be claimed among the living!

I could not follow Michael Esdaile's mind, since it was safely hidden behind the mask of Priesthood. He may have been pre-occupied with placing before God the souls of the newly de-parted; but I think he was also aware of some of the living in his congregation. His beautiful voice lingered over words that could strike a specially painful chord in the breast of his young wife.

If ever a man believed in God, in His Church, in the position of Man as a regulated Mouse-ling of an Eternal Cat, Michael Esdaile is that man. I do not speak irreligiously, for I think a man without a religion is as empty of purpose as an idiot. All I ask is that he should be a little intelligent about his God — or better still, a little more honest. Either a man's religion is the aim of his whole life, or it is nothing — a mere black speck dancing in the sun before the eyes of a patient suffering from the liver.

One thing we know: we were created, and therefore in us must move something of the Creator, and of His responsibility for this power of creation. I do not find we are in any position to ask anything of this Unknown God; but has He not the right to ask something of what He has created?

He had asked something of James and Eunice, and of Rose-mary; and I think that they all three gave Him very successful answers. There was nothing to bury; so as I saw that the service was drawing to an end, I slipped out at this point in my re-flections, into the bright and empty day.

1st February 1941

I THINK there is one new, great hope — Russia. Churchill said some enigmatic words about Russia not long ago. Maisky was featured visiting a London Shelter. Such straws show deep currents beneath them. America is still in the hands of that man of infinite courage and astuteness, Roosevelt.

The third term of Roosevelt, the London applause for Maisky reported in the Press, these may be the great landmarks of history. Without them, this small sea-set Island with its vulnerable distant children might not be able to endure.

Up till now, Tom Wendover was only permitted by the Home Office to allow me to act as the screened head of this hospital; but now he has received permission to use me publicly as its chief. It makes no difference to my work, but it has greatly pleased Matron and Sister Tutor. I do not know why it has pleased them; but I am grateful, and perhaps it is natural for loyal fellow workers to wish their chief to have the full benefits of his position.

All my work interests me, but there is a single case that I find myself almost unduly anxious to cure. It is that of a young Dockland teacher, a man rather less than my own age, with shock blindness. He behaved heroically through a series of raids, but was finally trapped in a shelter on the fringe of a big explosion; and has seen nothing since. The eyes themselves, and the optic nerve, are quite intact. He had other injuries, which should not affect his eyesight; and which are clearing up satisfactorily. I give him all the spare time I have; for I think I know what is at the back of his trouble, if we can reach it together.

To-day I found him very much depressed. He had just been given Evans' (the eye man's) final report. There is nothing the matter with his eyes from an oculist's point of view. There is therefore nothing further that can be done for him.

"Now," John Stephens said to me, "I'm doomed — can't you

see I'm doomed? If there were any injury, however severe, there might be some hope I should recover my sight, even if only partially. But since there is no injury, there is no hope. As far as I can grasp this nightmare situation in which I find myself, I am incurable *because* there is nothing the matter with me!"

"There must be something the matter with a man who can't see," I ventured to suggest, "but I think you have now come into my province. My business is to find out with you, since I cannot find out without your help, *why* you can't see! Once we have grasped the cause, we may feel hopeful as to curing the symptom. My only fear is that you may not give yourself the trouble to make this search with me, since it may be a very painful one."

He said quickly and angrily, "Do you mean that you think I don't *want* to recover my sight?"

"I wish it were so simple," I answered. "It is — among other things — your very longing that sets up a barrier. You double-cross yourself with longing. The will is a very dangerous weapon to let loose in the mind. First we must free the mind from the dictatorship government set up by that master of Special Privilege, the Will. A wise man once said, 'Do not ask if the Will is free; ask rather if the Mind is free to will.' We must now train your mind till it gains enough courage to be free to will!"

It is an awkward business to tell a schoolmaster that he is in any need of training; but this young man was highly intelligent; and it was terrible to him to be blind. I had therefore good hopes for his cure. Also, from the first we had talked easily together as friends.

He frowned and tossed his head wearily from side to side, staring into the bright daylight with his self-darkened eyes. "You speak in riddles," he said fretfully, "but I suppose in time you will explain them. Anyhow, I have nothing to do except lie here and listen. If that is any help to my cure, you can count on it. I will listen."

"You must also talk," I reminded him, "but that is a part of listening — it is usually, also, the less difficult part! You will have to tell me things about yourself that you hardly know, and occupy yourself between our talks with your memories — especially your early memories."

"And if you do not trust my mind, how can you tell whether these things I tell you are the truth, or not?" he demanded, with a certain triumph that must have helped to relieve his terrible depression.

"That will not matter at all," I told him, "whether you tell me the truth or not, since the lies also will be yours. You are inventing them; and it is the mind that invents them that I shall be studying. I mean, it will not matter to *me;* it will perhaps matter to *you;* that depends upon how much you value the truth. To a mind that values the truth, it is very unsatisfactory to tell lies. I think that is one of the worst tortures of a Nazi concentration camp. They try to make liars out of men who once valued the truth. But this is not a Nazi concentration camp, and the truth is not denied you. Do as you choose!"

"There can be no torture," Stephens told me, "as severe as I am suffering now."

I did not dispute this point with him, for there is no thermometer for human suffering. Personally, I think there is no torture so terrible as the torture inflicted by a fellow man, because you have to feel for him, as well as for yourself. You cannot believe that you are not evil if your brother gives you wilful pain; nor can you believe that he is not evil for giving you this pain.

I watched the tragic mask of this young man's face with the greatest pity and interest. I can imagine he was a charming-looking child; and that when he fell down, his mother always picked him up and pitied him. One always suspects the pampered child in these sensitive, thin-lipped faces, with early-wrinkled foreheads.

"Dictatorship government!" he muttered. "I don't know what you mean! Mustn't a man control himself? I tell you I have seen wrecks all round me of uncontrolled men! Don't think my life's been easy either — even before this horrible accident. Penury and ambition are bitter bedfellows. If I hadn't learned to control all my wants and live close to the bone, I could never have been in the job I suppose I've now lost, as teacher in one of the best L.C.C.

Schools in London! I'm only twenty-nine — how old are you?"

"I am thirty-four," I told him. "Do not think I undervalue your success or your hardships. I simply say that you have always lived under too great a strain. Perhaps this is impossible to avoid, except for the specially privileged, under our present economic system. Those who, by their hard work and good characters, should be assured of financial security, are forced to struggle from the cradle to the grave, in the deepest mental anxiety; while those who really need the spur of insecurity are sometimes lavishly surrounded by every form of material protection. I am convinced that this Dole system — whether it functions in the realm of investment and inheritance, or in the more hand-to-mouth realm of the government-kept unemployed — is wholly wrong. Security and the willingness to work should always go together. Every child should have his equal chance of both. He should be trained for work, and know that when trained, he would be given work."

"Oh, yes, yes!" he said impatiently. "Of course our system is bitterly unfair; but if it were fair, should I be any better off than I am now? I am willing to work all right. I have been trained for my work — and I am blind! I suppose you are going to propose now that I should study Braille, as Sister did this morning! If she hadn't been a lady, I should have told her to go to hell!"

"I should not study anything," I told him, "until you see a little more plainly why you are blind."

"And you really think you can tell me why?" he demanded scornfully. "I don't mean your dictatorship-analogy stuff — but *really* why?"

"Tell you — no!" I answered. "Telling by itself is not of much use, but I could perhaps *show* you why you are blind. I do not imagine that, as a teacher, you found it much good telling your students what you wished them to know, did you? But when you showed them how to think — why then they might arrive anywhere with their own knowledge!"

When he smiled, his thin, pinched, eager face looked very intelligent. "A tight-rope walker, but a good boy!" I told myself. I saw that all his life he must have cramped and tensed himself to walk upon the air, with only a rope between him and the sheer precipice of disaster. All the while he had ignored the easy earth beneath his feet which was his to walk on. One cannot go very quickly with such cases.

"I wasn't allowed much time to teach my boys how to think," he said. "Our modern educational standards are pretty rigid. We cram their little minds as you stuff a goose. Not to make children think, but to overload their thinking power, seems to be the bright idea! Still, I did what I could, of course. With a class of forty that ought to have been fifteen; with a set of text books that were some of them lies and the rest of them inadequate presentations of the truth; with a classroom that stinks, and children that weren't properly fed, I think I gave the richest country in the world its full equivalent for the salary it gave me! I went to a training college once where I had a real teacher. He taught me how to work — so I'll work with you now, Doctor. I'll do my darnedest if you think you can really help me, and won't try to make me learn how to read Braille!"

This was how we started to work together.

I have my own idea of shock blindness. I believe it to be always confined to people who have already borne as much as their over-sensitive nerves can carry. Such over-sensitiveness comes invariably from some form of early spoiling. Often the patient has had to live up to ideals that are too high for him, or highly unnatural to his sex or circumstances. Among those affected are a high percentage of tight-rope walkers, like this patient. They are determined (it is part of their childhood's life-plan) that life itself is dangerous and not to be trusted, so naturally, being courageous people, they try to control it, as well as to control themselves; and to meet dangers that have never existed, they manipulate each fresh emergency to fit their over-cautious minds. Like Atlas, they run off every morning to school — the world on their shoulders — trying to arrange in advance how to meet disasters that will never happen to them. Their sense of responsibility is frightful; they have, as it were, chosen the career of the Lord God Himself, and how dearly they must pay for it!

Such children dictate to life itself, as Hitler dictates first to Germany; then if they conquer it, to the world. No doubt Hitler prefers to feel himself responsible for the world, since he was never able to become responsible for himself.

Men like this young Stephens order about the accidents of Time. They plan, they sweat, they agonize; and all the while they cannot keep back one drop of that great stream of life from taking its predetermined way in spite of them.

Stephens alone lost his eyesight in that burning shelter. Others lost their lives when the roof fell on them; some crawled out unhurt — and a few saved others as well as themselves. But Stephens, forced into immediate catastrophe upon so large a scale, cried to himself, "I can't manage this; therefore I can't bear it. I won't even look at it! It is not within my powers!" His eyes helped him out. They instantly refused to see. Unfortunately the body, once it has granted the order of the Will, never knows where to stop. As we used to say in Wien, "Why throw the baby out with the bath water?"

Many pianists with an overwhelming desire to shine in public cannot play at some particular concert where they suddenly fear they may not be able to play to great advantage. Their wrists oblige them for this purpose; but they also go on disobliging them when the concert is over and the patient would be genuinely glad to return to his piano.

These alibi illnesses were diagnosed and treated with great success by Adler, who alone understood the grievous discouragement that lay behind a varying flock of symptoms. Illusive domestic eruptions, broken careers, or even too many motorcar accidents, always follow the secret directions of the hidden Will. Stephens is not responsible for being blind, but he is responsible for something happening that prevented his being a hero on too large a scale. His body did the best it could to stop him. It took away the sight of his eyes.

There was a boy of twelve years in the same shelter. He dug out, with his own hands, his mother, a little sister of six, and his baby brother; an hour later he was discovered sobbing behind a wall because in his desire to save them from the flames, he

had lost a torch when his father had told him he would beat
him if he mislaid it again.

Real heroism comes without effort. Long ago Thomas à Kempis
wrote of the mainspring of all human actions: "Love — and do as
you please."

As yet, this young teacher John Stephens, with his thin set
lips, and peevish expression, does not love enough for it to be
safe for him to do what he pleases. He has none of the ease of
a generous giver. Tommy Baker, whose hands and feet were badly
burned, and his arms covered with septic cuts, was so happy in
digging out his family alive that he did not notice the pain for
several hours afterwards. He was seen to brush the flames away
with his bare hands, as if he were shooing off intrusive insects.

One should not use comparisons between individuals since
each acts from a different aim, except to show that the facts
themselves can be considered differently. What was unbearable
to the man, was to this child a barely noticeable hindrance.
This boy Stephens was an Idol, whose mother excused him from
the simple duties of a man only to expect of him the virtues of a
God. No doubt he had badly overstrained himself in a wholly
useless manner before there were any Air Raids.

I do not know if I can gradually get him to realize that life
is easier than he thinks; and that he no longer needs his blindness.
Time will help, as it does in all shock cases, except the most
determined depressions, since it will push him further away from
the shock period. Also, he must have fairly strong nerves since
he has never had any other form of nervous breakdown in spite
of being under so heavy a strain from his earliest childhood;
and this too will help his recovery.

I have talked over his case with Matron, who has had him
put into a specially safe, small room on the first floor near the
staircase, with two other educated patients, not too much better
than he is himself.

I must try to re-train him in a different kind of courage;
and since he has courage, this will not be so difficult as if I had
first to rouse a courage he had never used at all. He has previously
used a courage forced to distinguish itself by unnatural efforts;

now he need only use a courage that will do what is necessary, because the thing in itself will seem to him more worth while than either distinguishing himself or running away.

One learns very much from such patients because they are intelligent and do not let their teacher get off scot free from delusions not dissimilar to their own.

The day I came back to visit Stephens, straight from the Requiem Mass, he said to me at once, "Doctor — your voice is different!" I asked him, "How is it different?"

"You are sorrier for me than you were yesterday," he told me; and he cried a little, because he is very sorry for himself. His mother developed this self-pity in him that she might have the joy of giving him consolation. I knew that it was bad for him, but I had forgotten that it was still worse for a doctor to despise self-pity in a patient.

I had had too much contempt for this poor being's unhappy burden. In the Mass, I had thought out the qualities of my dead friends so as to see how best to serve them. I never saw in Eunice that she felt contempt for anyone; and I shall serve the purpose she lived for better if I never despise self-pity again in anyone but myself.

6th February 1941

WHEN Gillian said, this morning, with her hand covering the mouthpiece of the telephone, "This is Father — shall I answer it?" I was wholly taken by surprise. Tom had never yet seen his hospital. For four months it had been in working order, and week by week we had expected his visit. The air war came; the London Raids; the death of James and Eunice: all these things had held him away from Silver Fountains. It had seemed as if he had forgotten, or indefinitely postponed, the problems of his own home; his wife; Adrian and Virginia.

We had been at first all keyed up to receive him. After all we had spent thousands of pounds on the reconstruction of Silver Fountains. It was Wendover's money that was spent on changes in his property; but time had blunted our sense of personal responsibility to Tom. We felt responsible now solely for human emergencies; so I said, without lifting my head from my writing, "Why should you not answer it; it is your father speaking!" I got up to leave the room that she might speak more freely, but she said with a curious urgency in her voice, "It's about the hospital! He wants to see it!" and then in her clear, casual telephone voice she spoke into the instrument, "Yes! Yes! As soon as you arrive; I'll tell him." "Father will be here in an hour," she added to me, hanging up the instrument. "We must have the whole hospital ready for inspection; we'll have to hurry. Will you tell Matron or shall I?"

Had she forgotten that none of us had met since we had lost Eunice and James; and Rosemary?

I saw from the expression on her face that ceremony came first. Red carpets must — metaphorically — be laid down; and I must be prepared to give an account of my stewardship. Emotions were out of place.

There is a saying in this singular country: "Possession is nine points of the law." With this overwhelming superiority — does not the spirit escape? I saw that what we had made of Silver Fountains now came before the death of James.

A stir passed through the hospital. The Matron gave her orders. Sister Tutor and Sister Lawrence passed like tonic breezes through the Wards and corridors. Sister Peters cleared away the last imaginary vestiges of the theatre's recent activities. There was practically nothing for me to do except to stand in the hall and wonder what I could say to the man who had lost his only brother, and my best friend; and I need not have wondered this, for when Tom Wendover arrived, I said nothing.

Against that casual, unconcerned manner, that unaltered granite face, what could I say? One glance at Tom Wendover disinfected emotion out of existence.

Matron, Sister Tutor, Sister Lawrence and Dr. Reed stood in a group about me. I made the necessary introductions; and Lord Wendover asked immediately what, if anything, the hospital still needed; and how he could best serve them. I do not know that he listened to their answers, or if the question was merely a rhetorical one — but after he had asked it, the situation came into his hands and remained there. All I had to do was to follow him about, answering technical questions.

We went over the hospital from roof to cellar. I was amazed at his mastery of every detail; and his searchlight powers of observation. He might have been brought up in a hospital, he knew so much about its every need. A great Englishman is almost always a great organizer; and it was obvious to me that this man had, to the fullest extent, the English power of controlling institutions and bringing out the latent capacities of everything under his control. It made it the more difficult to understand why he had so completely failed to control the relationships, and inner forces, of his own personal life. It was equally curious that though he was ready to do all in his power to smooth the running of our new organization, as far as I could see, the patients themselves made no personal impression on him whatever.

The only moment I saw him emotionally touched was when he found Virginia with the children. His eyes softened for a moment

into tenderness as they rested upon her. "Does she work here
every day?" he asked me.

Virginia was standing by a baby's cot with her back towards
us. Slowly she turned, as if Tom's glance had summoned her.
It is difficult to take a woman by surprise socially, especially,
perhaps, an American woman.

Virginia did not turn a hair. She came forward swiftly to
meet us, smiling pleasantly, with her hand outstretched. "How
splendid to see you," she exclaimed; and then remembering
James, her eyes clouded, and she said quickly, "We've all felt so
terribly for you, dear old Tom!"

I don't think he objected to her standing there beside him,
breathing beauty and sympathy — he merely tossed her words
aside from him, as if they were just a piece of social routine.
She was more used to him than I was, for she let the subject go
as easily as he did, and added quickly, "What do you think of
the fine new hospital we've turned your fine old home into?"

"I don't know yet," Tom said smiling down at her, "I only
think of the fine V.A.D. you've turned yourself into! What's
become of Jill, by the by? I suppose, as she's only a secretary,
she can't have pretty arm bands with coloured letters on them;
but I have a hunch, as you Americans say, that arm bands or no
arm bands, she does as much as all the rest of you put together!"
I heartily endorsed this statement and told him that I supposed
we should find Gillian where I had left her, working in my room;
but when we reached the library, it was empty.

Lord Wendover looked round his familiar quarters and his eyebrows lifted a little, but he made no comment. He fetched us both
drinks, and cigarettes, and with a jerk of his head in the direction
of the Ward we had just left, he said, "You've made a good job
out of all this, I fancy."

It is all, I think, that he ever means to say about my work
for the hospital; and perhaps it is enough.

Now we *had* to speak of James — at least I was preparing to —
when he so completely took my breath away that I could never
really speak of James again as I had meant to speak of him.
Tom Wendover said abruptly, and yet pleasantly, as if it cost

him nothing, "I thought I'd like to tell you myself, before the lawyers start up, my brother James, and Eunice, have left you all they had. The estate amounts to about six hundred a year under present taxation. It's all correct and straightforward. They made identical wills leaving everything to Rosemary, and, failing Rosemary, to you."

A moment before, I had been his servant, rootless, with no certainties of time or place, no assets beyond my medical training; and now I was independent and secure. I could only think how like James and Eunice it was to give everything they had to a disinherited, disenfranchised speck of Austrian dust! I could only think that once more I could allow myself to give as well as to take.

"No one else in all the world . . ." I said, and could not go on; but I began again after a moment because he too said nothing, "If you don't know James and Eunice — "

"Yes, yes," he said quickly, "but you see I *do* know them! After all, why else do you suppose you're here? I had the devil of a time getting you appointed! James was never in the least like me, but brothers understand each other pretty thoroughly. I knew you were his best friend. James didn't make friends easily — he didn't fall in love easily for the matter of that. You'd hardly call Eunice an easy girl to fall in love with, would you?"

"Perhaps not," I murmured, "but I think she was impossible to fall *out* of love with!"

"Yes," Tom agreed a little impatiently. "Well, that's what I mean: one always found he'd had good reasons for his few affections! I dare say he thought I was a tyrant and you'd better be free of me, free, anyhow, to say what you liked to me. In a sense you know you're my partner. You don't want to throw up the hospital because you've got this money, do you?"

I told him truthfully I would rather throw away the fortune, for what besides a man's work counts in the end? Probably Tom had guessed the truth: James thought I would do better work if I felt free of Tom's control.

We were silent, thinking out our private thoughts. At last he said, "How about my wife, and the situation, for I suppose

by now you know there *is* a situation?" Perhaps the money had
done another thing: it had given me in Tom's eyes a certain
positive value so that my opinions became worth having. Property to him meant more than persons, and I doubt if he really
felt a human being *was* a person without it. He was not wilfully
greedy, as many rich men are, but he considered property a duty
and that the more property you possessed, the more likely you
were to do your duty. Tom might have admitted that bad rich
men existed; but he would have thought them the mere exceptions
that proved the rule.

I told him first how his wife was, and then I said, "And the
situation: well, as I see it, you yourself are the situation, Lord
Wendover. She thinks that you no longer love her."

He was silent for a very long time, smoking, sipping at his
whisky, and looking into the bright wood fire. Then he said,
without looking at me, "Well — why should I? A man's got to
have something, hasn't he? What do you suppose *she's* ever given
me? Now I'm nearly fifty, and for the first time in my life I've
got something I want to live for; something, I mean, that's worth
the upkeep, cost what it may! Mind you, I don't like what's
happened. I realize a lot you said last time I saw you was true.
I haven't broken my wife's heart, because, as far as I know, she
hasn't got one; but I've hurt her damnably, and I'm sorry for it.
I'm still sorrier about the children. I suppose I've lost them as
well as my wife: she'd naturally take good care that I should.
Well, children grow up anyhow. They should live their own
lives, and always do! Why shouldn't I live mine?"

Of course, as long as he knew what his life was, there could be
no reason against his living it. I was not to know — but I had a
feeling that at fifty one cannot start all over again from scratch;
and I knew that what Tom Wendover built on was not really
sound. Though he was a good constructor, he had missed the
foundations of happiness. Did he himself know that? Was what
he cared for in Virginia only her beautiful young body? Did he
feel that he had bought it, and could keep it? But did he know
what he had bought it by! It was not money: it had been the
trust of his heart that he had paid for Virginia — and how could

he stop paying? If he still trusted her, he must trust himself to give her whatever it was she most wanted, even her freedom. I said at last, "Well — a man's life, what is it? Each has his own knowledge of it. A wife and children — these mean a lot to some men; to others little; I cannot judge for you, Lord Wendover, because I do not know your values. But I can tell you this, that you appear to have been too good a father to throw away your responsibilities quite so easily. Both Adrian and Jill seem to be in a bad condition. They are shaken, and do not strike me as being capable of living altogether upon their own wits. It seems they have a great opinion of you as a father; and that this present situation does not satisfy it?"

Tom Wendover shook his head, and went on smoking. After a long silence, he said, "Not now, they haven't. But I did what was necessary for them while they needed me. They're healthy, well-educated, game; if this country holds, they'll have money enough. Now I'm going to take what I damn well want out of life for myself alone — and nothing is going to stop me. I've stood three months of London under bombing attacks. Twice the house I've been in was struck, and I've stopped counting the chipped and shaken ones. I've stood and listened above burning rubble to hear if the people under it were alive or dead. For hours I've listened. I've seen Westminster in flames, though, by God, we got 'em under before much damage was done! I know all the holes there are in our defences. I know just how rotten our chances are, and I believe we'll win through in spite of the rottenness. What do you suppose my life is worth to me now? It's worth what I can damn well get out of it while the going's good!"

There was nothing to say to him. This great rule "to get" — if it's been taught a man as the core of his heart, then he but follows its logic when he takes life as a quarry and hunts it for his own pleasure; and to his own doom. I liked Tom Wendover — but I knew that he was doomed. I could not alter his doom by liking him; still less, by personal criticism; so I poured him out another drink, and we started discussing the hospital again.

8th February 1941

AFTER Tom had gone to the Dower House, I tried to think a little about the money; but I couldn't.

My mind was in a turmoil of anger and frustration.

It was no business of mine, but why had Gillian refused to welcome her father? Was not her grief deep enough to drown resentment? Why had she too acquiesced in this cold storage of grief?

Gillian should know better than to lower the pulses of her own heart and her father's by driving back the sympathy that once bound them into so close a comradeship!

What does it matter — what should it matter to her — that this defrauded man has looked elsewhere for his comfort than to my poor patient, who was always so little of a wife? Must his child be less his child because he has not starved himself to meet her ideals? Has she, this cruel little household judge, been such a success in her own love relationships?

I wanted to hurt her with my anger. I suppose that I felt she despised me as well as her father, and I despised her back! But did I? Well, I suppose since I write this diary for the purpose of telling the truth, I must tell it. I was angry because I loved her! Or I should love her, if my heart were alive and free, or if I had been sure of the heat of the centre that was in her. Perhaps I would not have admitted that I loved her, even to myself, while I had no money. Perhaps I also am smirched with the property sense of the British. I suppose I have what they would call a "right" to love her now. These puny, paltry "rights" that are made out of material possessions! Did I not love her when I first set eyes on her and saw she would not smile? Anyhow, I know her for what she is — a good girl, as reliable as a man's right hand; but reliable to what — a real or an unreal standard?

We meet half a dozen times a day. About my work she has

never once failed me. I have learned exactly upon what I can count. How without this help of hers could I have run this little British World, a hospital unit? I am a stranger to all their ways, to their very tongue. I sometimes feel a stranger to the pulses of their hearts. Gillian has proved herself my friend in the deepest sense of the word, whatever else she may be to my gladdened eyes, or to my eager senses. It is *her* lookout if she prefers to be an icicle, not mine; yet how could she be so cruel to her father!

I became more and more excited with my anger, and at last I started to look for her all over the hospital, for she often stays on long after hours, seeing to things that affect its running, or talking out problems with Sister Tutor and the Matron, who are both greatly attached to her.

But she was not with them, nor could I find her anywhere. I went back to my desk. I took up problems that could well have waited till the next day; and I made a hash of them. Then I rang up the Dower House. She must be at home by now, and I could at least say something disagreeable to her about one of these unsolved problems, down the telephone.

But she was not at home. To my astonishment, Miss Fitchett, who had answered the telephone, told me that Gillian was staying the night with the Esdailes at the Rectory.

I could hardly believe my ears.

"With Virginia?" I stammered.

"With Virginia!" Miss Fitchett repeated.

"— And our patient?" I gathered myself together to demand.

"Well," Miss Fitchett said consideringly, "Lord Wendover has been with her for half an hour. He has gone out now to see someone in the village. I gave Lady Wendover an aspirin afterwards."

I said, "Quite right!" and rang off. Miss Fitchett's mind and mine march together like twins. But although it was now late, I could not stay indoors. I felt as if a weight, as heavy and as cold as stone, had been lifted off my heart.

The night was thick and dark. The wind sang and sighed in the branches of the trees. Every now and then some low cloud let down its stinging drops. At sea, it must be what sailors call "a dirty night."

I walked through a grass ride to a little hillock of land from which you can, in daylight, catch a glimpse of the sea. Looking towards the coast, I saw the sky in flames; and knew that "something," as they say here, when the enemy visits them, "had been dropped," near Plymouth. London they had postponed rather than given up.

I had been expecting these Raids on the seaports. The Nazis strike, as a lunatic always strikes, at the nerve-centre of a man's being. So far, Plymouth has had only little Raids, with trifling damage, a night of horror for some poor householder, a lonely haystack on the moors; but to-night they must have found a bigger target: perhaps the gas works burned! I stood there smelling and listening. Curious that man is destroying all that he has earned from his expanding knowledge of the laws of his Universe. He has made the earth his home. He is no longer a stranger upon an unawakened planet; and to-day with what he has taught himself, he destroys all his new and dear possessions! And he destroys them because he has not learned to love his brother as himself.

The raiders passed. The flames died down. Very distantly upon the waves of the air, I heard the "All Clear" sounding. I walked on through the soft windy darkness towards the Rectory.

It was too late for me to intrude upon them. Perhaps they were all in bed and asleep; but I liked to be near them. My heart felt soothed and happy. I knew very well what this visit of Gillian's to Virginia meant — Lord Wendover, too, would know it. It meant she was no longer angry with her father; for his sake, she had forgiven even Virginia.

It was, I thought, a beautiful strange way of showing her forgiveness — altogether English. It satisfied everything — and expressed nothing. To-morrow she and her father would meet tranquilly as if nothing had ever happened to disturb or break their old relationship.

I felt very proud of Gillian; and ashamed of myself for having doubted her. She had taken what she needed out of the deaths of James and Eunice; perhaps they had helped her more, dead, than if they had been alive. I felt strangely and deeply comforted. What I had minded most about the loss of my friends was that their particular value had seemed wasted; but now I began to see that, after all, it was being used where they had been most loved. Adrian as well as Gillian had reacted strongly to their grief. Adrian had gone to London to his father. He had not come here to Virginia.

Being partly a Jew, by race though not by faith, and partly a scientist, I have never thought very seriously about the immortality of the human soul. To a Jew, what is important is that God should be immortal; to a scientist, that Truth should be handed on intact from one generation to another. But to-night I thought that perhaps immortality is just as certain as mortality. The force, call it what you will, that was in James and Eunice, and in their child, has it not passed into something else? The magnificent cool strength of James, the lucid honesty of Eunice, even the beauty and the innocence of Rosemary, do they not still stir in the hearts that understood their value? Who knows whether these lights of the Living do not always remain, when breath and consciousness — what we call "identity" — are blotted out? They may even grow stronger by joining the new hearts they reach out towards after they lose their own.

Now, everything seems to go down into darkness. In each country struck by War, more than a generation — young and old alike — the landmarks of history, the light of the ages, seem put out. Flames destroy whatever is destructible; but they themselves die down with what they destroy. What is indestructible, in nature or in man, remains unchanged and incorruptible; perhaps it is even strengthened.

By now I had reached the walls of the little churchyard; and beyond it, only a few steps away, I felt the gate of the Rectory garden move under my hands.

Michael is very careful about his black-out; not a chink of light showed anywhere. It was so still that you could almost hear the earth breathe.

Suddenly a flood of music broke upon the darkness. It was Schubert's "Unfinished Symphony." I suppose the London Orchestra must have been playing it for the B.B.C.

Of all the music in the world, this is to me the nearest ecstasy.

Schubert had lived in the Hohe Warte close to where we had our home. The café he loved best, and where many of his songs were written, still stands, pear-espaliered. I have seen its white blossoms, sweet-scented in the moonlight, as he must also have seen them.

I do not know what Schubert thought when he wrote the "Unfinished Symphony" or even where he wrote it; but I have always felt it must have been born there in the spring, under those blossoms.

The Hohe Warte dips into the little village of Grinzing, where every house used to have its own vineyard running up into the hills; and each householder drank his own wine, under his orchard trees.

Schubert was too poor to buy even his food. He sold his songs for sixpence; but often the householders of Grinzing — for the sake of his music — gave him food and wine.

Schubert possessed nothing but his music. The hopes that built up the walls of the "Unfinished Symphony" ended in failure, an early death, and incredible immortality! What a contribution this man gave to a world that would not even pay enough to keep him alive!

There is in this great music such freedom, such triumph over material obstacles! How high it helps the heart to climb where his own feet faltered! What power there is in us to surpass ourselves!

The violins are drowned at first, they sing under the weight of the orchestra. But at last they rise — they come together — they beat their way forward into the light. The weight falls away from them — they are free — they soar — they make fresh creatures out of their own transparency. Such creative life there is in Love, and in nothing else!

This symphony is the most near, the most unhidden, the most released music in the world. Whatever grief broke the heart that made it, once, at least, Schubert had risen higher than the stars.

I dedicated Gillian to this music before I went back to Silver Fountains.

10th March 1941

IT is more than a month since I wrote this Diary; and I must ask myself why I have not written. Nothing that I feared has happened, nor has anything happened for which I hoped.

Freud would say, probably with truth, that I wished to forget what I have been observing. I cannot say that I have been too busy to write because one does what one wants to do, no matter how little time there is to do it in. Besides, for the first few months of this job, I was naturally still busier; and yet I wrote. Now the routine takes me along with it easily, though the work is heavy.

It was such a little thing to make me feel a thousand miles away from Gillian — to make me feel that I *wanted* to be a thousand miles away from her.

She came into the kitchen, where Caroline and I were having a chat, and gave us a look that froze us both. "You are talking to a servant!" her look said to me; and to Caroline, how much more unforgivably, "You *are* a servant!" Caroline got up, and stood smoothing down her apron; and I — I would not stand up, to pay her any homage. I was so angry I did not even take my cigarette out of my mouth. Caroline and I are friends; and both of us are servants. What else should any man be who serves a cause? But he must never be another *man's* servant, not even while he earns his bread from him. A man works for this bread; he should not be asked to give up his self-respect for it as well as working. Bread is not worth any man's self-respect. Even life is not.

In Austria we had always too many servants and we fell because of this — for among our servants were the Slavs, who have always known that they could not be servants.

Perhaps just because our country fell from too much mastership, people like myself — and there were many of us in the New

Austria that the Dictatorships strangled — based the structure of our new-born state upon social freedom. We poured out of our thin pockets money enough to build the best workmen's dwellings in the world; and we drove out of our lives the chains with which we used to bind our brothers.

Poverty still bit our heels; but we divided fairly what we still possessed. Our schools had begun to teach a new learning based upon social responsibility; and in spite of our poverty we had fewer child delinquents than in any other great city in the world.

When I came to Silver Fountains I saw only the human beings who were in it; and of them all I think the easiest for me to talk to was — Caroline.

Every afternoon Caroline and I took our coffee together, and while we drank it I told her much that was upon my mind; and she told me much that was upon hers. She was one of twelve children, all living, and all successfully employed.

Caroline herself is a skilled cook, a kind, plain, unmarried woman. Once she had a child that is dead, but she has kept her mother's heart for every child. I talk as freely to her about the human needs of the hospital as I do to Matron. Perhaps more freely because Caroline is of the class to which my patients belong. Matron is not.

It is of Caroline — not Matron — that I ask, "Why will not this woman eat?" or "Why do you think this child's temperature should rise, not every night, but once a week, to 103° — and always on a Friday?" It was Caroline who helped me to find out that the woman could not eat because there was no one to cook her husband's meals for him in Bethnal Green; and that the child's temperature went up every Friday night because his own Staff nurse was off duty upon that evening and the nurse who was on duty was less favourable to his claims.

While Gillian looked at us she stood as still as an icicle below freezing; then she gave an order to Caroline, as curtly as her father gives his orders. Afterwards she turned to me, and said, "Are you ready now to dictate those reports?"

"Go," I said as curtly, "and do whatever you choose! I also, when I am ready, shall do the work I choose!" She turned crimson, as if I had struck her; and since that day there has been an unspoken barrier between us.

After she had gone, Caroline said to me, "You shouldn't have spoke so to Miss Gillian! She's a good young lady, but she doesn't understand us! It's not in her blood to — if you know what I mean!" "What is it that she doesn't understand?" I demanded. "You or me? Or our being friends? I presume hers is the same blood as any other human being's!" "In a manner of speaking, of course it is," Caroline explained, but she did not sit down again, even while she explained, "only you know as well as I do what her mother and father are! She and Master Adrian — I'm fond of both the children — I wouldn't say they put on airs, but airs is what they have — and what they are — and you can't get away from it. Something's going on in this country that hasn't reached them yet either. I don't know what it is rightly myself, but my brother Jack says it's Russia, and we've all got to come to it; but if you'll excuse me, Doctor, I must be getting on with my work."

I left the kitchen then, but I have found myself remembering ever since then a part of a sonnet of Shakespeare's: —

> Farewell! Thou art too dear for my possessing,
> And like enough thou know'st thy estimate:
> The charter of thy worth gives thee releasing;
> My bonds in thee are all determinate.

She is too expensive then for me, this flower of the British aristocracy. But curiously enough, although I think so, I cannot be sure that those bonds *are* quite "determinate," for as the days passed Gillian relented to me, though I myself held back.

There was a moment when I touched her hand by accident and she did not draw it away; instead she lifted her fringed eyes to mine, and I read in them that tenderness a woman only shows a man when she is making herself ready for a supreme surrender. Suddenly I felt, to the depths of my being, afraid. I have known and conquered in myself the fear of death; this was a more terrible fear — it was the fear of Life. And yet I need Gillian as a man upon a raft with only the salt sea round him needs fresh water. I need her; but I dare not touch a woman who might one day remember that I was a Jew.

When I was not on duty I occupied myself with sharing out my new fortune with my fellow refugees. It is, alas! but like a drop of water, so little, when one thinks of all the Austrians over here with nothing but their bare lives and empty hands. But at least I have been able to lift some of the agony from a few of them. As manpower decreases in this country, and the crass, cruel blindness which keeps locked up friends with foes alike is a little released to meet England's needs — never, alas! in one single Democracy yet is it released for the needs of others — my countrymen will get work again; and what they must crave — work for Freedom — against Hitler. But alas! Some of us are by now too exhausted, too depressed, too long persecuted, to be able to make the best use of ourselves when the chance occurs. We need to be re-educated in courage; and for this there is no time, no money, no wisdom, since there is not enough love.

Now perhaps I come to the heaviest load upon my heart, heavier than not having had the courage to free my heart for Gillian. I am unsure if the spirit of this country is freed to fight successfully against the Nazis.

We talk here of Freedom; and thank God there is still in this dear Island freedom enough to be able to talk of it; but there is too little! Each action, each order, each plan, is checked by rigidity. Not yet has this country been awakened to the fact that it *is* a Democracy. This country does not yet belong to its People; they have too low a stake in it — too little hope that the future is to be their future, and not that of their overlords. Until this is assured them, there can be no unity; and without unity who can conquer Nazis? Hitler knows this: that is why he always appeals to the worst in his enemies; and how he has succeeded in rousing it!

Many of the rulers of this country are not bad men; one, the most important of all, is a superlatively good man, though he has a despotic streak that may mislead him; but none of them are single-minded.

The rulers of England want to fight against the Axis, but

they want to stop the turning of their own Axis! Against the Axis Powers you must move: you dare not stand still. I wake at night with the sweat on my forehead, saying to myself, "Perhaps England will move, perhaps in time there will be an awakening!" I hear overhead the light murmur, five thousand feet above me, of a lonely boy's wings; and my fists clench that he may not risk himself in vain.

When Tom Wendover comes down for his week-ends, we talk together of these things. But he does not want any change, except from War to Peace. I learn from him what, as they say here, I am up against. A benevolent, blind strength, perfectly certain of itself and absolutely uncertain of anything else. Life itself escapes such men as Tom Wendover.

During these two dark and heavy months, London has had a rest; only night after night the other great centres of the Island's industry have been harried and broken open — as an expert thief breaks open a locked safe.

Once I went up to town with Tom Wendover for two nights' holiday. One of these I spent in a Dockyard Shelter. I talked all night to one or other of the working people I found there. They do not sleep very much by night; but they work all day. That is why they are still in London, close to the target of the Docks.

The second night I spent with Tom, in his beautiful London house. They talk a great deal of equality of sacrifice in this country. It is quite true that bombs do not discriminate; but the discrimination is there; and more universal than the bombing. Tom has had severe losses. Part of his great City offices were wrecked. Incendiaries dropped on his own roof, which has been mended. His house has been on fire three times; his windows broken and the glass renewed. His life has been in constant danger; but he could, had he so wished, have gone into safety. He did not wish it; this is to his eternal honour. But the humble workers who could not go away however much they wished it, have they not too an honour, perhaps an even greater honour because it is unconscious and anonymous?

I came back to Silver Fountains chilled and sad. It is not because London has been wounded that I feel sad and chilled; but because I am afraid these cruel wounds have been in vain. To lose and learn hurts no one; but to lose and *not* to learn — that is a lasting tragedy!

How can I love Gillian when I am so unhappy and she cannot understand the cause of my unhappiness?

The pause in my heart is part of the pause I find in the War itself. But the War seems to pause because it is still being fought in patches; and if one is not in the patch itself, one feels nothing. Am I, too, making a patchwork of my life?

If the War were all the same for everybody, then we should all feel stronger; but we have not yet this strength.

Everyone in a bombed town becomes automatically a hero. Even those towns and villages close to the victims seem to gain some of this strength through sympathy. "When you see people's furniture coming along just anyhow, in the rain, being spoiled, on trucks and lorries, then you want to take in evacuees!" a woman who lived near a target area told me. But we have to see the broken furniture; as yet, there is not enough. Shocks do not carry far, not yet from one heart to another in an unbroken chain.

When I was with Tom in London I meant to go alone to the place where my friends were killed; but to my surprise Tom said to me, "I'll go with you!"

James and Eunice had thought it was a safe place they had chosen, near the Heath and with open spaces all about them. A direct hit had struck the apartment house they lived in and an oil bomb drove the flames through it. One of the outer walls still hung a blackened screen against the empty sky.

When I saw what had fallen on them, I could at any rate let Tom believe that it must have killed them at once.

Tom turned his back on the heap of rubble. "We did what we could," he added, after a pause, looking out over the untouched stretch of Greater London, "but it was no use whatever."

"All death is like that to a doctor," I told him. "Each time — with the death of each patient — it is a useless defeat. Something black has come into the picture and got the better of us. We know the direction from which it comes, but we can seldom tell whether

it will come or not. I advised James at least to stay just outside
London. Had he been down there in the heart of it, they might
still be alive!"

"No one can foresee luck," Wendover said. "They oughtn't,
Eunice and the child, to have come near the place; but, well,
they were a queer couple, very devoted. I dare say they'd
prefer to go together. It's the child's death that sticks in my
throat!"

"The child knew nothing," I reminded him. "She was not
responsible, as her parents may have felt themselves to be, in
that last moment; as we feel now, clogged with our security!
Rosemary escaped everything, except death."

"Ah — " said Tom, with a sort of grim relief, getting into his
car and preparing to drive away as quickly as possible — "what
more could you want the poor child to have to face? It doesn't
bear talking about! I stood there — on top of them — trying to get
things done for about six hours. I can only hope, as you say,
that being a pretty hefty bomb it knocked the life out of 'em
before they knew what struck 'em! A damned, messy, useless
business!"

I said no more. I had wanted to go there alone, but I was glad
now that Tom had come with me. If he hadn't, I should never
have known that he had stood there those six hours.

They were out of it, James and Eunice and the child; and
Tom and I had to go on fighting what had taken them out of it.
Their share was perhaps the easier.

14th March 1941

WHEN one does not want to be fascinated, the only way to avoid the danger is by seeing as little as possible of the Fascinator. A needle in search of a magnet is doomed. So, for the last two months, although I could not help seeing Virginia daily, I have succeeded in reducing our contacts to the open civility of the children's Ward. The hierarchy of the hospital helps me here, as in an English hospital a V.A.D. hardly comes within the scope of a doctor's notice.

If I am alone with Gillian, I am starved and dry although my heart is hers; but if I were to be alone with Virginia, I know well how quickly she would apply tinder to my dryness and send me up in flames.

I was therefore not best pleased when — while I was finishing my desk work for the evening — Gillian dashed into my room with an unusual air of speed and determination, saying, "Will you see Virginia please — here, in private? I know it is not allowed, but she's in such trouble, and — and I think you ought to see her!"

Gillian always controls herself too much, but I was aware of a trembling in her, as if she were holding on to something with an even more inflexible desire to hide it than is normal with her. She stood near the desk, and looked down at me urgently. Her colour — she has very little, although it is exceedingly clear and fresh — came and went in waves; and her eyes sparkled with a sort of angry intensity.

Whether she *wanted* me to see Virginia or not she was, I saw, quite determined that I *should* see her; and I was equally determined that I should *not!* "You know the rules of this hospital," I told her. "Nurses do not see doctors alone after hours, under this roof. If Virginia really wishes to see me, she must get special permission from Matron; or she must make some arrangement to see me to-morrow outside the hospital precincts. But if she is in trouble, why do you not help her yourself?"

"If she thinks *you* can, *I* can't!" Gillian explained with more heat than lucidity. "Anyhow, what are rules when a person's in trouble? I thought you'd see that; so did she!"

She spoke jerkily, with the quick uneven breathing of a person who is emotionally disturbed. I thought that either Virginia must be in some real danger, or else Gillian was using her friend's trouble as a sort of red herring, to confuse the scent of some deeper trouble of her own.

It was important to me to find out which was the actual fact and which the red herring.

"Well," I said consideringly, "that depends upon what Virginia's trouble is. I could imagine troubles that were greater than the need for keeping rules; but you must not forget that I am in charge of this hospital, and, although I did not make its rules, I am responsible for seeing that they are carried out. You are a person who appreciates order in your work — you must know you cannot maintain order without rules!"

"Then why did you see her — here alone — late one evening, once before?" Gillian flashed out at me. I wondered why Virginia had put this particular weapon into her champion's hands.

"I *did* know Virginia's trouble then," I answered as mildly as I could, "and I gave her a piece of advice which I have no reason whatever to suppose that she followed. The same thing might happen again if I saw her now, and I don't think it's worth breaking a rule for advice that will never be followed."

"Then you're a very poor friend!" Gillian exclaimed with a scorn I hardly thought I had deserved. I said nothing. If she thought me a poor friend, I knew no argument against it. A long silence followed. Gillian still stood above me, like an avenging Fury, but she shifted from one leg to the other as if she were not wholly satisfied with her aggressive tactics. One hand rested on my desk. She has very well-shaped and beautiful little hands, well-kept and unexaggerated by cosmetics, but I prefer looking at a hand that is open rather than at one that is clenched.

Gillian looked away from me, but I felt if I could not see the angry glittering of her eyes. "I suppose you don't want her to come," she said at last in a low uneven voice, "because this time it wouldn't be a secret! If she'd asked *herself* — instead of *my* asking you — you'd have let her come!"

"On the contrary," I said gently, because I began to believe that Gillian might be a little jealous, "now I have two reasons for seeing her, instead of one. *You* want it, and *she* wants it. But since you have every right to be here and she has not, do you not think you could tell me what her trouble is? Then we could give Virginia — after talking it over together — the advice of two friends instead of one — if it is advice that she really needs!"

"What do you mean," Gillian asked me, her eyebrows shooting up as her father's do when he is annoyed, "by 'if it's advice she really needs'?"

This put me in a corner, for I was certain the help Virginia sought was a little sympathetic drama with a male companion as an audience. I should like to have said this to Gillian, but I feared in her ferocious championship mood she would not make good use of my suggestion.

"People very seldom do need advice," I ventured to remark in a more soothing manner, "and when they need it, they even more seldom take it. I should suspect that what Virginia wants is sympathy and that, as you seem to have an even greater supply of it than I have at present, *you* are the person to whom she should take her trouble. If either of you need any more practical form of help you are right to count upon it from me; but I need not break a rule in order to find out what the trouble *is* — if you will be so kind as to tell it to me!"

"You can be more hateful than anyone I know!" Gillian burst out, withdrawing her clenched hand from the desk, and turning her back on me. "I wish Virginia *had* come herself instead of sending me!"

"Did she send you?" I asked in surprise, for I always thought Gillian had the master mind in this friendship and that Virginia was the clinging vine — although of course Virginia would not cling unless she found it a comfortable attitude. "It really interests me to know she sent you," I added, "because if she had walked

in here herself, I couldn't very well have avoided seeing her; and
if she were in any great trouble, this would surely have been the
simplest plan!"

I think Gillian would have thrown something at me if she had
not been brought up to think that physical violence is not a per-
missible retort.

"It seems Virginia made a mistake," Gillian said at last, and
looking at her back I could well imagine that she had slipped
a poker into it, "and so did I! She thought you would do what
I asked you!"

I now began to see a little daylight. The two girls were determined that I should act as Paris, and throw my apple to the one
I preferred. They wanted to settle once and for all this question
of my preference. Virginia might have other troubles; but this
was also a trouble, to them both.

But I was not Paris; and for the moment I intended to keep
any apple I possessed in my pocket. I hesitated, and then I altered
my voice. "Gillian!" I said. She turned once more towards me,
and her eyes ceased to sparkle with their hidden rage. "Do you
think Virginia is the only person who has troubles?" I asked her.
She shook her head.

"Sit down then," I pleaded, "and if you think it will do any
good to talk about what is on your mind, or on Virginia's, let us
talk about it together!"

She sat down, not far from me, and I watched with relief the
rigidity sink away from her young, resilient body.

"I suppose it's like this," she said at last, still reproachfully, but
without anger. "You know the Nurses' Ball is coming off the end
of next week? Mother's made it into a terrific affair, as I knew
she would, and personally I think it is a pity, but you *would* let
her! She has to invite Virginia, though of course she doesn't want
to — especially as Adrian will be home on leave. And now Daddy
has just telephoned he's coming too, and Virginia hasn't told
either of them anything!"

I hadn't supposed that Virginia would have told either of them
anything. My wolf dog, Luchs, when he was a puppy, had been
extremely fond of finding himself rolling down a steep bank in

our garden. He had not quite the nerve to fling himself volun-
tarily down this little precipice, so he used to creep nearer and
nearer the edge till the slope did the rest. Virginia reminded me
of Luchs. She, too, wanted the slope to take her.

"There will be trouble if Virginia does not tell Adrian," I said
reflectively, "and there will be trouble if she *does* tell him. She
must choose her trouble. She cannot avoid it because the situation itself is a false one. No woman can make two lovers happy
at the same time; but she can make them both unhappy at the
same time. In my opinion, if Virginia does not tell one of them
the truth, she runs the risk of making them both unhappy — as
well as herself, of course!"

Gillian looked at me with her pure candid gaze that fills my
heart with pleasure. "I think that is true," she said gravely. "If I
were Virginia, I should tell them both! But Virginia won't make
up her mind to tell either. I thought perhaps you could make her,
if I couldn't. After all, I'm not doing this — bothering you to
break rules, and disturbing your work — simply for Virginia's
sake, Rudi! I've got Daddy and Adrian to think about as well!"

I knew that she had, and I saw that she was thinking about
them with love and understanding. She had grown beyond her
own pain into theirs, but neither of their troubles was the reason
she had undertaken this affair.

"Yes," I said, "I know. I too think about them. But only
Virginia can act. I have not the power to make her; and I do
not want to have this power." I wondered if Gillian would understand what I meant; but the guard was down over her eyes,
and I could not guess. She went on, after a pause, as I had said
nothing, "She says she will try to tell Adrian, if she has to — but
not Father! It's funny, because in some ways she seems to be
more afraid of Adrian than of Father. I can't understand why,
because Daddy can be quite awful when he's angry, and Adrian's
only a boy! Yet it's as if she minded hurting Father more than she
minds hurting Adrian. Doesn't that make her seem fonder of him
— or is it just because he's old? If only people would make up
their minds who it is they're fond of!"

"Minds," I said, half to Gillian, and half to myself, "are not the only factors in these cases. However, I don't think Virginia is shirking telling Tom simply because he's old! After all, he's not crumbling, and wouldn't crumble if Virginia did tell him; he'd simply harden up. I'm not even sure that I think she's fonder of him. At the present moment, I'm pretty sure she's fonder of Adrian; but she's more secure with Tom; and if she tells him, she would be throwing her security away. Tom would forgive her many things, but he wouldn't forgive her for breaking the heart of his son. I think Virginia likes security better than anything else. She hasn't got enough of it in herself. That's why she needs so many of us, to give her affection and sympathy. It makes her feel safer than she feels by herself. You do not need any security from other people, Gillian. You do not even need to make me obey your wishes. You can obey your own!"

Gillian said nothing for a long while, but she did not stiffen up again as I had half feared she might. At last she said, not looking at me, "You *did* see Virginia when she wanted you to, before, even though it broke the rules!"

"What rule would you like me to break?" I asked her smilingly, "besides this one, which wouldn't do any of us any good?"

"None!" she said angrily, but perhaps not very angrily.

"That is what I should suppose," I answered her. "You don't need a rule broken for you, but if you needed it, be very sure that I would break it, I would break them all!"

Gillian turned her head away from me so that I could only see the shape of it, and the line of her throat leading up to her delicately moulded chin.

"I don't know what you mean!" she said at last. I saw that she knew very well what I had meant, so I said no more.

"I am really frightened," Gillian added after a long pause, "about Adrian — this week-end! If she doesn't tell him, oughtn't I to tell him myself?"

"To tell him is Virginia's business," I answered. "It is the fact itself that is dangerous. We might make it more dangerous by telling Adrian now; and it is possible that Virginia could make it less dangerous. But none of us can help it being dangerous. We must just be prepared to stand by if the storm breaks. The

most important thing you have already done — and in my
opinion, you have greatly improved the situation by doing it. You
made friends with your father. You are standing by Virginia, and
when Adrian comes he will find that your old relationship with
him has been restored. Now if things go wrong, they can all three
turn to you, instead of turning away from you; and they could
not do better than turn to you!"

"I do hope things won't go wrong!" Gillian said in a low voice.
"But if they do, you'll be here anyhow, Rudi!"

When a man has such a signal from the woman he loves, he
must be a stick if he fails to respond to it.

I sprang up, but before I had time to touch her, the telephone
bell rang and Sister Curtis told me one of our babies had con-
vulsions. Most people are at the mercy of their own accidents,
but doctors are at the mercy of everybody else's accidents. Still
I snatched her hand and kissed it before I hurried away to the
threatened child.

I do not know if there were restrictions at the bar because I do not drink cocktails, and was well satisfied with a glass of wine with my supper, but I noticed no one in the least drunk even towards morning. Many of the officers were gay, but one does not grudge those who give their lives the extra exhilaration of a little alcohol.

I had no intention of dancing with Virginia at all. When I had finished dancing with my many colleagues, I had arranged to seek out Gillian, who was busy doing *her* duty as the daughter of the house towards her chief guests.

Suddenly, as Virginia passed me, there was a moment's pause in the music. Virginia said to Adrian, looking at me over her shoulder, "You *must* dance with someone else sometime! Rudi will take me on now — you haven't asked me once, Rudi — for anything at all!"

I took her in my arms. It was of course a mistake for I had already seen how she danced. Once in a blue moon a man comes on a woman who can dance with the abandon of a Bacchante, the swift lightness of a swallow, the wicked rhythm of a gypsy. Virginia was such a dancer; and I was unfortunately altogether too good a partner. We were married into the music; and people stopped dancing to watch us. I had always realized that Virginia's body was not merely resilient, but trained to absolute control of physical movement. She had mastered the laws of her craft by prolonged practice so that she could create out of it fresh laws of her own. I had only to understand what Virginia was going to do next; and give her the necessary support. I understood, through some subtle alchemy of the blood, only too well. How could we stop this flying joy that penetrated into the very sources of our being? God knows how long we danced together, or how beautiful Virginia looked while dancing!

For many months I had had hardly any physical activity, or any relaxation of my over-controlled senses. Now that the chance came, I swiftly forgot everything but the fun of that terrific dancing.

I suspect that Frances finally signalled to Miss Fitchett not to put on another record. We came up against silence as abruptly as if it were a stone wall.

I saw Tom's face first; and then Adrian's. Tom looked roused, but more amused than angry. I think he had merely seen a new Virginia; and wanted to make her his. But Adrian's face made me wish I had had no feet to dance with. Poor boy, the controlled sick anger of his eyes will always haunt me! He loves Virginia with such a wild and wilful determination to possess her utterly; and the dance had shown him that she could no more be possessed than an Atlantic wave.

"You did not dance with *me* like that!" I heard him say to her. I caught her answer — bewildered a little, but soothing, as if she were addressing a sick child, "But Adrian — darling — I couldn't help dancing like that with Rudi — he's a Viennese!" I hope this was a comfort to him!

I went to look for Gillian. She stood in a doorway with behind her a row of little pink trees called fairy begonias. When I asked her to dance with me, she said, "Certainly not!" as if I had no right to touch even the surface of her world.

There is no lightness in the young of this country. If they feel at all (and they check their emotions as much as possible) they feel with the hardness of a nail hammered down into the wrong hole.

Now, even if Gillian were in love with me, she needn't have minded my dancing with a Bacchante — perhaps with a little of the abandon of a Faun to match her! Such a dance is a mere emotional cocktail. It is not a drink from the waters of life. I wanted to explain this to Gillian but one glance at her steel-set face warned me to hold my tongue. Perhaps in the far future I might be able to soften this barred and bolted expression; not now.

It was a pity, for I had waited half the night for this supreme pleasure of dancing with Gillian.

We had shared work together, sorrow together, anxieties and efforts together, but so far we had never shared the liveliness of a common secret of the blood.

"You've got to let him take it as easily as he can!" I urged the father.

To my surprise, Tom yielded. "Come inside," he said to me. "I suppose we'd better get together over this infernal mess!"

When we reached the library, he flung himself onto the nearest arm-chair with a deep sigh. He did not look at me, though he spoke in my direction. "It's all your damned fault, you know," he told me. "You and your confounded dancing stirred my blood! I brought her back here. Well, I felt I had to! God knows why — or how — the boy turned up just now. I thought everybody was in bed ages ago. Of course it's all rot about him! Virginia may pretend to herself it's serious, but there's nothing in it. Why he's little more than a child! Still, I must admit I thought he knew about us. His sister does, but he appears not to! These young people are as shrewd as an old roué half the time, and as innocent as a baby the rest! Of course I've been as careful as possible these last three years but I thought a boy of his age was bound to have spotted something. After all, both the children were Virginia's greatest friends. Get me a drink," he added, "like a good chap. I need one. I suppose it's going to be hell for the boy."

I poured him out a double whisky before I answered him. Then I said, "*Only* for the boy, Tom?"

He was silent for a long time, drinking slowly, as a man does who knows how to drink and is in no hurry. He swung his crossed leg backwards and forwards with a jerky uneven motion; and I knew that his heart was not steady under this sudden blow.

"What do you feel about her yourself?" he asked finally in a surly tone. "You danced with her. Is she the sort of girl a man of my age gives up? People talk a damned lot of nonsense about young love — but it's when you're head over heels for the *last* time that you really know what letting go of a girl would mean!"

For myself, I do not think of women as objects for letting go or holding onto — I think of them as fellow human beings with equal rights. Tom's problem was not solely whether he would give Virginia up or not. I did not know what Virginia wanted; nor did I think that Virginia herself knew what she wanted.

I thought it best simply to answer for myself. "I've never been her lover," I said at last. "Perhaps that makes it more difficult for me to see eye to eye with either of you. Naturally I regard Virginia as a most beautiful and attractive girl, but has she not a right to make her own decisions?"

"She's committed to me," Wendover said after a pause. "The boy's a minor without rights or possessions."

"He has the rights of a lover," I ventured, "whatever those rights may be."

Tom sat bolt upright and stiffened like a dog that suddenly sees what he has got to fight. "D'you mean she's taken that boy on seriously as a lover too?" he asked me in fierce astonishment.

"You ought to know your own son," I told him. "Would Adrian speak to you as he spoke to you to-night, if he had no rights? Would he have asked you that brutal question, 'Is Virginia your mistress,' in the face of the girl he adored, unless she had given him everything, and was now — by her relationship with another man — destroying the value of what she had given him?"

There was a long silence. Wendover relaxed slowly as if he no longer wanted to fight what he saw. He looked older. His leg began again its short uneasy jerking. At last he said, "D'you know for certain?"

"No," I told him, "I only know that I *am* certain."

Tom said slowly, as if talking to himself, "Well, it would account for a good deal lately that I haven't quite understood! But you don't think Virginia cares seriously, do you? I mean, even to-night? Well, I think I had a right to suppose it only a flirtation. I ought to have got a divorce and married her long ago! It was the thought of the children stopped me. I thought — till they married — both of them ought to have their own home. But these illicit relations aren't fair to a married girl who's only been unfaithful because her husband didn't know how to behave like a man. I neglected her for my work; I had to! If she'd been my wife, I think she'd have stuck to me all right, but she's been too lonely!"

"Yes," I agreed, glad to have reached a point we could agree upon, "I think she has felt cut off from everybody's life. She hasn't had any of her own; and she's felt unable to make a new one, at least without a new lover. What are you going to do about it?"

"Well," Tom said, passing his hand across his forehead with a helpless gesture that was strangely unlike himself, "what can I do about it? It's a damned sight worse than I thought — but it's still the same thing, isn't it? Adrian can't keep her, and he'll have to make up his mind to do without her."

"I think that's already made up. He won't forgive her," I told Tom. "But about Virginia: do you think that losing Adrian will make her stick to you?"

"I don't see what else she's got to stick to!" Tom said, holding out his glass for more whisky.

As I filled it up for him, I wondered if it had yet struck Tom that we neither of us knew how hard Adrian was going to take it.

20th March 1941

THE blessing of hospital life is that you can't break off from caring for sick people to indulge in private anxieties. For several hours, until my rounds and theatre work were over, I got the incidents of the dance, and even Virginia and Adrian themselves, out of my conscious mind. Neither of the two girls turned up the next morning. I wasn't surprised not to see Virginia in the children's Ward; but not to find Gillian working at her desk was somewhat unexpected. She came in at about three o'clock, looking very white and harassed.

"Rudi," she said, "no one knows where Adrian is. I've been ringing people up all the morning — without of course letting on that he's missing. But he didn't sleep in his room last night; and Dad rang up his air field just now. He hadn't gone back, and anyhow he has three days more leave."

Gillian was too much in earnest to be angry with me any more. The tie between us, even if it is only a work tie, is too strong for us not to share each other's anxieties.

"Have you seen Virginia?" I asked her. Gillian shook her head. "I rang up Michael," she added. "He hadn't seen her either, but she's in her room with the door locked. She said she didn't want anything except to be left alone."

"She would see you perhaps," I said after a pause. Gillian shook her head again, this time with more emphasis. "I'm furious," she said in her low, gentle voice that can say such astonishingly cruel things, "simply furious with her, Rudi. Couldn't you go, and find out if she knows where Adrian is?"

"No," I said, after thinking this over, "I don't think I'd better. Michael hasn't asked me to see her, and I don't think he'd understand it if she *did* see me without his asking. Besides, Virginia needs another girl just now — not another man — to stand by her."

"Why should she be stood by?" Gillian asked inexorably, her

soft brows meeting in fierce displeasure. "Hasn't she made all this trouble?"

"Well, just because she *is* chiefly responsible," I told her, "the worst of it falls on her. Even if you don't particularly *want* to spare her, she may know where Adrian is. After all, that's the point: someone *must* see her!"

"She wouldn't talk to Michael through the door," Gillian said hesitatingly. "She just said, 'Oh, leave me alone!'"

"Perhaps not," I answered, "but I think she'd talk to you!"

Neither of us said anything for a minute or two. I went on working while Gillian reduced her will to reason, not in anyone an easy process; and where the will is strong, a highly difficult one. It is to Gillian's credit that I have often watched her succeed in this struggle.

"All right," she said at last, "I'll go . . . if you can manage the work."

I went on working for another hour; then Gillian came back. She looked softer and younger. I could see that she had seen Virginia. The young are generous; and Gillian had been unable to refrain from sharing Virginia's grief. I knew too that she must have lightened it.

"She doesn't know," Gillian said quickly, "where Adrian is! She's just as worried as we are — and Rudi, I'm getting *horribly* worried! We've put Mother off till now, but we're not going to be able to go on putting her off!"

I put down my pen and took up the house telephone. Dr. Reed is a good colleague and mercifully, though it was her time off, she happened to be in. She agreed at once to be responsible for the hospital till I returned. I was going to do something that I knew Gillian wouldn't like, so I asked her to go away, and come back to me in half an hour's time. I was going to talk to my friend Caroline, the cook.

I knew that Caroline had lived in Silver Fountains for many years. She came as a kitchen-maid, and rose to be assistant cook to the French chef, who left when the War began. Caroline then became the household cook, but Frances did not like her and took the kitchen-maid with her when she went to the Dower

House, leaving Caroline to the hospital. I had the feeling that Caroline might be able to help us.

She had finished clearing up for the day and was dressed for the afternoon, so that she willingly took me into the little sitting-room that used to belong to the chef. She made me coffee because she knows I hate tea; and as I have taught her how to make it, I can enjoy drinking it. We sat down comfortably together and I smoked a cigarette.

"Are you fond of Mr. Adrian?" I asked when we had relaxed sufficiently to sink into gossip.

Caroline said that she was, particularly fond of him, all the servants were. He was less reliable than Miss Gillian, but of course he was a young gentleman, and they were fonder of him.

I said: "Caroline, he's in great trouble and no one knows where he's gone to. There was a row last night at the dance and it would be best to keep his having disappeared, and the cause of it, to ourselves. We are his friends and must stand by him. Can you tell me where you think he's likely to have gone? We've rung up his field training corps, but he isn't there."

Caroline smoothed down her apron, and poured me out a second cup of coffee. "Well — no one can be surprised, can they?" she murmured confidentially. "What I always says is, 'Married women is married women and should be left alone!' If they run about like young girls and don't look after their own nurseries, then anything can happen; and this one doesn't! She looks like a schoolgirl, and behaves accordingly! Not that she isn't nice-mannered, and even nice-hearted in a manner of speaking — none of us having anything against her, not the household staff I mean. She's downright human, being American — and I dare say that's against her too over here! The Master, he should know better at his age, and have left her alone! But the pore feller, what's 'e got 'imself? That's what you've got to look at, isn't it?"

Caroline and I looked at it together; and I tried not to be drawn too deeply into the spectacle. I was aware that everyone in the household knew of the conflict between master and mistress; and took sides upon it. Most of them were upon Tom's side; and of course they wanted to know where I stood; but when

Caroline saw that she could get nothing but a head shake out of me, she went on with her own reflections.

"Of course if you was to ask me where Master Adrian would go, if he *was* to fall out with his pa, which is only natural under the circumstances, and a dance was about bound to set them both off as we all knew, I should say it might be to his old nurse, Mrs. Curtain, Sarah Bellows that was, as likely as not! She fair worshipped that boy, took him from the month after she'd lost her own, both of 'em with the diphtheria, and 'er 'usband at sea, and not much of a 'usband when he wasn't! Drowned later on or stayed in some foreign part with another woman, I'd say, like as not! But the Master saw she'd got enough to live on after 'er Ladyship sent 'er out of the 'ouse. Jealous, if you ask me! Wouldn't be a mother 'erself, and couldn't bear for 'er children to 'ave any other! Nurse Curtain — she was all of a mother that them pore children ever had! But far and away 'er favourite was the boy! Master Adrian 'e gives 'er Christmas presents to this day that'd startle a millionaire! But 'e don't go and see 'er as regular as Miss Gillian."

I thanked Caroline, and left her. Mrs. Curtain was not on the telephone and lived fifty miles away. Gillian agreed to drive me over, but said that Adrian wouldn't dream of going there. "People in this country," she explained to me rather severely, "don't make friends with servants like you do, Rudi! We love Nannie, and always shall — but neither of us dream of telling her things about ourselves. You see, after all she left us when Adrian was nine and went to his prep school, and I was twelve then and had had a governess for years!"

"Still, he may be there," I said obstinately, "even without telling her things."

He was there. He had turned up, Mrs. Curtain told Gillian afterwards, at nine o'clock in the morning in his little sports car, still in evening dress; unshaved; unwashed; unslept; and looking like a ghost. She'd given him a hot breakfast, and by and by had persuaded him to have a good "lay down" on her bed upstairs with a hot-water bottle. He was so cold his teeth chattered; and his feet were like ice; and there he'd been ever since,

tossing about in his sleep and crying out sometimes as if someone
had hurt him. She'd been upstairs once or twice to take a look
at him.

I found him sitting on the edge of his bed, tidying. His revolver
lay on the dressing table near him, with a letter — probably the
usual farewell letter — addressed to Virginia. He wasn't going to
shoot himself till he left the cottage. There was a wood near;
and he had decided it would suit his purpose. He didn't want to
upset his old nurse, though how he was going to avoid doing so
by shooting himself, even in a wood, he didn't explain; and of
course he hadn't let her agony occur to him.

He had wanted to see her again before he went "out" because
on the whole he'd liked her better than anyone else he'd ever
known.

He didn't tell me all these things at once, but they came out
by degrees, while Gillian sat downstairs talking, she told me
afterwards, about the garden to Mrs. Curtain.

I explained to Adrian that I hadn't seen Virginia myself, but
Gillian had; and that she was fully as heartbroken as he could
wish. "If you kill yourself," I explained to him, "you a good
deal worse than kill Virginia! Whatever her mistakes may
have been, she loves you; but I suppose that is what you want
to do?"

He lifted up his head angrily at that; he had, after he'd finished
talking, put it down on his arms, to hide his tear-stained face.
"That's nonsense!" he exclaimed fiercely. "Why should I wish to
hurt her! I've written and told her: it's just that I can't bear my
life! She knows I've forgiven her — even last night I forgave her
— I saw she couldn't help it, and she explained it wasn't your fault
either. She *made* you dance like that with her! You see, she
married too young, and right out of her own line; and Father
took advantage of her being so young and so unhappy, and our
friend, Jill's and mine. Of course I'll never forgive Father! That's
one of the things I've told her! She must never speak to him
again! She promised me last night not to, and to give up everything; and look after her children."

"She's only twenty-four," I said a little acidly, "but I dare say she'll give up everything if you kill yourself. It won't make her care very much for what's left. Your mother and Gillian, too, may find it a little difficult to go on with the business of living. I should think, too, that your father — for a time at any rate — would be unable to work for the safety of his country — but I suppose you've forgotten England."

Adrian said, "What d'you mean, forgotten England?"

"Well," I said, "if my country, instead of being raped and trodden under by the Nazis, still had a fighting chance, I should choose to die defending her rather than in defending my own personal pride; if you don't want to live, there are more useful ways of dying at the moment than by committing suicide; that is merely the unkindest and most wasteful way!" I spoke the last words very slowly and deliberately, because I saw by the way he jerked his head back that he was taking them in; and didn't like them.

However, probably what saved us was the old nurse's putting the hot-water bottle in his bed, and tucking him up. I imagine by the time we'd reached the cottage, the fixity of his intention had already begun to loosen. Still, it was as well we came, for he'd written that letter to Virginia which he was going to leave for his old nurse to post.

He didn't say any more about England but he told me how sorry he was for Virginia. He couldn't marry her now. He couldn't look at her again — that was all over. She'd lied to him, and worse than lied to him — given herself away behind his back, as it were, to his father. She wasn't the same person to him any more. Her beauty was still cruel and it hurt him that she was unhappy; but he took no further interest in her. Let her do what she liked: go back to America; go to the moon; go anywhere, or to anyone, except, of course, his father. That would be too base; and quite unbearable.

Adrian had reached the gist of Hamlet's speech to his mother. Virginia, like the Queen, wasn't to get any pleasure out of her sin. I let him go on playing Hamlet, with a touch of King Arthur making a farewell speech to Queen Guinevere; and indeed from the way Adrian talked about Virginia, he might well have been her wronged husband, rather than a lover who had helped to wrong him.

It was curious how completely both father and son ignored the rights of Michael. Still, the grander Adrian felt, the more unlikely he was to take his life, so I encouraged him to be as grand as possible. Keats, like all good poets, was right when he said "Beware of Passion, that's both meek and wild." Adrian's passion was considerably less wild by now; and it was not at all meek.

When we went downstairs, we found Gillian sitting on the floor with her head on Mrs. Curtain's lap. She volunteered the information that she hadn't been crying though it might look like it.

Mrs. Curtain said that what we all wanted was a good strong cup of tea; and she proceeded to make it, accompanied somehow or other by cream, plum cake, and lavishly buttered toast. We commented upon these luxuries, and she replied, with a twinkle in her eyes, that what with cows and chickens all about the place, you couldn't help what turned up.

In spite of our own insoluble problems, we all ate a remarkably good tea. Mrs. Curtain wanted to know how her Ladyship and Miss Fitchett were; all about Caroline and the older members of the Staff; but curiously enough, though she owed him her pension, she neglected to ask after Lord Wendover. She had been told nothing; but she knew everything.

I marvelled at the strange relationship between her and her former nurslings. She waited on them hand and foot and talked to them with tender freedom. Once or twice she even scolded them — Gillian for not wearing enough clothes on a cold March day; and Adrian for using bad language, although I fancied she was used to it from him, and rather liked it.

Adrian leaned back in an arm-chair by the fire, his fine sculptured face in the repose of complete exhaustion. He looked as beautiful as he had looked in joy; and just as young. For those nine radical years of a child's initiation into life, Mrs. Curtain had ruled over him with a rod of love. She understood him inside out; and yet she never for one moment forsook what they call in this country "her place." In my country, the relationship would have been as deep, but much simpler and more open. We should have felt that our fostermother was our true mother, if she had loved us as Mrs. Curtain loved Adrian and Gillian. She would have spoken with authority of all our needs, and we should have told her everything. Mrs. Curtain gave her nurslings only her ministrations. She asked no questions but conventional ones.

When we left her, she took Adrian's hand between both of hers, and looked at him with the tears running down her cheeks; but she did not try to kiss him, or to warn him; she only smiled at him through her tears.

Gillian *did* kiss her, and thanked her for the tea; and then ran back from the gateway to the open door where the old lady stood waving, and pushing her gently inside so that she wouldn't catch cold, kissed her again.

We didn't ask Adrian where he was going. He had his own car, and went off in it, we gathered, to see some friends who lived in the neighbourhood, till his leave was up. His farewell to us was extremely cold and casual, but Gillian told me afterwards that it didn't matter and was quite all right.

I was still a little anxious about the letter to Virginia, which he'd slipped into his pocket before we went downstairs.

I explained to Gillian how I felt about it; but she said, with a kindly reassuring smile, "Well — he couldn't very well tear it up under your nose, could he? You know, Rudi, you do sometimes expect people to do such impossible things!"

10th April 1941

NEITHER Gillian nor I spoke much on the drive home. The moors swelled up all round us, a deep violet-blue. The honey-coloured air was fragrant with the scent of gorse and heather, and loud with the sound of flowing waters.

When we reached the Rectory Gillian went straight upstairs to Virginia, and I telephoned in Michael's study; first to Frances and then to Tom Wendover. I told Frances little or nothing; and left her annoyed, but without anxiety. I told Tom everything. He listened without comment, and when I had finished the silence was so long that I nearly laid down the receiver, thinking he had gone away.

"Well — " he said at last, rather as if he were speaking to an accommodating tradesman — "I'm sure I'm much obliged to you."

I walked about the room after those two abortive communications, studying the craftsmanship of my shock patients in their new setting.

I liked the room: it was simple and austere and suitable for its new purpose. Quite contrary to my expectations, Michael had succeeded in drawing fear out of their shaking hands and panic-invaded minds.

I found myself wondering what he had put into them instead. There must be something in his trained spirit stronger than sacerdotal vanity, or he could not have reached them. Suddenly I found he was in the same room with me. He switched on the light, and I saw that he looked like a man in the sudden grip of a mortal illness.

"Could you spare me a few minutes' talk?" he asked quietly. I said I was only too pleased, and he knelt down in front of the fire and lit it. I had not noticed how cold the room was, before. He pushed forward an arm-chair for me, and took one opposite.

"I must ask you," he said in his low controlled voice, "what happened last night — at that dance! You see, I don't know anything. I can't ask my wife — she hasn't let me into her room! Nor can I ask Gillian, since what happened may concern her brother. I beg of you to tell me." He had not said why he had not asked Tom Wendover.

"I think," I said after a careful pause, "that what happened was in the nature of a final parting between Virginia and Adrian. Whatever their relationship was, I think you may take it that it is now over."

There was a long silence between us.

I have never known a man who had such complete physical control as Michael Esdaile. Whether he felt anger, self-pity, or relief, he revealed nothing by either movement or expression. At last he said, "Some time ago you spoke of this matter to me. I did not know you then; I felt, forgive me, a certain hostility to you, as a man who did not share what I believed. Now we have worked together, and I have talked with the patients about you, and I feel in a queer way that we *do* share something fundamental. Do you know what it is?"

I hesitated for a moment. He was asking me a question that had been often in my own mind. "Perhaps," I said, "our aim for our patients is the same, though we may reach it from a different starting point. We both believe in personal responsibility; and we try to rouse and increase this sense in our patients."

"Yes," Michael objected with a slight frown, "but why should you hold each person so responsible for his actions, since you are not a professing Christian?"

"I am not a Christian at all, in any dogmatic sense," I agreed, "any more than I am a Confucian, though I find much to believe and act upon in the sayings of Confucius. Probably, however, we both believe that to admit the truth of any creed is to put it — or try to put it — into practice — otherwise we do not believe it. You, as a Christian, believe the admirable sayings of Jesus, for instance, and you act upon them. To you He is God; to me He is not God, but as I also try to put His admirable words into actions, both of us become equally responsible for what we accept as true. I doubt if I have accepted nearly as much as you have accepted; but all my life I have been busy trying to find out what is true."

"Yours is a curious dialectic," Michael said uneasily. "I am sure about most questions we should find ourselves deeply at variance, but I admit that we *are* directly responsible for carrying out what we believe to be true."

"Perhaps there is not so great a difference between us," I said, looking at his worn and troubled face. "Only no doubt you have a much more exacting standard than mine. Also you have a master— and I am conscious of no power other than the laws of nature. The laws of nature, I admit, are very exacting sometimes, but we can get away from them oftener perhaps than you can get away from the laws of God. It is an interesting moment, I find, when at last Scientist and Religious see quite clearly that man has to choose between being his brother's keeper and being his murderer. Time and space and all scientific thinking are upon your side, this time; they agree with the religious person that man must love his neighbour as himself, or the whole race of man must perish."

"That is a great part of the Christian religion," Michael admitted cautiously.

"It is the whole of mine," I told him, "and I find it enough."

Michael did not at once answer me. I smoked a cigarette through before he spoke again.

"I could not live without God," he said then, slowly and without taking his eyes from the fire, where the flames had reached the core of the coal and burned it scarlet. And I believed him; but I waited for him to say more, for it was necessary to talk about Virginia, and I have never found it necessary to talk about God.

Suddenly he turned his head and met my eyes, with the sincerity that is his greatest virtue.

"I do not know," he said simply, "what happened at that dance. In fact there is very little that I *do* know about my wife at present."

"What is it that you want to know?" I asked him cautiously,

for I did not wish to seem impertinent to him, and to have access
to more facts about his wife than he had was a kind of imper-
tinence.

"I want to know what their relationship really is," Michael
asked me relentlessly.

"*Exactly* what the relationship between Adrian and your wife
is," I replied, "I cannot tell you! But I presume it to be a serious
business."

"Yes," he said with a long curious sigh that was neither impatience nor relief, "I know she thought it serious — but was
this folly about Adrian all? And why is it over? There is surely
something behind it — and behind this parting. It is this something that I want you to tell me! There is nothing on earth so
terrible as a fooled suspense! How can I help her if I do not
know the truth?"

I wonder how much one can help any other human being,
even if one knows the truth, unless one trusts them? I could not
exactly say to Michael, "As long as you are looking at Virginia
from above to below you will be of no use to her. Go and be
unfaithful to her if you can't find any other way of feeling yourself to be equally in the wrong!"

"The barrier between you," I asked tentatively, "it is not a
recent one, is it? Would you mind telling me what caused it?"

"The cause was the same," he said in a voice so low I could
hardly catch his words. "She was unfaithful to me. We had
been married only three years."

"About this suspicion of yours," I said consideringly, "Virginia
has herself spoken to me. I should say that I believe her when
she tells me that the flirtation you objected to at that time was
not a serious one. I mean that I believe that she was physically
faithful to you when you thought that she was not."

I lit a cigarette, and watched the flames redden into the heart
of the coal. I smoked it through before Michael spoke again.
"Perhaps by faithfulness we mean different things," he said at
last. "I thought that Virginia meant the same thing as I did. I
cannot divide the senses and the soul!"

"I am bound to tell you," I replied, "that I think you made

life too hard for Virginia. You forgot — if you ever knew — her background in her own country. It was built up on devoted swains, a variety of them, but the procession was continuous and started in her earliest childhood. I am sure that she wanted to be all that you thought and believed her to be. Perhaps she wanted it too much! Perhaps what you asked was impossible! At any rate, she failed. What was she to do when she saw that she had failed? She took the only way she knew of remedying her faltering self-esteem: she found fresh adorers. I am not defending the way she took. She imagined that as a wife and mother she could play that card-sharper's trick of winning hearts without losing her own. This is not a very honest game, even when one is without other obligations; but *with* them, it is still less workable. Believe me, she has found no satisfaction in it!"

"She had my whole heart," Michael said in his low, unexaggerated voice. "She knew that she had it. How could I help it if she preferred inconstancy?"

"She was a stranger in a strange land," I urged upon him. "She needed a great deal of confidence, and she could not find it either in herself or in her husband."

"She did not look for this confidence in the right place," Michael told me, "nor did she contribute to it! She believed in God. Could she not have found her confidence there? Had she done so, she would have needed nothing outside her normal life. After all, what other safeguards does a woman need? A devoted husband, a home, her children — she had them all!"

"I do not know anything about God," I told him, "beyond of course what I find in human beings who are, I believe, supposed to represent Him to each other. Where Virginia looked for trust was where all women look for it, in the heart of her lover. You ceased to be her lover when you ceased to trust her. She therefore found another man who *did* trust her."

Michael got up and began walking up and down the room behind me. "I suppose I am right in thinking," he said at last, "that she looked for it in Tom Wendover."

So he knew at last! Perhaps he had only just guessed it; perhaps he had known it subconsciously all these years. A jealous man knows much; sometimes it would be better if he knew all and therefore realized how little there was to know; but sometimes what he has not admitted to himself could be true suddenly bursts upon his horrified vision and is far worse than his suspicions. I think Michael had not really known before what he knew now, and it appalled him. I said nothing. He walked slowly about the room, as a man who has gone suddenly blind feels his way among familiar things that may now hurt him.

"It's inconceivable to me," he said at last, "that a man of Tom Wendover's age, position and responsibility could be guilty of so base a betrayal of a friend's honour! I have worked for his interests; I have served the spiritual needs of his family. I thought he would have looked upon my wife as I looked upon his daughter, Gillian — as a sacred trust — almost as if she were his own child!"

"You forget," I told him, "that Tom Wendover was himself a sex-starved man, with a wife whose chief interests were elsewhere. Cannot the soul be as unfaithful as the senses? And when it is divided from them, is it not necessarily unfaithful? I do not like illicit love affairs any more than you. Both by theory and practice I am a monogamist. But to my mind, this prolonged and devoted relationship between two defrauded mates has not been a base one. If we are to speak plainly, I think it was less base than your refined and inconclusive relationship with Frances Wendover!"

I had startled and shocked him — as indeed I had intended to shock and startle him. I was myself in a nervous state and kept seeing Virginia lying stricken on her bed upstairs, motionless all day long; and then again I would feel her in my arms, dancing. There are more things than muscles and limbs that need their share of exercise; emotions need them.

"My relationship with Frances Wendover!" Michael exclaimed in astonishment. "But what madness — I have no such relationship!"

"I speak as a scientist," I explained. "I know that morally speaking, both of you are pure as lilies. But she is sterile, with all her senses misdirected into rigidities and escapes. For that I hold you partly responsible. She is not an easy-loving wife. Had she been, Tom Wendover, I am convinced, would have been an easy-loving husband, and then Virginia would not have found that particular escape."

"But even then," he said in a puzzled voice, "if Virginia's own heart was not sincere, she would have found some other escape, some different unfaithfulness!"

"It is always a little suspect," I mentioned, "when a jealous husband looks upon himself as a Hound of Heaven; and it very often brings about the thing he most dreads! But it is particularly suspect to be a Hound of Heaven to your wife while you are enjoying a Platonic friendship with another woman. Forgive me; there has been so much pain caused by so much holiness in this business that I speak perhaps too forcibly. Besides, I am thinking of Adrian, of Tom's boy, and how he nearly took his life when he found out about his father and Virginia! What you say is perfectly true. Virginia's heart was not as sincere as yours, or nearly as hard!"

"Was he — was Adrian — also her lover?" Michael demanded fiercely, ignoring my accusation.

"Not now, he isn't," I told him. "He's on your side all right, though a little late in the day. He's shocked to death too, quite literally to death, by the failure of Virginia to wait to be unfaithful till he grew up!"

"You speak with cruel irony," Michael said, after a long pause; not without justification, for I felt ironic. "To you it is evident there is no such thing as sin! Even if Adrian has come to realize it is too late to save either Virginia or myself, if he has saved his own soul, I can still rejoice!"

"Well, I'm glad you can rejoice," I replied. "You certainly have all the facts before you now, as far as I myself know them."

Michael stiffened and stopped short. "By Heaven — " he said, with fierce but controlled passion — "you may know the facts, but the truth has escaped you! You can't get rid of me and my religion so easily. Nor can Virginia. This religion was also hers — she loved God — she believed in His love! She made her vows beside me at the altar. It is this that she has thrown away. You do not know what she was to me; and, I still believe, what I was to her. Why I loved Virginia only less than God!"

I turned my head and saw him standing as if he were made out of stone, with his hands clenched at his side. I was silent because I thought that perhaps he was praying. Besides, what could I say? To love Virginia less than something neither of them had ever seen or knew anything about was, from my point of view, ridiculous.

"Do you suppose that boy who tried to take his life — or who would have taken it if you had not stopped him — cared for her as I care?" he burst out again. "I who have lived under the same roof with her for these three years and *not* been her lover?"

"Well, you see," I said cautiously, "we come back to this question of responsibility, the tie that binds us together. You are more responsible than Adrian; therefore you dare not put upon him a weight that you have trained yourself to bear! Why should we suppose that morals need less training than athletics? They do not; they need more, because they are more fundamental, and we need them until we die, whereas the use of athletics is practically over at forty, if not before. You are an athlete in the spiritual world; Adrian has hardly left the nursery slopes upon which skiers in my country practise their first turns. What I venture to suggest is that you have expected, and exacted, from these two young — and presumably pampered — children the virtues of a muscle-trained saint."

Michael's fierceness lessened. He even came back to his armchair and sank back into it, as if something in him had freed itself.

"Do not think," he said quietly, "that I shall be sorry if you take from Virginia part of the burden for what has happened."

"I am no man's judge," I answered, "but I think where the intimacy is as great as that between husband and wife — there should be — perhaps there must be — some interchange of responsibility. You married a very young and untried girl; have you not perhaps asked rather too much of her? And even of yourself? It may have been hard for Virginia to share you with God; but it was, if I may say so, impossible for you to behave with kindness to her while you did not treat her as a lover."

I saw his flushed face turn white, as if something had hurt him to the heart; and for a while I think that he forgot me altogether — and forgot himself. He was thinking only of Virginia, and of what he had made her suffer.

I too thought of her. I heard Gillian come downstairs, but I did not think it right to leave Michael to join her, and after she had paused for a moment in the hall to listen to our voices, she went home alone.

"Will you go up and speak to her," Michael said, at last, in a low voice. "She will not let me in."

"Shall I tell her that you now know everything?" I asked him.

He hesitated for a moment, then he said, "Yes — tell her!" and as I still paused at the door to see if he wished to give me any further message, he said, trying to smile, "Do you believe, Dr. Ritterhaus, that to understand everything is to forgive everything?"

"Perhaps," I said, "but it would be equally wise to say, if we said it of ourselves only, 'To understand everything is to forgive nothing.'"

Michael stood up and came to the door with me. "That is Virginia's room at the top of the stairs," he pointed out to me. He laid his hand upon my shoulder before he let me go. "Perhaps that is the safest plan," he said to me.

12th April 1941

I FOUND Virginia lying face downwards on her bed in the dark. Gillian had fetched a hot-water bottle for her feet and covered her with a rug, but the hand I took between my own was still ice-cold.

"Rudi," Virginia murmured, "it is Rudi?" For I had not even knocked, I had gone straight in.

"Adrian isn't dead," I whispered, bending over her, "and he won't now try to be! These cruel partings — you may not believe it, Virginia, but they pass. They are not the end of us: they are only the end of themselves."

"Yes, but Rudi, he loved me," she whispered, "and now he doesn't, he can't, never any more!"

Poor child, she was defeated! As she lay there trapped in her great beauty my heart ached for her. She was in the first flush of a young triumphant love. It had been no mere chance physical contact between these two young people — such contacts are as light and featureless as summer gnats coupling in the air — they do not alter the structure of the heart. But Virginia's love was as real as Virginia herself; perhaps it was herself that had escaped so gaily, so precipitously, so generously into the clear fresh senses of a young boy. Each had truly belonged to the other and felt themselves glorified by their supreme contact with each other. But it was a love born of an idea to escape, and against the law of human obligation; such loves are always tragedies. Hamlet cannot enjoy the innocent Ophelia because he has set himself to slay his mother's lover. Othello possesses Desdemona as a loved object, without the respect due to another human being, and so he throws "a pearl away richer than all his tribe."

Lear will not take sane love and so beats himself against insane hate. Macbeth kills his own loyalty; but cannot remain a king after he has killed it.

Virginia was in the throes of just such an ultimate disaster. In a sense she would never get over Adrian, although I do not think she loved him as she might have loved Michael — if he had taught her how.

I knelt down beside her. "He's very young," I said. "He doesn't know yet how despicably we all act sometimes; you have something to be sorry for, but so has he!"

"Oh, no!" she whispered. "He didn't know; I'd never told him about Tom!"

"He knew about Michael," I reminded her, "and the children."

"But Michael," Virginia said, "he didn't seem to count. Michael's so long ago!"

"I know," I admitted. "When you leap into a cataract you can't remember the ground you stood on before you leapt; but it is still there, and you may still climb out of the torrent, and onto that safe ground again."

She did not say anything.

I went over to the window and drew aside the curtains, to let the fresh spring evening touch her, with its chill sweetness. In spite of her reddened eyelids, crumpled dance clothes and colourless cheeks, so white against the one scarlet sleeve, which fell away from them, Virginia was still beautiful.

"Michael must know something is wrong," she said after a pause. "I wouldn't let him in."

"He knows everything," I told her quietly, "and of course it is better that he should. He is a strong man, and doesn't like cobwebs. Now he knows — and is thinking about it, and will understand."

"But — but — " she said, looking distraught and appalled, like a bewildered Rhine maiden looking for her lost gold — "but — he'll never forgive me, Rudi, not if he knows about Tom!"

"At present," I said, "he is not thinking about forgiving you. He's trying to forgive himself. But he won't succeed. As for you, you think now that being despised by Adrian, who has no great right to despise you, is worse than being dead, but it isn't, not while Michael is alone, and needs you."

"But Michael doesn't need me," she whispered. "He has God."

"Well, he's perhaps beginning to realize that you and God are not so different after all," I said, laughing a little. "We only have God's creatures to know Him by — how do we know that if we fail them, we do not fail Him? Perhaps there is no other way of failing Him than by failing them!"

"But he can't respect me," she whispered with a tortured look at me. "No one can respect me after Tom! You don't know everything, Rudi: it's far worse than you think. You say 'my children,' and so they are both mine, but not both Michael's! He can't know Jock's Tom's — but I think he thinks — he isn't his!"

"That I have always known," I said reassuringly, "and I always respect women more for having children than for *not* having them, even though it would be simpler no doubt if they were all their husband's children. Now I am going downstairs to get some hot broth for you. Lie down again till I come back, and remember there are still things to live for: the Nazis are not here; the Channel ports are open; your house is not bombed; your children are alive; you are twenty-four and very beautiful, and you have a husband who can learn! Very few wives are so fortunate; for I must admit husbands as a rule cannot learn either from their wives or about them! After all, Adrian was a most difficult young man, and one who would require a great deal of any woman, in the long run more perhaps than you could have given him. He was *really* a problem!"

"Oh, Rudi," Virginia said, with a rueful laugh, "how you go on about problems — he was the man I loved!"

She, too, said "was" I noticed.

"Yes," I said, "and so were Michael and Tom once men you loved, and you survived them. Believe me you can survive many more lovers. And now I shall fetch the broth." I believe she laughed aloud as I left her.

Virginia is like that! She is a flying Mercury carrying her swift heart between Hell and Heaven. She is contact-making — dynamic and made for love.

It is true that her heart is sick, but where there is laughter there is always more health than sickness.

She has lain on that bed for more than twelve hours, without food, trying to die against her youth — but she could not — her youth was too gallant and too strong for her vanity to subdue it. She has lived.

The house helpers were both out, and Michael came with me into the kitchen, to make the broth; but he allowed me to take it up to her.

"She is very unhappy," I told him, "but perhaps it is better to let her be unhappy for a little while longer. You see, she feels ashamed."

Michael stood at the bottom of the stairs while I went up. "Tell her," he said in a low voice, as I took the tray from him, "tell her I, too, feel ashamed."

19th April 1941

I HAD a disquieting talk with Barrow to-day. He said he and Datchett, the surgeon, were both very disturbed over the state of unpreparedness in Plymouth. There are neither enough, nor sufficiently strong, shelters; there are not enough fire watchers, and many of them are untrained; one man often holds two or three official jobs, so that if he fall out in an emergency there would be no one who could, at a moment's notice, take his place. There is a bad division of power between Town people and naval control; between the benevolence of the great and the needs of the poor — who are powerless to express them.

There are altogether too many unevacuated children, hospitals, maternity homes and helpless people in exposed positions.

I can't imagine Barrow rattled, nor was he rattled, but he was decidedly gloomy. "If somebody or other," he told me, "isn't prepared for this God-Almighty smash due to us, we shall get it in the neck. I'm tired of hearing about people in bombed cities 'taking it' when a little common sense, foresight and intelligent preparation could at least prevent their having to 'take it' in an overwhelming and panic-driven manner. If it comes to us, as it did to Bristol, we're bound to be knocked to bits.

"The Fire Service has never been brought up to the needs of the attack it's liable to have to meet. We ought to have the assistance of London firemen to help in directing all our coastal Fire Defences, and all our engines and material inspected regularly and brought up to date. Fire service should be standardized so that it can be used equally well anywhere. Perhaps it's been done already, but they're so hush-hush about what elementary steps they have taken, or mean to take, in defence of dangers created by — and therefore presumably known to — the enemy, that none of the general public has the least idea how safe or how unsafe it's likely to find itself. That's why we can't get evacuation taken seriously. That's what I came over to see you and Wendover about. Datchett and I sleep in the town now, and naturally the hospital people consult us as to where they'd better send their cases. Bodmin will do what it can for us, and we have a general arrangement for what's possible in the neighbourhood. We rely mainly on Tavistock; but you know what it'll be like, with the moors round us, and not knowing what roads we can use, or as far as that goes, what roads will be usable. I'd like to reckon on a possible two hundred beds here, if you thought you could run to it? Datchett and I could, I suppose, if we're alive, get as far as this to give you a hand with them. We've both got motor-cycles in one garage and our cars in another."

"We could let you have a hundred beds," I told him, "and I suppose we could jam another hundred into the passages and halls if we could get camp-beds. Fortunately, Wendover's still here. He goes up to-morrow. We'll ask him what he'll do for us. Does the Navy think you're going to cop it?"

"Well, they won't say what they think," Barrow told me, "but they're beginning to give advice . . . canvas water tanks in the main streets in case the reservoir — put up on a height where it can get the first bomb — *does* get it. Unfortunately the Navy's advice is too like 'instructions' and the Town authorities don't like it. It's a pity nobody but a few lowdown crawlers like us study human nature! If people weren't so brisk when they give advice, a good deal more *would* get done by the people who aren't going to do it! The officials of Plymouth are mostly what is known as 'hard-headed business men.' That means self-willed old tartars, who've got their way so far by looking after their own pockets. Who is going to prove to them *now* that this isn't the way to deal with what's dropping down on them, *and* their pockets, from the skies? They've *employed* experts, but they don't listen to 'em! Of course we've got half a dozen first-rate fellows working their hearts out to get things ready. Tennyson may be right when he said 'Kind hearts are more than coronets,' but when it comes to getting things done in this little Island, give me coronets — or what can buy them up — every time!"

I rang across to Tom, who was alone in his old quarters. He was, as I expected, irritable. I knew that Virginia had refused to see him since the dance; and for some reason or other, he thought this was my fault. However, he agreed to come to my office, although he wanted to know through the telephone, with Barrow beside me, why Barrow hadn't come direct to him. If he'd got cold feet. And why he hadn't taken his problems to the proper local authorities. At the moment, I felt rather tired of Tom and all he stood for, so I answered him pretty curtly. I said Barrow had come to see me because he was my friend, that he hadn't got cold feet, but *had* got common sense; and that the local authorities were themselves the problem. Then I rang off; and in five minutes Tom was with us.

"What's all this about Plymouth defences?" he asked Barrow in his bright, blustering way. "Haven't you got the Navy on your front doorstep — let alone the Bellinghams and the Ashendens, and other local johnnies, to look after you? Laboratory's got enough sand to put out incendiaries, hasn't it?"

I suppose Tom *had* to talk like this to a man to whom he paid a thousand a year; and I suppose Barrow had to look dry and disgusted while he was taking it. Tom knew nothing about the Laboratory; he didn't even know, or if he knew, he'd forgotten, what sort of an explosion a direct hit on an X.R. plant would be certain — not likely, but *certain* — to cause to anything in its near neighbourhood. All Barrow's life was based on ascertained knowledge, and all Tom's on a sort of triumphant juggling with forces about which he only knew that he was in control of them; and therefore needn't understand them.

Barrow said wearily after a long pause, "All the sand at the bottom of the sea won't be much use, you know, if the Laboratory gets a direct hit — but let it take its chance! What I've come to consult you and Ritterhaus about is the hospitals. Datchett and I are pretty uneasy about the hospitals. We want to know how we can dispose of our worst cases quickest, if we have to. We haven't got nearly enough ambulances, either."

"Well, ambulances," Tom said reflectively, "they're expensive things, you know, Barrow, especially in war-time!"

"Oh, yes," said Barrow with deepening exasperation, "and human lives are cheap, I know, especially in war-time!"

"Well, it won't do to take a sentimental view of things," Tom reminded us.

As he spoke, the siren started up. Silver Fountains is a very silent place. Beyond the occasional hoot of an owl, or the wind in the trees, there are no night sounds, so that the siren churning the air up and down in its curious, uneasy, awakening manner has its full effect upon human nerves and ears. We all three stopped talking until the last banshee wail died out upon the air.

"I suppose you may have heard," Barrow then said quietly, "what happened the other night. We won't say where — we won't say to what; but it's possible that you, Wendover, were told. I know you are chief Air Raid Warden of your district; if so, you realize what damage befell us, and what assets had to be written off our national defences."

He spoke with bitter gravity, and I noticed Wendover lost his jaunty air. I had of course as an alien been told nothing, though I knew there had been a Raid over the coastal district of more than usual length and severity.

Wendover said, after a long pause, "Each side gets such losses in war-time. We've been extraordinarily lucky so far. I admit what happened the other night was extremely unfortunate. It couldn't have been foreseen, or as far as that goes, avoided. Naturally I was told; I didn't know *you* were."

"Doctors," Barrow observed dryly, "are sometimes necessary when such disasters take place. I happened to live the nearest to the scene, and I know exactly what the destruction was; and it convinced me, Wendover — that is why I am here to-night — that Plymouth itself will get the next knock.

"Remember it's a smaller city than Bristol, and if I may say so, it is psychologically far less sound. Bristol is a great city, with old traditions of self-help. Such places can stand up to almost any disaster. Bristol — when hit — *did* take care of itself, or what was left of itself; but can a city that has always been taken care of take the right precautions in time? We have the added drawback, too, of living under a dual authority."

"The Bellinghams are the best people in the world," Tom said stoutly. "They'll stick to Plymouth, both of 'em, with their fur flying!"

"But not even *their* fur flying will save Plymouth," Barrow told him patiently. "There are things the 'Best People' can't do; don't know how to do; and won't know ought to *be* done! Cities must depend upon their citizens. Their chosen officials should be their backbone. Rich fairy god-parents scattering largesse from the skies won't amount to much when the Germans start scattering *their* largesse from the skies! You don't know it yet, Wendover, but the age of transformable Pumpkins is definitely over."

"What do you want me to do then?" Wendover demanded rather sulkily, swaying his foot about as he always did in a quandary. "I've got to go up to town to-morrow. I don't live in Plymouth. My job's in London."

This action of Tom's with his foot interested me, because I believe that it is symbolical of his attitude towards life. His emotional and intellectual powers are equally uncertain. Behind his air of mastery and prompt decision, I believe there lurks complete uncertainty. He literally does not know where to put his foot down.

"I think we must have some more ambulances," I put in, "and if you could order a hundred camp-beds, and get them here as quickly as possible, it would be wise. Also, I should like to give you a list of extra things, bandages and instruments, which may be necessary. And I dare say Matron would like to add her own list of household needs to mine."

The noise of planes and anti-aircraft fire had increased. I knew Tom's chief gamekeeper was acting as his deputy, but I was not surprised to see him become restless; and finally he took up the telephone. I signalled to Barrow that we had better leave him for a few minutes.

We went through the children's Ward and reassured the Night Sister that the Raid was a long way off; then I took Barrow back to Tom's room to await him.

He joined us in a few minutes looking graver than he had looked before, but also, I thought, more accommodating.

"Make out your lists," he said to me, "and I'll come in and O.K. them before I leave to-morrow. They won't let me control more than a dozen ambulances, on the off-chance of a big Raid, but I'll see what I can do about getting another eight. The beds I'll send down, and what stores you and Matron need. Fortunately I've been saving petrol for at least two years. What about drivers? They won't leave me the extra men."

"We can raise six drivers from the hospital Staff," I told him, "and I suppose you can provide the other six from your own people on the premises?"

Tom nodded. "I got onto the Bellinghams," he added a little shamefacedly. "I don't think there's anything serious doing to-night really. They're fully prepared, of course — as I knew they would be — splendid people — absolute liaison with the Navy and Town officials — ready for all emergencies. Of course, I quite agree with you fellows; there may be a big Raid any time now; but mind you, no one can say our anti-aircraft gunnery is less than first-rate; and — and under the circumstances, our defences, I'm sure, are more than adequate for what we may have to face. I can't help thinking you two, no offence meant, mind you, but, well, are taking rather too gloomy a view of the possibilities! Doesn't do at a time like the present, you know, not to keep our heads!"

"The occasion for losing them has not yet arisen," Barrow dryly reminded him. "Failure to keep our heads might very well take place in a catastrophe when there was nothing handy to meet the catastrophe *with!* Did you ask the Bellinghams, when you were onto them just now, whether experts who had had experience in big Raids are satisfied with our fire defences, and think that we have sufficient and adequately trained fire watchers?"

"That," Tom reminded him, with an air of slight rebuke, "would be interfering with what isn't our business, wouldn't it?"

Britain — I thought to myself — how she clings — magnificently — idiotically — to her own formulas! How like the British are to the ancient Romans! Dying gladiators — every man of them! "He who is about to die salutes you" they cry in turn. They won't leave it out; not even when the salute itself, and the time it wastes, costs them their lives. Whose business is the fire defence of any city? Everyone's, surely, who has a home to burn, or a life to save. Is *no one* to be made responsible except those whose interest it would be to hide what they hadn't done?

"The gas main is very old-fashioned," Barrow said, after a prolonged, uneasy pause. "It was never made of sound material: too cheap. I doubt if it will stand another bad jolt. It's being run on very low pressure still, after the last hit."

"Well, we must put up with this sort of thing in war-time," Wendover told us still more reprovingly. "It is just one of our necessary hardships! The Germans no doubt suffer worse still; but I doubt if *they* complain."

"We haven't the advantage of concentration camps over here," Barrow said in his measured unemotional voice, "to put the complainers in; so we still make complaints; but do not be uneasy, they're not listened to, Lord Wendover! Poor people are dependent on gas, and might become restive if it was completely denied them by enemy action. What do you suppose would happen at Plymouth, for instance, where there are a good many poor people, if our main got knocked out beyond repair next time and they had to live without gas to cook with till the end of the war?"

"My dear fellow," said Tom, with an air of shocked incredulity, "you really mustn't let your imagination run away with you!"

I am extremely fond of Tom, but this was too much for me, and I said rather sharply, "Look here, Tom, we don't either of us want to be nasty, but we are scientists and we are producing facts for your serious attention. It is quite true that by the use of *your* imagination you can escape thinking of what's going to happen to a city without gas, without water, without electricity, without transport — possibly without food or houses; but in actuality, the only possible escape is in having made some kind of provision beforehand to meet these needs. It is therefore in the present instance *you* who are being too imaginative."

"But I thought I'd just told you," Tom protested, "that the Bellinghams have been, with the Plymouth officials of course, making all possible arrangements. They're in constant touch with the Navy too. Plymouth hasn't really anything to do with me. I can't keep butting in like this!"

Barrow and I exchanged glances. If a man adds irresponsibility to his lack of expert knowledge, there is very little that can be done with him. He's no longer an asset in danger, but a burden. Even in prospective danger he is a burden. Tom remained in a position of power and could use it, but how could we persuade him to use it in the right direction? This was our problem — and indeed, it is Britain's problem; and it remains insoluble.

Barrow took the drink Tom remembered to remind me to offer him, and drank a double whisky himself; then he rather wisely left us to ourselves.

"Perhaps we've done the best we can," Barrow said encouragingly after he'd listened to Tom's footsteps dying away. "Thank you for your support. I doubt if an Englishman in your position would have cared to say so much to Tom. You see he pays us both."

"Well, he's a good fellow," I said tolerantly. "He won't bear either of us any grudge for speaking plainly to him. He simply — well, I suppose we've both got to face it — won't do more than he feels good form suggests; and that won't be enough because we're not dealing with 'good form' upon the other side — we're dealing with the Nazis."

Barrow got up stiffly, and walked up and down the room, his shoulders hunched and his hands in his pockets. He is a lean, long, parched fellow, and looks much leaner and more parched than when I first met him. I like him for the funny little twinkle that comes and goes in his colourless grey eyes; and for his fundamental qualities beneath the twinkle.

"I can't get my wife to leave me," he said abruptly, with the uncontrollable pride of a man in the woman he loves. "Poor girl, she believes she has a right to make me as uncomfortable as possible. All she'll do to meet me half-way is to send our two children to my mother's in the Midlands. We've done that, thank

God, a week ago. We have one of those reassuring Anderson shelters in our bit of garden, double exit, blastproof doorway, oil stove inside — all the right gadgets . . . unless it happens to be hit. I think I'll be getting back to her now, Ritterhaus, if you don't mind. One has a curiously homing instinct after an Alert nowadays, hasn't one? Funny world we're living in, isn't it? After it's blown up a bit more, p'raps we shall find out what it's made of, and who it really belongs to! Good night!"

I shook hands with him, and I suppose I ought to have gone straight to bed, but I wasn't quite happy about one of our babies, a pneumonia and shock case sent in from the coast; I thought I'd sit up with the little fellow a bit, especially if he was awake and frightened.

While I was just making up my mind to go to him, Gillian knocked at the door. She was smiling a little as she came in, and did not ask me with her usual over-polite docility if she was interrupting me. She had cocoa on a tray, with two cups. "It's too late for Dr. Barrow," she told me, "so it will do for you and me. What did you say to make Dad so furious?"

"I told him he was imaginative," I replied.

"What was he being imaginative about?" Gillian asked me with a chuckle.

"All the Invisible Airy Nothings the British think are coming to their rescue," I explained, "while they content themselves with whistling for them! It *is* imagination, you know, to expect rescue or to fancy that whistling is an adequate provision for the Day of Judgment. Tom doesn't know what to prepare *for* — he doesn't know what to prepare *with;* and why should he? He hasn't ever, I suppose, *had* to prepare for anything, by any efforts of his own, in his whole substantial life!"

"Now I suppose you feel better!" Gillian said, handing me my cup of cocoa. I took it gratefully, but I couldn't help wondering what sort of shelter Klara and Andreas had got against the R.A.F. It had come into my head while Barrow began talking about the wife who wouldn't leave him. It is curious that we cannot always get rid of our responsibilities when they have gone beyond our powers.

"You're rather down on poor old Dad to-night," Gillian sug-

gested, "aren't you? I thought he'd been behaving rather hand-
somely for him, *not* having much of a row with Mother over the
dance. He hated it, you know, and it cost an awful lot. And he's
been steering clear of Virginia — and getting heaps of things he
doesn't think we need, for the hospital, and yet he doesn't stop
us having them!"

"In many ways your father is a paragon," I told her, "and of
course I like him; but I don't like what he stands for: the Humpty-
dumpties of English life. I don't belong to 'All the King's Horses
and all the King's Men' who are on his side. Once he's knocked
over, and he will *be* knocked over, you won't find *me* trying to
help Humpty-dumpty climb onto his wall again. You see, I just
don't happen to believe in walls or in Humpty-dumpties either.
But I'll drink to one of the last and best of the Humpty-dumpties
in cocoa with you, if you like! I suppose if we want drivers for
these fresh ambulances I've been asking Tom for, in case there
were to be trouble in any of the Plymouth hospitals, I've got to
let you drive one of 'em?"

"But of course," Gillian answered serenely. "You're quite
silly sometimes, Rudi. Can't I drive a car?"

"Like hell — you can!" I agreed gloomily, thinking of a road in
the process of being blitzed and Gillian on it. "And so can
Virginia," I added.

"Yes, I expect she will too," Gillian agreed with equal serenity.
"Virginia says she's quite all right now — and do you know, Rudi,
in some ways I think she's really happier for having got rid of
poor old Adrian."

"When an escape turns into a complication," I suggested,
"people are always glad to get rid of it! Of course she was desperately in love with him, while he represented something without
pain or obligation, and gave her the adoration that was very reassuring to her discouraged heart; but when the pain started up,
and obligation set in once more, and when, above all, Adrian
began to criticize and disapprove of her instead of adoring her,
well then, no doubt, she might begin to feel better for having
broken her heart. For all that, Gillian, she *was* broken-hearted!"

To my surprise, Gillian agreed with me. She nodded gravely.
"Yes," she said, "I think she was! But it's all rather funny, Rudi,

as well as sad. I thought Michael would make her go away; I
thought she'd want to; but he isn't going to make her; and
Virginia wants to stay. I think it's the hospital really! Not you
and me, though she does rather cling to us. But she actually *likes*
the work, and Michael, well, you can't tell exactly what Michael
means ever, can you, he's so good?"

"If I knew what goodness was, I might know if I think Michael
is good," I replied, "but I don't think he's a quitter, anyhow. I
mean, I'm sure he is not afraid of meeting Tom. It might far
rather be Tom who is afraid of meeting *him!* The only danger I
see arising out of his particular problem would be if your mother
should find out what has happened."

Gillian nodded again. She sat quietly for a while, sipping her
cocoa, while I applied myself to mine.

"There's the All Clear sounding!" she said at last, springing
to her feet. "I'd better go back now, but it's long after eleven so
I don't want you to see me home. If we're going to have bad
nights soon, we'd better prepare for them by a few good ones.
But, Rudi, you don't really know Father — he's not as stupid as
you sometimes think he is!"

"Perhaps he isn't," I said with a sort of released exasperation.
"Perhaps the whole British Empire isn't! But I can't help thinking
it *is,* and in a sense being thankful for it. Anything more intelligent would die of despair! How can one expect this one little
vulnerable dumping-ground of an island, this broken-open bun
for a bear, to be able to withstand the fully prepared force of
the greatest fighting Power in the world, with the skies under its
feet and all Europe in its pocket, and another murder-trained
Power equally equipped on the other side of the Pacific waiting
to come in! Good night, Gillian!"

She stood in the doorway looking back at me, with her grave
and candid gaze, so sweet, so sound, so sane, and so utterly
vulnerable.

This is the worst night I have spent in England, since I now
realize what I had never before so fully realized, both what there
is to lose in this great country, and how little care has been taken
in order to preserve it.

23rd April 1941

THE nights over Plymouth have been increasingly noisy lately. We can hear the gun fire coming up the estuary every evening with a punctual menace.

After the second warning which I got last evening privately over the telephone, I went upstairs to Stephens. I knew very well how he always felt after an Alert had sounded.

I left the door of his room open so that Gillian might signal to me if there were any further warnings.

"I didn't hear you shut the door," Stephens told me in his usual suspicious, fretful way.

"It is a warm night," I answered, "and besides, I like open doors. It is our habit in Vienna to have communicating doors between our rooms. We are a friendly people."

"Well, *we* like *our* doors shut!" Stephens said irritably. "Not that it makes much difference to me in this place, and I hear noises whether the door is shut or open. Both the other fellows are fast asleep as usual. They don't have to be in the dark all the time and wonder what waking up is for! That's the reason *I* can't sleep. I'm afraid I might forget, and then wake and find there *is* no difference between night and morning. I suppose you've heard I've quite given up that fancy of yours that I shall ever recover my sight? And as I *have* given it up, I've consented to learn Braille. If I'm to be blind for the rest of my life, I must be able to read to myself at least!"

"It will not be a waste of effort," I hastened to assure him, "for when you recover your sight, you can still teach the blind to learn Braille, and of course you will be able to teach them better than anyone who has never been unable to see."

I did not tell him so, but I felt very much encouraged by this new step forward, since I felt sure that one of his main reasons for remaining blind was his inability to loosen the force of his own driving will. He had had to loosen it in order to learn Braille since he had made up his mind, against all persuasion, *not* to learn it.

His cure depended on more than the removal of his shock symptoms. Something had to be created in him to take the place of the fear that had caused his loss of sight; and I do not believe that anything has ever been created by force, least of all by the force lurking in that profound and subtle double-crosser the human will. The only creative power I know is that of what might roughly be called "love"; not of course a sentimental love: a far more impersonal and less individual emotion. I sometimes think that migratory birds may have it for each other. They fly in the same direction, and have never been seen to interfere with each other's flights.

"There seems to be an awful lot of noise going on to-night," Stephens said nervously.

"We have some new and very powerful anti-aircraft guns on the coast, I believe," I told him. "We are well-defended. But I have been thinking there might be a serious Raid over Plymouth itself one night soon. If it should take place, they will need more doctors. I am making a few preparations, in fact, so that we might send a small contingent — just one or two nurses, and ambulances; and I think I should go myself, with them."

He became very angry. "But Doctor," he said, "you have no right to think of such a thing! Naturally you ought to take in surplus Raid cases, but you yourself ought to stick to your post — and to take our nurses — Why, I never heard of such a thing!"

"I shall only take one or two volunteers," I hastened to reassure him, "and I don't quite see it as you do. You'll all be well looked after here by Dr. Reed and young Burdock. A big Raid in a small city is apt to be disintegrating. You can't get emergency cases to hospitals quickly enough. An extra First Aid centre of a mobile kind is worth its weight in gold at such a time. But of course such a Raid may never take place. I only told you because we are friends, and I thought you might like to know, in case it happened suddenly."

"To-night, you mean?" John said in a frightened whisper.

"It might be to-night," I agreed, for I already saw Gillian standing in the doorway, and knew this meant the final warning.

I stood up and he grasped my hand – a quick strong grasp that I liked to feel, for I knew that energy was coming back to him, and without energy there can be no human miracles.

"Well," I said, "if I go, I shall rely on you to support the Staff as much as possible in my absence."

He said in a quick moved way, "You bet I will!" and then, "Good luck, Doctor – " I thought there was a note of regret in his voice, almost one of longing. Suppose that he began to desire to *meet* a danger rather than to flee from it, might not this too be a step forward in the recovery of his sight?

Plymouth had got its blitz, Gillian told me, as we hurried downstairs side by side. I saw no way to keep her off the road. I hardly wanted to, for the use of courage is a beautiful thing, and she seems made of courage.

We had arranged all that we needed earlier in the week. We had our ambulances stacked with First Aid appliances, and for ourselves, steel helmets, goggles and gas-masks, so that we were off in five minutes, Gillian driving me in the first ambulance; the others following. We picked up Michael and two of his Church workers in the village. It was not until later I knew that Virginia was also driving one of our ambulances.

The sky was lit up towards the coast, a flaming red mass, with a smoke pall blown to one side of it. We could not see the city, even when we came near, only the flames ringing it round.

It was a fine April night, the air was sweet as honey, and the sky brilliantly spaced with stars.

Fire-engines from surrounding districts were mostly on the main London and Exeter roads, so they did not hold us up. Many were there before us. They had come, hell for leather, from every part of Devon and Cornwall, to serve Plymouth, but very few of them could operate to help their sister city. Miles and miles of hose lay idle and useless all night long because it could not fit into the type of the Plymouth engines. These brave men stood cursing helplessly, with black anger in their obstructed hearts, watching the walls of flame they could have put out rise higher and higher until the city they had come to save was hidden from their sight.

We got in fairly easily ourselves by back-ways known to Gillian. Sometimes a fresh crater stopped us suddenly.

"Something dropped here!" Gillian would say to me over her shoulder before she backed out from the yawning death ahead of us.

Occasionally we had to slow up for the people pouring out towards the country. I thought them a grand crowd. Some even stopped to cheer us as we passed, or to advise us which road to take. These were, perhaps, official traffic directors, but I did not myself see them that first night. The people spread out over the moors, the roads and the fields; and why stop them? They would have been killed had they stayed where they were; and it was their business to keep alive. They were even blamed for their flight in some of the newspapers afterwards. I should have liked those who blamed them to have been on the spot those people left! They were helpless, and had they stayed where they were we should have had to try to save them. As it was, they saved themselves; and that the loss of life in this, and all the following Raids, was so small compared to what it might have been, is largely owing to the fact that the country *was* near; and that the people had the sense to walk out into it.

Our main difficulty was where to put our ambulances. I meant to get in touch with one or other of the hospitals. But several were already struck, and though I got some of the buses near enough to help in their evacuation, we decided to rig up a First Aid station in the centre of the city for ourselves, where it was most needed.

I do not say there were no competent authorities to tell us what to do or where to go; in the course of the night several spoke to us, asking who and what we were, and begging us to carry on. But there was no sense of an organization or of order. Events had, as it were, romped in like a tide against sand castles, and all forms had been washed away.

The only order I gave during the night was to the ambulances to fill up and get out.

We had plenty of light from the burning buildings, and I was aware of Sister Tutor at my elbow, handing me what I needed without my having to ask for it.

Once we organized a Raid of our own and dashed into a house on fire to bring out an extra table we needed to put our blood-transfusion tubes on. I suppose it was a sort of glorified looting, for we never found the house to put it back into again; but no one stopped us. It was as if everyone that night in Plymouth were cut off in a special hell of his own, and had to do what he could about it. Whenever I looked up I would see Michael climbing over burning rubble, or smouldering masonry, with a child in his arms, or shepherding a forlorn old lady out of some flaming shell. Once I saw him carrying a crippled girl, her crutches sticking up behind him like the grotesque wings of some early Gothic angel. The expression upon his face, too, was like that of an angel. A red-hot belief in eternal glory is probably the best antidote to human panic that there is.

But the rest of us did not share Michael's intoxicant drug. For us it was a most disgusting night.

It was difficult to get used to the variety of noises. The barrage alone shook the eardrums nearly out of our heads. No one could guess where or what was going to drop next, so there was no use paying the least attention to the noise; and personally I got used to it after the first two hours, though I could not quite get over the feeling that I was a Piccadilly Drill. I had to say pages out loud to myself of Goethe's *Faust* while I was working, just to make sure I was human. No one could overhear me, so the German language didn't matter. Two men whose names I never knew, but whose faces I came to depend upon like a brother's, helped us all night long, carrying stretchers, or bringing fresh patients, or scouting to find out where the ambulances were likely to be, for the next batch. One had to bear in mind that the cars might have had to move from any arranged spot, or even have been forcibly removed from it, by a direct hit. We ourselves had to move hurriedly more than once during the night. Nor shall I readily forget the expression on Sister Tutor's face — rather like that of a disdainful giraffe — as she picked her way over streaming gutters, carrying a lighted spirit lamp guarded in a biscuit tin, and a handful of freshly sterilized instruments on a once spotless tray. An incendiary dropped close by her, a little whirl of dangerously expanding lights, standing as high as a cat. She acted before it had time to do more than splutter. She gave it a kick a footballer might have envied, into an empty stone-yard, and an unconcerned warden, with a bagful of sand, finished it off. Sister Tutor barely glanced to see what had become of it before walking away with her spirit lamp intact, and her instruments uncontaminated.

It was no use making plans, as fresh things happened every moment. There wasn't just the damage already there to consider, but the damage there might be, in the next thirty seconds. Mortal danger and perfect security jostled each other by inches. There were no precautions you could possibly take, and after a while this became a great relief, since there was only immediate activity left for consideration.

Sometimes there were helpers, and sometimes, when you wanted them most, they were prevented from being anywhere near you.

As I finished with a patient I simply laid him on the ground, with a shot of morphia to keep him, I hoped, fairly comfortable until someone could pick him up and carry him off, to wherever the nearest ambulance or motor vehicle was stationed. Even when in his bus, he was not much better off for a time, for quite apart from his perfectly open chances of being bombed again, he might have to go four miles in a wrong direction, in order to get a quarter of a mile in the right one.

Shock cases lay before me, blue all over, with bits of their houses in their hair; choked with plaster; their hearts failing, so that one expected instant death; but after one had got the plaster out of them and pulled them about a little, they would get quietly up and walk off as if nothing whatever had happened to them. I lost count of broken limbs to be set in splints, or severed arteries to be tied up. The burns were the worst, but fortunately in the most desperate cases shock completely anæsthetizes these patients. I was terrified the morphia would run out, but it lasted like the Widow's Cruse, till morning. Every now and then Sister Tutor's

voice rose behind me, saying, "I think we need so and so . . .
I will go and fetch it," just as if she were in the theatre and had
her cupboard handy. Off she went, through God knows what
lurching walls or flying obstacles; and my mind did not set evenly
into its groove of work again until I once more heard her slightly
grating voice saying, "Here it is, Doctor!"

Nurse Amory, too, showed dauntless courage, but her white
strained face haunted me. I did not like her being so young.

The patients were no trouble at all. What with extreme shock
added to plain human grit, none of them seemed to make a
difficulty he hadn't got. I never handled easier or calmer patients.
I think by the time they had been hit, they had passed the panic
stage. When they reached me, they were at the core of human
endurance. Perhaps they felt reinforced too by the human help
that had at last reached them. Even when they died from terrible
injuries, under my eyes, they died, as it were, as considerately as
possible. I dare say this sounds nonsense; but it was a fact. The
skies had fallen upon them. Their homes were mere shells of naked
flame. The streets they had tried to escape by had turned into
caves of fire; yet there they lay, in the frail and noisy little space
we had rigged up for our dressing station, looking up at us with
their kind unconquerable eyes. Men, women and children —
those who died in Plymouth, buried, burned and broken, or
those who survived it — *how* I salute them, flesh and spirit, for
they lived or died, these nameless heroes and heroines of Britain,
without either rancour or panic!

Neither saints nor angels have ever increased my faith in this
enigma Life; but what are called "common men and women"
have increased it.

They brought me a dirty little slum child, so extensively burned
that it was impossible to save her. As I lifted her onto the table
she smiled up at me, with relentless fortitude. "I'll be all right
now!" she assured me, and died as she spoke. This child died
gloriously. She made death, as Shakespeare says of Cleopatra,
"proud to take her."

Towards dawn the Raid shifted farther away from us. Even if
a Raid is not yet over, you get a curious feeling of security when

the sky above your head grows quieter. It is difficult to explain such a feeling, for each new patient is an absorbing problem, so that one is never consciously aware of danger *as* danger, while solving it.

But I was perfectly aware when danger lessened of a new extension in time, as if one were living in an elastic space that could contract or extend according to some unknown law. It is always a relief to feel that time is going to be given one to finish one's job.

As the night wore on, there was an occasional pause between patients when I could stand up and breathe deeply. What I wanted most was to wash out my eyes, for although the smoke was blowing in the opposite direction, the air was acrid and smarting and made one's sight misty. I protected my eyes as well as I could, while operating, but I could not altogether stop their watering.

Sister Tutor said suddenly, "I think, sir, you might take five minutes off now!" and produced from God knows where a priceless cup of coffee out of a thermos flask. I had not realized that I was shivering with cold until I drank it.

When I had given her back the little metal cup, she said in a slightly injured voice, "Virginia Esdaile is doing something extremely silly, and I've been unable to stop it."

"What is she doing?" I asked, with a pang of fear. I could not stop Virginia from driving one of our ambulances, but I had hoped Michael would. After all, she was a mother — with young children. She had more primary responsibilities.

Sister Tutor sniffed audibly. "Well," she explained, "there's a woman giving birth to a child in a cellar, buried under a house as a matter of fact. I don't know how Virginia *got* in, but she *is* in, and it's most unsuitable. She has never had any midwifery training and is indeed only a recent V.A.D. — but she won't come out! I've ordered her to do so twice; perhaps she'll listen to you. It's most unlikely she'll be able to deliver the child properly. Nurse Amory can carry on here for five minutes or so, can't she, while I show you where it is? The blitz seems clearing!"

Sister Tutor always speaks of Air Raids as if they were a manifestation of nature rather than due to any human agency. I think she feels that to depersonalize the Nazis is to reduce their effectiveness.

We made our way over the controlled, but still burning, heaps of rubble till we reached the collapsed building under which Virginia was trapped. The whole place was running with water, and a fireman was still on duty. He had managed to make a hole through the bricks, and by lying face downwards, I could see into the cellar. I could even hand Virginia through an instrument, but I could not reach her. She explained that she had got in through the back of the house, but the wall behind it had since fallen in, so there was no way out. There were two sailors farther down the road, experts in demolition; in a few minutes they would be coming along to help the firemen dig them out.

Virginia had managed to get the mother free of plaster and rubble, and into an open space where she could kneel beside her.

I don't know that I should have recognized Virginia, she was so streaked with dust and black, and her face covered with cuts — and bruises — but her voice when she said, "Oh, Rudi — that's you!" was just the same. I suppose she would have put that breathless pleased sound into it, if it had been Adrian or Tom, or any of the others who adored her; but it was a very delightful sound, coming up at me from a cellar full of dirt and danger.

The wall above them both hung like a bulging wave. The two women were in immediate and mortal peril, but they were bringing that child into the world as if their only business were with Life.

Virginia followed my instructions with absorbed precision; and the woman, looking up at her, obeyed her as if she were listening to the voice of God. It was much more the single-minded union of their intention than any instructions of mine that produced a safe delivery. Life, too, that amazing unaccountable force, acted against every adverse circumstance with a curious ease.

The mother was only a girl and it was her first child. One would have said she had everything against her, but she was not alone — another girl as determined as herself was helping her through her job. I sometimes think that women, in their special function *as* women, are as near to Life as bark is to the tree: you cannot separate them from it.

I saw the two sailors' faces as they knelt one on each side of me, loosening the bricks as quickly as they dared. I thought to myself that the Shepherds of Galilee in the legends of the Christ child might well have stared at the young Mary as these rough men stared at Virginia and the struggling mother. The sailors used the worst possible language in an undertone to each other, but their actions and their expressions showed that their hearts were awed.

Soon they had made a hole large enough for Virginia to hand up the newborn child. Sister Tutor took him from me — a fine boy — and wrapped him in my pullover. It took us the best part of an hour to get the mother out, but this too we accomplished safely.

Then the wall behind her caved in upon Virginia. She could not have seen it coming. I tried to jump in front of it as we saw the first bricks loosen, but the sailors hauled me back; and then with a rush the bricks struck her down, and the stream of them hid her from our sight.

We dug on until we reached her. She was still alive; but the hardest thing I ever had to do was to keep her alive. Her back was injured and both legs crushed. I knew she could never walk again.

I did what I had to do, to free her struggling lungs and steady her feebly beating heart, and then they took her away from me.

It was broad daylight. I found myself sitting alone on a block of fallen masonry, surrounded by running water. A black cat picked its way gingerly over burning rubble and cast a look of bitter reproach at me for not preventing its discomfort.

"That's the cat on hot bricks!" I said aloud, and heard myself, laughing.

24th April 1941

As I leaned over Virginia to give the anæsthetic before Datchett made his examination of her injuries, she whispered, "Don't let me live, Rudi!"

There was nothing in the examination to lighten her plea. Datchett took the same view of her injuries that I did. She could never move of her own volition again.

I wonder how often not the intention but the desire springs up in a doctor's mind: "Can I let this human being out of the trap of Life?" Sometimes where the case is hopeless, the intention follows; but more often one is left longing to give release but realizing that Science was never given us to cut short life. Often a student may feel that he knows more about some special detail than his Teacher; and it may be that he is right and that he really *does* know more; but he is seldom so sure of himself as to violate his Teacher's more universal knowledge. Life has, as it were, more surprises for its student, Science, than Science has for Life.

I saw John Stephens before I went back to Plymouth for the next night. He hardly waited for me to reach his bedside before he said with heightened nervousness and irritation: "Didn't I tell you not to go! We're not supposed to know, but of course I've heard about — that girl — that nurse — Virginia Esdaile — the parson's wife — and now like me she's a helpless cripple! And it's all your fault! That's the worst of men like you — you risk other people besides yourself with your wretched heroism! Where *you* go, they think they've got to follow!"

He must have been in great pain to want to hurt me as much as those words hurt me. A man does not lash out at his friend unless he is also lashing out at himself. I had to remind myself of this; and I did not answer him.

"Well — are you going again?" he asked angrily after a pause.

"Oh, yes!" I said; but again nothing more, for now I knew that his anger was part of his friendship for me: he had wanted to stop me. I patted his shoulder before I left him, to show that there was no ill will between us, for in these uncertain times it is well not to leave rawness on the feelings of our friends when we go into danger.

On my way down I saw through a window overlooking the Park a group of deer moving across a glade with the ineffable lightness of a girl dancing. I wished for a moment that I was blind like John.

In the old legend *Quo Vadis*, Saint Peter, persuaded against his will, flees from Rome during the Persecution. While he is seeking safety in the desert of the Campagna, he meets his Master, carrying the Cross.

"Lord, whither goest Thou?" Peter demands.

"To Rome — to be recrucified," the Christ answers; and Peter, turning, "rushed on Rome and death." I saw Gillian come out to the ambulance to drive me into Plymouth. Saint Peter was lucky to be alone when he met his vision.

At the same moment a servant came to tell me that Tom was on the phone. Tom told me he was bringing with him from London one of the greatest English surgeons to see Virginia. Money can do these things, but not the greatest surgeon living can give back to Virginia the use of her young body.

Tom's voice over the phone had been hoarse with fury. "Why the hell did you take those girls into that inferno?" he demanded. "Why didn't you stick to your post? You have no right whatever to leave the hospital!"

"But all of us who can help must go where help is most needed," I expostulated. "You yourself are going there to-night, I believe?"

"Yes, of course," Tom answered impatiently, "that's another matter. I shall stay with the Bellinghams; and I've brought a lot of stuff with me. But for God's sake stop playing the fool and stick to your own hospital! I got your telegram about Virginia — is there any change?"

"No change," I told him. There was a pause before he asked: —
"Is she disfigured?"

"She's bandaged up," I told him. "I doubt if the facial dis-
figurement — mere cuts and bruises — will last. Her eyes are
uninjured. She fell forward shielding her face. The worst injuries
are to the spine, and both legs are crushed. We may not have
to amputate. We think she will live, but of course with such
extensive injuries that is still uncertain."

Tom said "Good God!" and was silent for a long time. I wondered if he too thought it better that she should not live. I think
he did. I think he felt that her living was a responsibility upon
his affections — difficult to accept where there was no reward.
As for Adrian, he has already repudiated *his* responsibility. He has
not even answered my telegram. The Wendovers were both, I
thought, in their different ways fair-weather lovers.

When Tom spoke again it was of Gillian. He said she was on
no account to go anywhere near the target area.

"I think she intends to drive me in to-night," I told him.
"Do you forbid her?"

"Yes!" Tom shouted with terrific emphasis, banging down
the receiver.

I found Gillian waiting for me in the driver's seat. "I have
something to ask you," I said hurriedly. "Please do not go to-
night. Let Michael take your place. He cannot be with Virginia.
It will help him to be in danger. It will help *me* if you are *not*
in danger."

She gave me a curious look. There was no surrender in it;
but there was an appeal.

"I will do anything *else* you ask me," she said gently, "but
not that!"

"But that is what I *must* ask you!" I pleaded. "You know what
I am already responsible for! Do not add to it!"

"I am responsible for myself," Gillian said after a pause. "If
you thought it right to stay here, then I should stay with you,
because I am working for you. I can surely choose now! I am
not a child!"

"Your father forbids you to go," I told her then, drawing on my goggles, for I knew the argument was over.

"If you had said that to start with," Gillian murmured with a grim little smile, "you would have saved time! Get in!"

It was broad daylight still, a grey spring day without energy; only the larks were still alive in it, rising up from the moor, singing their hearts out, over the dead heather.

When we reached Plymouth there was a new and ugly feeling in the air. At the first surprise attack the city's heart had risen to meet it, with the whole courage of man untainted by defeat or exposure; but now in many this courage had become exhausted. Hour by endless hour, shocked and homeless people had stood without food or shelter, by their little pieces of furniture, in the open streets, unwilling to leave their last possessions, not knowing what else to do or where to go; and all the time exchanging their terrible stories.

Others stayed, crushed utterly, in their stricken or shaken homes, unable even to ask for advice or information, clinging to their familiar rooms and few possessions, however spoiled or threatened. There was very little transport and not enough advertisement of what there was or where it started from. What authorities were on the spot did what they could, but many of their own homes were destroyed, and all had their homes and families equally threatened.

I was aghast, before the fresh Raid started, to see these huddled groups in the open, standing by a baby's cradle, or an old armchair which they had dragged from the flames the night before, crying aloud in the streets with grief and anger — shouting even for "Peace!"

I thought it tactless and ill-timed to offer as consolation a loud speaker promising equal destruction to German homes. At this moment the only human relationship these exposed and shell-shocked people could accept was with the homeless. An injured German would have felt far more of a friend to them at the moment than a British official with his home intact.

This country has never been ideologically trained against the Nazis as the Russians have been trained. On the contrary, through all those dangerous, gritless years of appeasement what training there was pointed the other way. WHAT DOES HITLER THINK OF THE WORLD? I was shocked to see up on placards all over London when Czechoslovakia was pushed under the knife; not WHAT DOES THE WORLD THINK OF HITLER? for knifing his neighbour!

It was not surprising then that in a moment of such complete physical and moral destruction as the Plymouth Raids there were people found who preferred peace with the friend of some of their own politicians to an inexorable hail of bombs. What was surprising was that so few did, and that these pitiful cries so soon died down.

We arranged our First Aid station near a street that had been partially destroyed and was still smouldering. Much had been done in the last few hours to meet the return of the raiders. Help of all sorts had been pouring in from the surrounding villages and more distant towns; but the amount of dislocation that had taken place the night before made it in some ways more difficult to face the new flood of destruction. The storm, too, fell upon nerves already shaken, not upon healthy ones.

There had been in the first night's havoc an element of fierce joy springing out of the use of unknown forces set free to meet the onslaught of the danger. But now that exhilaration of the spirit roused to fresh triumphs had wholly vanished. What was left to most of us was the colder, tougher quality of endurance. And even this did not come at once. In my own heart I felt, and was conscious that those around me felt, something inimical and beaten down. It was as if a voice told us with authority — "This is too much. Do not bear it! This ought not to be asked of human beings!"

Sometimes, between the perpetual arrivals of fresh cases, I saw people running in and out of the struck and flaming houses who neither belonged to them nor were in them to save those who needed help. They were looters.

I think if Sister Lawrence had not been by my side that night, I might have become unskilful or even reckless in my work. Perhaps I might have lost a surgeon's patient economy, upon which so much of all after care depends. But Sister Lawrence prevented me from giving anything short of my best. She made each patient human to me by the strength of her own pity. I think she was more frightened of the flames and clamour than Sister Tutor had been, nor was she so highly intelligent as that tough and admirable woman; but Sister Lawrence had courage enough to do her duty beautifully. She had in her some quality that makes a man know he can count upon it to the uttermost, as — when he was a helpless child — he counted upon his mother.

The noise in the skies above, the senseless bumps and crashes, the screams and the flames — smoke always in one's eyes and throat, bitter and sharp, like the taste of death itself — all this went on without cessation or relief.

I hated everything I heard or saw; and I rebelled against everything. Worse even than the loathing I had always felt for the Nazis and the brute force they stand for I felt the indignity to life itself. A doctor is a man who, if his career is well-chosen, looks upon himself as a guardian of life; he cannot take lightly what infringes the rights of his great charge.

And yet can life be made undignified by any act of man? Life is being interrupted on these nights by man's obscenity, as nature is interrupted by storms, or by the explosions of pent-up gases; but such catastrophes are not permanent, as are the laws of nature. Nor are these cruel obscenities from the innocent skies, made by man against his brother, capable of inflicting any real indignity upon life. They will cease, and life itself will be unchanged by them. Still, if there be Powers of Evil, they were very free in the city of Plymouth that night. They had taken the driver's seat, and dashed with their freight of helpless passengers over the precipice. My mind felt like a pit of black and red flame. I was sickened at the thought of Gillian standing by that unwieldy bus of hers in the dark, with the cries of the wounded in her ears, alone and at the mercy of chance. What was the use, I asked myself, of doing anything to save these sunk and shattered people brought to me, one by one? Why not collect those I had ready, and take them and Gillian into comparative safety? What I saved here, in the open, might be destroyed the next minute. Even if this child Sister Lawrence had just laid before me, with its

leg torn off, *did* recover because I stopped the bleeding and gave
her a blood transfusion, would she thank me? If she survived the
agonizing, bumping drive ahead of her, and reached a slightly
safer area where she might be bombed again to-morrow, what
profit would there be for her, in her impoverished and broken
life?

The bombs rained down like an endless series of ghastly
accidents.

I heard the howling mutter of angry people, a cry that is worse
than fear because it is fear turned aggressive and pointed like a
weapon towards others. I heard authority checking these demoralized groups by force. Commands were not readily obeyed,
and sometimes they were not obeyed at all. But the anger and
the disobedience were sporadic and trifling compared with the
apathy of most of the people; and apathy is a worse sign in a human being than anger.

Morale is not a single instinct. It has many ingredients. A sense
of personal responsibility, the natural courage of an individual,
the amount of his acquired self-discipline — and above all his
interest in others — these together make up the spirit of morale.

A plan helps all nervous people; and where there has been no
plan, there is always more fear. Those who are accustomed to
make themselves responsible for their own good behaviour, go
far in helping to maintain the good behaviour of others. There
must have been many such people out in the streets of Plymouth
that night or there would have been far more active mischief
than there was.

I do not say the school-teachers were the best people in Plymouth, but I think their courage must have ranked very high,
for Michael told me that in the shelters with the children they
kept a wonderful and easy order; and without sleep, baths or
hot food they went back next day to their battered school-
houses and re-lit the hearts of their shocked and frightened
pupils.

I saw most myself of the sailors who helped us from the ship-
yards and the docks. All of us were cheered whenever we caught
sight of their eager, lively faces questing for those in danger like

hunting dogs; and knowing what to do to save them, when they found them. Hundreds — perhaps thousands — of the bewildered inhabitants of Plymouth must owe their lives to these sailors who dug them out of fallen houses, scaled threatening walls and shaken roofs to reach them; and sometimes even ran to and fro through walls of flame. Urging them on and guiding their grim efforts were their officers. The undefeatable face of an admiral driving a motor lorry into a sea of flame will never be forgotten by those who saw him. It was as if he said: "Let the skies fall! And if there is a German behind those falling skies, I will still get him!"

My own stretcher-bearers, nurses and ambulance drivers never failed to meet an emergency. They made my work easy.

To-night, the firemen and the sailors had got what they most needed — water. We were less, though it did not always seem so, at the mercy of the flames.

The dawn was slow in coming and the night air very cold. I found Gillian waiting for me with reddened eyes, and a face curiously hollowed by the struggles of the night. "She will look like this when she is old," I said to myself.

"All night long I have felt like a bad dog," I told her, as she tried to make her stiff lips smile at me, "but now I am losing something of this sense of evil. Do not think me heartless! But after all, you are alive, and so am I! What has happened to all the hours of the night? Well, they are perhaps in store for us to-morrow, but I do not feel limited by them any more. Instead, I am thinking of hot tea and bacon and eggs, and also that Caroline will find in her store cupboards a comb of honey, or a pot of strawberry jam!"

I would have liked to take the wheel away from her and have driven myself, but I thought perhaps it helped her to drive. There is nothing that steadies the mind more than its own skill in action.

The light was thick and soft upon the newborn leaves. A little wind crept up behind us from the sea, and made them shine and tremble. The great gates of the Park opened and closed upon us. I had not forgotten, but I had postponed, what I must do to save Virginia.

25th April 1941

WE had barely passed the gates when a small figure darted out perilously upon the drive, waving to us to stop. It was Miss Fitchett, breathless with hurry and agitation.

"Please, please, Dr. Ritterhaus, come to us at once!" Miss Fitchett gasped, springing onto the running board before we had time to pull up. "Lady Wendover must see you immediately — she really must!"

"You're mad, Fidge!" Gillian said indignantly. "He's got to clean up and get his breakfast first! Think what a night he's had!"

"Oh, yes, I know, but he *must*, dear, he really *must!*" Miss Fitchett moaned. "I *do* know how inconsiderate it sounds; but you don't realize, Gillian dear, how necessary it is, and I can't tell you!"

"Is Mother *ill*," Gillian demanded, "or is it just plain temper again? Because if it's temper, she won't have time to die of it before Rudi's finished his breakfast!"

"Please turn for the Dower House," I said sternly. I had not often spoken sharply to Gillian before and, after a startled look in my direction, she obeyed. I knew that Miss Fitchett was an adept at Lady Wendover's tempers; and I did not think she would have run across the Park at eight o'clock in the morning for anything short of a catastrophe.

She did not tell us what it was, and none of us spoke again until after we had arrived. Gillian, with an uncertain and exasperated glance at us both, ran upstairs to her room and Miss Fitchett drew me carefully and secretly into a small room off the hall. Even then she came up close to where I stood, and whispered.

"Gillian must never know! No one must ever know!" Miss Fitchett told me. "She tried to commit suicide. She knows about Virginia and Tom!"

"*How* does she know?" I asked her incredulously.

"An anonymous letter — we think it's one of the nurses. There was a little trouble a week ago with one of them; and now of course all this fuss Lord Wendover's making over Virginia has made her inclined to believe it." Miss Fitchett ran on breathlessly: "I saw the letter myself. It *sounded* true, Dr. Ritterhaus! I *should* have believed it I think, even if I hadn't known it *was* true! She didn't show it to me at *first*. She rang up Lord Wendover at Silver Fountains — this was late last night — an hour after he and that famous surgeon from London had arrived. He put her off and wouldn't come over. I heard her say on the telephone, 'But I can't wait till morning, Tom!' I suppose he said she *must,* and slammed down the receiver. But she doesn't, you know — wait! She just went into the bathroom and locked the door. The maids had gone to bed, and I couldn't get her to answer me, so I went to the tool-house and got out the ladder. It was moonlight or I couldn't have done it. I'm terrified of climbing ladders but somehow or other I *did* climb it — it's less terrible when you can only *half* see — and fortunately she always leaves the bathroom window open because of her heart — although I had no idea it was so difficult climbing off a ladder into a window, even when it is open.

"There she was, with both her wrists cut, in a bath full of blood! Fortunately she hadn't severed an artery and the cuts weren't *very* deep, but oh, the shock! Then she told me; and now she's in bed. I've cleaned everything up; and I took the ladder back after she'd settled off. I don't think anyone need ever know, except Lord Wendover. She's bound to tell him of course, because she cut them *at* him, if you know what I mean!"

I considered that Miss Fitchett's diagnosis was correct. Lady Wendover had certainly cut her wrists open *at* her husband. That she had not succeeded in her efforts was simply due to the heroism of Miss Fitchett and to the fact that Lady Wendover did not know how to do things very well.

I found her lying with her eyes shut; and her face turned to the wall. She had lost a good deal of blood and was suffering from shock; otherwise, her heart was in a fairly good condition.

It is wonderful what a nervous heart will stand, when it has accustomed itself to frequent self-produced upsets.

I knelt down beside her, and she said between quivering lips, with her eyes shut, "Dr. Ritterhaus?"

"Yes," I said, "your friend, Rudi!"

She moved her poor, rather ineffectively bandaged wrists so that I could see them. The tears streamed over her cheeks but she did not try to hide them from me.

I went into the bathroom and cleaned myself up a little, and then re-bandaged her wrists for her.

"Now," I said, "tell me, are you so troubled about this old business of Tom's?"

"Yes!" she whispered. "Oh, Rudi — I have loved him so — I have loved *only* him all my life. And now to find after all these years that he has betrayed me — now I really know that I have lost everything!"

I patted her shoulder, feeling sorrier for her than I could put into words; besides I could not contradict her. She had in truth lost everything; and worst of all, she had for the moment lost that blind auto-intoxication through which all her senses were accustomed to function. She was bereft not only of her husband, but of her myth about herself. For the first time she realized that she had not given Tom enough to live on; so that he had had to seek for it elsewhere. And yet surely she was the most generous of women? Somewhere, poor Frances had always believed, within herself lay all the heroic virtues which she had never taken the steps to acquire; and now for the first time she knew that she had *not* acquired them.

She was stingy; she was *not* generous. She was jealous; she was *not* magnanimous. She was weak; she was *not* strong.

"But you still have something," I urged. "You have the work you are doing for the hospital. Believe me, that has an actual value. There is one thing more that you can do, and you only, through this cruel stroke of fate. You can comfort your husband. He too has lost much — in losing Virginia; and he *has* lost her. She will, if she recovers, be an invalid for life. Their friendship was not like yours and Michael's; it could not exist *without* a physical tie. Whatever he may say to the contrary, in his heart Tom was faithful to you. He did not replace you with another woman — mature, and his equal — like yourself. He took instead this young girl for her swift beauty, because she was to him like a child easy to satisfy, and not a serious obligation; because, too, he had the needs of a man long left unsatisfied. You can very easily forgive him, if there is anything to forgive!"

She opened her eyes then and looked at me. She did not speak but I know that she meant me to see in her poor drowned eyes all that she was too proud to say. She made no more excuses for herself, nor did she again find fault with Tom. The look she gave me was questioning and self-distrustful, as if she wondered if she had the power left to bring comfort to her husband.

"I have never known a woman of your age still so beautiful!" I told her quite truthfully.

"But not," she whispered, "*after* Virginia!"

"Oh but you were *before* Virginia," I explained. "Not now, perhaps, while he is still too shocked to look for love; but soon — but soon, if you are kind enough, he will turn to you for comfort! You might even tell him that you know about Virginia, and that you understand."

"But not — not this?" she whispered, looking at her bandaged wrists.

"No — certainly not," I said firmly. "That was a hostile act. He should *never* hear of it. I shall not let him see you till those wrists are healed; but they will heal readily."

I think that she was disappointed to hear that they would heal so readily, but this was a disappointment that I knew was good for her. Naturally she would have liked her wounds to be more serious. To decide to die in order to show your husband how badly he has behaved requires a good deal of self-stimulation; and it is hard to feel that your efforts were both inadequate and inconspicuous.

"There is only one person I think you would do well to share this knowledge with," I said. "I think Gillian should know!"

"But why Gillian!" exclaimed her mother. "She is utterly unsympathetic to me and has never shown me either respect or understanding. How could she, a young girl, even realize what has brought me to this?"

"I think that is where you make a little mistake," I told her. "I believe Gillian to be really sympathetic where the need is real. Besides, I believe that all daughters, even when most aggravated by their mothers, have a secret respect for them. They believe perhaps that they can do everything better than their mothers can, and many things they *can* do better, but they have not yet lived long enough to be sure how successfully they will meet the major emergencies of life, which lie, sometimes quite creditably, *behind* their mothers!"

Lady Wendover frowned. "I do not think it suitable," she explained, "that a girl of Gillian's age should know such a horrible thing about her father and her childhood's friend."

"But she *does* already know it," I told her mother, "and her first reaction was nearly as strong as your own. She was deeply horrified and shocked at the wrong done to you; but since then she has learned to understand Tom's and Virginia's difficulties, and she will not make too much of what has happened in the past. And indeed, why should either of you — for it is over."

"That dreadful girl!" Frances moaned. "How *can* Gillian understand her? What is there to understand about her, except that she is light and base?"

"It will not comfort Tom if you think that of Virginia," I told her firmly, "nor make Gillian admire you more; but if you understand that Virginia was lonely and very young, and had far too high an ideal set before her to live up to — an ideal for which her early training had not in the least fitted her — well, then I think it will be nearer the truth! To call Virginia light and base though she has behaved with lightness and even at times perhaps basely is a little unreal. You know how she got her injuries. She saved the life of a woman in childbirth, and brought a living child into the world, at the expense of her own life."

Lady Wendover closed her eyes again.

"I wish *I* had done that," she whispered. "I should like to go into Plymouth with you to-night, Doctor!"

"No, you are far too weak from loss of blood," I replied hastily with secret anxiety, for I could not imagine a worse companion in a blitzkrieg than Frances. No one would be able to stop the blitzkrieg to attend to her, and it would be equally impossible to stop her, in order to attend to the blitzkrieg. Still, I considered it a favourable sign that she should wish for Virginia's crown, since that was to acknowledge that she had won a crown.

"But there is something of value you can do," I suggested cautiously. "You can be brave and let Gillian see you, as you are. She has had two bad nights and is physically worn-out. I think if she could see you and feel that you depended upon her young strength and understanding in your trouble, she would stay at home to-night."

Lady Wendover whispered, "I'll try!" I leant over her and kissed her hand. She opened her eyes, and gave me that look of confidence that passes between friends with a common purpose who have trust in each other. "Why, Rudi!" she murmured. "How red your eyes are: have you been crying too? No, of course not, how stupid of me, that must be smoke. Go down at once and get your breakfast!"

I found that Gillian and Miss Fitchett had prepared the breakfast of my dreams. There were bacon and eggs; there was a dish of honey as golden as the sunshine, and plate after plate of hot toast to eat with the fine butter belonging to their own dairy farm.

I ate like a wolf in spite of my fatigue, and Gillian ate like another wolf, with me. We were enchanted with each other's appetites.

The little room we sat in was called the Breakfast Room. It was full of early sunshine, and so open to the trees and birds that we might ourselves have been a part of the April life. Miss Fitchett had left us alone with each other.

Still, there *was* that shadow of Plymouth upon Gillian's face, and perhaps upon my own. We had come up against too many horrors to lose this shadow yet. All those who worked in Plymouth through those nights had it. It was like the shadow you see often, though not always, upon the faces of the dying. Once a doctor or a nurse sees that shadow on a patient's face he knows there is no more hope, for you cannot turn back death. I suppose we had as it were caught the semblance of this shadow, although we were full of life, and would soon get rid of it again.

I did not tell Gillian about her mother till we had finished breakfast. When I came in, she had asked at once, "*Ought* Fidget to have fetched you?" I nodded; and she asked me no more questions.

"Now —" I said, pushing away my empty plate — and God alone knows how much I had cleared off it — "I will tell you everything. Your mother knows about Tom and Virginia! I suppose sooner or later it was bound to leak out: an eavesdropper, something overlooked and forgotten like Virginia's yellow scarf, enough, at any rate, to cause an anonymous letter which has convinced your mother. This knowledge has been an overwhelming blow to her, and she tried, though unsuccessfully, to take her life."

Gillian got up, took a cigarette, lit it, and swung herself up onto the window-seat. I could see the profile only of her shadowed face. I am sure that she had received a shock, but her voice was hard when she spoke to me. "Well," she said, "what do you propose that I should do about it, if she has?"

"You can comfort her," I said quietly, lighting a cigarette for myself, and thinking as I leaned back in my chair how curious the silence was; the nerves seemed to sink into it as if it were made of velvet.

"Why should I comfort her?" Gillian demanded. "I've thought quite a lot about Father and Virginia, Rudi, since we talked about it. Mother gave him nothing all their married life. Well, now she has found out for the first time that she has got nothing back! I hardly see where comfort comes in!"

"I should hardly call two children, and over twenty years' companionship, *nothing*," I answered. "It is quite a lot to give another person, Gillian."

Gillian frowned. "You know perfectly what I mean," she said severely. "It amounted to nothing because she spoiled it. It wasn't ever — for one moment — the honest-to-God sort of thing Daddy managed, somehow or other, to give her."

"Very few of us are honest either to God or to each other," I reminded her, "and probably none of us are honest the whole time. Anyhow, your mother's grief was real when she, perhaps for the first time, realized that she had failed both herself and your father. She could not bear to go on living. Certainly if Miss Fitchett had not climbed that ladder, your mother would have been found dead in her bath."

"Suppose she *had* been?" Gillian said, turning her face fully towards me, and speaking with passion. "After what we've seen last night — how much would it matter?"

"If we saw anything at all last night," I said, "it would matter exactly as much as the wilful destruction of any other human being."

She was silent for a while, though I think the feeling in her was still that of extreme impatience. After all, she had experienced horrors enough to fill an ordinary lifetime in the course of a few danger-shaken hours, and at the end of this, it was not surprising that she felt irritable when asked to soothe a rather selfish outburst of personal feeling. Yet I knew well enough, if she saw her mother's face white as death, drawn and old with shock and loss of blood, every nerve of her being would respond to it; and I knew that only if she *did* respond to it, should I be able to heal her mother's broken pride.

"Remember what you felt yourself," I urged, "when you heard of what your father had done to Virginia, a girl your own age; and to Michael, a friend! Yet you had no responsibility for such actions. All wives feel, and rightly feel, that they are responsible for influencing their husbands' emotions. They cannot *make* a husband happy if he chooses unhappiness for himself; but they can certainly lighten or deepen the happiness of a person so intimately bound up with them. Your mother had not deepened your father's capacity for happiness. She had never been, with him, intimate *enough!*"

"But what's the use!" Gillian exclaimed, throwing her half-smoked cigarette into the dew-drenched grass beneath her. "Why should *I* be dragged into it? Nothing will be of any use now —

after Virginia! Fancy being 'forgiven' by Mother! Wouldn't it make you sick if you were her husband?"

"It's curious," I said, "but I have often noticed how readily men return to wives when they have lost their mistresses, if the wives give them half a chance! After all, wives, when you come to think of it, were a first attraction, and a pretty deep one, or no man would be fool enough to take on the obligation of marriage. Your mother won't, I think, be too forgiving about it now. She has looked into the pit of a human being's loneliness; that makes one humble enough to try to earn companionship."

Gillian made no reply to me but I was under the impression that when I had gone, she would stay with her mother.

26th April 1941

I HAD expected an explosion from Tom about Plymouth but we did not have so severe a one as I had imagined. Gillian had returned safely and Tom is a man of quick and passionate temper leading to immediate action, but easily deflected once this action has not taken place. All he said was that I could do as I chose personally but the hospital, which had now been filled to the brim, must close its doors, and none of the Staff be used elsewhere. All our ambulances had already been handed over to the Plymouth authorities. If I could carry on my duties with four hours' sleep in the day for another night or two, and yet not neglect my hospital responsibilities, I was free to carry on. I knew very well what support and co-operation I should receive from my colleagues and the Staff generally, so that what I proposed to do was altogether easy. Tom readily promised *not* to visit his wife for the next few days. His own quarters in Silver Fountains had been taken over. He was sleeping at his game-keeper's, and he was rather glad, I could see, not to go near the Dower House. He was wholly absorbed in the hopes he had built up about Griggs's fresh diagnosis of Virginia's injuries.

The examination had been postponed to the afternoon so that I might take part in it and get my four hours' sleep first. Dr. Reed gave the anæsthetic. I merely assisted Griggs; and showed him what Datchett had already done. I was against the second examination, in my patient's interests. She was still fighting for her life, and I thought the extra fatigue of a further anæsthetic unnecessary, particularly as I had every confidence in Datchett. Still, Wendover insisted, and if Virginia died under the anæsthetic it was after all more in her interest than living.

I could not have given her an easier death myself. But Fate is seldom so accommodating as to do one's work for one. Virginia survived the second anæsthetic.

Griggs confirmed Datchett's diagnosis and approved our treatment. He merely made — to earn his fee — one or two minor suggestions which may or may not prove to be improvements. He asked me to break the news to Tom after we had discussed the case, and promised to confirm it. He was afraid of Tom; and had reason to be, since he had done what is basically false in a medical man: given an optimistic opinion in advance of fact.

Tom took it as I had expected. At first he was indignantly incredulous. All his sentences began with "Surely — " He meant to dragoon Science to carry out his will, at least approximately. I was patient but firm, and finally he shrugged his shoulders and went to the window of the little office I both worked and slept in, standing with his back to me, and looking out on his great possessions.

At last he said, "Well, Rudi, there's one good thing about it: now I can look my boy in the face again! It's a queer thing, but at my age women aren't the chief thing in a man's life. I thought the world of Virginia. I am prepared to stand by her now in any way that'll help her, though of course we must consider Michael. I've lost, and I know that I've lost, everything else. No one will ever know what that girl was to me. She was Paradise and plenty, after twenty years' starvation in a desert. I'm damned cut up about this business; but I won't deny that I didn't like that trouble about my boy. If he had done himself in — and he has a bit of his mother's hysterical strain or whatever you like to call it — it would have queered my pitch even more than this has."

"I can understand that," I told him. "You see, I too have a son."

He turned round quickly, and we looked at each other. It was curious, that shared moment. We were literally at one with each other. It was then that Tom said, "Go and do your damnedest in Plymouth to-night again if you must! After all, I shall be there as well. I'm going to stay with the Bellinghams until the Raids are over. By the by I saw Virginia this morning."

"She's under opiates," I told him, "all the time."

"Yes," Tom said, "I know. The Sister told me. You'll keep her like that, won't you?"

"I shan't let her suffer," I told him, "any more than I can help." But I did not tell him how I was going to carry out my intention. Tom was too conventional to accept mercy as part of the scheme of things.

Before I left the hospital I made my second round and found John Stephens in a highly excited state. I hesitated whether or not to order a sedative; but I decided against it. After all, sooner or later he would have to learn how to control his nerves, and I thought that he was strong enough to begin. I merely warned Sister to keep an eye on him. He was, if anything, more hostile to me than he had been the day before, but Sister told me he had taken his first walk that morning with a great deal of courage.

Michael called at the hospital to take me into Plymouth in his small car. It was odd how completely Virginia's accident had taken her away from him. She belonged to the hospital — to the village — to Plymouth, now — as she had never belonged to her husband. She was a Public Heroine. The anonymous letter had been written only just in time. A few hours later probably even its writer would have fought anyone who breathed a word against Virginia. She had become immaculate overnight; and perhaps after all what everyone thought of her now was as true as their meaner estimate had been earlier, before she had had the opportunity to prove that she was a heroine as well as a witch!

I found it strangely restful driving into Plymouth with Michael. He did not want anything from me. He had his God. Nor did he try to do anything for me, since his powers were taken up with his driving, which he did extremely badly, and in fighting his own heartache.

In a sense, Michael was more to be pitied than Tom Wendover. Tom had paid for Virginia's accident. He had arranged without reference to Michael, I afterwards discovered, Griggs's superlatively expensive visit; but in what the English call "wear and tear" I do not think Tom paid as much as Michael.

Michael, who had remained perfectly unshaken by his Plymouth experiences, looked ten years older since Virginia's accident.

Still, pity for Michael did not disturb me. Pain for pain, he had given Virginia quite as much I considered, during their married lives, as she was suffering now; and a pain for which there are no opiates. Let those who try to lessen the self-esteem of another human being think what they do!

We found Plymouth in a wholly different condition. The authorities and those chief citizens who had already proved their competence to face emergency were now in full control; and the people answered to it. Defeatism had stopped. It had never been more than the reaction against unanticipated and over-whelming odds.

I do not believe courage by itself can stand against this War. It has to be courage equipped, trained and in a sense spiritually prepared for social interest before it can dare to meet success-fully the illimitable dangers of mechanized science welded against us by the ruthless hearts of our enemies. When men know that they are responsible for part of a combined plan to meet a com-mon need, they function well; but no man can function well where the plan does not exist, the leadership is irresponsible, or the danger unequally shared.

The night before I had found that the organic life of the place was treacherous and unsound; but now, though all the city's func-tions were still awry, the beat of life was behind them.

We found a well-arranged First Aid station awaiting us. Bar-row was to have shared it with me; but he and his wife had been killed the night before. I was glad they were together when death took them. I told Michael. "Some people have all the luck," he said. "Yes," I said, thinking of Klara and of how easy it would have been to die together, "they seem to — " but then I thought of Gillian and I lost the wish that I had died with Klara.

The night was like the former ones except that once I was caught by the tail end of a blast and blown across the road. All I felt was a maddening sense of physical constraint — I couldn't get away from that blast — and then a bump. I landed against a wall, and broke two ribs, but I did not know this till afterwards.

Michael wanted to take me back, but I was soon quite myself again. I only had to wait for the tremulous stage to pass, while

a hospital student took my place. Michael made me comfortable
with his coat, while I was waiting, against a heap of fallen bricks;
and two barmaids from a Public House next door brought us
each a bottle of beer and plates of sausage and mashed.

They told us they had stuck to their functions through the
blitz because their customers might miss them.

When they left us, Michael asked me: "Are you well enough
to talk?" "When I'm not, I won't be well enough to live," I told
him, for as is the case of all good Viennese, conversation is my
favourite pastime. His head was close to mine so that I could hear
what he said quite plainly, and we saw each other's face by
flashes.

"I have come to a very strange conclusion, Rudi," he told me.
"Since Virginia's accident I do not think that I have ever understood God."

"Well," said I, looking round me at the blitz activities, "surely
that's not very strange. Who could?"

"This is what *we* have done to God — not what God has done
to *us*," Michael told me with grave certainty. "This much I
still believe that I understand: to me, God has always been the
one overwhelming Reality, and I had thought that whoever
studied Reality must learn to understand it, and therefore to
represent it, but I suppose only so far as they themselves *are* real?"

The whole thing was funny — Michael talking like this in a
blitz — even though I admit there was a sort of lull — but the
flames were lighting up the sky not far from us, and the guns
were banging and spluttering all round. My head worked to and
fro like a concertina; and words like "Reality" never have meant
much to me at the best of times.

But I was suddenly touched when he whispered or shouted into
my ear — I don't know which but anyhow I heard it — "I know
now my faith wasn't real! I know that I tortured my poor girl
worse than these diabolical engines of man have tortured her."

"She also tortured you," I reminded him.

"But not until I had clipped her wings and barred her into
my cage," he told me. "You can't think, you who have never
seen her before I interfered with my Maker, what a marvellous

creature she was! So full of life you held your breath to look at
her. Do you remember, from the Greek, the line 'the innumerable
laughter of the waves'? Virginia was like that line, and now she
laughs so little, and has almost no life at all. And I am responsible."

Someone came and gave me a cigarette.

What happens when a city is being methodically blitzed is a
succession of bangs and thuds, followed by the roar and tremble
of explosions; and then if you're not so near as to be blinded
by dust and fumes, you look up, and perhaps you watch a building totter and subside upon itself — or perhaps you just see a new
empty space in a row, like a knocked-out tooth. I had to try to
drag my mind back from these spectacles, even to Virginia.

"Virginia should have known better than to let you remake
her," I told him, in a sudden pause. "She ought to have fought
you back. She had the weapons, but she was afraid of you. She
thought you too strong an antagonist. Besides, you'd loaded
the dice against her: you'd got God! She preferred to use her
weapons against lighter men. You know, Michael, I think you
cheated Virginia by dragging in God. You made it, as the
Americans say, 'too tall a proposition' for her."

We watched in silence a little street upon the hill crumble up
like a table napkin. The noise seemed to come a long while afterwards; and then the dry long whisper of the flames. In the sky
there was a much longer pause. Even the naval guns took a short
holiday.

"God was on her side," Michael told me. "He knew her for
His own; and gave her the greatest of His opportunities. But I
am not afraid that He has deserted me, now that she lives. If she
had died, I should have been afraid. All the love I never knew
how to give her I shall give her now; and all my life henceforward is hers."

I wanted time to think before I answered him. I did not want
to give him the shadow of a hope which the future might take
away. I have written, and I believe, that I mean to take Virginia's
life; and I also told myself that I had only postponed this action
because the day of the examination was not suitable for my
purpose. I needed to be alone in command, and also to rest my

nerves. But now I asked myself, Why did I have all these needs? Why had I not insisted on giving the anæsthetic instead of Dr. Reed? I had only to manipulate the anæsthetic for the fluttering of that enfeebled heart to stop. Is it true, as Adler once told me: "He who has not done a thing after the moment necessary for decision does not intend to do it"? Had I ever really intended to take Virginia's life? Did I now so intend?

Perhaps if I had not talked like this between the sounds and furies of Death itself, I might have done it. How can we tell what changes or influences us to change ourselves? We are so bound up with one another — so together at one moment — so divorced and alone the next. I think on the whole this third night was the noisiest of the three I spent in Plymouth. It made me dislike destruction more than I had ever before disliked it. Besides, Michael would now give Virginia what she wanted most: a relentless, sacrificial devotion. Perhaps she might not mind her crippled life so much after all, if she could count forever upon his devoted heart?

"But dare I believe," Michael demanded, "that she'll still take anything I have to give? She's so used to my torturing her!"

"No! No!" I told him. "After all, she still loves you! I dare say you think this is nonsense, but when she went off under that anæsthetic she kept muttering, 'Michael — Michael!' — never the names of any of the others! She'll soon begin to stop being afraid of you — and to tyrannize over you to your heart's content!"

My tremors had stopped now. I'd been trying while we talked to see what I could do with my right hand and arm, and I saw that I had regained full control; so I got up and we went back to the First Aid station. I did not think, whatever happened, Michael would torture Virginia again; but I doubt if he won't make her sometimes feel more in a cage than ever.

30th April 1941

PAIN is an interesting problem and it is a pity that doctors do not experience it oftener, as we should then perhaps have more understanding of how to deal with it in our patients. After the blow I had received, fracturing, as we afterwards discovered, two ribs, I worked on for some hours without much trouble, partly no doubt because I was anæsthetized by the shock effects of the blast, but also I think because absorption in a necessary task side-tracks, as it were, that summons of the nerves to the brain which produces pain. Almost any task that takes a man's full attention inhibits other subjects from reaching his brain centre. We notice this even without pain, when for instance a person's brain clenches down — like the action of a fist — against any intrusion from another person or against any subject that they regard with hostility. Many people also, with untrained or over-exalted minds, fail to register a new fact unless it falls in with their own prestige occupation. Of course in the long run, any severe injury sends its signal along the nerves to the brain, no matter how deep the victim's preoccupation. Still, when the poet said, "The ruling passion strong in death," he struck upon a too little studied fact. Any passion that rules a man's life survives practically everything else, except personal extinction, and we do not even know for certain that it does not survive that!

What I noticed after I went back to work at the First Aid station was a strange sense of inner calm, as if all about me the threatened city were being reinforced by a new spirit. "The Jameses and Eunices have come back," I thought fancifully to myself. "They are at work all over the city. Its attacked and wavering life is safe in their hands."

All about me I saw the faces of unaggressive common-sense authorities. Sometimes they brought the patients to our station; sometimes they gave us necessary information about the Raid;

but whenever I came across them, I knew them instantly as the people who will — if it is to be saved — save England.

I do not know if more or fewer bombs were dropped that third Raid night in Plymouth; if there were more or fewer fires to be fought; more or less casualties; nor whether a greater or less destruction of buildings took place. I only know that there was some new power, a different kind of power, to meet them.

Because I love such people and because I know what they are like in danger, I can only call them "the James-and-Eunice power."

I dare say I was a little light-headed, for although the outer surface of my brain saw the needs of my patients and prompted me to the right reactions, beneath this outer surface I was aware of a constant stream of alien images. Lines of poetry haunted me and came back again and again, and I remember in a very warning manner one special verse haunted me.

> Cover her face!
> Mine eyes dazzle.
> She died young.

None of my patients died upon the operating table this night, nor were any of them beautiful, and yet each one as they came before me, under the blue light, stabbed at me with that message.

Our station was a surface shelter well blacked out, so that I could not tell, as I worked, when the light came; but it must have been near morning when I heard running, stumbling footsteps just outside the shelter as if someone were in urgent haste.

I had just finished with the last batch of patients, and taken off my overall, when a man stumbled through the blast doorway and caught me by both arms. "It's you! It's you, Doctor!" he panted. "I can see it is you!"

It was my patient, John Stephens, who was blind. I do not to this day know how he had guessed which of us was me, for Michael and the Warden were with me, and John had seen none of us before. His eyes shone with a brilliance I have never seen in any human eyes, even in Klara's when she first loved me.

"It's the dawn," he said, shaking me in his excitement, "and I can see the ruins, I can see the flames, and the walls of this cellar, and your face, and you're alive! We thought you were killed — but you aren't, you're safe — so it's all right!"

I, too, felt my heart beating fast with his joy, and I sat down on a box and tried to look as soothing as I could, but I admit that I was almost as excited as John himself.

"How on earth did you get here?" I asked him.

"Someone who'd just got out of Plymouth told Caroline," he answered. "They'd heard you were hit, and Caroline told a nurse, and then it spread in whispers all over the hospital. I was crafty about it — I got hold of my clothes somehow and found one of the under-gardeners who could drive, and I made him bring me in. There was Miss Wendover's small car in the yard still. When they told me where your First Aid station was, why then I just came along here by myself. I ran."

There was a nearby crash, and the shelter rocked, but the boy gazed at me with his brilliant, friendly eyes cleared of all fear.

I had not expected to see this miracle. No natural law had been violated. The suspension of a natural function had simply been released. What touched me was that the releasing factor should have been my danger. The boy saw because he was more concerned with my safety than with his own.

"Can you remember," I asked him anxiously, "exactly *when* and *how* you first saw?"

"I don't know," he said, almost impatiently. "I could guess Nurse had heard something. She moved about as if she had, and sniffed. I felt sure she was crying, so I said, 'Have you heard any bad news?' Then she said, 'Well, I suppose I oughtn't to tell you — but they say that Doctor's been hit!' I saw her face then, and the tears running down it, and I closed my eyes; and when I opened them she'd gone to tell one of the other nurses about you, I suppose. So I just hopped it. I don't believe I actually took in that I was *seeing with my eyes*, if you know what I mean, until I got outside and saw the fires burning over Plymouth."

I didn't ask him if he had been afraid, because of course he hadn't. That was the real miracle. He had gone towards the flames.

Soon after John came the All Clear sounded and we pushed

aside the black-out curtains and found broad daylight outside. The water sparkled in the gutters and a strong wind, blowing in from the sea, drove the smoke away from our eyes. We looked across the road and saw Nelly, one of the barmaids who had fed us in the night, standing in the shattered doorway of the Public House.

"Hi!" she called out to us. "You men like some breakfast?"

Over we went, Michael, John, the Warden we called "George," and myself. We couldn't wash because there was only water enough for our hostesses to make the tea; but I never enjoyed a more perfect meal.

Nelly and Gladys cooked and served it; but after they'd served it, they sat down and ate with us.

I do not like dyed hair — Nelly's was that red-brown concoction that is the poorest form of human camouflage, while Gladys had merely what may have been a pleasant sand colour burned into a washy-lemon tint; but with the sunshine upon their neatly tidied heads, not Botticelli's Venus rising from the seas had more entrancing locks.

Nelly may have been my age; Gladys, the publican's niece, was distinctly younger. They had been left in charge of the Lamb and Flag overnight because the uncle was worn out. They had kept open as long as they dared, they explained, to cheer their customers, and the rest of the night they had just sat up and watched.

"If you'd needed help," Gladys told us, "we'd have come over and helped you. We're both of us First-Aiders, but George here told us you didn't need us because you'd got the Parson and him; so after we'd seen you blowed across the road, we thought we'd cook something and bring you out some beer whether or no it was after hours. You got to break rules sometimes, haven't you?"

"It was some night though, wasn't it?" Nelly observed proudly. "I *had* thought I wouldn't stand any more of it, but go to my married sister in Wales till the blitz was over — but there, your customers get sort of dependent on you, don't they? And as long as you've got a nice set to serve, I believe in sticking to them, and so does Gladys. We do commercials mostly here — them and dockers — mind you, the *best* dockers — not a rough lot, but good skilled men that it's a pleasure to talk to!"

The sun shone full on the kitchen table through the glassless windows. They gave us bacon cooked as people can only cook their natural dish — each rasher was succulent but crisp — and eggs that Nelly had fetched the day before, with a pint of milk, from a farm. It must have been the best tea, and the freshest eggs, in England.

It has never surprised me that Chinese and Japanese geishas have been considered the finest conversationalists in the world. They were trained from their earliest childhood to entertain intelligent men; it was their vocation. So, too, these English barmaids had trained themselves. They had no fine wits or great scholars to entertain, but they had mastered the art of making a man feel at home and able to speak easily of what concerned him most. They were sunny-tempered, sensible girls who wanted to be pleasant, and knew how: my God, but they knew how! The table shook with our laughter.

I dare say they found us easy to amuse. To begin with, we were all alive, and a few minutes before nothing had seemed less likely. Before we had finished our first egg and rasher, they knew our first names and had discovered John's miracle. This put the crowning touch upon our festivity.

They had never heard of such a thing in their lives — it was Hollywood come to breakfast. For the first five minutes they kept up a perpetual fire of "Gosh, it isn't true!" "You're pulling my leg!" "What do you take me for?" "Boy, what does it feel like?" I doubt if they would have believed the fact either from John or from me, but they believed Michael. They respected him more than they did us, but they treated him the same. They knew all about him, of course, because he had become by then a Plymouth Legend; and they must also have known about Virginia. But with that tact of the heart which lies so much deeper than any social variety, they never mentioned her or anything that could have reminded him of her.

They had already formed a fast friendship with "George." He was their Warden and had proved himself an habitual hero.

In earlier times it was enough to establish one's reputation as a hero, to be one, once a lifetime; but "George" had been one, on an average, every ten minutes for the three worst nights of Plymouth's martyrdom. "George" was a modest fellow, but if he had not already known before he sat down to breakfast with Gladys and Nelly what a hero he was, he would have been an idiot had he not known it long before he got up.

I wish I could remember the jokes that Gladys and Nelly told us, they were so good; but they vanished with the succulence of the bacon, and the almost heady flavour of the strawberry jam. The palate is generous enough to give us these pleasures of taste, but memory is too stingy to let us relive them. Long years afterwards we can recall the actual events of a good meal, course by course; but one mouthful of its taste — never! Such was this meal, and such the irreplaceable flavour of our hostesses' wit.

I only know that as we looked at each other's grimy red-eyed faces, helped each other to our needs, and listened to each other's voices, we must have been the happiest and friendliest group of people in England.

A doctor always knows when a patient is weighing the dice against him by a desire *not* to live; even quite a small illness may kill such a patient: he is already dying, and his doctor a mere hindrance to his carrying out his purpose. On this occasion I had exactly the opposite feeling. This party sitting at the Lamb and Flag's kitchen table after their third blitz night were livers. Whatever might attack them, they would contribute nothing to the powers of death. They were against death. Every nerve in us rang with fight, with victory, with a sense that to have survived so much was to have survived everything.

We sat in the kitchen as near as we could get to the stove, for the morning air was keen, and as far as we could get from the glassless windows. But we were not cold; the sun was on us, and within us. I think we kept thinking of the light more than we should otherwise have thought of it because we were all seeing it through John's new eyes. I had made him sit with his back to it, so as to rest them.

"Enjoy to-day," I told him, "because you'll never see with

quite the same dazzling clearness again. You are like a man who has been a long ocean voyage away from the earth and all that grows on it; the first day he touches land he is overwhelmed with the scent of land and can talk about nothing but the different smells. He knows the earth as he has never known it before, and as none of those who have never left it *can* ever know it."

On our way home I told him to shut his eyes from time to time so as not to tire them. I did not say anything to him about not looking at the wounds of Plymouth — its still smoking, smouldering streets — for although all the fires were, as they say, "under control," this did not mean that they were out — only that they could not spread farther. Michael sat in front of the car with Peter, who was driving, and John and I behind together, so that we could talk if we wanted. I was in pain now, and the jolting of the car increased it; but I could hear what he said. We had reached the outskirts of Plymouth, and the unharmed country once more intersected and relieved the ugly damage of the night.

"You see," John said in a low voice, "it isn't only seeing that I'm glad about. That wasn't more than half of it — though I'm afraid I made an awful fuss about that half. It was being *afraid* to see I minded most! That's what I got over last night. I found I didn't *need* to be blind any more!"

I did not say anything, but I thought to myself what a good thing intelligence is in a patient. Many patients might have had John's experience; they might even, through unconscious processes of the same nature, have recovered their sight; and yet never have learned the root of their trouble. But this man knew his own roots and could now be trusted to attend to them by himself. I need say nothing more to him; and for my own sake I was glad of this, for the pain had now taken full possession of me.

I do not remember much more about the drive since before we reached Silver Fountains I had pitched forward onto the floor and lost, to my considerable relief, all remaining consciousness.

14th May 1941

LET any doctor who wants to know what good nursing can do for a patient get nursed in his own hospital. I had already made up my mind that English nurses are the best in the world — both an Englishwoman's qualities and her defects fit her to this skilled task — but not even my high estimate of the professional Sisterhood had reached the standard of perfection set by Matron at Silver Fountains. It seemed almost a pity that I had not broken *all* my ribs. I became automatically, as I was carried across the hospital threshold, the most pampered man in Europe.

Nevertheless, I was not happy during the ten days I was forced to remain in bed, for I could not see Virginia and I feared that she needed me; but I was more *comfortable* than I have ever been in my life, and I hope that I learned something from these faultlessly skilled and kindly women.

I had many visitors, including Lady Wendover and Miss Fitchett. Matron, Sister Lawrence and Sister Tutor, all three called upon me daily, but the one visitor I looked for and would most have welcomed, Gillian, did not come.

On the last day of my seclusion Adrian strolled in. He had got his wings and looked astonishingly handsome in his blue-grey uniform. In some indescribable way he had altered since I last saw him. He had always looked smart in a careless and rather offhand manner, as if whatever clothes he wore were bound to be the right ones; but now it was as if a slight rigidity — a kind of spiritual frost — had settled over his smartness. He had the bloom of the best Gainsborough portraits. A trifle more grandeur had been added to his slim figure. He held his shoulders with a more conscious correctness, and carried his fine young head with a firmer poise. Even the straight glance of his large bright eyes fixed itself with a greater steadiness. He had not dropped his casualness but he now controlled it, whereas before it had been the only uncontrollable quality I had observed in him.

"I thought," Adrian said, rather quickly for him, and before he straddled the small cane chair the nurse pushed forward for him, by my bed, "as I had a spot of leave I'd come along and see for myself how you were. Doctors talk such utter bosh about themselves when they're ill!"

He didn't smile at me, but his gravity had a certain austere friendliness in it. I thought to myself that it was like being visited by a masterpiece of antiquity, when antiquity was young.

Nature was young in Adrian and quite perfect. I had never in any other country seen quite so beautiful a specimen of young manhood. I thought to myself bitterly, "If the Nazis break this mould, there will never be such another," and I was sorry for Virginia when she looked at him.

I was not however at all prepared for the fact that she wasn't going to have a chance of looking at him.

"Very nice of you to come and see me," I told him, as soon as nurse left us, "but surely you are going to see Virginia, too? She has made a marvellously quick recovery. She will be, as you already know, injured for life; but she has already got over most of the shock effects of her injuries. I think she could safely see you — for half an hour — either to-day or to-morrow."

"Oh, no," Adrian replied with extreme coolness, getting out his cigarette case and lighting a cigarette for me with expert courtesy, "why on earth should I see her? I'm not a doctor. I couldn't do her any good." He looked at me with a sort of sedate indifference that I found oddly touching; because it wasn't indifference. He was, beneath the shield of his imperturbable manner, nervous. He remembered perfectly well that the last time he had seen me he had meant to take his life, and he wanted me not to remember it. I said nothing.

"We decided," he went on after a pause, "after that dance, that we wouldn't meet again. Much the simplest, you know, under the circumstances. Of course socially, if we turned up together, we wouldn't funk it, but that's not particularly likely to happen at present, is it?"

He wanted to give me the impression that he was quite heartless. Perhaps he wanted to give it to himself as well as to me, and thought that he had succeeded.

To Adrian, emotion itself is indecent; not only emotion exaggerated or out of place — as it is to every sensible person — but any emotion at all, however appropriate. The British young do not want to feel emotion, or to express it, or let it function as the mainspring of their lives; and yet emotion *is* the mainspring of every human life. Every animal, every bird, one might say every vegetable for the matter of that, lives because it feels. But the English have so suppressed their right to emotion that they often give an impression of extreme lightness where they feel most deeply. I thought Adrian dared not trust himself to see Virginia.

I was not certain that seeing Adrian would benefit her; but I knew well enough that she lay there longing for a sight of him, fearing to see once more his forbidden beauty, but counting, too, on a mercy that had been denied her before her physical disaster. "Now," she would be saying to herself, "he will forgive me; he will be sorry he was so cruel. He will come quickly. He will tell me, just once more, that he loves me!" She wouldn't, I knew, dream of taking advantage of his pity, but it would have been an advantage to her, at least spiritually, to be sure it was there. I believed it was the reason she had flung off her shock effects so quickly. Now she could not have this advantage, not because it would upset *her*, but because it would upset *Adrian*. I could not swallow this dignified selfishness very easily.

"I am certain," I told him, "that a visit from you is in Virginia's mind. Everything between you in a practical sense is over, but after all, there is a continuity in human feelings. They do not become a rabbit one minute and a pocket-handkerchief the next. Virginia has been cruelly hurt. She will have years of quite hopeless suffering ahead of her. Do you not suppose that your sympathy might help her?"

"Is there anything *but* a practical sense to love?" Adrian demanded, with his wilful lift of the brows. "What good will it do either of us if I go into her room, where she's all tied up, and say, 'My good girl, I'm awfully sorry!' If she isn't a complete moron, Virginia must know that I'm awfully sorry, and she must know that I'm not anything more than sorry."

I gave it up. I suppose it hurt me too much. He wasn't feeling like a human being. He had never loved Virginia like a human being. She had been a highly prized object that he wanted to possess. Well now — he no longer wanted to possess it.

He began to talk about his squadron, and for an hour he gave me the gist and tingle of his new life. He loved it, and was alive in it, and was no longer thinking of it as a good substitute for suicide, but as a reasonable and highly thrilling gamble with a bunch of good fellows in it with him.

This was the sort of life Adrian was fitted for, and he knew it. But I was to find it was not the whole of him. Little silences began to creep into his vivid snatches of talk. He paused deliberately every now and then as if he were waiting for me to say something that he wanted to hear; but I had nothing particular to say to him since I had not got over his refusal to see Virginia.

He got up at last, and walked about the little, spotless, empty room, looking out of the windows that give a rich green glimpse of his future estates — if he is to be granted a future. At last he stopped at the foot of my bed and looked at me with a strange urgency.

"Well," I said at last, "what is it?"

"*I* can't do anything," he said almost reproachfully, "but can't *you?*" He was talking again about Virginia as if we had never stopped.

"You mean," I said to make quite certain, "that there is such a thing as *useless* suffering?"

"Well — you shoot a horse, don't you," he urged, "if it's too much hurt to enjoy life? Why not put *any* animal out of its pain?"

"I have often asked myself the same question," I said cautiously, "but you know, I suppose, that a doctor, particularly, is out to protect life. To take it is to violate the *raison d'être* of his profession. Besides, it goes against the very instinct that makes a decent doctor choose such a profession. It would be like giving way to an enemy."

"Oh, yes — there's all *that* of course," Adrian said scornfully,

"but what's the odds if a person's life isn't worth living? Why
not take it? What's particularly sacred about human life? Isn't
all that bunkum? Quite healthy people are dying in flat millions
now as far as that goes, and the rest are cheering them on!
Nobody can take a very serious view of human life under the
circs, can they?"

"If you and Virginia had been all in all to each other," I
said after a pause, "and she had given up her children and
Michael, and all the other obligations she had taken on in the
world she lived in, for you alone, you could have made, together,
such a decision, and counted upon me to help you carry it out,
although I should even then have put before you the fact that
life is a changeable business and has surprises in store for us, of a
beneficial as well as of a disastrous nature. Even injured people
may change their minds about living when they have got used
to their injuries. Besides, there is such a thing as owing a debt to
life, and as long as we can contribute towards paying it, perhaps
we should go on living. Virginia will have to decide for herself
whether she wants to pay this debt to life. She is a generous giver,
and she still has obligations within her power to fulfil. There
is Michael and her two children. She even has friends; and now
the world that didn't approve of her is at her feet. Virginia has
her niche in it. She may like to stay in this niche. It is not altogether painful to be a great heroine."

"That's bunkum too!" Adrian responded promptly, but I
thought with a little uncertainty behind his promptness. "Do
you want her to string herself along on her vanity?"

"No doubt she *has* vanity," I admitted, "and no doubt you
added to it to appease your own, whenever it suited you. But she
gave you more than flattered vanity. Virginia was generous to
her lovers; and if she loves the world, she will be generous also
to the world."

Adrian turned his back on me and strolled to one of the
windows. "Then I suppose you won't do it," he said to me at
last over his shoulder.

"I have made no decision yet," I told him. "I am her doctor
but I am also her friend. She has conflicting claims upon me.

All I can promise is that I shall try to reconcile these claims to suit her needs; and when I am sure of what her needs really are, I shall exercise my skill upon them to the best of my ability."

Adrian turned round quickly, and held out his hand to me. I had no idea what his expression meant. I cannot fathom the English beyond a certain point. I am exasperated by them. I admire them. I am shocked to the core by them. I suddenly find I love them; but I do not understand them. I saw that Adrian's young eyes were giving me some kind of message and I fancy that it was a friendly, or at least not an inimical, message. He shook my hand with an abrupt strength, and then saying nothing whatever more — not even one of those strange mock phrases they use over here for "good-bye" — walked out of the room.

He left next morning without having seen Virginia.

16th May 1941

I WENT out for a walk in the Park when I could move again, before I paid my first visit to Virginia.

The hart's-tongue ferns upon the banks of the stream that runs through it are so bright a green that they make a light for themselves. You look up the watercourse from them, to the pale silky beech leaves, and your eyes are dazzled by their beauty. That wide-open flower, the primrose, has a child's face, and grows everywhere at Silver Fountains. All the hedges are alive with the swift secrets of the spring.

I tried to get accustomed to them before I went into Virginia's room.

The bandages have been taken off her face now, so more than ever, since they still fit her head like a cap, you feel that abrupt Greek beauty of her forehead and the set of her splendid brows. She had no colour in her face but she had painted her lips, and her eyes were full of light.

"At last — Rudi!" she whispered, holding out both her hands. Well, of course I knew that she was pleased to see me, but not as pleased as all that!

I had said she was not to be told about Adrian's visit, nor had she yet seen anyone from the outside world since Tom's one short visit after her accident.

I kissed both her hands. They were still bandaged but she could move them now. Last time I had looked at them they were producing life. "That was a fine baby, they tell me," I reminded her, "that you brought into the world. I am going to arrange that he shall be one of your first visitors."

"Oh, Rudi," she said again, "fancy your thinking of that baby now!"

It was to be a real visit, not a medical one, so we were left alone. I sat down beside her.

Her whole room was, as I had expected to see it, filled with flowers. There were bowls of priceless orchids as well as roses; plates of hothouse grapes and peaches. I cannot think where Tom got them all from, but he had managed to rake them in. Piles of the newest books and papers were strewn about within her reach. She had no single small want left ungratified.

"Aladdin's Palace?" I said, smiling at her.

"Does it matter now what he gives me?" Virginia asked with a rueful smile.

"Well, you haven't got to get rid of him now," I told her. "Michael has learned not to mind. You're rather rich now, Virginia — you've got a slave, that's Michael — a thief, that's Tom — and a friend — that's me! And you've got them all at your feet, as well as the permanent admiration of this extremely loyal island. It seems to me that you did rather a good night's work for yourself!"

A shadow crept over her face. "Yes," she said in a small uncertain voice, "but Adrian hasn't written, Rudi! He hasn't come! He won't now, I think!"

"No," I agreed, "I don't suppose he will, but why want him to? If he came it would *really* hurt you; and after all, he's intelligent — I think he knows that it would hurt you! Besides, if he'd come, it would, I think, have been because he cared *less* rather than *more* for you — cared, I mean, in such a way that he *could* come! Fancy coming to see you like this, and then having to go away again! But we may take it that whenever he serves his country he will think of you."

"I'd have *sent* him away," Virginia said with firmness, "you know that, don't you, Rudi? I'd never have let him hang round me for life, like poor old Tom's going to do, at intervals, which, between you and me, will grow longer and longer! I wouldn't, having just said once to him 'Forever,' have let Adrian see me again."

"Yes, I know that," I admitted, "but can you imagine saying 'Forever' to Adrian? Wouldn't he have replied 'Rats!'?"

"He might *say* 'Rats!,'" Virginia answered with a half smile, "but he'd *mean* 'Forever,' Rudi! And if I saw his eyes, they wouldn't be angry any more."

"Well, if Adrian is still angry with you, which I entirely decline

to believe," I told her, "he simply isn't worth saying either
'Rats!' or 'Forever' to! No, Virginia, you'll have to pay for your
fun like all the rest of us — only rather longer. But at any rate,
you've *had* it! Adrian isn't going to owe you a grudge for the rest
of his life; and any girl he marries is going to have to take a back
seat in his imagination. Whenever he's annoyed with her, and I
fancy he gets easily annoyed with women, he'll remember you
and down she'll go, just one peg farther than she'd have gone
anyhow."

Virginia laughed. She nearly laughed her little soft, eager
laugh, as if she were amused.

I don't think it hurts her to laugh. We were both silent for a
long while afterwards. She was thinking of Adrian, I suppose,
and I was wondering if there was any way of easing the weights
attached to her spine.

"Rudi," she said at last, "I wonder if you remember something
I said to you, when I first came round. It was to *you* I know,
because I saw your eyes, with a funny white thing over your face
before I went off again. I knew I was half-dead. I wanted to be
sure I could be *all* dead. I said, 'Don't let me live, Rudi!' "

"Oh, yes," I said, "I remember."

"Well," Virginia persisted, "are you going to make me live?"

Virginia has the most searching and unsecretive eyes I have
ever seen. You have only to look into them to know the *whole*
of what she is asking you; and to see that she will find out, from
looking into yours, what your answer is.

I was perfectly aware that Virginia could stand the pain she
was now bearing. Her pulse was good, her organs were all sound;
and she would have to stand it intermittently, and not much
lighter, for the rest of her most unnatural life. I was equally
aware that Virginia knew it and that she had made up her mind
not — if she could help it — to bear it. I was in the tightest corner
I have ever been in; until Virginia herself let me out.

"But it wouldn't be fair, Rudi," she told me, "to ask you
to do it, because you don't want to, and if you don't want
to, it must be because you think I *can* bear it, so I suppose I
can!"

"I think you can," I told her cautiously after a pause, "but I haven't made up my mind that you *should* bear it. I intend to make it up once and for all within the next half-hour. Once I have made it up, nothing that you or anyone else says will make me change it. Because you wouldn't have any peace, nor should I, if you thought I could.

"The question in my mind is not so much whether you can bear the pain, for of course you can, and we shall see that you are helped, as medical science can more and more help in the lessening of pain, *to* bear it; also you will have long periods altogether free from pain; but you will be inactive. Is your life, as an invalid, worth living, is the real problem. If it isn't worth it to *you*, it won't be worth it to Michael and the children — or all the rest of us. But *isn't* it worth it to you, when you once try to realize what you can make just still *having* you to so many other people? I'm not going to ask you to churn your heart upside down, but putting the dream of Adrian aside, just as an intellectual fact, have you ever loved anyone as deeply, as *wholly*, body and spirit, as you once loved Michael? Think of Michael when he wasn't a tyrant, a priest, a heavenly poop, or a sadistic bully, but just plain lover. Wasn't he worth more to you, weren't you actually more *entranced* by him, than by any of your Escape Substitutes? I saw him with two barmaids at breakfast in Plymouth the other day, and the barmaids liked him the best, though they'd three other attentive men to choose from!"

"Did he really have breakfast with them?" Virginia demanded with her eyes sparkling. "What fun! I wish I'd been one of the barmaids, Rudi!"

"Well, in a sense no doubt you were, to Michael," I assured her. "You're a highly skilled girl in your sex life! I know very well that you are, for you can make me forget that I'm in love with Gillian, and you must have some skill for that! Why don't you use some of this skill of yours on Michael? Physical life doesn't matter to him more than a row of pins — he's proved that to you over and over again — but he's human. He likes to feel that a beautiful girl takes the trouble to please him. Put him back into the sunshine again — let him live!"

"But where *is* the sunshine now?" she asked me with those cruel, truth-compelling eyes.

"You know as well as I do," I replied with a sternness I was far from feeling, "that sunshine is not made by sex, though sex can be used, and should be, to enhance it. Your sunshine comes from your own spirit; and if you think that a few broken bones are going to alter all your spiritual faculties, you think human beings more easily demoralized than I do!"

I turned my eyes away from hers, so that she should not see what was always there, whether I tried to hide it or not, that I *had* seen men demoralized from physical torture by their brothers. I also made up my mind that if the Nazis came, I would kill her immediately, no matter what else happened.

"But, Rudi," she said after a pause, "I'm so afraid of Michael! What you say is partly true: perhaps I am afraid of him because I once cared so — more than for anyone — so that other people seem like echoes afterwards. But now he's hurt me so often that I don't care any more: I'm free of Michael! And I don't want to begin feeling less free again!"

"You won't!" I said. "You forget the weapons have changed hands. You can use them against him if you want to now, but I think you won't! Michael will never torture you again — unless you let him. He'll pamper you instead; but after all, I think you could allow yourself a little pampering! It's heaps of fun, you know, being pampered!"

"Yes," Virginia said in the low voice I couldn't quite get accustomed to, for as a rule she talked louder than Englishwomen, "heaps of fun, Rudi! Only, I hope it doesn't sound mean, but I've always been in a cage since my marriage, behind bars; and Michael has been what's *kept* me in the cage! Now I'm in a different kind of cage, and it's not his fault this time, of course, but shan't I still go on thinking he's my gaoler and responsible for the bars, even when he's being so awfully good to me?"

I nearly broke down then, for I remembered Sterne's starling that couldn't get out. I had to be silent for a moment or two before I dared answer her. Then I said, "Each man makes his own cage; and is his own gaoler whether he knows it or not. Michael made too much of an obligation that you were making too little of; well, now that situation is over. You are in a perfectly new situation as regards both Michael and your entire household. I think it rests with you what sort of a cage you inhabit."

She closed her eyes and we were silent for a long time; and then I asked her if she had heard about John Stephens. She opened her eyes and said she had, of course, but she wanted to hear more; so I told her everything. She was quiet again for a long time after I'd finished; then at last she said a little mockingly, "What a happy story, Rudi!"

"Yes, it is happy," I said savagely, "because he *made* it happy. He got rid of something much worse than his blindness. Structurally, his accident was not like yours — it could be got rid of; but that was not what made him happy — and you know it! It was the knowledge that he needn't be a coward again."

"And you think *I* needn't?" she whispered.

"I *know* you never *were!*" I told her from the depths of my heart. She believed me then, and looked up at me, and smiled; but I could not smile. I stood up, burning with the anger Hamlet felt when the decision he hated was forced into his hand to carry out: "O cursèd spite — that ever I was born to set it right!"

"The time's up," I told her. "Now you've got to tell me which you want: an easy, painless, unanticipated death (for I shall choose my own time over it and you will not know when it happens), or else you must be prepared to take Life with your chin up, and on its own terms. No one can help you to do that, I least of all, since I am your instrument!"

I dare say I sounded bitter, but I couldn't help it. I knew that I could *do* what I had required of myself. I could kill Virginia; but I knew that I would not survive it. I felt ashamed because I wanted to live: I wanted to marry Gillian, to have a child again, and to go on with my work; but I didn't want these things enough to kill Virginia and go on living; nor did I want Virginia to have to go on living.

I didn't look at her while she made her choice. I looked over her head at Tom's expensive orchids. Money can buy everything in the world, I thought to myself, except life.

"All right," she said after a pause, I did not know whether short or long, "I'll go on living, Rudi — only I think you'll have to help me live — sometimes!"

"If you've decided," I said, looking down at her, "I'll help you all I can. It was only about the decision that I couldn't help you."

Then, for the first and last time, I kissed her.

19th May 1941

I SAW Gillian again the day after Virginia had made her decision to live. I wanted to go to Plymouth in order to consult Datchett. The night Raids had stopped but the services were still bad, and it was better to see him personally to talk over Virginia's case, and others equally serious; and I knew that Gillian would drive me in.

I had not seen her since my accident. She had not asked to see me; and I had not sent for her. I did not know her reason; but I was sure enough of my own.

If Gillian had seen me knocked out and spectacularly pitiful, as people are even after quite slight Raid injuries, she would have found it very easy to let me make love to her; and I, physically weakened and clinging to my suddenly restored life, might have made it.

She would not then have ever given me a bright and equal passion, organically perfect, but a forced plant, unequal, shadowed, founded on pity rather than desire. Such love between a man and woman sets it wrong for life. Either a woman loves you because she cannot help loving you — as a man loves a woman — or else she will have a deeply hidden, unacknowledged grudge against her lover, vitiating all true growth in comradeship. I could not afford this mistake with Gillian. I was too proud of her to be her weakling lover. A man can all too easily be loved as a child by a woman — and then he can be replaced by a child — but a mate is her mate for life, and if he has achieved this goal, he need never fear replacement.

When I came out, she was already sitting at the wheel of her car. She said quickly and rather nervously that she hoped I was all right. Words mean very little to English people, and they spend most of their time trying to avoid speaking them, or in saying carefully only those words that further their own actions, or those of other people.

It was a fine spring day when, in this country, all the objects of the countryside seem to be moving quickly in a bright light. The blossoms were out upon the trees, and bluebells stretched like shimmering patches of sea or sky, under the fluttering pink-leaved oaks.

We drove in silence through the Park, until we had passed the gates. Then Gillian said to me, "You saw Adrian? It was a very short leave but we took a long walk together, and talked a lot. He likes his work. Do you think he was right *not* to see Virginia?"

I found this a difficult question to answer, because I did not know what she felt, and I did not want to strike against her feelings. I thought, from the way she looked at me as I came down the steps — only once but a long look — that her heart was as open and alive as the day itself; and I wanted to keep it open and alive.

"If you had been Virginia," I asked cautiously, "would you have wanted to see Adrian?"

"No," she said quickly, "he'd have been too sorry for me! I'd rather he stayed angry — and in love. After all, the thing that parted them was the same. An accident couldn't make it better or worse, could it?"

"Perhaps not," I said cautiously, for there was in this accident of Virginia's something that to my mind *should* have got the better of Adrian's anger. "You see there is one great difference between you and Virginia. You have the pride that acts like a kind of armour to you in all your emotional life. Virginia has not got this kind of pride. She is defenceless."

"Oughtn't everyone to have it," Gillian demanded, "every girl, I mean? Isn't it simply self-respect?"

"You can call it by any name you like," I answered, "but it remains armour just the same. An English modern poet wrote a nice couplet on Pride: —

> The Proud have all the pain;
> None of the pleasures of the vain.

But they have that particular pleasure unknown to the vain — they keep their self-respect. Virginia could not respect herself; and at last she has done something to be proud of! Need any of us be afraid of spoiling Virginia a little now?"

Gillian made no answer. I looked at her and saw that I had made her cry. She has a very tender heart and I was not sorry to see this sign of it, because unless she had this tenderness, I would not care to possess it.

Neither of us for a time said anything more about Virginia; but nothing that we had said had weakened Gillian's friendliness. She looked only ahead at her road as a careful driver should, but I had a feeling that none of the voices of the day escaped her. We shared the south-west wind with its eager softness, the sudden tossing into the air of a lark's song from the close fields we drove beside; the shining of the rounded white clouds sweeping onwards across their wide floor of blue, with equal rapture.

"I'm quite friendly with Mother now," Gillian began at last, in a gayer voice. "I mean — I'm terrible sorry for her! Poor dear, she's been awfully sensible about getting well this time. You know it's a funny thing, because they aren't a bit alike, but she and Matron have made great friends. Mother hates Sister Tutor of course, and despises Sister Lawrence, but she seems to like Matron. Fidge has been awfully clever about her wrists; actually they don't show at all. She's put long sleeves with frills into all her nightdresses, and managed to make them look quite natural. Mother showed me the cuts, of course. They were quite deep ones, for her! I told Adrian about them because I thought it would make him nice to her; and it did. He was nice, too, about the work we'd done in Plymouth. He didn't think we oughtn't to have done it. He didn't see Father. He said he wouldn't just yet, but he would some time or other. It didn't matter, because by then Dad had gone back to London, so he couldn't be hurt. I think Adrian's leave went off rather well — the home part of it, I mean, don't you?"

I agreed.

"And your mother and father?" I asked. "I have not had a talk alone with her since just after her accident. When she visited me at the hospital with Miss Fitchett, she only told me that she had seen your father, not how things had gone between them."

"Yes, she saw him almost at once," Gillian said eagerly, "the morning after you — the morning after Plymouth — when I didn't go. And of course it was rather raw, but I fancy she didn't rub it in terribly! Anyhow I could see when he came out of her room, and he stayed quite a long time, that he'd been *really* cut up. Directly he came downstairs he sacked one of the maids for leaving a tack on the carpet, and you know what it means to sack a perfectly good maid now! I begged him not to, afterwards of course, but he said 'he was 'wholly justified,' and I think it showed he took rather an interest in the house again, don't you? I mean as if he were really the master of it, and not just walking in and out as quickly as he could, as he has done for the last two years."

"You understand your father," I said, "a great deal better than I do."

"Well, he takes some understanding," Gillian admitted. "Besides, perhaps he looks at things the way I do myself. He went to see Virginia, you know, at once."

"Yes," I said, "I know." It was as near as Gillian could get to telling me that she wished Adrian had done the same.

I asked Gillian to meet me, after I had talked with Datchett, by the steps of the Mayflower Monument. From there we could see the devastation — it was in fact all round us — but we looked towards the sea.

"Why did you want me to meet you just where the Plymouth Fathers sailed from?" Gillian asked me when we'd sat down on the steps together.

"Because it was a great venture," I told her, "and a happy one. They were driven forth into exile, a persecuted group, and it is to their descendants that England now looks for bread and hope. I thought it would be nice to meet where they had stood looking out, as we do now, into the unknown."

Gillian did not answer this, but I was looking at her face and I saw the sensitive shadow of her sympathy pass over it. She was thinking that I too was in exile and had been persecuted; and

that I wanted not to be a beggar in the land that had opened
its doors to me. I said quickly, "There is also something that
I wanted to explain to you in this special place. Look round you
a little at this desolation. It is what the Nazis have done far more
dreadfully by *spiritual* devastation, in their own country, to
their own ruined hearts, and to those of every hopeless little land
they have overrun and forced to serve their own ends. They have
done it most of all to France, for they have prostituted her great
strength and her pride. This they have not yet done here — perhaps they never can!"

We looked in silence at the ruffled sea, alive as it is sometimes
near the coast, with the uncertain life of little ships. Each single
ship has now such a dearness to those who live by the sea that
none of us can watch a boat go towards the horizon without our
hearts following her, until she sinks from sight.

"Why do you say '*perhaps*,' Rudi?" she asked at last, turning
her eyes back from the sea and looking at me in a troubled way.
"Don't you believe we *can* win, even with the sea?"

"I think it still depends," I told her, "on what is most important to us. Whether what we want is the old world for ourselves,
or whether we are building up a new world *not* for ourselves but
for others to share with us, an Everyman's World."

"Everyman's World?" Gillian asked me slowly, with a little
lift of her brows.

"Yes," I said firmly, "in other words, Caroline. And this is
what I have brought you here to talk with me about: Caroline!"

Gillian stared at me incredulously. Her lips opened to speak;
and then closed again.

I looked at her as a man looks at the woman he loves. I knew
she thought that I had brought her here to speak of our love.
And so I had; but I knew also that it must begin — and might
end — with Caroline.

"You see," I said, taking her hand in mine that she might feel
as well as see what I was meaning, "unless you understand what
I feel about Caroline, I cannot dare to ask you for your love.
You know that I love you; and that I have it in my power to

rouse your love, if I do not already possess it." She did not lower her proud clear eyes from mine.

"Oh, yes," she said letting out her breath in a long sigh of surrender, so that my heart rose exultantly to match her courage.

"But I am not going to try," I said as firmly as I could, "unless I can make you understand about Caroline. Why do you despise her, and make her get up and stand before you as if she were of different flesh and blood from you, or from me? Can money mean so much to you? She is an older woman, a very wise and good woman. She loves you. She is a friend both of yours and mine. You did yourself a very great wrong when you looked at her as you did the other day. It was the look of a Nazi, the *Herrenvolk* look; do you belong to them? My wife Klara belonged to them; and she looked at me, as you, the other day looked at my friend Caroline; because I was a Jew!"

"Oh no — Rudi!" Gillian protested, the swift colour mounting up towards her forehead. "Oh no! I mean it wasn't like that, not really!" She withdrew her hand but not because she was angry with me, only because she had suddenly become uncertain of herself and of me.

I took out a cigarette and lit it though my hands shook. I was risking much. "Is it so different?" I asked her.

Gillian lowered her head a little; and I think she was ashamed, nor could I spare her that, for to despise any other human being is a shameful thing; and she *had* despised Caroline.

"You do not know the real Caroline," I went on after a pause, "for if you did you could not despise her. It is true that compared to you there are many things she does not know; but as far as life itself is concerned, and life is after all our main concern, she is highly experienced. I find her of great value to me. You probably owe to her Adrian's life: this tired old woman whom you made get up and stand before you as if she were in the wrong. She knew better than you knew where to find a boy in trouble!"

"Oh don't, Rudi — don't be so cruel!" Gillian said in anguish; and then I knew I had made myself unhappy enough; and also that it was worth while for us both to be so unhappy. I threw my cigarette away and said quickly, taking her hand again: —

"It is not your fault; I mean you have been brought up very falsely. I don't suppose you were in the least more to blame than Caroline for what occurred the other day — both of you reacted to a very false point of view; old-fashioned too — and of no further use to the world! But before we let ourselves be as happy as two people can be who should have learned to love and trust each other profoundly, I must know exactly what you feel! Not twice will I stand before the woman I love and find in her a stranger! I could not survive it!"

"How I feel, about Caroline?" Gillian asked in a low voice. I nodded. "Well, *now* I feel ashamed because I see that I ought not to have minded your liking to be, well her friend, in a way I couldn't be, even now I couldn't, not a friend in exactly the same *way* to Caroline; but I do see that I ought not to have minded *your* being! Only, Rudi, it wasn't altogether what you think. I suppose you mean a sort of caste feeling, but I was jealous as well! Jealous because everybody is so exactly alike to you! I mean those women who poured all over you, when you were hurt, and that Stephens boy who can see now, but who keeps wanting to talk to you; and then of course Virginia, she means so terribly much to you! And even Mother; and Uncle James and Eunice and I know Rosemary though you never speak of her. There seems so little room for me, Rudi, and if you've got to love Caroline too — " She looked at me with April eyes; but her lips shook.

She was all the world to me. All the pure and vivid world of spring: the clean-washed sea and sky, the hedges full of life and birds' songs; the bluebells and the primroses.

I had this year begun again the old and deep tranquillity of mutual love, in which everything that lives blossoms afresh. I lit my life by her eyes — and she thought that in my heart there was no room for her.

"If you can love these people too," I said cautiously, "it will be, for both of us, wholly easy. I *do* love them. I admit it. I've learned to. I was broken up into them as it were by the Nazis. You've got to choose to-day between being a person who hates, a Hitlerite, or his chief enemy, a person who loves, a lover of Life! Life is universal, it belongs equally to all of us. If you are a lover, you can't despise, if you're a hater, you can't respect, another human being. You can't even respect yourself, unless you respect everyone else. There must always be some part of you that is at the mercy of shame! I can't very well tell you — how I find myself in the ranks of the lovers — perhaps all doctors — and all artists by right of their creative faculty — belong to them — for only lovers create Life, otherwise we should fail as scientists or artists; and this would be to us the one failure we cannot afford. As I see it, we have to get rid of this top-dog world out of which murder springs! Russians, Americans, Chinese, we ourselves! We must prove ourselves the spiritual enemies of the Nazis. This sense of superiority is the dead tissue of the cancer cell that must be cut away from us, before victory comes, or else a new cancer will form itself. When we are fighting side by side as brothers, to win a world that belongs equally to all of us — then we shall win the war; if enough of us do not want this new world — then we shall lose the war and with it human brotherhood. But I believe that enough of us are wanting it! I believe that we shall win this war; but not soon, not top-doggishly, not until we have beaten the Nazi out of ourselves as well as out of Germany! Look behind you at the ruins of Plymouth. What was within those walls was not clean enough. Plymouth was no worse than many other commercial cities, though perhaps it was more fascistically and despotically governed; but I think it will now be better — sooner — than many other cities. The flames we saw and fought together burned to the bone." I paused, but she made no answer, and I began again: —

"You ask me — or rather you tell me — that Virginia means so much to me that there is no room for you. Perhaps it is natural that you should feel that, but I should have to be a wholly different person to want Virginia as a wife. Such quick, responsive lovers as Virginia seldom make good wives. Her hand is always on the latch of her window. I am only one of the birds she would let in if I tapped. But I have never tapped at her window. I am not at all like a bird. I am a man who loves a home, who has once had one; and been deeply rooted. I was torn up by the roots before I left my home. Very slowly and very carefully I have looked, before I found, where to replant my roots."

Gillian was silent for a long time, then she said softly, "I'm like that too, Rudi, I shan't change."

For a long time we sat motionless, looking out to sea, her hand in mine, both silent so that we might better know what our blood said.

Occasionally and in the distance people passed us; but the Hoe is a wide place, and stretches away into a sort of empty blueness upon both sides.

One of the Sunderlands moved out of the sky above the Sound. We saw it a long time before its deep roar reached us.

It was the rescue flying ship. I wondered how many men in rubber boats, or taken straight out of the cold sea, were being carried home in safety. As their hearts felt mine also felt.

Gillian looked up at me with a sudden smile. "It's quite all right about Caroline," she said reassuringly.

I heard deep within me a voice calling for the last time, as in my sleep I have so often called aloud: "Klara! Klara! Klara!" It is strange that I have never been able to see her face since she turned and looked at me with loathing. I saw it now, beautiful and cruel — but no longer mine. It was fading out forever; and my voice calling her faded out with it.

THE END